TWISTED

MAGGIE GILES

Cover Illustration © **Nat Mack**
Distributed by **Blackstone Publishing**

ISBN: 978-1-990253-70-6
Ebook: 978-1-990253-64-5

FIC031010 FICTION / Thrillers / Crime
FIC031080 FICTION / Thrillers / Psychological

Follow Rising Action on our socials!
Twitter: @RAPubCollective
Instagram: @risingactionpublishingco
Tiktok: @risingactionpublishingco

For my Bella girl. I miss you every day.

TWISTED

Chapter 1
Melanie Parker

THIS WASN'T THE FIRST GIRL THEY'D ENCOUNTERED IN the street, and Mel knew she likely wasn't the last. Her sour attitude pervaded as her best friend Jackie crouched next to the girl, trying to shake her awake gently.

The location was strange enough to put Mel on edge. They'd found the girl, whoever she was, slouched against the wall in a back alleyway behind a closed club with a swollen cheek, cut lip, and what looked like a forming black eye. Her bright red hair was mussed and matted with blood. She wore jeans and a cropped shirt, the latter torn. Whatever had happened to her hadn't been good.

As Jackie tried to coax the girl awake, Mel reached for the girl's discarded purse, a square silver clutch. It was empty except for an orange bottle of pills prescribed to someone named Lexi. The drug—Solydexran—was unknown to Mel and the pills looked big and painful to swallow. Otherwise, the girl had nothing—no money, no ID—though Mel did find the glinting diamond bracelet wrapped around her thin wrist quite appealing.

1

"Hey, sweetie," Jackie asked. "You okay?"

Jackie was always so kind and gentle, and often Mel wondered how they'd grown so close over the past year. They couldn't be more different. Not that Mel didn't care about the girl or what had happened to her, but this wasn't the first one they'd come across and, more than once, it had meant bad news.

The girl blinked several times before her brown eyes focused on Jackie. She drew a sharp breath, then her hand flew up to her head, and a groan escaped her lips.

"Hey, sit still." Jackie caught her hand. "You look pretty beat up." She glanced back at Mel with a concerned gaze. Mel didn't budge. She knew exactly what Jackie wanted to do. She was always the saviour, bringing home lost and broken girls. The whole thing was getting old, especially when the girls disappeared the next morning ... usually with something precious stolen from their house.

"Lexi?" Mel asked, trying the name on the bottle of pills.

The girl's gaze found Mel and her brow crinkled. "No, Candice ... Candy usually." She glanced around, a nervous look in her eyes as if trying to find an escape. There was nowhere to go, and even if there were, she wouldn't get far from the looks of her. She possibly also had a concussion.

Mel grimaced. Why would this woman have someone else's pills? In her twenty-eight years, Mel knew that meant only one of two things. *Druggie. Thief.*

"I'd say it's a pleasure to meet you, but you don't look so good." Jackie reached out and touched the bracelet Mel had been admiring. "That's pretty."

Candy's eyes darted to it. Confusion clouded her gaze.

"Uh, yeah, thanks." She tried to shift and winced. "How did you find me?"

Jackie glanced back at Mel. "We were taking a shortcut home. And I'm glad we did."

Mel crossed her arms, certain the girl was hiding something. "Do you remember what happened?"

"No." Candy closed her eyes for a moment. "I can't remember anything."

Mel gritted her teeth. *Definitely a druggie.*

"Can you move?" Jackie asked. "I'll help." She slipped an arm around the girl's back and instructed her to go slow.

Mel stood back and offered the small purse. "This was next to you."

"That's not mine." Candy didn't even reach for it. "I've never seen it before." She swayed and fell against Jackie, who steadied her.

Mel glanced down at the clutch in hand. Either she'd stolen it, or she was lying; Mel couldn't be sure, and neither boded well.

"C'mon, let's get you out of the street." Jackie walked alongside Candy as the girl limped, clearly favouring her right leg.

"Should we go to the hospital?" Candy asked, drawing a slow breath as they exited the alleyway.

Mel followed them. "You don't have any ID, nothing. They'll ask a lot of questions. Ones I don't think you can answer."

Jackie shot Mel a cool look over her shoulder before focusing back on Candy. "Do you think you were robbed?"

"I ... uh don't know." Candy's gaze dropped to the sidewalk.

"Don't worry," Jackie said. "Blaine has stitched me up more than once. He'll say if you need a doctor."

"You're taking her home?" Mel asked. She'd been expecting it but hoping Jackie would have sense this time. They had to be more careful about who they welcomed into their lives.

Again, Mel received another glare from her friend. "She needs help, Mel."

Mel pursed her lips and didn't respond. The girl needed help, but did Jackie always have to be the one to provide it? This girl was just some prescription drug addict or thief. Why did she have to be their problem?

Main Street was busy that morning. Everyone's day was just beginning as Jackie and Mel's was ending. The hottest restaurants and boutiques lined the busy road. People of all different classes scattered the sidewalks. Some looked at them as they passed; others didn't even glance.

Across the street from where they walked, a noticeable commotion sprung up. Several police cruisers sat outside a small store roped off with caution tape. A large sign outside indicated it was a jewelry boutique, and even across the four lanes of traffic, Mel could see the shattered front window. Her mind immediately went to Candy's mysterious diamond bracelet.

"What happened there?" Candy asked as if reading Mel's thoughts.

Jackie shrugged. "No clue. Robbery or something."

"It looks pretty bad." Candy reached down and fiddled with the bracelet on her wrist.

"Whatever, shit like this happens all the time around here," Mel said, though she hadn't heard of anything that looked this severe in weeks, and she always made a point to keep up with the police. The more she knew about their movements, the easier it was to run her operation without disruption. And the safer it kept her and her girls.

Candy glanced back at Mel, who only looked at her with disdain. She swayed on her feet again, and Jackie reached out to support her.

"Where are we going?" Candy moaned, resting her head against Jackie's shoulder. "I'm exhausted. I could use a rest."

"Don't worry," Jackie said. "His place isn't far."

Mel cleared her throat. Sure, the house was Blaine's, but Mel had considered it home for the past two years she'd lived there with him.

Jackie ignored her. "I can't let you rest. What if you have a concussion?"

"Is it safe?" Candy asked, her voice quiet.

Mel scoffed at the idea of Blaine being dangerous.

"It is," Jackie said. "Blaine looks like a bull, but it doesn't match his personality. I promise it will be fine. We'll make you all better."

"Okay," Candy said, the tone of her voice still uneasy.

"Where are you from?" Jackie asked, trying to keep her talking as they turned off the main street toward a row of houses.

It took a while before Candy answered, "I've lived here all my life."

"And where are you living right now?"

Candy frowned. "Nowhere. My boyfriend kicked me out last week."

This made Mel hesitate and rethink her theory. Maybe

she wasn't just some deadbeat druggie; maybe her ex-boyfriend was abusive.

"What an ass," Jackie said.

"Tell me about it," Candy grumbled.

"Do you want to stay with us for a while?"

"Jackie!" Mel said, stopping before they climbed the cobblestone path to the front door of the large, two-story home.

"Only until she gets back on her feet," Jackie said. "We can't just leave her alone with nowhere to go."

Mel narrowed her gaze. They didn't know anything about her. What if she was some informant for the police? What if she could bring their whole lives crashing down? Mel had more to think about than just herself. Blaine, Jackie, and the other girls would be implicated if the police ever got word of how she kept so many women employed and off the streets.

Mel didn't answer as she stormed past them to the red front door. The brick was darker than the other houses on the street, and the three front windows on the lower level were shuttered. Only the silver sedan in the driveway confirmed Blaine was waiting inside.

"Hey, babe," Blaine called from the kitchen.

"Hey." Mel tossed her keys on the side table and kicked off her shoes, not bothering to look back as Jackie and Candy entered the house. Instead, she continued toward the kitchen.

Blaine sat at the counter, slouched over the day's newspaper, and glanced up with a beaming smile when she entered. His wide smile was bright, and he offered his arms for a hug. Mel held back, too pissed to enjoy his affection. However, part of her wanted to crumble into his arms and let him deal with Jackie's nice streak.

"What's wrong?" His arms dropped to his side, and he slipped off the barstool he'd been sitting on. "You look annoyed. Did last night go badly?"

"No," Mel said. "The job was fine. Christine took the clients to meet Jackie at a bar in town and from the sounds of it, they gave a show. Hopefully, it get us some returning business."

"Then what's wrong?"

Mel grimaced. "It was after, when Jackie and I were on the way back from the hotel, and she found someone to bring home."

Blaine ran a hand through his thick hair. "Another stray?"

"You know Jackie."

He rounded the corner and caught Mel's hips. "How's this one look?"

"Worse than all the others." Mel slipped out of his hold and tossed the purse she'd found with Candy on the counter. "I was thinking a drug addict, though now I'm not so sure." Then she waved toward the entrance hall. "Go see for yourself."

Blaine nodded and left the kitchen.

Mel waited, listening as he spoke to Jackie in a hushed voice and then to his steady footsteps as they climbed the stairs. It was only another few seconds before Jackie entered the kitchen.

"Don't be mad," she said.

"I'm not mad."

"I know you better than that." She cracked a smile.

"Hmm. Just make sure to hide the silverware."

Mel hummed her disapproval, then reached for the bag on the counter. "What do you make of this?" She rolled the pill bottle toward Jackie, who caught it.

"No clue." Jackie examined it. She cracked the lid and poured the large grey and white pills into her palm. "What do you think it is?"

"Who knows? It isn't prescribed to our lost girl."

Jackie frowned as she read over the name. "Solydexran. Never heard of it."

"Me neither," Mel said. " If we're dealing with a drug addict—"

"We're not," Jackie cut her off. "We've seen enough of those. Candy isn't using. She's hurt." She placed the bottle on the counter. "Considering she was kicked out of her boyfriend's, I thought you'd be more sympathetic."

"Yeah, well, until I know who this girl really is, I'll keep my sympathy to myself."

Jackie flashed her a sardonic smile, then turned away. "I'm going to go check on Candy."

Mel let her go, then reached for the bottle again. She didn't know why the pills put her on edge since she'd never even heard of the drug before. She tipped one into her hand. It looked like a pain to swallow, and according to the instructions, whoever Lexi was, she should take these pills twice a day. Unsure what else to do, Mel snapped the bottle's lid shut, tossed it into the top drawer, and went searching for Gabi. Maybe finding out about Gabi's night would take Mel's mind off the morning, a lost girl, a jewelry theft, and strange pills. Could the day get odder? Mel sure hoped not.

Chapter 2
Detective Ryan Boone

APPEARANCES SUGGESTED A TYPICAL BURGLARY—THE large front window shattered inwards, thick metal bars pried out of place, and yellow caution tape blocked the crime scene from the busy main street—yet the twisted feeling in Ryan's stomach said something different. After weeks of heavy caseloads, this one seemed too easy. Ryan ran a hand through his brown hair as his partner Brad Archer stepped to his side from the front seat of the cruiser. Archer instinctively straightened his suit jacket, something he did whenever he felt uneasy.

"Yikes," Archer said.

"What? Too heavy for your first case after taking leave?" Ryan cracked a playful smile at his partner, who'd been off for two months with a new baby.

"Waking up this morning was too much," Archer retorted, then waved a large hand in front of them. "Shall we?"

"Sure," Ryan said. "Though I'd bet getting up to an alarm

9

to chat with adults is a bit better than a screaming baby and shit-filled diaper."

Archer only chuckled. Ryan had never been great with kids—only one of the reasons he didn't have them.

The two detectives ducked under the police tape and entered the front door. Inside, two uniformed officers stood near the back of the store, speaking closely with an older man. Two others dressed in dark forensic uniforms snapped pictures of the scene and spoke quietly to one another as they gathered whatever evidence they could find.

"Ah, Boone, Archer," Superintendent Jasbir Singh said, stepping away from the other two. "About time you two arrived."

"Sorry, sir," Ryan said, cocking his head toward Archer. "You know we're still on the baby's schedule."

Archer nudged him. "What happened here?"

Ryan found it obvious. The window had shattered inwards, scattering glass across the dark, carpeted floor. Inside, the square storefront was lined with plastic cases filled with various sparkling jewelry pieces, all intact except one. He crouched next to the broken-in case and pulled on a plastic glove before running his fingers along the edge of the giant hole in the side of the case.

"We're looking for a bad guy with a blowtorch?" Ryan asked.

"What do you mean?" Singh asked.

"The case has been melted." Ryan straightened and pulled the glove off with a soft snap. "Why didn't they touch any of the other ones?"

Singh frowned. "Mr. Donovan has described an exquisite piece of jewelry. A silver bracelet encrusted with hundreds of tiny diamonds, worth a pretty penny." He looked back at a short man with shock-white hair and chubby cheeks. "He seems to think that's the most valuable piece they took."

"Must have been some bracelet," Ryan muttered as he scanned the cases filled with gold watches and thousands of sparkling gems. "Might be a good time to shop for the wife, eh Archer? Isn't your anniversary around the corner?"

"I don't need you reminding me," Archer said.

"Of course not." Ryan laughed. "She won't let you forget it." Ryan scanned the case again when something caught his eye on the opposite side; a single pill resting in the crease where the wall met the floor. It was a cylinder, half white, half grey, clear against the clean carpet. Ryan tapped the closest forensic officer and directed her to the pill.

"Ever seen one of those before?" Ryan asked Archer when the woman picked it up and placed it in a clear bag. Archer only shook his head. To the woman, Ryan said, "Get that tested and let me know what it is."

Then he turned back to the other officers and Mr. Donovan. "Are we only looking at jewel thieves out for your bracelet, or are they more basic, just looking for anything of value?" He could see the cash register open and empty.

Officer Jerry Quinn, the rookie on the team, shook his head. "They jimmied open the register, though Mr. Donovan says there wasn't much cash there. They busted into the back room and found the safe, I guess."

Archer frowned. "Still doesn't explain why they left the other cases."

"Thieves with a particular taste?" Ryan walked closer to

Mr. Donovan. "Do you have an inventory of all the stolen items?"

"Of course," the man said, handing him a package with the items' descriptions and photos.

Ryan flipped through the pages and found the bracelet Singh referred to. "This is the piece worth the most?"

"Indeed," Mr. Donovan said.

"And the safe?"

"Cleaned out," Quinn said.

"Broken into?" Archer asked. "How did they manage?"

"They must have had the code, or they were killer at breaking them." Quinn ran a hand over his wavy, long hair, wiping away a layer of sweat on his forehead.

Ryan glanced around the room. "Hey, look, Archer." Ryan pointed to the corner of the ceiling. "We're on camera."

"Do you have surveillance for the night of the burglary?" Archer asked.

Mr. Donovan clicked several times on his computer to bring up colour footage.

"No audio?"

Mr. Donovan shook his head.

Ryan scratched at his chin as the video played. It didn't show the break-in, just the two culprits moving through the store. The smaller of the two deactivated the alarm and turned to the partner. In the quick turn, Ryan saw a flash of red hair. The figure's slender form suggested a woman; the other figure was much bigger. The larger person went to the camera; his face was covered, but Ryan saw his green eyes as he broke the camera lens. The picture went blurry and cut out.

"They move through the place with ease," Ryan said, looking back to Singh. "Maybe a former employee?"

"Donovan is compiling a list," Singh said. "It will be at the station when you are done here."

"And current employees?" Archer asked.

Mr. Donovan shook his head. "Cory is a reliable worker. He wouldn't have done this."

"We'll need to speak with him just the same. Maybe he saw something or someone checking out the place." Ryan stepped closer to Singh. "Pull the last few weeks of surveillance too. Maybe they were in, casing the place as a customer."

"That's probably a long shot," Singh said.

Ryan cracked a smile. "Sure, then you can spend the next few days sitting in front of the TV. Isn't that your favourite thing to do?"

Singh raised an eyebrow at Ryan but said nothing about the quip.

"Put a rookie on it," Ryan said when his joke fell flat. He glanced over his shoulder at the two forensic officers. "Any prints or DNA you've found?"

The woman he directed to the pill shook her head. "Hundreds of prints, likely from daily customers. What was left of the camera and the empty case were wiped clean."

"Let me check out the back. Then we can head to the office. Archer and I can contact the former employees when we return."

A wave of relief washed over Singh's stern expression. He reached out and took Ryan's hand in a firm shake. "Thank you, Detective," he said. "I have no doubt you'll figure this one out quickly." When he released Ryan's hand, he reached for Archer's, then nodded to Quinn. "We'll head back to the station. Don't hesitate to contact me if you need anything." Singh headed toward the door with Quinn on his heels. "See you back there."

Ryan watched him go before turning to Archer with an amused grin. "He sure bolted fast."

"Does that surprise you?"

"Nah." Ryan waved it off. "I know better than to expect more than donuts and coffee out of Singh." He turned and followed Mr. Donovan to the back of his store to look at the safe.

Archer followed with a soft chuckle. "I can see my time away hasn't hindered your obnoxious humour."

Ryan glanced over his shoulder at his muscular partner. "Did you miss me?"

"I guess your terrible jokes do beat the screaming baby." Archer grinned. "Still, I'll stick to my wife and kid for snuggling."

"No argument here."

Chapter 3
Melanie Parker

MEL PACED THE TILED FLOOR IN THE KITCHEN, RUBBING at her temples in an attempt to stay calm. "God dammit, Jackie. You're trying my patience."

"What was I supposed to do?" Jackie asked from where she sat perched on a barstool. Her wide eyes made her look younger than twenty-seven, and she cowered under Mel's accusing gaze.

"You're supposed to get over this need to help people."

Her soft-hearted friend had not only brought home Candy several hours before, but she'd also now offered her permanent residence until further notice, something Mel hadn't agreed to. If this were the first one, then maybe it wouldn't have been so bad, but Jackie had brought home more than one helpless girl in the past. Mel's operation had little to show for it. Jackie had promised it wouldn't happen again, though, of course, it had.

"We don't even know who this girl is, and by the sound of it, she doesn't know either."

"She got kicked out of her boyfriend's house, and it looks

like he beat the shit out of her," Jackie said, dropping her gaze to the floor. Though her blonde hair fell forward and shielded her face from view, Mel knew the familiar look of sympathy.

"You think it was the boyfriend who hit her?" Mel hated considering the idea, wanting no reason to pity the girl—having come from an abusive relationship with her ex, she couldn't deny the pattern felt familiar. Still, a part of her was convinced the drugs had something to do with it.

"I don't think she just got in a bar fight," Jackie said, looking back at her friend.

Mel chewed on her lower lip as her blue eyes darted around the bright room. She didn't speak for a while, and Jackie didn't push her to. Finally, she let out a long breath.

"Fine," she said through clenched teeth. "She'll stay until she's better. After, if she's not willing to work, she has to go. I don't care what you promised." Mel wouldn't have any free-loaders in the house longer than necessary. She had a duty to her girls. The house was there for them whenever they needed it, not for the strays Jackie tried to bring home.

"Okay, thank you. I wouldn't ask you to take care of her for free or anything. I'm sure she'll be willing to pay her way."

The front door opened with a loud creak. Mel turned to leave the kitchen but hesitated. "Go upstairs and check on her. See if Blaine needs anything else."

Jackie headed upstairs by the back staircase, and Mel went into the front hall.

"I wondered when you were showing up," Mel said. Gabi stood in front of the door, kicking off her shoes. The black cocktail dress she wore stretched around her round middle. Her wavy onyx hair was a tangled mess pulled back her round, tawny face. The dark makeup she wore last night had mostly been wiped away, evidence of its remains resting under her eyes.

Gabi said nothing, only dug into her purse and tossed a plastic grocery bag at Mel.

Mel caught it and opened it, checking the contents. "How was last night? I expected you hours ago."

"Fine." Gabi pushed by Mel, who reached out and grabbed her wrist.

"Where's the money?"

Gabi laughed. "You're looking at it. You said to grab."

Mel released her arm, and her grip on the bag tightened. "Fine."

Gabi had been with Mel for only six short months, and as much as she liked to question Mel's authority, Mel had a soft spot for the younger woman. Mel remembered being twenty-two and carefree. It was easy to excuse her juvenile behaviour. Plus, Gabi had been there for Mel when she needed to get out of a bad situation and couldn't involve Blaine. Gabi held some of her darkest secrets in a way Jackie could never understand.

"Hello to you too, hon," Gabi said, standing on her toes and kissing both of Mel's cheeks. Mel's response was stiff, and when Gabi pulled back, she frowned. "Something going on?"

"Jackie brought home another stray," Mel said.

Gabi linked her arm and steered her into the sitting room to the waiting couch. "Who's the stray? You don't seem happy about it."

"Am I ever happy about it?"

Gabi laughed. "C'mon, tell me. I miss all the fun."

"Her name is Candy," Mel said. "At least, that's what she claims. We found a pill bottle on her that suggested differently. Her memory is foggy, and she can't remember anything. She was all beat up in an alleyway downtown. I'll admit she looks awful. Jackie thinks her ex beat her or something. I'm still on the theory she's a no-good druggie."

"Are you letting her stay?"

Mel frowned.

Gabi gently nudged her. "What's bugging you?"

"How many girls has she brought home now?" Mel shook her head in disbelief.

"This is four," Gabi replied.

"And how many of them are still here?"

"I see your point. Anna did stay for a bit. You don't think this one will be any different?"

For a moment, Mel didn't respond. Candy appeared too scared to be a druggie and too out of it to be a thief. Her story about where she came from seemed true, but Mel couldn't be sure.

"I don't know. You know Jackie; she couldn't just leave her there."

"Yeah."

Before either could say anymore, Blaine and Candy entered the room. Mel stood to meet them. The red-haired woman's cuts had been cleaned, and her swollen cheek was bright red like it had been iced. Blaine had given her a set of Jackie's clothes to replace the torn shirt and dirty jeans she'd shown up in. She still looked like crap.

"Feeling better?" Mel asked.

"Yeah, thanks," Candy said. "I appreciate your help."

18

Gabi stood. "I'm going to have a shower and get changed." She stepped closer to Candy and took her by the shoulders. "I'm Gabi." She leaned in and kissed Candy's cheeks, then smiled. "Welcome to the family." Gabi glanced back at Mel before turning and hurrying up the stairs. Typical Gabi welcome.

"You can stay as long as you need to heal," Mel said. "I don't know what happened to you, and I don't know if I want to. You look like shit and can't remember if you have anywhere to go, so stay. Get better and see if your mind comes back."

Candy frowned. "Are you sure?"

Mel ignored her question and looked at Blaine. "Can you go make up the pull-out bed in Jackie's room?"

Blaine leaned against the doorframe, arms crossed. "I thought Jackie was going home."

"Change of plans," Mel said. "She's staying, and so is Candy."

Blaine's eyebrows furrowed. He turned and went toward the stairs.

"So, you'll stay," Mel said. "At least until you're better."

Candy only frowned for a moment, lowering her gaze to the ground. She then glanced back at Mel, her eyes lit up with a smile.

"Yeah, that would be great. Thank you."

"Get better. It will make Jackie happy."

It had been three days since Candy arrived at the house, and Mel's irritation with her grew daily. She worried about the life the twenty-five-year-old couldn't seem to remember. She worried about the drugs that remained in the kitchen drawer. She worried about the supposed ex that might come breaking down their door. Mostly, she worried about the state they'd found Candy in and if the cops would come knocking one day.

Mel stepped out of the primary bedroom and paused when she heard Jackie speaking at the bottom of the stairs.

"Are you sure you want to go back there?"

"It'll be okay," another voice said. "I won't be long."

Mel descended the stairs, where Jackie spoke with Candy, who was dressed and looked ready to leave.

"What's going on?" Mel asked.

"Candy is going back to her boyfriend's place," Jackie said. "I told her it was a bad idea."

Mel frowned. "If she thinks she needs to go, then she should."

"What if he hits you again?" Jackie turned away from Mel.

"We don't know if he did hit me." From the look on Candy's face, it was clear she thought he did. Mel had seen abused women return to their husbands; Mel had seen that look. Mel had *had* that look.

"Maybe Jackie's right."

Candy shook her head. "I have to."

Jackie grabbed Candy's wrist. "What if you don't come back?"

"I will." Candy pulled her arm from Jackie's grasp and reached for the door. Before touching the handle, she hesitated, unclipped the silver bracelet from her wrist, and handed it to Jackie. Then she looked up at Mel.

"That's for letting me stay here," Candy said. "It's my guarantee I'll come back and repay you for taking care of me."

Jackie's hand closed around the bracelet, and she shook her head. "You've only been here a few days. You're not better yet."

"I'm well enough." Candy reached for the door. "I'll be back. I promise."

Mel stepped forward. "Do you want Blaine to take you?"

"That would make things worse," Candy said. "I'll be fine." She didn't wait for either to answer before slipping out the door.

Jackie frowned and glanced down at the bracelet. "Why wouldn't she listen?"

"She's going through something you can't understand," Mel said. "She has to figure it out on her own."

Jackie looked up and held the bracelet out. "Take it. It's all you care about."

Mel shook her head. "I thought you knew me better than that, Jackie."

"You never cared about anyone else I brought home." Jackie planted her hands on her hips.

"I know," Mel said. "And I don't care much about this one, but I know an abused woman when I see one. She's been hurt. That much is clear."

"Then why didn't you stop her?" Jackie's voice was desperate.

"What was I supposed to do?" Mel said, losing her patience. "If you think I'm okay with letting Candy go back to her fucked up boyfriend, then you have me all wrong."

Jackie dropped her eyes back down to the bracelet. Her

mouth curved down. Mel, for a moment, felt terrible for snapping. Stepping closer to Jackie, Mel put her hands on her shoulders.

"Keep the bracelet safe," Mel said. "Candy will want it when she comes back."

"*If* she comes back," Jackie mumbled.

Mel gave her a little shake. "*When* she comes back." She directed Jackie to the stairs. "Stay here tonight."

"You don't want me to work?" Jackie asked.

Mel laughed. "No, I want you to relax."

Jackie looked to protest but didn't and eventually headed upstairs. Mel watched her go, then turned for the kitchen.

She entered to find Blaine's back to her.

"What are you doing?" she asked.

His shoulders jumped at the sound, and he quickly discarded the phone he was holding.

Mel frowned, realizing the cellphone in his hand was hers.

"Are you going through my phone?"

"No." Blaine shifted under her gaze. "I was just going to plug mine in." He waved his phone at her, then turned back to the charging dock.

Mel didn't answer, finding his reaction strange, and took her phone from where he dropped it. The screen was blank, and she tucked it away without another thought.

"Are you driving Gabi to her job tonight?" Mel leaned against the counter, mind on the clients she had booked for the evening.

"Yeah." Blaine glanced back at his phone when the screen sprung to life. "What's your plan tonight?"

"A little accounting," Mel said. "The girls need to get

paid. I gave Jackie the night off, so I'll have to call one of the others in."

"Christine will always work."

Mel only nodded her agreement. Most of the girls would jump at a job. Cash was cash.

The front door opened with a noisy creak before Blaine or Mel could speak again.

Mel raised her eyebrow. "I thought you said you oiled the hinges."

"I guess I forgot." Blaine gave her a sheepish smile as she rounded the counter and left him alone in the kitchen.

"About time you made it," Mel said to Gabi, who stood in the front hallway. Gabi was due at her job in an hour. Mel usually liked having a bit more time to prepare.

"Something came up," Gabi said, and Mel didn't pry. She didn't ask the girls for details and expected them to do the same.

"Are you ready?" Mel looked her over.

"I am." Gabi wore a tight red dress that hugged her curvy shape in all the right places and complimented her bronze complexion. Her long black hair was curled and framed her smiling face. Mel had to admit she looked great.

"Good." Mel raised an eyebrow. "Why do you look so pleased with yourself?"

"I got you a new client," Gabi said.

"Did you? Who?"

"Paul Dorian."

"The lawyer?" Dorian was a well-known defense attorney in the city—one with a huge office building and a record for winning. He didn't seem like the type who would seek out Mel's services.

Maggie Giles

"The very one."

Mel crossed her arms. "How?" It was unlike Gabi to bring home such wealthy potential clients. She was still new to the game, so the idea she could bring in others like Dorian was appealing.

"You know Mr. Kyles has a thing for me."

"The short banker?" Mel snorted. "What of him?"

"Seems he and Dorian have done business in the past. Mr. Dorian was at Liam's last night," Gabi said.

"Liam?" Mel asked with an amused smile.

Gabi's cheeks went red, and she looked away. "He asked me to call him that."

"I'm sure he asked you to scream it." Mel cackled. "What about Dorian?"

"He pulled me aside before the end of the night and asked if the rumours about Melanie Parker were true."

Mel leaned forward with a raised eyebrow. "And what rumours would those be?"

"My question exactly," Gabi said. "Said he was interested in getting to know you. Said he'd like to take you out."

Mel laughed. "I don't go out."

"You will for this one." Gabi pulled out a business card and passed it to Mel. "Call him; see what he wants." She crossed her arms with a smug smile. "I imagine a group of girls and a ritzy party. Probably better than what Liam would throw."

Mel's fingers traced over the textured writing on the card. "Enough games. What does he want?"

Gabi shrugged. "He wouldn't tell me. Said he'd only speak with you. Call the guy. You know it'll be worth it."

"I'll consider it. Maybe it would be a good assignment for

Candy if she decides to stick around." Candy would be good for the job. Mel always looked for diversity in her girls. A flavour for everyone. Candy would bring in good money. Some men loved a feisty ginger.

Gabi frowned. "The new girl? Really? *I* brought him in."

Mel stopped and sneered. "Mr. Kyles is one thing, and a top-notch lawyer who's willing to pay big money is another."

"Nice." Gabi scoffed.

Mel smirked. "You know I'm not."

Gabi opened her mouth to retort when Jackie came down the stairs with her bag packed.

"Where are you going?" Mel asked as she brushed by Gabi, finished with their conversation.

"Home," Jackie said. "You don't want me to work and I don't want to stay here doing nothing. My roommate is probably hanging around. I might as well go see her and catch up."

"I'll be here tonight," Mel said. "Stay with me."

Jackie glanced behind her toward the kitchen and shook her head. "You and Blaine could use a night." She lifted her bag and moved passed Mel. "I'll see you in the morning, or maybe in a couple days, depending on how I'm feeling."

Mel narrowed her eyes and wanted to protest further, but Jackie didn't wait for an answer, instead reaching for the door and leaving with a quick goodbye.

"What's her problem?" Gabi asked.

Mel only shook her head and shooed Gabi upstairs to put on her final touches. Mel watched Jackie from the window as she climbed into a waiting cab and disappeared down the street.

Footsteps from behind her drew her attention away from the window.

"Everything okay?"

Mel sighed and stepped to Blaine, resting her head against his chest. He wrapped his arms around her.

"Jackie went home," Mel murmured. "I think she's mad at me."

Blaine gently kissed the crown of Mel's head. "She'll be okay after she cools off. You know Jackie. She always gets caught up and worried about the ones she brings home."

Mel didn't answer, only allowing herself a moment of peace in Blaine's arms. Maybe Jackie was right; they could use a night together. Too often, Mel knew she was cold with Blaine and too often was he beyond patient. Sometimes she wondered why he loved her.

"Do I look okay?"

Mel untangled herself from Blaine's hold and turned to address Gabi. The shorter girl stood on the steps, rocking her red dress and significant, black stripper heels. She'd touched up her makeup and the winged liner looked so precise it could have been tattooed on.

"Perfect." Mel took Gabi by the shoulders. "You were requested for six hours. There will be drinks and a nice place to stay—a beach house. Blaine will be here if you need him. He's your third number on speed dial. Hold it down if you need him fast." Gabi knew all this, but Mel made a point to repeat it for each job.

"I'll be fine, mother hen." Gabi winked.

Mel dropped her hold and looked away. "I've told you not to call me that."

Gabi laughed. "I know, but you take such great care of us."

"Be safe."

"I always am."

Blaine grabbed his coat and the keys, then motioned to the door. Gabi smiled and headed outside.

Before leaving, Blaine leaned down and pecked Mel on the lips. "Don't worry."

"I won't."

Blaine half-smiled. "You will. I'll pretend you won't."

He turned and headed to the car where Gabi waited. Mel watched from the doorway until the car pulled out of the driveway and disappeared down the street.

Alone in the silent house, Mel reached for her phone and unlocked the device. There was a voicemail. Her brow furrowed. She checked her call history but didn't have any recorded missed calls.

Clicking on her voicemail indicated the message had been left three hours before.

"Patsy, cut the bullshit and call me back. I'm tired of your games."

The voice was harsh and familiar. It sent chills down Mel's spine. She couldn't place it. The name Patsy made her pause. She didn't think she knew anyone by that name, yet she was sure she'd heard it before. Though unsure what the feeling was, she hit delete and removed the message.

Mel chewed on her lower lip as she flipped through her call history again. *Patsy.* She made a mental note to ask Blaine about it.

Chapter 4
Brielle Jeffries

THE BRIGHT SUNLIGHT WOKE BRIELLE FROM A RESTFUL slumber. She hadn't slept well in months, but last night was okay. She felt rested, revived, and actually happy. Until she looked around and realized she wasn't in her bedroom.

The room's walls were eggshell white and featured only a single window. The box room was small, smaller than anything in her parent's home. Her heart began to race. Something wasn't right.

Brielle flipped her legs off the bed and looked around. Her purse rested on the floor, discarded against the farthest wall. Her wallet was still intact, and there was no one to be seen.

Sweat prickled on her brow line, and she pressed her eyes shut. She was hot. Too hot.

Brielle reached into her bag to pull out her prescription and found it missing. Her eyes crawled to the desk in the corner. An orange pill container, tipped on its side, sat on top. Brielle grabbed it—the bottle belonged to her—and only one pill remained. She popped the white and grey pill into her mouth and swallowed. She'd gotten good at swallowing pills dry when she was high every day.

On the other side of the desk were stacks of papers and a pile of bills made out to Jacqueline Biggs. This gave Brielle pause. She was in Jackie's apartment. According to the address, she was on the other side of town. How did she end up here?

Brielle's parents had been away for the last week, and expected to return in four nights. She'd been alone and drinking at a bar, something she'd started doing whenever her parents left her by herself. It probably wasn't the best habit, but it made forgetting everything easier. Plus, it beat getting high. She wasn't allowed to do that anymore.

Brielle waited for a moment and listened. She couldn't hear anyone moving in the apartment, and she wondered where Jackie could have gone.

Closing her eyes, she thought back to the previous night. It was the same as every night. Drinks at the bar, slow intoxication, a handsome face, a trip to the bathroom, and an escape home. Except she couldn't remember going home. Or seeing Jackie. It didn't explain how she ended up here.

She gathered her things, not willing to face her estranged friend after so long and headed to the front door. A bright digital clock made her stop. The date was written in bold, blue lettering. Brielle had difficulty believing it. If it was true, she was missing more than a night of memory.

Shaken, Brielle hurried from the house. She hailed a cab when she reached the street. As she climbed into the back seat, she noticed a black SUV sitting a few car lengths away. There was someone in the front seat, though the windows were tinted. Brielle was sure she'd seen the car before. She shook her cloudy head. How could she be sure of anything when several days seemed to be missing from her memories?

Brielle gave the driver her address and grabbed her phone from her bag. The device was dead; who knew for how long.

"Is it really the twentieth today?" Brielle asked the driver.

"Yes."

Brielle frowned. She'd lost three days, and her parents would be home tonight. It was happening *again*.

The cab pulled up to her parents' house, and she hurried inside. There, she was met with her housekeeper's bright smile. Rose had worked with her family for many years.

"Good morning, miss," Rose said.

"Good morning," Brielle said as she brushed passed the older woman and ran up the stairs to her bedroom.

She threw open the door to her pristine room. Even if she had slept here in the past three days, Rose would have been through to clean it already. She tossed her purse on her bed and started rifling through it. Not enough to justify leaving for three days. Only her wallet, a pack of half-finished gum, cigarettes—only one remained—and a blue BIC lighter. She ran her tongue over her teeth. Her mouth felt dry, dirty. When was the last time she'd brushed her teeth?

Grabbing her phone, she plugged it in. It would be a few minutes before she could use it. That was when she caught her reflection in the mirror. Brielle was wearing a pair of jogging pants and a T-shirt she'd never seen before. Quickly, she removed the shirt for a bigger surprise. The bra wasn't hers either. Had she been staying with Jackie in a drunken or drug-induced coma?

Looking at her dead phone, Brielle considered trying to call Jackie to see what had happened, but from what Brielle remembered, there wasn't a number to call. Brielle had no idea how Jackie had found her. Had she stumbled across her at the bar? Or maybe Brielle sought her out after too many vodka sodas. There was no way to be sure.

Brielle quickly changed and headed back down the stairs. "Rose?"

Rose looked up from her work. Her thinning white hair was pulled back in a tight bun, stretching the lines around her eyes as she smiled.

"Yes?"

"Someone has been in my room," Brielle said. "I'm missing a necklace."

Rose's smile immediately faded. "It's not possible, miss. No one has entered your room since it was cleaned after your departure. It hasn't seen a single step for two days."

A cool shiver ran down Brielle's spine. So, she hadn't been home in days. Quickly she shook her head. "I probably just lost it on my own. I'm pretty spacey like that." Then she headed for the front door.

"Where are you going?" Rose asked. "Your parents will be home tonight."

"And I'll be back," Brielle said. "I'm just meeting a friend for lunch."

Rose glanced at the clock; Brielle did too. It was only ten in the morning.

"Brunch, I meant." She turned, grabbed the keys from the hanger and left the house before Rose could comment. Taking her mom's car, she headed to the last place she could remember being: the small bar off the main stretch.

She was there in minutes and was surprised to find the place closed. Brielle hadn't really thought it through. *Typical.* She parked and went to the door, hopeful someone had come in early for their shift. She knocked. No one answered.

Brielle waited a moment more before turning back for her car and resolving she'd have to return later. As she climbed in, a bang resounded down the alleyway. A young man flipped a large bag of garbage into the outside bin.

"Excuse me!" Brielle called, rounding her car and entering the alley.

The man looked at her. He was young, probably in his early twenties, with dark brown hair and matching eyes. He regarded her for a moment before his confused expression melted into a steady smile.

"You're that girl from the other night," he said.

"You remember?" Brielle asked.

"I couldn't forget the performance you gave!" He chuckled.

Brielle frowned. He seemed to notice her reaction before his chuckling silenced and he mumbled, "Sorry. You looked like you were having a bit of fun."

"I likely was. I just can't remember," Brielle said. "Do you have a minute to talk?" She waved to the door. "I know you're not open; however, I could use a drink and a bit of insight on what happened while I was here."

The man looked like he would refuse but said, "Yeah, sure. C'mon in."

Brielle followed him into the bar. It looked different during the day. The lights were bright, the tables and chairs stacked. The liquor behind the bar was covered or locked away.

"I'm Brielle, by the way." She sat on one of the bar stools.

He'd moved around the bar, unclicking locks and then mixing a drink. She hadn't even ordered anything. When he finished, he plopped the glass down in front of her. She knew it immediately—an amaretto sour.

"I know," the man said. "You told me. I told you I was Gary."

Brielle winced as her eyes were still fixed on the drink. She reached for it and scrunched her nose as the smell of the amaretto hit her. Then she set it back down.

"Please tell me I was drinking something else when I was here."

"You started with martinis, then that other girl showed up and you two started downing these. I assumed it was your favourite."

"Other girl?" Brielle looked away from the glass and back at Gary. "What other girl?"

"I don't know. You didn't say." Gary moved around the bar and sat on the stool next to her. "You two were mighty friendly, though. A lot of hugging, drinking, and laughing. Then the show started."

"What show?"

"You both got up on the bar and started dancing." Gary smiled. "The manager came over to boot you off but your friend wouldn't hear it. Claiming you two were allowed to do whatever you wanted. Then you started kissing, and, well, no one was gonna stop you."

Brielle shook her head. "It's not possible." The actions he described were the exact things she used to do with Jackie. Then, dreading the idea, Brielle asked. "Did we leave alone?"

"After that performance?" Gary said. "Hell, no!"

"Who did we leave with?"

Gary frowned, placing a finger on his temple. "Come to think of it, I think the girl may have arrived with two men, and they took you home."

"This girl," Brielle said. "What did she look like?"

"Uh," Gary said, then he looked Brielle up and down. "A lot like you, actually. Pretty, thin, blonde, with a friendly smile."

"That's it?" Brielle said. "We drank and left with some guys?"

"Yep. You came back the next night alone. You didn't come to talk to me and you didn't stay long. Some man came and met you for a drink. When he left, you did, too, both going your separate ways, it seemed."

"Thanks." Brielle stood and moved away from the bar.

Gary grabbed the drink he'd made her. "Didn't you say you needed a drink?"

Brielle looked back at the amaretto sour, scrunching her nose again. "I hate amaretto."

"You'd have fooled me." Gary moved around the bar and tipped the drink into the sink. "I'll remember for next time."

"Great," Brielle said, then left Gary alone in the bar. She shook her head when she breathed in fresh air. Everything he described was identical to the nights before she went to rehab, when she used to see Jackie. Drinks, dancing, likely drugs, and anonymous sex. It worried Brielle she had no memory of the events. A part of her wanted to find Jackie and tell her it couldn't happen again; the other part didn't want to see her. Jackie did something to Brielle, something she couldn't control, and it terrified her.

Back in the car, Brielle drew several steady breaths. She'd have to be careful. Her parents were back tonight, and if they knew how she'd spent the last few days or who she'd spent it with, they'd send her back to the clinic, and after a year away from there, Brielle didn't want to go back.

Chapter 5
Melanie Parker

MEL PUSHED THROUGH THE FRONT DOOR WITH groceries in her hand. She'd taken to keeping the house in order since she'd moved in with Blaine nearly two years ago. Along with their joint operation, it made her happy to keep the place fully stocked. It gave her a sense of order with all the comings and goings. On any given month, she could have three or more girls living in the house, though many opted to get their own places once the money started rolling in.

Sometimes she wondered how their operation could be different if she could turn Blaine's place into a full-fledged brothel. That was a dream for a foolish woman. While sex work was legal, purchasing sex was not, so clients would not be willing to attend a place where they could easily get caught.

"Blaine?"

"In here." His voice came from the kitchen. How convenient.

Although Mel hated the "mother hen" nickname, she

always wanted to be the caregiver to her girls. Someone they could turn to. Someone to help support them.

Business was one thing; safety and care mattered too.

Mel entered the kitchen with a smile that faded when she saw Blaine's concerned expression and Candy's bottle of pills on the counter in front of him. She set the bag at her feet.

"Everything okay?"

Blaine rolled the pills across the counter to her. "I found these in the top drawer."

"So?" Mel caught the bottle before it fell to the floor.

"So?" Blaine scoffed. "Where did they come from? And who the hell is Lexi?"

"I found them." Mel set the bottle upright on the counter. "Candy had them on her in the alleyway. In the purse I brought home. She said they weren't hers." Mel shrugged it off and turned back to the bag of groceries on the floor which she scooped up and placed on the counter, starting to unpack the contents.

"Are you sure they aren't hers?" He stood from the barstool and rounded the corner, catching Mel's wrist to stop her from loading the bag of apples into the fridge.

"No," Mel said. "What can I do about it? They clearly don't belong to her."

The annoyed expression on Blaine's face told her he disagreed.

"This is serious, Mel." Blaine released her arm and ran his hand through his hair. "Do you know what this drug means?"

"Who cares? It's just a prescription and it isn't even hers."

"I'm not so sure," Blaine said. "She was confused when you found her, maybe she's lying."

Mel planted her hands on her hips. "What do you care?"

Blaine had never been so skeptical of the other girls Jackie brought home. He always went with what Mel said and felt when it came to the business. He usually trusted her.

"It's a dangerous prescription to have." Blaine's eyebrows folded together as he looked from Mel to the bottle and back again.

"Dangerous how?"

"It's just a really intense drug."

"Because you're an expert now?" Mel scooped the bottle off the counter and pointed to the name in the top corner of the label. "Know anything about Dr. Miranda Konch? Seems like a pretty standard prescription to me."

"I've heard of her. A renowned author and psychiatrist." Blaine took the pills. "I don't like the look of these and if they were found with Candy it could mean a whole other problem."

Mel returned to unpacking the groceries. He was worried she was a druggie, which Mel had initially thought too. "If she is a druggie, like I suspected, then I doubt we'll hear from her again. I wouldn't worry too much about it."

"Fine," Blaine said, though he looked to disagree. His hand closed around the bottle. "I'm keeping these out of sight just in case."

Mel waved him off. "Do whatever you want."

He stood in the doorway for several seconds, watching her move about the kitchen until finally he turned and left her alone. She listened for his steps as he ascended the stairs.

Then she abandoned her task of unloading the bag to search for her phone.

With the device in hand, she researched the doctor who prescribed the medicine. She was a best-selling author and a well-known psychiatrist, as Blaine had said. There were rave reviews about an institute she had opened outside of town, and she was praised for her extensive work with young people—particularly women—who suffered from extreme anxiety and depression. Nothing triggered a response in Mel, but her name and photo were oddly familiar.

She clicked on the institute and noted how much the photos of it reminded her of one she'd been sent to years before. No surprise, really. Don't most mental institutions look the same?

When Blaine's footsteps sounded on the stairs again, she exited her search and returned to the groceries.

Blaine entered the kitchen wearing his black leather jacket as if ready to leave.

"Where are you going?" Mel finished with the fridge and tossed the plastic bag.

"Out," he said.

"Where?"

"I'll be back in a few hours." He headed for the front hall.

Mel followed. "That doesn't answer my question."

"I'll be back," he said.

"Is this about the drugs?"

"Leave it, Mel." Blaine reached for the door but Mel grabbed his arm.

"You can't just walk away from me. We have work to do."

He shook off her hold. "I said I'll be back." Blaine was out the door before Mel could protest further.

She followed him out to the front steps and watched him climb into his sedan and drive down the road. Arms crossed and brow furrowed, she returned to the empty house.

Chapter 6
Detective Ryan Boone

RYAN INSPECTED THE INTRICATE PIECES OF JEWELRY that lined the metal table in the evidence locker. Each one resembled a piece described and pictured in Mr. Donovan's detailed report of the stolen items, though many were still missing, including the bracelet that seemed so precious to the store owner.

"Case closed?" Archer said with a chuckle as he entered the evidence locker. The door swung shut behind him.

"Yup, that's a wrap. Let's grab lunch." Ryan grinned.

"What about a suspect?"

"Oh, right." Ryan scratched at his chin. "I guess we're tasked with finding one too. Any leads?"

"None, same as yesterday." Archer stepped to his side, looking over the rows of jewelry. "I guess that's the catch of finding evidence in an alleyway."

"It is, isn't it." Ryan placed the ring he'd been examining aside and pulled off the rubber glove. It was weird enough that they'd found half the merchandise ditched in the alley behind the store, and stranger still, they couldn't find any way to track it. Ryan knew this case was turning into a tough one. They'd have to figure out something quickly, or the trail would go cold.

"Any luck with that elusive employee?" Ryan asked.

"Chase?" Archer said. "She's still the only one we can't reach." They'd been able to contact all former employees except for a woman by the name of Lexi Chase. Mr. Donovan had implied she was a reliable employee though suffering from anger management issues, which was clear by the arrest record Archer and Ryan found on her. She'd been charged with assault and was attending mandated counselling.

Ryan reached up and scratched his chin. "Too bad we can't find her."

A knowing smile crossed Archer's face. "I think we did. Her old boss, Darko, called back."

"Well, hot dog! What did the big guy say?" Ryan asked, remembering his brief conversation with Lexi's former employer a couple of days before. She'd quit over a month ago, and Darko hadn't had any information for them.

"She called him."

"She did?"

"She needed a reference for a new job at the law firm Dunn & Dorian. He called as soon as they were off the phone."

"So, she's likely interviewing soon," Ryan said.

"I'd say so, yes. Darko seems to think tomorrow. I'm sure we could call the law office and find out more."

"Without alerting Ms. Chase?"

"Get Jade to call. That's why we have her."

Their assistant had always been good at vague explanations and discouraging further questions. She'd been with them for nearly four years and had learned the ins and outs of discretion from following their cases. Ryan had come to appreciate Jade over the years. She was young, enthusiastic, and had a way with empathy. Plus, she tolerated his stupid jokes.

Jade had only just started her job when Ryan's wife of five years died in a car accident. It had been nothing short of tragic, and for months, Ryan threw himself into work, hoping any distraction would stop him from remembering Lilian and the way the accident had bruised and battered her once beautiful face. That image haunted Ryan for longer than he'd like to admit.

Jade had been a light. Cleaning when he couldn't manage it. Grocery shopping and cooking so he wouldn't starve. She'd owed him nothing, barely knew him, but took it upon herself to lift him up.

Since then, he'd become the workaholic he'd always feared he'd become and made sure Jade got a raise. There were no romantic prospects. No one would ever be Lilian.

Ryan agreed. "As long as Jade doesn't actually mention Ms. Chase."

Ryan left the evidence locker and Archer followed.

"I'll let her know," Archer said. In Ryan's office, Archer took the seat across from him. "What about the pill?"

Ryan reached for the report given to him by the lab. "It's called Solydexran. A drug on the market typically used for anxiety or stress. It was launched just under five years ago. Why, need a pick me up?"

"Funny," Archer said. "Any tips where it could've come from?"

"My best guess is this one came off our suspect."

Archer didn't respond. He just waited for Ryan to stop grinning.

"Any pharmacy, really."

"If you find anything else."

"I'll be sure to keep it to myself."

Archer groaned. "I really didn't miss you much."

"You don't say." Ryan shot him a smirk.

Archer only shook his head. "You heading home?"

"Not yet." It was early still, and Ryan was used to longer hours. Going home meant re-watching *Schitt's Creek* and trying not to drink the entire six-pack he'd stashed in the fridge. Work seemed safer.

"What more do you have to do?"

"I want to check out the tape again." Ryan meant the one from the robbery. He'd already watched it a few times. The rookie who sifted through the store surveillance hadn't found any matches.

"There's nothing on it."

"I'm not so sure. Something about the robbery still feels off."

Archer chuckled, standing and tucking his hands into his pockets. "I'll leave you to it."

"You're heading home then?"

He glanced back at Ryan. "You know I never leave until you do."

"Really?" Ryan asked. "That's why you're always hanging around?"

Archer shook his head and turned for his office.

When Ryan was alone in his office, he closed the door, sat at his desk, and opened his laptop, pulling up the footage again. It was quick, showing the suspects as they moved through the store until the green-eyed man cut the footage. Ryan started the video again.

He did this three more times until his vision focused on the mirrored wall on the backside of the store. There was a single bit of light being reflected in the mirror and an outline of a person standing in front of it. Could there have been another person involved? A look out of some sort.

Ryan buzzed Archer's office. "You need to come in here."

"I don't want to hear about the officer that got his zipper stuck ... again." Archer groaned.

Ryan laughed at the terrible joke he'd told earlier, then composed himself. "That was a good one, but no, I think I've found something."

"Be right there." Archer was in his office in a few seconds and staring at the video.

"See." Ryan pointed to the person he was sure stood outside the store. "There's someone else involved. Three people."

"It's hard to tell if he's even there," Archer said. "It could be anything."

"Anything is a bit of a stretch." Ryan traced the outline. "There's a clear head and possibly an arm? We're looking at a humanoid, at least. Maybe alien?"

"You know what I mean," Archer said, ignoring his partner. "It's not clear enough to make a call."

"What about other surveillance? Other buildings on the stretch?"

Archer shook his head. "Nothing that faces toward the shop."

"We should check anyway; maybe we'll see them drive up." Ryan stood. "You can never be too sure."

"I'll get on it." Archer moved to leave just as Ryan's office phone buzzed.

"Ryan." Jade's voice came through the speaker. "Is Brad with you? I've just tried his office."

"He's here."

"Great, I've spoken with the recruitment at Dunn & Dorian, and Lexi Chase will be interviewing in two days. I've got the address and exact schedule waiting for you on my desk."

"Thanks, Jade."

"Always a pleasure." The phone clicked.

"Guess we're off to see some lawyers," Ryan said, rubbing his hands together like a gleeful child. "Think I should try out my new material on them? Did you know when chickens graduate from law school they become ... legal tenders?"

"Please don't." Archer clapped Ryan on the back. "I think you better get some rest."

"Yeah, yeah." Ryan looked back at his laptop. "I'll head out soon."

Chapter 7
Brielle Jeffries

BRIELLE SIPPED A GLASS OF WHITE WINE WHILE HER parents finished getting ready for the evening. The car was already out front waiting for them, and, knowing her family, the function would probably start before they arrived. Her mother finally strutted into the room dressed in a long lavender ball gown. The dress was embellished with sequins and tiny gems. Brielle rolled her eyes at the tacky garment, though it was a rather typical outfit for her mother. Brielle's short, black cocktail dress paled in comparison. Mary Jeffries had always liked to stand out.

"Mary!" Brielle's father's voice echoed down the twisted staircase. "Where are my cufflinks?"

Mary stopped putting things into her small shoulder bag. "In the top drawer, where they always are, Leonard," she called back, then she turned to Brielle, who was seated on one of the dining room chairs.

"Did you really need that before leaving?" Mary nodded to the empty wine glass on the table in front of Brielle.

"Yes," Brielle said. "Who knows who I'll see tonight."

"Aren't you excited, honey?" Mary asked. "Many of your friends will be there. They're excited to see you."

"Hmm." Brielle looked away from her mother. The friends she referred to were the children of *their* friends. People Brielle had grown up with, not necessarily liked, though she wouldn't complain. Since her return from the institute with Dr. Konch one year ago, this was the first event her parents were willing to take her to and only after they had been out of town for a week and there had been no incidents. Brielle didn't mention to either of them she had little memory of what happened the previous week. They'd blame the alcohol or accuse her of doing drugs again if she did.

Her mother turned back with a hard look. "Please try to be a bit more pleasant. I understand it's not in your nature, but you could try."

"I didn't say anything," Brielle protested.

"Honestly, Brie, sometimes you don't have to." Her mother sighed and turned away from the dining room.

Brielle took the free moment to return to the bar and fill her glass again. Two glasses deep would be enough to keep her buzz on until dinner was served.

"Another one?"

Brielle turned to see her mother standing in the doorway with her lips pursed and hands on her hips.

"I'm twenty-seven, Mom," Brielle said, sipping the drink again. "I spent five good drinking years locked in an asylum for crazies. Let me drink now."

Mary's pinched expression tightened. "You weren't locked in an asylum. You were home nearly every weekend."

"Except when I was too busy 'working abroad,'" Brielle

said, making air quotes. Her parents never told anyone Brielle was seeing a psychiatrist after she had been kidnapped as a child. They were ashamed—no member of the Jeffries' family had ever needed psychiatric help before, at least as far as the family knew—and when things got hard for Brielle as she aged, her parents shipped her away to her doctor's psychiatric hospital claiming their intelligent, beautiful daughter had been accepted for a prestigious internship at a company overseas. Nobody ever questioned a Jeffries.

"Brielle," her mother said. "You could stay here tonight."

"That would be a waste," Brielle said. She gulped down the rest of her drink. "Besides, I'm sure it will be fun." She put on a fake smile, and her mother's cold expression softened.

"Exactly, honey. Just be positive."

Brielle held her smile steady until her mother turned from the room, went back to the bar, and filled her glass again when alone. She gulped it back in one go when she heard footsteps descending the stairs.

Her father stepped into the dining room dressed in a fine black suit, golden cufflinks glimmering on his wrists, and smiled at Brielle. "You look lovely." He took his daughter by her shoulders and kissed her forehead.

"Thanks, Dad." Brielle smiled and placed the glass in the sink of the bar. Someone would get it later.

Her father looked at the glass. "Feeling a bit nervous?"

"A little," Brielle said.

Leonard put an arm around her. "Don't be."

"There will just be a bunch of people I haven't seen in a while," Brielle said. "I don't know if I want to see them."

"Will you be okay?"

"Yeah, I have to do it eventually, right?"

"Right, you'll do great." He gave her a one-arm squeeze around her shoulders.

"Leonard!" Mary's voice came from the front hallway.

Offering his daughter a smile, he and Brielle left the dining room to find Mary in the front hall, poking her head through the curtain on the window.

"What's wrong, dear?"

"That car is there again," Mary said, drawing back the curtain so Leonard could see. "It's parked on the other side of the road. What is this, the fifth time this month?"

Leonard shrugged. "I wouldn't worry about it."

Mary frowned and lowered her voice. "What if it's drugs?" She said the last word in barely a whisper, and Leonard looked over his shoulder at Brielle.

"I'm not deaf," Brielle said. "And I'm not going to crumble hearing the word *drugs*."

"Of course not, honey," Mary said with a sympathetic smile.

"Can we just go?" Brielle grabbed her red pumps from the front closet.

"Lead the way," Leonard said.

Brielle took her black pashmina from the coat rack and headed out the front door toward the limo. She looked at the waiting car down the road, which unnerved her mother. It was black, with dark windows. It was still early enough in the evening to make out the license plate. It was just a jumble of letters and numbers; it didn't mean anything to Brielle. She'd seen it, too, though she wouldn't worry her mother by telling her. She was beginning to think it was following her. With one last glance, Brielle climbed into the back of her family limo and tried to forget all about it.

THE BANQUET HALL where the A House for Women's charity event was being held was grand. The modern space opened into a large ballroom with round white-clothed tables featuring several large, embellished chandeliers. Hundreds of people were scattered about the massive room dressed in varying degrees of formal attire. A gentle tune could be heard among the buzz of conversation from the string quartet tucked in the corner.

Mary nodded toward a tall brunette woman dressed in a dark blue ball gown with long sleeves and a high neckline standing next to a good-looking man with dark slicked hair and a pinstripe suit. "You must remember her, sweetie."

Brielle cocked her head to the side as she regarded the woman. Despite being caked in heavy makeup, she was young and looked no older than Brielle. Her cheeks were sunken, and even despite the makeup, Brielle could see the dark bags beneath her eyes. The blue in them still lit up when she smiled, a smile Brielle remembered.

"Is that ..." Brielle trailed off as she tried to remember the name. "Patsy Reese?" Brielle had gone to high school with her. She had been captain of the soccer team and held student council president for their final year. Wow, did she look different.

"Patsy Morrison now. She's married and heads this committee."

Brielle could have figured out the married part by the gold band on her finger and the way the man held tight to her waist. Patsy held a steady smile. Brielle could see how it strained on the sides; she was forcing the expression.

It grew wider as an older woman in a tight red dress approached them and kissed Patsy's cheeks. They had a quiet conversation. Patsy couldn't seem to stand still. Her discomfort was a clear giveaway.

"Let's say hello," Mary said when the other woman moved away. She reached out, grabbed Leonard's wrist, and pulled him away from the conversation he was having with another guest. Brielle followed behind them, unsure of what to say to Patsy. It had been ten years since they last saw each other, and they were never close.

"Mrs. Morrison!" Mary called, dragging her husband behind her. Patsy's smile twitched and seemed less forced when she acknowledged Brielle's parents.

"Mrs. Jeffries," Patsy said as she clasped Mary's hand. "What a pleasant surprise. I wasn't sure whether to expect you and your husband."

Leonard took her hand, leaned in, and kissed her cheeks, and then Patsy motioned to the man beside her. "You remember my husband, Fraser?"

"Oh yes, of course," Mary said as she greeted Patsy's husband. "It's been ages since I've attended one of your events. We couldn't resist this one. I knew it would be well worth it and I am not disappointed. As always, a beautiful engagement; your ability to throw a flawless event never ceases to amaze me." She blinked her long eyelashes at Patsy before glancing at her husband. "Isn't that right, Leonard?"

Leonard smiled. "All Mary has spoken of since last year was this function." He motioned toward the party. "It's truly a good cause." The AHW was famous for its support of women who had suffered trauma.

"The charity has always been close to my heart," Patsy said. Her gaze lifted and glanced past Mary and Leonard to where Brielle stood. "Oh my goodness, Brielle?"

Brielle forced a smile when she heard her name. "Hi Patsy, it's been a long time."

"Far too long," Patsy said. "We must catch up soon since you're back."

"Right," Brielle agreed. "We should." Though she knew they never would. That was all girls did these days, fake smiles and false sentiments. Did anyone have a real friend anymore?

Patsy smiled again and waved them into the large banquet hall. "Please, find your seats and enjoy yourselves."

"You'll come by our table later, won't you?" Mary called as Leonard led her away.

"Of course. See you later, Brielle."

"See you," Brielle said, following her parents. As they made their way through the banquet hall, Brielle looked back at the couple greeting guests. Patsy's smile had disappeared, and Fraser pulled her close. His jaw was stiff and his gaze hard; his easy expression upon greeting them was gone.

Patsy didn't meet her husband's gaze as he spoke to her; his grip on her waist tightened, and she winced before he released her. When Fraser stepped back from his wife, Patsy's eyes quickly darted around. Her gaze met Brielle's, and she immediately dropped the contact.

If it wasn't age her makeup was trying to cover up; was it something else? Maybe those weren't bags Brielle had noticed, but fading bruises. Perhaps that was why the charity was so close to her heart.

Brielle turned away as Patsy and her husband entered the grand hall. How had the most confident girl in their high school ended up here? Patsy never touched drugs; she never drank a drop. She was most likely to succeed, and now it looked as though she had fallen the furthest, and for once, Brielle didn't hate herself for the life she'd endured.

Chapter 8
Melanie Parker

"I WON'T ALWAYS HAVE THIS OPPORTUNITY, PATSY," HE said through gritted teeth. His voice lowered, and he breathed hot air on her as he huffed out the words. He took her hand in a tight grip. Too tight. "It's like you don't want me to succeed."

She flinched. "You know that's not true."

"I don't know anything when it comes to you," he snapped.

She glanced around them, worried about who might be listening. They'd always done a good job hiding their marriage flaws in the past. Recently, his displeasure with her had been getting more erratic by the day.

"I'm sorry," she whispered. "I didn't mean it." She risked a glimpse behind her toward the beautiful setup in the banquet hall. She hoped this night would be one when his anger was forgotten, and she could pretend their marriage was as picturesque as it was when they first met. She was always fooling herself into silly dreams.

She released a breath when his grip on her loosened and his expression softened. "Of course. You were confused." He reached up and affectionately smoothed her hair, and she stood stock still, hoping he wouldn't notice how she always winced at his touch. Not that anyone would blame her. These days she didn't know if a pat or a hit would come from his initially loyal and loving hands.

He pulled her back against him, his mouth at her ear. "Now, let's join those women you call your friends and forget you ever said anything."

She closed her mouth and forced it into a confident smile as he led her further into the banquet hall. Her strained smile only caused pain to shoot through her face. The bruise had been so prominent yesterday and had faded enough today to cover up. It wasn't enough to stop the discomfort he'd caused, physically and emotionally. It was really hard to feign happiness when you were dying slowly inside.

MEL JOLTED awake at the sound of her phone. Groggy, she reached for it, trying to silence the annoying alarm. Patsy. She'd dreamed about a Patsy.

The alarm wouldn't let up, so Mel grabbed the phone, realizing it was a call.

Jackie's picture covered her screen.

"It's early," Mel said. She placed her hand over her eyes as she listened to Jackie on the other end of the phone.

"How are you asleep? Do you have any idea what happened?" Jackie's voice was breathy. Her words came out too quickly.

Mel sat up, goosebumps making her arm hair stand on edge. She was alone in the room. Blaine must have gone out early. Or had he not come home? Last she remembered, he was taking one of the girls to a job and planned to be home once everything seemed in order.

"What are you talking about?"

"Mel," Jackie said, her voice harder. "Blaine assaulted someone last night. They have him at the police station."

That had Mel out of bed and on her feet immediately. Blaine knew better than to get caught by the cops. Already Mel could see her operation spiralling out of control. Blaine would be charged. He'd get a record. The cops would keep an eye on him, then discover the truth about her line of work and how she kept so many young women employed. What was he thinking? Immediately, she brought up a mental list of each woman who had worked for her and started considering the best way to dispose of the paper trail.

"Have you talked to him?" Mel switched her phone to speaker as she frantically peeled off her sweat-soaked nightshirt and pulled on a pair of leggings and a t-shirt.

"No," Jackie said. "I spoke to Amara. She told me he attacked the guy she'd been servicing. The police were called and took all three of them in for questioning."

Mel closed her eyes. This was not good. She descended the stairs, about to head to the police station to get Blaine.

"Is Amara okay?"

"She's fine, but she's gone."

"Gone? What does that mean?"

Mel didn't hear Jackie's answer, as the door swung open before she responded, and Mel pulled the phone away from her ear. There in the doorway stood Blaine, looking exhausted and angry.

"Jackie. I have to go. Blaine just got home."

Mel ended the call and gaped at him. "What the hell happened?"

Blaine's jaw clenched, and he slammed the door shut behind him. He didn't say a word. Instead, he brushed by Mel and headed toward the kitchen.

"Blaine!" Mel reached out and grabbed his arm. He shook off her hold. She followed his steps. "You have to talk to me. Did you get charged?"

"Of course not. Not unless *he* wants to be charged." Blaine growled the words at Mel as he turned to face her. Mel didn't step away. She only continued to glare up at him.

"What happened?" she asked again. "Because you attacked somebody last night ... like the idiot you are." Mel spat the words at him without thinking.

Blaine's hands curled. "Don't."

"Not until you tell me what happened," Mel demanded. "You got picked up by the cops. You're putting our whole operation in jeopardy. Did you even think?" She reached out to grab him again. Blaine's hands flew up and caught Mel's wrists.

"I said, *don't*." His eyes flashed as he shoved Mel away from him. He stormed toward the stairs.

"You'll have to tell me eventually," Mel said, following. "I'd rather not have cops come knocking on our door."

He turned sharply and held his cold gaze on her. "That asshole lied to you," Blaine said through his teeth. His chest rose and fell quickly. "I dropped Amara off and waited. Less than an hour after I left her, I got a call. There was no one on the other end. All I could hear was Amara screaming no."

Mel's eyes widened. Her stomach twisted with guilt.

"When I got back to the house, he was laughing his ass off with a camera while one of his fucked up friends held Amara down so the other ones could ..." Blaine looked away as he trailed off. He closed his eyes for a moment as if not willing to relive it. He didn't need to say. Mel understood they were raping her.

"So you attacked them?" Mel snapped. Despite what happened, Blaine put them all in danger with his actions. She wished their lives could be different and they didn't have to hide what they did. She wanted to give absolute security to all working girls. That wasn't a reality, and Blaine knew better than to jeopardize their lives and the lives of the women they employed.

Blaine's eyes narrowed. "I saw red, Melanie. There was nothing else I could do."

"Yes, there was," Mel said, matching Blaine's glare. "You could have gotten her out of there without putting someone in the hospital."

Blaine's jaw clenched again, and he shook his head. "He didn't go to the hospital. His sleazy friends took off once the sirens sounded, and I was left to pick up the pieces. He told the police we were fighting over a girl. Amara didn't speak a word."

He looked away, and Mel knew what he was thinking—a part of him wished she had. Maybe Mel would step away from this life if Blaine and the other guy had both been charged. He was an idiot for thinking it.

He turned back to her with a sad, merciless smile. "You

don't need to worry. You may have lost a girl, and she may have been assaulted thanks to you, but *your* operation and life are safe."

Blaine turned on his heel and headed up the stairs.

Mel opened her mouth to retort and found she had nothing to say. His words had been both cruel and true. She didn't ask about Amara. She was supposed to be better than this. She was supposed to be the one to help girls like Amara, to give them a liberating job where they were in control of their bodies and not ruled by men. How could she have been so careless?

Mel went to the kitchen and lowered herself onto the barstool. Then she reached for her phone and dialled Jackie.

"What happened?" Jackie sounded out of breath when she answered.

"He's home. He's not happy." Mel placed her forehead in her free hand. "There wasn't a charge against him. He was free to go. Still, he put us all in danger with these actions."

"It's not like he wanted to attack them."

Mel paused, knowing Jackie was right. Blaine was the farthest thing from an aggressive person. She'd only seen his anger come out twice in the two years they'd known each other. The first time was when a John got too pushy with Mel and wanted more than what was agreed upon. Mel had always been able to hold her own, and when things got out of hand, she called Blaine in. He'd made quick work of the man and had Mel out the door in under five minutes.

The second time was only a few months back when Mel decided to go back to her ex. She still didn't know why she went to see him or what she'd done to cause him so much anger. He was always angry these days.

Blaine interrupted a particularly rough morning, finding Mel cowering on the kitchen floor with her ex standing over her, ready to hit her again. The only thing Mel remembered now was seeing Blaine in the doorway, eyes narrowed, as he stormed across the room, grabbed the back of the other man's shirt, and swung him across the room. He punched him too many times after that, and it was all Mel could do to beg him to stop. The loser wasn't worth Blaine going to jail for homicide.

Mel let out a long sigh. She'd been unfair to Blaine.

"It must have been pretty bad," Mel whispered after a while of silence. "For Blaine to do that."

"Be glad it wasn't you, or they'd all be dead, and we'd be dealing with a murder."

Mel couldn't deny it.

"Instead, we're a girl short, and Blaine is pissed."

"I think he's upset. He was protecting Amara. It's not like he punches every asshole we come across."

"I was too hard on him." Mel stood. She needed to talk to him. "Jackie, I'll call you later, okay?"

"Don't bother," she said. "I'm here." She ended the call as the front door creaked open.

Mel left the kitchen to find her in the front hallway. "You didn't have to come."

Jackie didn't speak; she walked to Mel's side and took her in a firm hug. "We'll be okay."

Mel didn't answer. She just let her friend comfort her.

When Jackie pulled away, she frowned, reached up, and touched Mel's cheek.

Mel quickly swatted her hand away as pain shot through her face.

"What happened to you? Are you bruised?"

"Nothing." Mel reached up and touched her tender cheek. She couldn't remember anything hitting her in the face that would have caused such discomfort. She glanced in the hallway mirror and saw the faded yellow splotches around her left eye.

Mel quickly laughed it off. "Blaine rolled me off the bed the other night when things got a bit passionate. You know how clumsy I can be."

Pretending with Jackie always came easy. The girl would believe anything Mel told her. However, Mel couldn't so easily convince herself. It had been a while since she'd suffered severe memory lapses. Or discovered unexplained bruises. Maybe she'd been drinking too much. Stress sometimes made her go a little heavy on the sauce.

She couldn't let Blaine find out. The last time a boyfriend found out about her blackouts, she was sent away for psychiatric help. It had done nothing but cause her more distress. She wouldn't go through that again.

The idea made Mel's stomach twist; however, she had no idea what may have caused the faded bruising or any idea why she hadn't noticed a bruise in the first place.

Jackie cracked a smile that disappeared quickly, and she chewed on her lower lip. "What do we do now about the Amara thing?"

Mel turned back to her friend. "We change our tactics. Get better at screening. I won't let that happen again."

Mel went for the stairs, resolved to find Blaine. She owed him an apology.

Jackie didn't speak again, only let Mel walk away. They

both were thinking the same thing. In their line of work, how could they ever be sure they were one hundred percent safe?

MEL'S EARS perked at the sound of the front door opening. It had been over three days since Candy had left, and Jackie had gone home the day before. For once, Mel and Blaine were expecting a quiet night alone.

"Hello?" The voice sounded from the front hall. "Anyone home?"

Mel rolled her eyes and threw her legs over the side of the bed as she discarded her day planner on the bedside table. Blaine looked up from the book in his hand as she moved toward the door.

"What an astute question," she mumbled more to herself than Blaine. Why would the front door be unlocked if no one was home? She glanced back when her phone chimed on the bedside table and almost went to pick it up.

"Hello?" the voice came again.

Mel resolved to answer whoever it was later and headed down the stairs to find Candy at the entrance.

"You're okay."

Candy smiled, kicked off her shoes, and placed a small bag she'd been carrying on the floor. "Yeah, though the asshole didn't give me much."

"You're lucky he gave you anything." Mel paused, then added, "And didn't hurt you more."

"I guess."

Mel's eyes narrowed. "You are. To think otherwise is

pretty naïve." Or lucky. Candy had never seen the abuse Mel had.

Candy grimaced, shifting uncomfortably under Mel's gaze. She looked as she did when she left. No worse for wear.

She really was lucky.

Mel shook her head and turned for the stairs, uninterested in Jackie's pet.

"Uh," Candy said, forcing Mel to look back in her direction. "Is Jackie here?"

"No," Mel said.

Candy hovered in the doorway, seemingly unsure how to proceed.

"Come with me." Mel waved Candy to follow her. Mel had hoped Jackie would be here when Candy returned. Without her, Mel would have to tend to her in her friend's place.

Candy picked up her bag and followed Mel up the stairs. Mel led her into Jackie's room, reached into the top drawer, and pulled out the bracelet Candy had given them days before. "Here." Mel held the bracelet out to her. "Jackie will be glad you're back."

Candy eyed the bracelet. "Keep it."

"I don't want your blood diamonds." Mel took Candy's hand and thrust the bracelet into it.

Candy frowned and ran her fingers over the diamonds before putting them back on her wrist.

"I owe you for taking care of me, for letting me stay. I don't have any money. This is all I can give you."

"You could work," Mel said as if their job was a basic career. "I lost a girl this week. I could use another who's cute, innocent looking." She waved her hand up and down Candy's body. "You fit the bill. What do you say?"

"I don't know what I'm agreeing to."

"You can't stay if you don't pay your way."

Candy lowered herself to the bed behind her as if to consider where to go from here.

"What do I have to do?" She met Mel's gaze.

Candy said nothing while Mel explained the complex operation she and Blaine had set up in the previous year. Her eyebrows were set in a hard line, and she seemed uncertain.

"So you're a madam," Candy said. "Is Blaine a pimp then?"

Mel laughed at the idea. "Not exactly."

"You arrange for girls to sleep with guys for money," Candy said. "That's a madam."

Mel raised an eyebrow at the younger girl but couldn't disagree.

"Call it what you want," Mel said. "As you get into the job and make good money, most girls start to love it. It's empowering, in a way."

Candy frowned. "So, what, now one girl is gone, you need another to fill her place. Is it just you and Jackie now? Oh wait, there was another girl too, right, Gabi?"

"Yes, Gabi works with us, too, and other girls don't live at the house. Most of them have their own places."

Candy didn't respond for several moments.

Mel let out a long huff of air. "No one is making you stay. It's only if you want to. You're welcome to leave at any time."

Still, Candy didn't answer.

"Look, you seem like a good person who's had a rough time. I'm not about to force you into something you don't want or cast you out onto the street. Take a few days, and if you can find cash another way, you're still welcome to stay."

Mel turned for her room, leaving Candy to consider her options.

"BLAINE?" Mel called when she found the bedroom empty. She looked at the bathroom door. It was closed.

Mel went to the bedside table to retrieve her phone and texted Jackie that Candy had returned. There she found the table empty and her phone gone.

Strange. She could have sworn it was there when Candy arrived home.

"Blaine?" Mel called again.

There was a sound of a toilet flushing, and Blaine soon emerged. He tossed her phone on the bed.

"Found it in the bathroom."

Mel looked at the phone and then back at Blaine. She was certain she didn't leave it in the bathroom. Had he taken it for some reason?

"Thanks," Mel said, though she couldn't stop the skepticism from creeping into her tone.

"Who was it?" Blaine asked, his posture stiff as he moved past her and climbed back into bed with his book.

"Candy is back." Mel didn't offer him further details as she reached for her phone and texted Jackie. She clicked into her messaging app and paused, looking over the texts. There was nothing new or unread. Had her phone chimed when she went to see Candy? She might have left it in the bathroom like Blaine had said and imagined the whole thing.

Clicking on Jackie's name, she quickly typed out a message.

Candy is back. She's going to look for work elsewhere. May be back again.

Then she set her phone aside and crawled back into bed next to Blaine.

He draped an arm across her shoulders but didn't once look up from the book. Mel rested her head on his chest, unable to stop the frown that followed. Something about Blaine and her phone was bothering her. She couldn't quite put her finger on it.

Chapter 9
Detective Ryan Boone

Ryan and Archer sat in the cruiser, waiting outside the tall office. It was at least twenty stories high, with floor-to-ceiling windows on each level. The building appeared to be made almost entirely of glass.

"You sure this was the time?" Ryan asked, casting a sideways glance at Archer.

"Yup," Archer said, still gripping the steering wheel.

"And still no idea where she lives?" Ryan asked. He hated ambushing people on the street, but it sometimes made for the best confessions, even if it felt cheap.

"Nope," Archer said. "This is our best chance. Besides, would going to her house be the best idea with what we've learned?"

Every other former employee had an alibi. Lexi Chase was the only one evading police questioning; it didn't help she had a criminal record.

Ryan glanced back toward the building and then at the picture they'd found with her file. At least he'd be able to spot her.

They waited another ten minutes, and then he was out his door when she stepped into the street. Her long red hair whipped in the wind as she pulled her blazer tighter around her and clutched her briefcase with her other hand. She seemed to stop and draw a deep breath before moving away from the building.

"Ms. Chase?" Ryan asked. He heard the door open behind him as Archer climbed out of the driver's side.

The woman stopped and turned toward them.

Ryan fished into his pocket and pulled out his badge when he saw her confused expression. "Just your friendly neighbourhood police officer."

"Yes?" she said, though her voice seemed uneasy.

"You sure are a tricky one to find." He tucked his badge away and offered her a free hand. "Detective Ryan Boone."

Lexi Chase took his hand and shook it, then Ryan nodded to the cruiser behind him where his partner stood. "Detective Brad Archer." Archer didn't move. He only tilted his head in acknowledgement.

"How can I help you, Detective?" Lexi said. She spoke slowly and seemed to shift under Ryan's gaze. The police always seemed to make people uncomfortable, which was one of the reasons Ryan hated the ambush tactic.

"We were hoping to ask you about a recent robbery at Donovan's Jewellers," Ryan said. "You were a former employee there, correct?"

"Yeah, I heard about that. Such a shame." Lexi glanced from Ryan to Archer. "Is Mr. Donovan okay?"

"He's quite alright, Ms. Chase. Thank you for your concern."

"Of course," Lexi said. "I'm glad to hear he's okay. I was a former employee of his over a year or two ago. I can't remember when I quit. He was a great boss."

"Why did you leave?" Ryan asked, pulling out a notepad and pen, poised to make a note if needed.

Lexi frowned. "Why does it matter to your investigation, Detective? I found a good job in another city. I didn't think I needed a better reason than that."

"Of course, Ms. Chase," Ryan said. "We are just trying to gather as much information as possible surrounding former employees. We aren't trying to offend you in any way."

Lexi's hand clenched into a fist that she almost immediately released. She looked away from Ryan's gaze.

"Am I being investigated?" Lexi asked, her posture stiffening.

"We haven't ruled out any options," Archer said from behind Ryan as he shifted his position on the car. He straightened, and Lexi stepped back, a typical reaction to Archer's huge form.

Ryan glanced back and waved him down. Archer stopped moving and leaned back against the car. His dark gaze stayed on Lexi, and she shifted uncomfortably before them.

"We need to know where you were on the night of May seventeenth," Ryan said.

"Two weeks ago?" Lexi put a finger to her lips as her brow line furrowed. "I had just moved back to town. I was moving my things into my boyfriend's apartment."

"Can we speak with him?" Ryan asked.

Lexi shook her head. "You could if I knew where he was. He kicked me out shortly after and disappeared."

Ryan scribbled the note on the page and smiled to himself. "Vanished without a trace?"

"Seems like it."

"Can anyone verify your whereabouts?" He cleared his throat, reminding himself his quips weren't well received during interviews.

Lexi was silent for a few seconds before she spoke. "Yeah, my current roommate, Marley. She works at Dunn & Dorian." She waved to the office building behind her. "But here—" she pulled out her phone and motioned to Ryan's notepad. He passed it to her, and she scribbled down the number. "You can call her there."

"A contact for you too, Ms. Chase," Ryan said.

"Of course." Lexi scribbled another number down next to the first and passed it back. "Am I free to go?"

"What's his name?" Archer asked. "The boyfriend?"

Lexi shifted. "Look, if I'm not under arrest or anything, I don't feel comfortable giving out any more information."

Ryan frowned. He understood. It was a bit suspicious but not surprising. They didn't have a warrant for her arrest, and she didn't have to tell them any more than she wanted to.

"We'll call if we think of anything else."

"Great." Lexi turned on her heel and headed down the street. She didn't look back. Ryan watched her until she disappeared around the corner. He looked to Archer.

"Do you want to call the roommate?" Ryan asked as he and Archer climbed back into the cruiser.

Archer shook his head. "You're better at the people relations part of the job."

"Only because you always refuse to call." Ryan laughed.

Archer grinned. It was probably better that Ryan called anyway.

~

He called the roommate as soon as he got back to the office.

"Hello, this is Marley speaking," she answered on the second ring.

Ryan tapped his pen on his desk. "Hello, Marley. This is Detective Ryan Boone calling regarding a case we're working on. Your number was given to me by Lexi Chase, a friend of yours?"

"Oh." There was hesitation in her voice. "Yes, of course. How can I help you, Detective?"

"We'd like to ask you about Ms. Chase's whereabouts after her return to the city a few weeks ago," Ryan said.

"Is Lexi in trouble?" Marley asked.

Ryan stopped tapping his pen and leaned forward in his chair. "Not at this time. Do you have reason to believe that she might be?"

"Well, her ex was pretty horrible to her," Marley said.

Ryan jotted the note down. "How so?"

"I'm not really sure, to be honest. I've asked her before but she doesn't like to talk about it. I'm glad the jerk is gone."

At least that lined up with Lexi's story. Ryan made another note.

"Is Ms. Chase currently living with you?" Ryan asked.

"She is," Marley said. "Moved in right after she left her boyfriend's. About two weeks ago, I think."

Ryan frowned. Didn't Lexi say she had been moving in

with her boyfriend at the time? He flipped back in his notes from earlier to confirm his thought.

"She mentioned moving in with her boyfriend," Ryan said.

"Oh, uh, yeah," Marley said. "She did that, only for, like, a day."

"Do you remember where Ms. Chase was on May seventeenth?" Ryan asked, dropping his pen and scratching at the stubble on his chin.

"The seventeenth? Hmm ..." Marley didn't answer for several seconds. "She called me to say she was back in town and living in her boyfriend's condo. We made plans to grab lunch the next day and she ended up calling me later to ask for a hand moving. I went by as soon as I finished work. Her boyfriend wasn't there, and when I saw her the next day, she told me he'd kicked her out."

"Do you know what she did that night?" Ryan asked.

"No, I don't. Sorry, Detective."

"And this boyfriend," Ryan asked. "Can you tell us anything about him? A name, maybe? Ms. Chase was rather reluctant to tell us more."

"She called him Bren," Marley said. "I never met the guy and didn't even know his last name. Lexi didn't like to talk about him. I think he might have hit her."

"Nothing was ever reported," Ryan said.

"No, I told Lexi to report him, but she brushed it off. I think she was scared of him." There was a commotion on the other end. "I'm sorry to cut this short, Detective; I have to go."

"Thank you for your time," Ryan said. "I'll call if I have any more questions."

"I will help however I can." The line went dead before Ryan could answer. He placed his phone back on the hook and glanced at his notes. The conversations were evasive. Ryan couldn't put his finger on why.

A knock at the door drew his attention, and Ryan glanced up to see Archer leaning against the doorframe.

"Does her story check out?" Archer asked.

Ryan leaned back in his chair, scratching at his chin. "In a way, though, something about it doesn't add up. I don't think we're going to get anything else out of Ms. Chase or her friend."

"What are you proposing then?"

"I want to follow her," Ryan said.

"Do you have time for that?" Archer crossed his arms over his broad chest.

Ryan laughed. "No. Besides, Lexi Chase knows who we are now. What about Quinn?"

"He's eager," Archer said. He never seemed to have another opinion about any of the officers they worked with.

"Do you think he'd be good for it?"

Archer only shrugged.

"Thanks for your help."

His partner grinned. "Any time."

"Do me a favour?"

"Sure."

Ryan slid the notepad across his desk, and Archer stepped into the room to grab it.

"Ask Singh if he'll give up Quinn for this investigation." Ryan motioned to the notepad. "My notes are there if he needs some convincing."

"Singh always does what you ask," Archer smirked.

"That's true. I'm just too damn lovable to say no to." Ryan laughed. "Isn't that why you haven't asked for a new partner after all these years?"

"Your jokes might be bad, but your work ethic speaks for itself," Archer quipped. "Call me lazy, but with a baby at home, it helps when your partner is a crazed workaholic."

"Be warned," Ryan said. "The day Alexis Rose speaks back to me I'll stop showing up here."

Archer rolled his eyes and took the notepad before exiting the office.

Ryan swivelled in his chair and faced the window that overlooked the street. Even if Alexis Rose spoke back to him during an episode of *Schitt's Creek*, she still wouldn't be enough to replace Lillian. He drew a long breath and glanced at the bright sun. A tension headache was starting to grow behind his eyes. He was getting tired of all the mystery and needed a decent lead.

His phone buzzed. "Mr. Donovan is here to see you."

"Send him in." Ryan turned back to his desk and looked down at the blurry still in front of him. It wasn't clear who this person was, but it was a better picture than what was in the video.

"Thanks for coming." Ryan stood to meet the store owner. Mr. Donovan looked more put together than he had the day of the crime. Less anxious, likely because the police had already recovered half the stolen merchandise.

"Of course." Donovan took the seat opposite him. "There was something you wished to show me?"

"A question, actually." Ryan slid the photo closer to Donovan. "Does this man look familiar?"

Donovan studied the photo. "Certainly. This is the man

who has been sleeping outside my shop for the last two weeks."

"Homeless?"

"I assumed so." Donovan looked up at Ryan. "He was there every morning I arrived, and every evening I left. Friendly sort, went by the name Tim."

"We think he might be involved."

"In the theft?" Donovan shook his head. "I very much doubt it. He's not nearly sophisticated enough for something like this."

"You're right." Ryan reached up and scratched at his chin. "We think he acted as lookout. And it's strange he's no longer outside your shop, isn't it?"

"Sure," Donovan said. "Perhaps he found a better place to make street money."

"Or he doesn't need it anymore. Can you tell us anything about him?"

"I'm sorry, Detective, I don't know much else." Donovan paused before adding, "I recall seeing Cory speaking with him once. I suggest reaching out to him and seeing if he has something he can offer on the subject."

"I'll be sure to do that." Ryan stood with Donovan and offered his hand. "Please let me know if anything comes to you. We'll call if something comes up."

"Thank you for your thorough service, Detective."

Ryan nodded, and Donovan left his office. Back in his chair, Ryan glanced back at the photo. One suspect who had little evidence pointing in her direction and one who was nowhere to be found.

With no other options, he picked up the phone and dialled Cory. Hopefully, he'd be helpful.

Chapter 10
Melanie Parker

W HERE HAD HE PUT IT? MEL SEARCHED FRANTICALLY for the account information from Sanders Boutique on Main Street. Candy had returned only an hour before, having been unable to find work. She'd agreed to join Mel's operation, and now Mel had to find some suitable clothing for the girl.

Jackie had been far too excited to go shopping. Mel would have to chaperone.

Unable to find the card in his usual hiding places, Mel went to Blaine's office. She rarely stepped foot in this part of the house. Blaine had made it clear the office was his personal space and off-limits to Mel's working girls. He'd never forbid her from using it, though Mel could take a hint.

At the desk, she pulled open a drawer to find it empty. Moving on to the next one, there were only files and she promptly shoved it closed. Why had she let Blaine manage the account information when she was usually the one to go? She made a mental note to make sure the card was more accessible in the future.

When she slid open the next drawer and moved a file,

she stopped short. There in the drawer were several orange pill bottles. She frowned. What was Blaine doing with these?

Picking up the first one, she realized it was the bottle they'd found on Candy, the one prescribed to Lexi Chase. What were the others?

Mel picked up one and almost dropped it. The name—Brielle Jeffries—was familiar. An heiress. Mel couldn't begin to imagine how Blaine had ended up with this bottle.

Three more remained. Her chest constricted as she picked them up and read the label. Patsy Morrison, the name Blaine swore he'd never heard before when Mel had asked him about the strange voicemail.

All of them contained Solydexran and were prescribed by the same doctor—Miranda Konch.

"What are you doing in here?"

Mel jumped.

Blaine's eyes fell on the bottle in her hand. He was across the room in a few short strides and yanked the bottle from her hold before throwing it back in the drawer and closing it.

"You're not supposed to be in here."

"What are those?" Mel asked. She didn't care what he thought. She wanted an explanation. "You told me the name Patsy wasn't familiar to you, but you have three pill bottles prescribed to that name? What is going on?"

Blaine placed his hand on the desk and closed his eyes. Mel only continued to stare at him, her chest heaving.

"Blaine?" She demanded. "Why do you have a bunch of pills that don't belong to you? You lied to me."

Blaine turned a stern gaze on Mel. When he spoke, his voice came out low, dangerous. "Get out of here."

Mel stood her ground. "Tell me why you have those."

"It's none of your goddamn business, Melanie," Blaine spat at her. He straightened, his hulking form towering over her. Mel instinctively stepped back, away from his rage. Still, she couldn't let it go.

"Tell me."

"Get out," he growled again. When she didn't move he spoke more forcefully. "Get out!"

He stormed toward her; his hand poised to hit.

"Please, I'm sorry," she begged, cowering away from him. "I didn't mean it."

The sickening slap sounded worse than the pain that rang through her skull. She'd gotten used to the agony.

Mel leapt back, the flash disorienting and confusing her. Blaine still stood by the desk, his eyes wild and angry. She turned on her heel and scampered out of the office. She didn't stop moving until she was in their shared bathroom with the door locked behind her.

She drew several steady breaths as she sat against the door. What had she seen? *Who* had she seen? She reached up and touched her cheek where the man struck her in her memories. It wasn't tender to touch but a phantom pain that seemed to reside in her mind. She'd felt him hit her and Blaine hadn't even moved.

Mel closed her eyes and pressed her forehead into her hands. Was she losing her mind?

"Melanie?" Blaine's voice came from behind the door and he gently knocked on it. All anger he'd had only moments before seemed to vanish. "Melanie, let me in."

Mel considered ignoring him, unsure who she was opening the door for. The sadness in his tone made her reconsider, and she clicked the lock then moved aside so he could push the door open.

Blaine found her on the floor, her arms wrapped around her legs, and he immediately bent down and took her into his arms. She stiffened at his touch but didn't push away.

"I am so sorry." Blaine buried his face in her hair. "I didn't mean to yell."

Mel stayed quiet in his hold as her breathing calmed. She didn't know what came over her, or where the fear came from. She'd never been scared of Blaine before. What had happened this time?

He loosened his hold and pulled away to see her face. "Are you okay?"

Mel nodded. She wanted to ask about the pills, to ask what happened and why he'd gotten so angry. She wanted to know why he had them. But she didn't want to see his anger again. She'd never had him direct his anger so pointedly at her. It wasn't something she wanted to relive.

Blaine cocked his head to the side, his thick eyebrows furrowed. "Melanie?"

"Yeah, I'm fine."

Relief washed over his face as he stood and pulled her to her feet.

"What were you looking for?"

"The account information for Sanders," Mel said. "We're going to take Candy shopping."

Blaine led her from the bathroom. He went to the dresser where he'd discarded his wallet, pulled out a card and handed it to her.

Mel took the card and looked away from Blaine. "Do you think it's a good idea?"

"Shopping?" Blaine asked.

"No, having Candy join us." Mel chewed on her lower lip. She didn't know anything about the girl and still wasn't sure about the drugs she'd found the first day they met. Blaine had acted strange about them even then. It seemed risky, though, with Amara gone ... Mel was having a hard time seeing past the potential of having another girl on board.

"You can trust Jackie's judgment."

"I hope so."

Blaine grabbed his book and settled on the bed. "Call if you need anything."

Mel didn't answer him as she left the room and headed back downstairs to where Jackie and Candy waited. As she approached the sitting room, she overheard them talking in hushed tones.

"You really think it will be worth it?" Candy asked Jackie.

Mel hesitated and peeked around the corner, gauging her friend's reaction.

At first, Jackie didn't answer, only looked away, but not before Mel caught a flash of remorse cross her face. Jackie rarely opened up about her past, and Mel only learned about the girl through glimpses. It wasn't the first time Mel suspected Jackie wished her life had taken a different turn. It was a question Mel didn't want to know the answer to. She needed Jackie more than anyone. Sometimes more than Blaine.

Finally, Jackie spoke. "Totally. You'll love the job and the money. Trust me."

Unwilling to give Candy a chance to respond, Mel

entered the room. "Got the card."

"Great." Jackie looked at her with a smile, though her tightly-pursed lips gave way to the strain. It wasn't genuine. They stood and followed Mel into the front hallway.

"We're not getting anything too flashy," Mel said as she slipped on her shoes. "Candy's innocence will sell enough."

Jackie frowned.

"What's wrong?" Mel asked. Jackie had been in a mood since she arrived at the house. Mel didn't care for the games. Sometimes she wished Jackie would say what she was thinking.

Jackie shook her head. "She's a person, you know."

"What are you talking about?"

"Sometimes you talk about us like we're nothing but props in your lifestyle," Jackie said. "I get it that in a way we are. It doesn't need to be reminded. Maybe if you were a bit more sympathetic, Amara would still be around."

Mel's expression tightened. "Jackie, you know it's not like that at all. I work hard to keep you all safe and employed."

"I know," Jackie said. "You can just be really abrasive sometimes. Someone needed to say something. I'm not the only one who thinks it."

"You choose to be here," Mel said. The girls were a means to an end in a way. She didn't treat them like they were worthless. She cared for them. Made sure they made good money. Made sure they were STI tested. Made sure they were comfortable with the clients they serviced. It wasn't like Mel just threw them to the wolves to fend for themselves. So she was a little rough around the edges, so what? She had to be in her choice of work. Someone had to keep things in line.

"I know." Jackie turned back to Candy and smiled. "You ready?"

Candy nodded.

"Good. I'll drive." Mel grabbed the keys from the hook near the door and led the other girls to the car. "We'll head to Sanders. They'll have more than enough that'll suit you."

Candy fiddled with the bracelet on her wrist as she climbed into the back seat. She didn't stop fidgeting even when they were waiting outside the store.

Jackie glanced back at her from the front seat. "You okay?"

"Yeah." Candy looked at Jackie before averting her gaze outside once more.

"You sure?" Jackie cast a sideways look at Mel.

"Yeah." Candy didn't look at her this time.

"You can tell us, you know," Jackie said. "We won't judge."

Candy looked at Mel then bit down on her lip and her gaze fell to her hands in her lap. She obviously didn't trust Mel not to judge her. After a moment, she looked up at Jackie.

"I guess I'm just not sure what to expect."

Mel frowned and exchanged a glance with Jackie. "You're not a virgin ..."

Candy gave a stiff laugh. "God, no."

"Oh, good," Jackie laughed. "That might have posed a problem. Then what's bothering you?"

"I'm a little scared," Candy said, avoiding Mel's gaze in the rearview mirror.

"I understand. I was too," Jackie said. "Mel looks out for us and I promise you, the money is worth it."

"I could use good money," Candy mumbled the words as she looked down at her hands.

"We all can," Mel agreed.

Jackie waved to the store they were parked in front of. "Makes coming to places like this much more fun. No window shopping for us." She winked and got out of the car.

"Don't worry about it," Mel said. "It's always scary at first. You'll do great."

It wasn't the first time she'd given this speech to a new girl, and it wouldn't be the last. Most of the women she came across in her line of work were frightened and vulnerable. It came with the territory. The majority of them opened up as soon as they realized they were good at it and the men who hired them were desperate for their attention. Also, the girls were the ones with all the power. Women who once felt used, abused, or tossed aside, found new confidence in the control of their bodies and the money they made off it. What happened with Amara was rare and really a fault of Mel's for not vetting the job better. It was a mistake she wouldn't make again.

Candy followed them up the sidewalk to the brightly-lit fashion store nestled between a fancy spa and an upscale jewelry boutique. Candy looked at it and started fidgeting with her bracelet.

Jackie caught her hand. "Relax, we go to places like this all the time."

The door chimed as Jackie pushed it open and three sets of eyes fell on them; saleswomen. One of them gasped and a short, fit brunette bounced to their side.

"Oh my gosh, Brielle Jeffries," the brunette saleswoman

said to Jackie. She looked no older than twenty and blinked her large hazel eyes at them. "What a pleasant surprise."

Mel rolled her eyes. This wasn't the first time Jackie was mistaken for the well-known heiress.

Jackie simply smiled and shook her head. "I'm sorry ..." Jackie trailed off and glanced at the woman's name tag, "... Debbie, you seem to have me confused. I'm not Brielle Jeffries."

Debbie glanced between Jackie and the other girls for several seconds before her eyebrows folded together and she lowered her gaze.

"I'm so sorry," Debbie said. "I heard Brielle and her family had returned to town, and you look so similar. Forgive my confusion."

"Of course," Jackie said. "You aren't the first."

Another woman approached from behind them. Mel knew her as soon as she smiled.

"Hello, Ms. Parker," the woman said, gently pushing Debbie behind her.

"Hi, Angela."

Angela's gaze went to Jackie. "Forgive Debbie. It's only her first week."

"It's no problem."

Mel shrugged. "It's happened too many times to count." She stepped aside and pulled Candy forward toward the saleswoman. "This is Ms. Long, and we are looking for a few outfits suitable for a fancy party. We're hoping to impress. There will be some very eligible bachelors there."

"On Mr. Roche's account?" Angela asked.

"Yes." Mel passed Angela the card Blaine gave her.

Angela smiled and took Candy's arm. "Very good. Come this way, Ms. Long. I'm certain we have something perfect."

Mel moved to follow them further into the store but Jackie grabbed her arm and held her back.

"Did you know the Jeffries were back in town?" Jackie asked in a hushed tone. The Jeffries were well known as owners of a North American industry-leading homebuilding company, Jeffco Homes. None of them had lived in the area for years.

A few months ago, when Jackie had been drinking, she divulged a past relationship with the heiress, Brielle. She didn't give many details, and when Mel asked about it the next day, Jackie was tight-lipped and embarrassed. They'd never spoken about it since.

"Whole family is back," Mel said. "As of last week. Don't you read the news? Or the tabloids at least."

Jackie frowned. "It's strange, isn't it?"

"Why?" Mel asked. "Are you expecting a phone call?"

"No," Jackie said quickly. "I'm just surprised, is all. I didn't think they'd come back."

"I don't try to understand the complexities of families like the Jeffries. Besides, they're a wealthy bunch. Maybe we can get a few clients out of it."

"Ms. Parker?" Angela called from a rack near the back of the store.

Mel glanced at Jackie, wondering if she would speak again. Jackie looked deep in thought. Whatever was going through her mind, she wasn't about to divulge.

Mel turned and went to join Candy.

Chapter 11
Brielle Jeffries

A COLD WIND WHISTLED THROUGH A CRACK IN THE STONE
wall. *The only light in the room was a dim candle that flickered every time Brielle shivered. She worried it would go out.
When it did, she'd scream and he'd return.*

*She watched the dancing flame, casting obscure shadows
throughout the small square room. She pictured demons,
monsters, ghosts—all means of terrible creatures could live in
the darkness. None were as scary as him.*

*Brielle pulled the covers over her head, willing herself to
be silent, to not make a sound. Even if the candle went out,
she'd be quiet.*

*Another breeze whistled through the crack and the candle
dimmed. Brielle withdrew her head from beneath the covers
and watched the shadows shrink, then grow, scaling up the
wall. Her breathing hitched when one looked like it moved
toward her, fingers stretching as if to grasp. Her heart thudded.
She'd been scared every night since he put her down here.*

*There was a thump above and she glanced to the roof as
another breeze extinguished the candle. She told herself not to*

scream. She told herself nothing could get her here. Then she heard another thud and couldn't stop the sound. She screamed. She screamed loud. Tears welled in her eyes and spilled down her cheeks until her screams turned into uncontrollable sobbing.

She heard footsteps descending the stairs. Her crying stopped. She held her breath as the door creaked open, and he entered, holding a candle in his hand. It lit up his round, youthful face. He looked like a boy, but Brielle knew he was a grown man. His hair was long, raven black, and his eyes were hazel, almost green.

"Poor little Relly," he said, placing the candle on the desk and coming to sit on the edge of her bed. "Were you frightened, my love?"

Brielle didn't answer, holding her breath as he reached out and brushed her bangs away from her forehead.

"You must not be scared, dear one," he said. "I will always keep you safe." He leaned down and kissed her forehead. "I love you, Relly."

When he moved away to light her candle, she released a quiet breath. Maybe he would go and leave her alone tonight. It wasn't the case, as he turned back to her with the familiar grin.

"I'm so glad you're here, Relly," he said, moving to the bed again. He cupped her face and leaned down to kiss her, this time on the mouth.

Brielle tensed, knowing what came next. She closed her eyes, freezing under his contact. Then something in her changed. She reached away from him, seeking for what she'd stashed between the bed and the wall. Her hand grasped it and swung, lodging the broken piece of metal in his arm.

He screamed, falling backwards from her. Brielle didn't hesitate. She jumped to her feet, hopped around him, and bolted up the stairs. She reached outside and found herself in the middle of a yard, the bright, round moon her only light source. Looking in every direction, she sought out the woods and ran toward them.

His screams came from within the bunker as he pursued her.

Brielle ran hard, dodging trees and other obstacles as she bolted through the thickly wooded area. When her lungs started to heave, and her legs started to slow, she sought cover, finding a space between the massive roots of an old oak tree and the soft ground below. Crawling inside, it looked like it may have belonged to an animal. Hopefully, the creature wouldn't return soon.

She crouched in the darkness of the home, hidden from sight, and fought to keep her breathing shallow and quiet. His footsteps echoed through the forest, snapping branches as he searched for her. Brielle allowed a single breath of relief when he ran past where she hid.

BRIELLE SAT UP IN BED. Her sheets and clothes were soaked with her cold sweat, and her heart raced as she gasped for a steady breath. She hated when her dreams used memories to haunt her. Shaking it off, she crawled out of bed and headed to the shower.

She'd had the dream before; she'd dealt with it more than once. Like every time, she'd take a hot shower and forget it. She was glad no one was around to see it happen. If her parents knew she was having these dreams again, it would be more evidence for them to prove she was crazy.

BRIELLE STARED out the fifth-story window, watching birds fly by and listening to the soft buzz of the moving traffic below. Seated in an oversized armchair, she had tuned out of the conversation with her shrink. These meetings felt pointless now.

Dr. Miranda Konch cleared her throat and drew Brielle's attention back to her.

Brielle glanced over at the older woman seated across from her. Her greying hair was tied in a tight bun on top of her head and accentuated her sharp, pointed features. Her taupe eyes bore into Brielle's and seemed to search for a reply. Brielle had nothing for her. After nearly fourteen years with this woman, Brielle neither felt closer to her nor comfortable in her presence. It was easier when she was still at the clinic. At least there she met with various shrinks and only saw Miranda once a month at most.

"Do you want to talk about the weekend?" Miranda asked.

Brielle looked back toward the window. "No."

A page flipped. "Are you sure? It's only your first gala back in your parents' reality. It's okay if you're having a hard time."

Brielle stifled a laugh. She couldn't be honest with the shrink, knowing her parents heard every last word they spoke in these appointments. Miranda had reported their conversations since Brielle was a little girl. Being an heiress and an only child didn't entitle her to privacy. Money could buy all the conversations in the world.

Brielle shifted her gaze back to the doctor and shook her head. "No, I'm fine. It's the same as it used to be. Socialites determining their worth by other socialites."

"You sound resentful." Miranda raised an eyebrow.

"For once, I'm not." Looking back at the window, Brielle wished there were other things about the plain, square office that she could focus her attention on.

"Your mother tells me you saw an old friend at the event," Miranda said. "She worries you might be comparing yourself to her success."

"What friend?"

Miranda flipped the page. "Her name is Patsy."

"Oh."

"Do you want to talk about her?"

"There isn't much to say," Brielle said. "We went to high school together. We were never close."

"Are you comparing yourself to her?" Miranda asked.

Brielle thought back to the night of the charity ball. She remembered seeing Patsy's forced smile and covered bruises. The woman was unhappy; she put up a good facade.

"I wouldn't say that."

"What would you say?"

Brielle looked back at the window and pondered the question. She found she pitied Patsy. She was the last person Brielle expected to fall under the spell of an abusive man, and she wondered what could have happened to her to end up this way.

"I don't know," Brielle said. "I guess it's a relief to see I'm not the only one who has struggled with growing up."

"And that helps you feel normal?"

"In a way, I guess." Brielle shrugged. She wasn't sure how she felt about it.

"Do you feel normal?" Miranda asked. "It's been nearly a year since you left my clinic."

"Yeah, I think so." Brielle didn't mention the memory lapses she'd been experiencing since her return to her parents' house; that would mean she was crazy.

"Nothing feels off?"

Brielle shook her head, though, in reality, everything felt off. She'd taken to drinking a lot since she left the clinic. All the nights her parents left her alone made it easy to start. Starting was always easy. Brielle chalked all her memory loss to her alcohol consumption. Drinking herself into a stupor wasn't hard when the only family around her barely paid her any attention.

Then there was the feeling of being followed whenever she stepped out of her house alone. It started a few months back, and when she couldn't shake it, she stopped going out as often alone.

"Are you still having your night terrors?" Miranda asked.

Brielle frowned. It sounded so juvenile. They weren't night terrors; they were reliving the past.

Again, she shook her head. "I'm fine."

"You don't dream about the abduction anymore?" Miranda glanced over her papers.

"No." Brielle looked away. She didn't want to relive being abducted as a child again. What happened last night wasn't a rarity; she often saw her prison when she slept. She heard his voice in her mind. They covered this in every session. Couldn't she escape from it for once?

"That's good, Brielle," Miranda said. "A huge improvement."

"I guess."

"What about Jackie," Miranda said as she flipped back in her notes. "Should we talk about her?"

"If you want to."

"This is about you, Brielle," Miranda said. "Not me."

Brielle didn't answer. Half of the appointments people made with shrinks were about the shrink, not the patient. Find someone crazy, then rack in the dough. Miranda had won big with her clients. Brielle was pretty confident her treatment funded this woman's lifestyle, from the Louis Vuitton purse on her desk to the countless pictures of glamorous ski vacations on her wall.

"Have you seen her since your return home?" Miranda asked.

Brielle shook her head. Another lie. She had seen Jackie too recently to be comfortable with. Brielle didn't want to think about how she woke up in a strange apartment on the opposite side of town or how the two of them had met up at a bar and been drinking together the night before. Several nights.

The last thing Brielle could remember was being at a bar across town. How she ended up in Jackie's room three days later was a mystery to her. She didn't wait around for Jackie, and Jackie never called.

"You seem healthy, Brielle," Miranda said, placing the notebook on the long desk behind her.

Brielle forced a sweet smile. "All thanks to you and your hard work."

Miranda stood and Brielle glanced at the clock. They

still had ten minutes left in their appointment. Miranda held her hand out.

Brielle stood and took the offered hand with a slight shake.

"I'm going to suggest we cut back on our sessions," Miranda said.

Brielle frowned. Was it a trap?

Miranda continued. "You seem well. If anything, a bit lonely."

Brielle still didn't move.

"If you are worried, we can schedule something for a few weeks from now," Miranda said.

Brielle snapped out of her shock and shook her head. "Not worried, just surprised."

Miranda laughed lightly. "Don't be surprised, Brielle. You've been seeing me consistently for years. I've seen you at your best and at your worst. You are at your best. You shouldn't make yourself suffer anymore."

"Thank you," Brielle said as Miranda directed her to the door.

"Of course. Call me if anything comes up or if you're worried about relapsing."

Brielle didn't answer as she gathered her things and headed through the lobby of the psychiatrist's office.

"See you later, Ms. Jeffries," the cheery receptionist said as Brielle walked by.

She forced a smile but said nothing, desperate to get outside and hopeful this new freedom was permanent.

Chapter 12
Detective Ryan Boone

A LOUD ROUND OF APPLAUSE FOLLOWED SINGH'S speech. Ryan shared a quick glance with Archer, who rolled his eyes. The police department praised the man. Ryan found him over the top and ineffective as a police officer. Too often had his work been put on Ryan's shoulders, though Ryan usually took the load willingly. Work was the only exciting thing in his life these days.

Archer stood from the table as a woman with russet-brown skin and a flowing dress made her way onto the stage.

Ryan knew her immediately as the head of the charity function, Jamila Cham. Ryan followed his partner's lead and, together, they walked to the back of the large banquet hall.

"Thank you so much," Jamila said, looking at Singh. Singh smiled as more applause followed.

Ryan stopped next to Archer, and together, they looked back at Jamila on the stage.

"If everyone would please take their seats, we'll be serving dinner shortly," Jamila said, smacking her large, red lips pressed into a painful-looking smile. "Thank you so much for all the money you have successfully raised for the regional police department. We have no doubt this will be yet another prosperous year."

More clapping and cheers followed Jamila's exit from the stage, and the surrounding crowd began to speak in hushed conversations.

"Prosperous?" Archer sneered. "Successful? Guess no one told her about this weird case."

Ryan shrugged. "We have unique cases all the time, and this one is no different."

"You don't think so?" Archer raised an eyebrow. "One suspect we can't find, and the other is suspicious, not solid."

"That isn't so unusual." Ryan scratched his chin. "We have problematic suspects all the time."

"One who seems completely unknown?" Archer frowned. "Not to mention, we can't even place one guy. The main guy, it seems."

"As you keep reminding me." Ryan ran his hand down the front of his formal jacket. "It's like you think I'm a rookie or something."

Archer's dark eyebrows furrowed at the mention. "Sorry."

"Don't be. I took the lead on this case. It's my ass on the line." Ryan tilted his head from side to side, stretching the tight muscles in his neck. He'd been slumped over his desk too much lately. His bad jokes weren't enough to take the chill out of this strange case.

"I didn't mean it like that," Archer said, though his deep voice lowered several tones.

"Are you mad I took lead without consulting with you?"

Ryan asked, turning toward his partner. "Is that why you've been cold lately?"

The sides of Archer's lips twitched, and he fought the smile that wanted to follow. "I'm always cold."

Ryan raised an eyebrow but didn't say anything.

Archer ran a hand through his short hair. "I'm not mad. I would have done the same thing. I guess I'm just frustrated that my first case back is such a trainwreck."

"Ah, so it's not about me," Ryan said. "And here I thought I had incurred the wrath of Archer."

"I wouldn't take it out on you."

Ryan cracked a smile. "No one would blame you. Someone has to take the office hero down a peg or two, otherwise, my head might get too big to fit through the front door. Did you hear the one about the police officer who couldn't make it into the interrogation room?"

"Yes," Archer said. "Too many times."

Ryan chuckled. "No, in all seriousness, being here doesn't help." He waved his hand around the room of well-dressed officers and their spouses. "Events like these are just a bunch of playacting, trying to get more funding. Time that would be better spent on the case."

Archer shook his head disgusted and glanced toward where Singh and the rest of his team sat around a large round table.

"Socialites and police officers," Archer groaned. "Why do they think we mix well?"

Ryan grimaced, and an empty place in his heart panged with longing. He didn't mention that many on the force were married to those socialites he referred to. Lilian had been one of them, and she and Ryan had been a perfect match.

As if realizing his blunder, Archer reached out and placed his hand on Ryan's shoulder. "Sorry. I didn't think."

"It's okay." Ryan forced a tight smile. "Be thankful we get all the booze we can drink. And a free meal."

"I'd prefer not to eat it."

"Then I'll be sure to take your plate, friend." Ryan clapped Archer on the back, trying to shake off the memory of Lilian.

Archer nodded toward a table near the front of the room. "It's strange, isn't it?"

Ryan followed his gaze to the oddly empty table closest to the stage. He recognized Robert Jeffries immediately, a surprisingly spry man in his late eighties with grey hair. The seat next to him was empty, as it always was at such events— a tribute to his lost wife. Though most of the family wasn't present, the oldest of Robert's sons was seated on the opposite side of his father.

Patrick Jeffries was a tall man with salt-and-pepper hair. Beside his father, they looked nearly identical despite the age difference. Patrick leaned away from Robert and whispered to the pretty, middle-aged woman seated next to him, his wife of thirty years despite the rumours of his infidelity. Ryan had heard talk that marrying into a family like the Jeffries was near impossible to separate from. She smiled at whatever Patrick said and brushed her long blonde hair aside. Then she reached across the table and grasped the hand of a younger man—her son, likely.

"Why? It's just a bunch of rich people trying to appear pleasant." Ryan chuckled. "With the company your wife keeps, I would have thought you'd be used to it by now."

"Har, har," Archer said. Then his smile faded. "I'd heard

the rest of the Jeffries returned to town. Why wouldn't they all be here? It looks like they were supposed to be."

Ryan glanced over the empty seats. Over half of the party was missing. It was weird, but none of the present Jeffries seemed to care.

"I won't even pretend to understand the complex world of the Jeffries family," Ryan said with a chuckle. "And I'm afraid I'm the wrong person to be asking for gossip to take back to your poor, deprived wife."

"Hey," Archer gave Ryan a nudge. "My wife is doing just fine."

"Really?" Ryan's eyes glinted. "Tell her to stop calling me then, would you?"

Archer punched Ryan in the arm.

"Head back to the table," Ryan said. "You need something to eat, and I need to find the bathroom." He needed a second to breathe—to recuperate and to forget about Lilian. Sometimes he wished the latter was possible.

Archer chuckled. "I need more than food. How about a strong drink?"

"Definitely."

Archer said nothing else before turning for a drink. When Ryan got back from the bathroom, he knew his partner would be sitting comfortably with a glass of scotch, Archer's drink of choice when he was stressed.

Ryan made his way through the room toward the hallway that led to the bathroom. Ryan pulled out his phone and started flipping through his email. Too much junk and not enough news. At least it was a distraction.

"Oh, excuse me," a quiet voice said.

Ryan stopped short and glanced up. Standing before him

was a thin woman in a ball gown with long sleeves and a high neckline. She didn't make eye contact with him and stepped back.

"Sorry," Ryan said, stepping around her. "My fault. I wasn't watching." He held up his phone to indicate his distraction.

The woman lifted her gaze slightly. "It's okay. I wasn't watching either."

Her eyes were a piercing blue; her hair was long and brown, worn straight down her back in a low ponytail. Though she didn't gaze at him long, it was long enough for Ryan to notice the caked makeup on her face hiding the purple bruise encircling her eye. Her left cheek was swollen, and there was a scratch trailing down her neck and disappearing beneath the gown's neckline.

She tried to step around Ryan. He held his arm out, stopping her in her tracks. "Are you okay?"

Her eyes widened, and she seemed to tremble under his steady gaze. "I—I'm fine." Her words spilled out in a quiet, stuttering whisper.

Ryan stepped closer, and she immediately backed away.

"I'm fine." Her voice came out stronger this time, still evident fear in her beautiful eyes.

"I'm a detective," Ryan said, holding his hands out to show her he had no intention of hurting her. "I can help you."

The woman bit down on her lip and looked back at the floor. "Really, it's alright, Detective. I'm sorry I nearly ran you over." She didn't wait for his answer before slipping by him and hurrying back into the banquet hall.

Ryan watched her return to her table; she never looked

back at him. As she sat, the man beside her glanced back at Ryan. His gaze was hard. Ryan immediately dropped it.

Shaking his head, he turned into the men's bathroom. Was she being abused, or was she simply clumsy? The latter seemed impossible with her wounds. Who fell on their face? Well, other than Officer Higgins from time to time.

The shrill ring of Ryan's phone interrupted his thoughts. It was the station.

"You've got Boone."

"Detective, glad we've been able to reach you." The voice on the other end of the phone sounded far away, like she was on speaker. "It's Janet." She was the video analyst who was reviewing the security footage and surveillance.

"Bit late for you to be still working." Ryan moved further away from the chatter coming from the main hall. "Don't tell me. Quinn tried asking you out again?"

"Very funny, boss," Quinn chimed in.

Ryan raised an eyebrow. "Shouldn't you be on assignment?"

"Winters has patrol tonight." Quinn let out a short whooping noise. "And thank your stars I'm here because I've found you a solid lead."

Janet protested in the background. "Actually, *I* found you a solid lead."

"Oh boy, Quinn. The girl hasn't even agreed to date you yet. Taking credit for her work is not a good start."

"Aw, c'mon, boss."

"What did you find?" Ryan asked.

"I've already forwarded you the picture," Janet said. "It took a while, but he slipped up. We got a clean shot on him.

It's in your email. We ran the still through the main database, and facial recognition did the rest."

"He's got a record?"

"Oh yeah." Quinn whistled. "About three arrests for petty crime."

"Any jail time?"

"None."

Strange. Repeat offenders usually got jail time. For this guy to avoid it, his arrests would have been handled as a particular case.

"So what is the name of the famous homeless Tim?" Ryan asked.

"Allen Kimball."

Ryan almost groaned. "Like Kimball Real Estate?"

"Couldn't be sure, boss."

It didn't matter, as Ryan had already switched the call to speaker and started searching for Kimball Real Estate. Olivia Kimball was a known real estate tycoon, and listed as one of her agents was Allen Kimball, a perfect match to the photo Janet had emailed him. Her son.

"Everything okay, Boone?" Quinn's voice lost his cheeriness.

"Yeah, fine. Thanks for the info. Forward it to me and start the process for an arrest warrant. I want him in custody tomorrow, if we can."

"Sure thing." The call ended, and Ryan tucked his phone away.

If he thought the case was complicated before, it's now even more so. A rich kid committing a petty crime was one thing, but this burglary amounted to more. Ryan would issue the arrest warrant, but within twenty-four hours, Allen

Kimball would be out on bail with an expensive lawyer in his back pocket. Convicting him wouldn't be easy.

Ryan headed to the bathroom then back into the banquet hall. Despite his distraction, he stole another glance toward the woman's table. She and the stern-looking man had gone, their meals untouched.

He returned to his seat, and Archer slid a glass of scotch in front of him, which Ryan reached for. His partner seemed cheerier, and Ryan resolved to tell him about the break the next day. Archer deserved one night of peace even if Ryan wouldn't get it.

Chapter 13
Brielle Jeffries

"I HARDLY THINK THAT'S REASON TO AVOID A function!" Mary screeched from down the hall of the upstairs level of their three-story home. "Now they're back, and you're going to let them run your life? You don't even care about the company!"

"You know that's not why," Leonard replied with as much venom.

Brielle stepped out of her room and glanced toward her parent's bedroom. The door was open, and Mary paced around the room, tossing her arms in the air dramatically with every word she spoke. She dressed in a long ball gown, and Leonard wore a suit. They looked ready to leave, as Brielle had expected them to do an hour before.

"You will have to face him eventually," she said, glaring at her husband.

Leonard was seated on the bed, his hands folded in his lap and avoiding his wife's gaze. *Why was he so ashamed?*

"I know," Leonard said. "I didn't think it would be

tonight. After the day I had, I'm more interested in a glass of scotch than a dinner party."

"It's for the police department," Mary said. "The one that helped your daughter, in case you've forgotten."

Leonard shrugged. "I don't care. I'm not going." He stood and turned from the room into their attached bathroom.

Mary released an exasperated sigh and turned toward Brielle, her eyes widening in surprise. She forced her stern expression into a stiff smile.

"Oh, hi, honey," she said.

"Is everything okay?" Brielle asked. "I thought you guys left already."

"No, we wouldn't without saying goodbye," Mary said, though they had left numerous times without seeing Brielle first.

"Oh. When are you guys going, then?" From the sound of the conversation, they weren't going at all.

Mary's smile faded, and she looked away. "We aren't." She reached up and pulled the clips from her hair, letting flat curls fall to her shoulders.

"Why not?"

Mary pursed her lips. "Your father doesn't want to see his brother."

"Daddy and Uncle Shawn always talk on the phone," Brielle said. "Why wouldn't he want to see him?"

"It isn't Shawn he's avoiding." Mary ran her fingers through her hair, continuing to pull it loose.

"Then Patrick?" Brielle raised her eyebrows. Her family hadn't seen her father's oldest brother and his son in almost two decades. They'd moved away when she was young and didn't stay in touch. Brielle still remembered the last time she saw her Uncle Patrick.

Patrick and Leonard had been arguing, much like every time they got together, but it was more serious this time. Uncle Patrick was yelling in her dad's face, spit flying. Brielle remembered watching as her mother rushed her out. That night, Patrick and his family left. Uncle Shawn's family quickly did the same. No one in their family had ever been close. Brielle knew her father had struggled with maintaining his relationship with Shawn in the past, but since her return from the clinic, they had grown closer. Leonard never mended things with Patrick, however.

"Yes," Mary said. "Patrick and Emily have returned."

Brielle frowned. "Is Derek back too?" Brielle hadn't seen her oldest cousin in over nineteen years. Would she even recognize him?

Mary nodded.

"Will we see them?"

"Not if your father can help it." Mary turned toward the bathroom and raised her voice. "Even a child knows he has to face his family eventually."

There was a muffled response from inside the bathroom. Brielle couldn't make it out, but her mother could.

"You *are* acting like a child," Mary screeched. "What are you afraid of? It's not like you are still children, and Patrick will punch you. You're adults now."

The door flew open and resounded off the stopper.

"I will not sit through an entire function listening to my brother and father talk about the business they cut me out of!" Leonard said. His suit jacket and tie had been discarded, and his white shirt was unbuttoned to mid-chest showing his undershirt.

"You weren't cut out," Mary said. "You chose to leave."

"I was told to leave," he hissed. "Leave or have nothing."

"Leonard!" Mary barked at him, hands planted on her hips.

"Leave it, Mary." Leonard shifted his gaze to Brielle and drew several breaths to calm himself. "We will be expected to see them before the end of the month. I'd rather the first time I see Patrick be when I have Shawn's support." He offered an apologetic smile to Brielle before turning and storming back into the bathroom, slamming the door behind him.

Mary shook her head. "What a fool." She muttered under her breath. Then she turned to Brielle. "I guess you will be seeing your cousins after all." Without another word, she stalked into their large walk-in closet and shut the door behind her, leaving Brielle alone in the hallway outside the primary bedroom.

Brielle stood there for a moment longer before turning and heading back to her room. She flopped onto her bed and stared up at the canopy overhead. What would it be like to see her cousins again? Brielle had never been close with any of them, and they'd all far surpassed the age where they would grow close through childish play. Would they be like strangers, or would their family connection make it different? Brielle only sighed because, like her father, she wasn't sure she wanted to see them again, and she certainly didn't want them to know where she'd been all these years.

Chapter 14
Detective Ryan Boone

THE SHRILL RING OF RYAN'S CELL PHONE JOLTED HIM awake. He glanced around his office. The sun had set, and the only light came from the small desktop lamp and his computer screen. His desk was lined with papers from the case; some had tumbled to the floor below.

Reaching for his phone, he accepted the call and said, "You've got Boone."

"Boone," Quinn said. "Did I wake you?"

Ryan shook his head, trying to clear his groggy thoughts. "No, I'm still at the station."

"Still?" Quinn said.

Ryan glanced at the clock. It was nearly midnight. "Yeah, I had work to do. Why are you calling so late?"

"Just heading home now," Quinn said. "I was prepared to leave you a message."

"Next time, email me." Ryan chuckled. "Is it about Lexi Chase?"

"Yeah," Quinn said. There were several clicks on the phone, and the next time Quinn spoke, he sounded farther away. "She is staying at the apartment she told you about, but she isn't *always* staying there."

"No?"

"Nope," Quinn said. "A couple of days ago, I followed her to a house in the middle of town. Nice place, gated neighbourhood."

"What's the address?" Ryan asked, grabbing a pen and paper to write it down. "I'll check it out."

"No need," Quinn said. "Already did. A Calvin Wright owns the house."

Ryan frowned. The name sounded familiar.

"You still there?" Quinn asked.

"Yeah, sorry. The name just threw me."

"Me, too," Quinn said. "I know I've heard it before."

"Did you look into it?"

"Yeah, he's a former research doctor. His license was suspended five years ago, but there isn't any record of why."

Ryan quickly scribbled down the name and made a note to look further into it.

"Did you try to contact the residents of the house?" Ryan asked.

"Yeah," Quinn said. "After I saw Lexi Chase leave with a couple of women, I went to the door."

"As a cop?"

"As a man looking for a nice family home. I said I'd heard the doctor lived in the area. The man who answered said he'd been renting the home from the owner for over two years."

"Did he say where Wright was?"

"No," Quinn said. "As soon as I mentioned the doctor's

name, he became much colder and less interested in answering my questions."

"Any way to confirm his story?" Ryan asked.

"Not without letting him know the cops are looking into him."

No, Ryan didn't want that. Then Lexi might know they were following her.

"Leave it for now, then," Ryan said. "Just keep an eye on her and let me know if anything strange happens."

"Boone, there was something else."

"What?"

"A man came by her apartment a couple of nights back," Quinn said. "He was pretty aggressive, banging on the door and swearing. Lexi wouldn't let him in. It was pretty clear they knew each other."

"My best guess is the ex-boyfriend." Both Lexi and Marley had mentioned an aggressive ex.

"Should I be worried about it?" Quinn asked.

"Not unless it gets out of hand," Ryan said. "Ms. Chase seems pretty capable of handling herself." Ryan glanced at the assault record they'd found on Lexi Chase. The woman was feisty and not afraid of a fight, made clear by the handled pint glass she smashed in a guy's face last year. She was lucky she only got an assault charge.

"Alright," Quinn said. "I'll pick it up tomorrow and let you know."

"Thanks."

"And boss?"

"Yeah?"

"Get some rest. You need it."

The line went dead before Ryan could answer. He

leaned back in his chair and yawned as he rubbed his eyes. Maybe Quinn was right.

With another yawn, he cleaned off his desk and piled the papers into his briefcase. He'd pick up the case in the morning. It wasn't like he was getting anywhere now.

Ryan followed Archer up the steps to the last known residence of Allen Kimball. His mother had been easy to find but little help. She cared less about her son than she did the crime itself. Allen was on her payroll for her husband's sake. She gave his address willingly, though she claimed she hadn't heard from him in a couple of days.

Now, in front of the house with Archer, Ryan wasn't sure what to think. No cars occupied the driveway, and three unopened newspapers lay against the door. An unanswered knock confirmed no one was home.

"Disappeared?" Archer asked.

Ryan shrugged. "Hard to say."

"Allen Kimball," Archer called through the door. "This is the police." Still no response.

"Uh, Detective?" Officer Collins asked. She was new to the team; only twenty-two and eager. "You should see this." She was peering through the front window. While large curtains shielded most of the view, there appeared to be a space large enough to survey.

Archer immediately approached the window. "Boone, come see this."

It was dark inside but light enough Ryan could see there

had been a struggle. The furniture was overturned and the TV on the wall was cracked in the middle.

When Ryan looked back at his partner, Archer's hand hovered over his weapon.

"Probable cause?"

Ryan agreed.

Archer grabbed his radio and reported their location, the situation, and the plan to enter. Ryan waved to Collins and the other young officer working with her.

"Head around the back of the house, look for any signs of forced entry. Be on alert. We don't know how long ago this all happened."

She nodded and headed off with her partner.

By then, Ryan looked back at Archer, who had approached the front door.

"Collins is looking for a way inside."

Archer didn't answer, only stared at the door, eyebrows furrowed. He reached out and tested it, pushing against the deadbolt lock. Then he touched the frame.

"What are you doing?"

Again, Archer didn't answer. Instead, he glanced at Ryan, then stepped back. Before Ryan could ask again, Archer moved toward the door and kicked it hard. He did it twice more before it swung open.

"Next time, warn me when you're going to Hulk out okay?" Ryan said. It wasn't the first door Archer had broken. Ryan admired Archer's handy work. "I swear that catches me off-guard every time. Remind me not to get on your bad side, Mr. Banner."

Collins came running around the house, gun drawn.

"Stand down, Officer."

She immediately did, holstering the firearm.

"Back to your search. Archer and I have this." Ryan waved his partner forward. Archer entered the quiet home, and Ryan followed.

The place was a mess. Furniture was tipped over, ripped, or broken. Picture frames had been smashed. There was either an intense struggle or a terrible tantrum.

Only two unbroken photos were still on the mantel, though toppled over. The first featured the suspect, Allen, with an unknown woman. The next was his family. At least they had the right place, even if they weren't sure what happened.

"Boone, get in here."

"You realize I'm your partner, not your dog, right?" Ryan joked. "I don't come running at your beck and call."

"Boone." Archer's tone came more sternly.

"Okay, okay." Ryan followed his partner's call into another room off the main entrance. It was a dining room with a long oak table and eight chairs. Most stood untouched, two had been bumped and turned.

"Over here." Archer stood at the room's far end, examining something on the floor. Ryan didn't see what it was until he rounded the table.

A stain on the grey carpet. Deep red and large enough to indicate someone had lost a lot of blood.

"Are we looking at a potential victim?" Ryan frowned. Had the others gotten to Allen first? He grabbed his phone. "Higgins," he said when the senior officer answered. "Put out a red alert on Allen Kimball and get someone in forensics to his address now. We're looking at a possible homicide."

"Sure thing." The phone clicked, and Ryan tucked it away.

"Let's keep looking." Ryan touched Archer's arm, and the large detective flinched. "It's okay. Just a bit of blood."

"A lot of blood." Archer's face scrunched with discomfort.

"Boone."

Ryan turned to acknowledge Collins before he could joke about the doctor who couldn't stand the sight of blood. "I told you to continue your search."

"We did, sir. The back door was wide open. Either point of entry or escape."

So someone had been through the house. His first real lead in this case, and it would be Ryan's luck the guy was possibly dead.

"Pig's blood?"

"You heard right." The young research assistant stood before Ryan with their findings in her hands. The blood they'd found in Kimball's house hadn't been his; it hadn't even been human. Pig's blood, nothing more.

"So it's a setup," Ryan said, more to himself than to the woman in front of him.

"Looks that way." She offered him the folder again, and this time he took it.

"Thank you."

He turned for Archer's office. The rest of Kimball's house had been a bust. Other than the blood and appearance of a struggle, there wasn't anything else to assess the scene. Now that Ryan realized it was a setup, it all seemed clearer.

"I guess you're going to stop eating bacon." Ryan dropped the folder on Archer's desk.

His partner looked up from his computer. "What?"

"Wasn't human blood making you sick." Ryan pointed at the folder. "It was pig's blood."

Archer flipped open the folder. "A setup. Kimball wanted us to think he was dead."

"To stop looking for him."

Archer leaned back in his chair. "Don't they know we don't close a case without a body?"

Ryan didn't mention the few times they had shut the door on a case without the remains, after they'd been open for months. No body, no crime. It was a hard truth for the police.

"So now we have to find the guy?"

"Yeah, There's an APB for him all across the city. If he tries to leave, we'll find him." At least a kid like Allen was well-known enough people would spot him. A catch of being rich and having your picture plastered on realtor signs.

Archer glanced back at his computer. "Any more on Chase?"

"Not yet. We'll find something."

"You and your damn confidence." Archer resumed typing as Ryan scooped the folder off his desk.

"It's not confidence." Ryan winked. "I'm just *that* good. After all, your wife—"

"I get it, Fabio." Archer looked up from his computer only to return Ryan's grin before getting back to work.

Chapter 15
Melanie Parker

MEL ENTERED THE LOW-LIT RESTAURANT AND NODDED at the hostess as she passed. "I'm here for Mr. Dorian."

The young woman at the front pressed her glossy lips into a tight smile.

"Mr. Dorian is at his usual table," she said. "Straight at the back, seated by the window." She reached for a menu, then made a move to lead Mel there.

Mel held up her hand. "I'll find him." She walked further into the restaurant before the girl could answer.

The restaurant was on the opposite side of the city, hidden from the main streets. It was dark, lit only by dim light and candles on the small tables. Paul Dorian had suggested the place, and it seemed like the high-profile lawyer did most of his meetings away from the usual venues.

Mel saw him seated where the hostess indicated, dressed in an expensive suit. His black hair was slicked back, and his eyes were fixed to the window, watching the few cars pass by. The windows were so tinted no one would see inside.

The click of Mel's heels seemed to draw his attention

and his ice-blue eyes flicked to her. They looked up and down her body before settling on her face; then, he smiled.

"Ms. Parker, I presume." He stood and offered his hand.

"You presume correctly," Mel said as she sat down. Once she did, a young waitress appeared at her side and Mel ordered a dirty martini.

"A pleasure," Dorian said. "On me, of course."

"Of course," Mel agreed. She kept her hands beneath the table, trying not to fidget. She hated meeting with clients, preferring to save a bit of mystery to her and her business. This was Blaine's job. Clients didn't mess with the brawn. They sometimes thought they could manipulate the brain. Worse were the ones who thought she was only the beauty.

Dorian motioned to the menu, and Mel shook her head. She wasn't here to eat. She was here for business.

"What can I help you with?" Mel asked. "I don't usually meet clients in person. I have an associate who does that for me."

"I understand. I believe one of your girls, Gabi, said as much," Dorian said.

Mel smirked. At least Gabi got it right. The waitress returned and set the martini down in front of Mel. She asked if they wanted to order. Dorian simply pointed to his nearly empty glass to request another cocktail, then shooed her away.

"I need to know all we discuss and do is done with the utmost care and discretion," Dorian said in a low voice.

"Discretion is our game, Mr. Dorian."

"Paul is fine," he said as if it were instinct.

Mel shook her head. "Mr. Dorian will do."

Dorian raised an eyebrow but said nothing about it. "I

have some clients to entertain," he continued. "Ones with particular taste."

"I have something for everyone," Mel said.

Dorian chuckled and tipped back the rest of his drink. "Why does that not surprise me?"

"Because you seem like a reasonable man."

They both fell silent as the waitress returned with Dorian's drink. Again, she asked if they wanted anything to eat, and again Dorian sent her away.

"It will be this Thursday night," Dorian said, then he slid a folded piece of paper across the table. "That address. I'm looking at ten girls."

Mel took the paper and raised her eyebrow. "Ten? You'll pay your party fees upfront. Whatever girls perform their duty will expect further payment. Half before, half after."

"You drive a hard bargain," Dorian said.

"It's the only way to keep things in order."

"Your operation fascinates me." Dorian twirled his drink, watching the amber liquid. "Tell me how you got started."

"That's not how this works." Mel leaned back in her chair.

"Satisfy a man's curiosity."

Mel pursed her lips. "Curiosity is a curse. Things like that can get you hurt."

An amused smile as he sipped his drink. "A threat, Ms. Parker?"

"I don't make threats," Mel said. "I have someone to do that for me." She glanced over her shoulder at the hostess before meeting Dorian's gaze. "Our business extends to the women you hire and the party you throw. Everything else is on a need-to-know basis. And about my operation, you don't need to know a thing."

Dorian's lips twitched. "Very well." He lifted his hands in mock defence. "Please forgive my intrusion."

Mel downed the rest of her martini and stood. This time he didn't reach for her hand but the lawyer did stand with her. "My associate will meet you tomorrow to confirm details and extract payment. Same number fine?"

"I expect great things from this, Ms. Parker."

"And you are right to," Mel replied. She turned to leave. Dorian caught her hand and pulled her closer to him.

"Until we meet again," he said. Then he planted a kiss on her cheek before releasing her. It happened too quickly for Mel to react. She hated when clients had the gall to touch her. No one would ever treat Blaine the way they treated her.

"Sounds good." Mel turned from Dorian and headed back the way she came. When she reached the hostess stand, she glanced back at him. The lawyer was still standing behind his table, eyes trained on Mel, staring at her ass. A big party, good money, and a sleazy lawyer that was easy to please. It was situations like these that made her job oh so fun.

MEL WAS ALONE by the time Blaine came home. He walked into the primary bedroom and shrugged off his jacket, tossing it on the bed. He placed a folder on the dresser.

Mel glanced up from her phone. "You're late."

"Happens," Blaine said. He tossed a stack of bills bound by an elastic band onto the bed.

Mel abandoned her phone and grabbed the money, flipping through the stack with her thumb. "He gave it to you like this?"

"What would you rather?" Blaine asked, sitting on the edge of the bed. "A brown sack with a dollar sign?"

"Funny." Mel placed the cash on the bedside table then moved across the bed and wrapped her arms around Blaine's shoulders from behind, resting her head against his back. "Everything go okay?"

"Of course."

"And what's your read on him?"

Blaine shifted, taking hold of her arms and moving Mel so she was seated on his lap. He rested his forehead against hers. "Hi," he said.

Mel smiled. "Hi."

He leaned in and kissed her. She let him for a moment; then she pulled away.

"Blaine, business first," she said. "What did you find?"

Blaine frowned and shifted again, placing her on the bed and standing. He moved across the room, grabbing the folder from where he left it. "Nothing at all. Dorian checks out, clean record."

Mel reached out and took the folder. As she flipped through it, she chewed on her lower lip. "I don't want something bad to happen again."

"I know," Blaine said. "You'll be there. It will be fine. Dorian isn't being coy about what he wants out of this party."

"I don't want Candy having to experience what Amara did," Mel said, glancing up from the file.

"You're giving him to Candy?"

"Yeah. A good idea, don't you think?"

Blaine only shrugged. He never did try to tell Mel how to do her job, only how to act.

"I think it is," Mel said, looking back at the folder. There were records of Dorian's cases what he'd won and lost. The former far outweighed the latter. There were reports of his personal life. He wasn't married; he had no family—just a rich, smart man looking for a good time.

Mel glanced up when Blaine hadn't spoken. He watched her carefully.

"What's wrong?" He'd been acting strangely for days, ever since she'd found the pills, and he'd lost his temper. She had not brought it up again, though she'd considered it.

Blaine shook his head. "Nothing."

Mel placed the folder aside and pat the bed, asking him to sit. "I want to ask you something. And I don't want you to freak out."

His posture stiffened, and he didn't take the seat she offered. It was as if he knew what was coming before she opened her mouth. However, she couldn't blame him. Mel had gone back once in the last few days to check the drawer when Blaine had been out. It was empty now, the pills gone. She couldn't find any evidence of them anywhere in the house. It was too weird. What was he hiding?

"I need to know about the drugs," Mel said slowly. "Are you using?" Blaine didn't have the typical indications of a user, though Mel couldn't imagine what else had made him so angry. First, when she found them on Candy and then when she found the stash hidden away.

Blaine's jaw tightened, and he looked away from her.

"Look, Blaine, I don't know what's going on," Mel said. "You haven't led me wrong in over two years, so if you tell me it's nothing, I'll believe you. You can't deny you've been acting different since Candy showed up."

He didn't react for a moment, only continuing to look away. Soon, he reached up and rubbed his eyes. With a sigh, he turned back to face her.

"You promise to accept what I tell you?" Blaine asked. "You won't ask questions after?"

Mel frowned, feeling trapped by his words. She'd said as much when she begged him to share his secrets, and now it seemed like he'd lie to keep her quiet. Still, she wanted to know, so she simply nodded.

Blaine lowered himself to the bed. "I've seen the drug before. I've seen it do bad things. I'm not using. It's not that type of drug anyway."

"Where have you seen it?" Mel asked, unsure how much she could pry before he'd cut her off.

"My sister had it," Blaine said. "Before she died."

Mel's stomach twisted. Blaine had never spoken about his family before. It was a topic they'd always avoided. Mel didn't want to share her past; she'd assumed he'd wanted the same.

"She died?" The words came out so softly, for a moment, Mel wasn't sure she'd spoken them.

"Yeah," Blaine said. "A long time ago. And, while I don't know for sure, I think the drug had something to do with it. So I can't have it in this house."

"Of course. I'm sorry."

"You didn't know." Blaine reached for her and pulled her against him. He cradled her in his arms and Mel allowed her head to rest on his chest, listening to the anxious heartbeat hidden below.

"They're gone now," Blaine said after they'd been quiet for some time. "You won't see them again."

Mel didn't answer. It didn't matter that she already knew they were gone. It only mattered that Blaine trusted her with his secret, and she'd make sure he'd never have to see Solydexran again.

CANDY SAT on the couch fiddling with the diamond bracelet around her wrist as Jackie spoke to her with a kind smile and encouraging tone; Jackie spoke this way with every young woman who walked through Blaine's door. The two of them made the best team—Jackie to coddle and Mel to get things done.

Mel leaned against the doorframe, watching them.

"Mel, c'mon," Gabi said from behind her. "Don't be stupid."

Mel turned away from the room, and Gabi led her into the kitchen.

"I should be doing this," Gabi said. "Jackie, at the very least."

"Jackie isn't interested."

"Then me," Gabi insisted.

Mel shook her head, glancing down at the low-cut outfit Gabi was wearing. "You'll have another client to attend to."

"What do you mean?"

"I mean it's not just a one-on-one," Mel said. "Mr. Dorian wants a party, a group of girls. Mr. Kyles will be there."

Gabi frowned and looked away.

"He'll be upset if he feels like you're choosing another,"

Mel said. She had worked with men like Liam Kyles for some time and knew how their attitude toward girls like Gabi were. "He's your number one client. Is losing him worth a sleazy lawyer?"

Gabi frowned but didn't answer right away.

Mel didn't need her to. She knew the answer before she asked the question. Mr. Kyles funded Gabi's lifestyle. Losing him wasn't a question.

"I still think you're making a mistake." Gabi crossed her arms.

"And what's new about that?" Mel said, glancing over her shoulder as Candy and Jackie emerged from the sitting room.

"What's going on?" Jackie asked with a bright smile.

Gabi frowned. "Mel's making a mistake."

"Get out," Mel said, her patience with Gabi running thin. "Go pick up the usual from Geoff and get out of my sight for a few hours. Or I'll be finding someone else to attend to Kyles, and you might find yourself a client short."

Hands on her hips, Gabi looked ready to challenge. She opened her mouth to retort and Mel took a step toward her, squaring her shoulders. Dropping her hands and her gaze, Gabi mumbled something inaudible, shot a cold look at Candy, then turned and left the kitchen. No one spoke until they heard the front door open and close behind her.

"What's her problem?" Jackie asked.

"You know Gabi, she loves to test my authority." Mel shook her head.

"Then why is she still here?" Candy asked.

Mel raised an eyebrow at the younger girl, finding amusement in her forwardness.

"Because I don't refuse a working girl," Mel said. "If you

pay your way, you're more than welcome. Speaking of." Mel hesitated and reached for the daily newspaper sitting on the kitchen table. "I've got a job for you."

She dropped the paper on the counter in front of Candy and Jackie. The front page highlighted the case won by Dunn & Dorian. Pictured beside the acquitted were the two well-known lawyers, Leslie Dunn and Paul Dorian. Mel pointed to the taller, better-looking of the two men.

"This is Paul Dorian," Mel said as Candy looked over the article. "Top lawyer in the city, also willing to pay good money for a dirty party. He's your first client."

Candy regarded the photo with hesitation.

"What is it?" Mel asked, expecting Candy to be happier about the job. He was rich *and* attractive. Most of the girls would have jumped at the opportunity.

"Are you sure?" Candy looked up at Mel. "He seems important."

"He's new. He'll like your innocent look." Mel waved her hand up and down Candy's slender body. "You'll be a kitten to him. It'll be perfect." Mel had been reading men like Dorian for years. She knew how to please even the most obscure gentlemen. Dorian was just another job and not a challenge.

"What if I screw up?" Candy glanced at Jackie.

"You won't, sweetie," Jackie said as Mel replied, "You better not."

Jackie shot Mel a hard look; she ignored it.

"I'm not going to lie to you," Mel said. "I expect Mr. Dorian to be a returning customer. He made it clear the other night. This is your test."

"Mel," Jackie said, reaching out for Candy's hand. "Don't lay it on so hard."

Mel ignored Jackie's comment. "I won't make you do it, of course; I think you'll surprise yourself. I wouldn't ask you to do this if I didn't think you'd come through for me."

Candy glanced between Jackie and Mel and seemed to consider her options. Pulling her arm from Jackie's grip, she fiddled with the bracelet on her wrist again.

"What do I have to do?"

A sly smile spread on Mel's lips. "Whatever he asks you to."

"Whatever?"

"Take the shots he offers; it will help. Lay off the drugs. I don't want you getting all coked up on your first job."

"I can handle drugs."

Mel laughed. "For some reason, I highly doubt that. Do what you feel you can, as long as you walk away with the cash."

"Will I be alone?" Candy asked.

Mel shook her head. "No, Jackie will go with you. Gabi, too. I'll be around until things get more intimate. There will be others; ten girls total." She reached out and took Candy's arm, leading her from the kitchen and up the stairs to the master bedroom. Jackie followed.

Mel left them in the doorway and headed to the closet. She pulled out a short black dress they had purchased a few days before and tossed it to Candy.

"Wear that," Mel said. "Jackie will get you anything else you need and get you ready for the night. Blaine will drop us at the party's location tonight after I confirm with Dorian.

We'll meet back at Hotel Chapuys the following morning. We always have a room."

Candy ran her fingers over the dress before looking up at Mel and nodding.

Mel smirked. "Good, glad to have you on board. It will be worth it."

Jackie nodded her agreement. "C'mon, hon, let's go find you some cute shoes for that dress before I head out."

Mel's eyes narrowed. "Where are you going? We have a job to do."

"I owe my roomie some cash for rent," Jackie said. "Don't worry about it. I'll meet you at the party."

Mel wanted to disagree, but her phone buzzed on the dresser, distracting her, and Jackie and Candy left the room.

"Mel here," she said as she answered the call. "Are you on your way back?"

"Hello to you, too." Blaine's deep voice came across the receiver.

Mel didn't answer him, and after a moment, Blaine spoke again, "Yeah, I'm not far now."

"Good," Mel said. "We need you to drop us at the party tonight."

"I always do."

"Candy agreed."

"Like you thought she would."

Mel laughed. "It helps when the client is a good-looking guy. I hope she doesn't get too used to it."

"I'm sure she understands what the job involves," Blaine said.

"Guess we'll find out ..."

"You okay?"

Mel frowned. "Yeah, I'm fine."

"You sound stressed."

"I said I'm fine. Just get home soon."

"Love you," Blaine said.

Mel hit end on the phone without answering him. It wasn't that she didn't love Blaine but saying those words in the past had always gotten her in trouble. People said they loved you, then the next day shipped you off to some mental institute. Love didn't guarantee anything—no loyalty, no safety, no real love even.

Blaine knew better than to expect those words from her.

She discarded her phone and started searching through her closet for something decent to wear. It had been some time since she'd been on a job. If it weren't for what happened, she wouldn't be going tonight, now she had no choice but to at least monitor the party for a bit.

Chapter 16
Brielle Jeffries

Mary poked her head into Brielle's room. "Oh, are you going out?"

Brielle was dressed in a blue skirt and a black crop top. She certainly looked ready to leave.

"Uh, yeah," Brielle said. "It's Gemma's birthday tonight. She invited me." Brielle had recently reconnected with Gemma at one of her parent's functions. They'd been in the same high school graduating year.

Brielle's mother frowned. "Is that Riley McLaughlin's girl?"

"Yeah," Brielle said, grabbing her bag. "I guess a bunch of people from high school will be there. It should be fun."

"Are you sure?" Mary asked, her tone and expression concerned. "There may be a lot of questions."

"There are always questions."

"You don't have to face them yet," Mary said. "You can wait. You can rest."

"I've waited almost a full year," Brielle said. "I have to

face the world eventually. Otherwise, what was the point of coming home?"

"You're right, honey. I only want to make sure you're okay. I don't want you to be overwhelmed and say anything you'd regret."

Or anything that would embarrass our family. Brielle held back an eyeroll.

"I'm fine, Mom," Brielle said. "I promise. I wouldn't go otherwise."

"Okay." Mary walked over and placed a kiss on her daughter's forehead. "That's all I needed to hear. Have fun tonight."

"Thanks," Brielle said, then headed out of her room and to the front door.

AT THE CLUB, she gave her name to the bouncers and was directed to an upper room. It was circular, with blue lighting and glowing neon paint on the wall. A heavy bass thumped through the room and several people danced.

"Brielle, over here!" A girl with teased blonde hair called to her, waving her hand overhead. She was seated with a group of people, some Brielle went to high school with.

"Happy Birthday, Gemma," Brielle said as the blonde kissed both of her cheeks. She looked the same as she did in high school, only with fake boobs and more makeup.

"I was so glad to hear you were back in town, babe," Gemma said. "You'll have to tell me all about it over coffee one day." This really meant Gemma wasn't interested at all. It didn't bother Brielle. She didn't want to tell the girl an elaborate lie either.

"Of course," Brielle said. "We'll set something up. Tonight is about you!"

Gemma's cheeks pinch in disgust. "Ugh, this old lady, you mean?"

One of the girls at the table laughed. "You're not thirty yet!"

"Thank god!" Gemma yelled. She grabbed a shot from the tray in the centre of the table and passed one to Brielle. She held up the shot to cheers her friends and said, "To me!"

"To Gemma," everyone murmured before tossing back the shot.

When Brielle placed the shot down, Gemma giggled and grabbed her arm.

"I'm so glad you came." Gemma rested her head against Brielle's shoulder and smiled.

"Me, too. It's honestly been forever."

"So tell me," Gemma said as one of her friends ordered another round of shots. "What kept the great Brielle away for so long?"

"A lot of things," Brielle said.

Gemma pulled away from her with a wicked smile. "A boy, no doubt."

"There were boys."

"*Boys!*" Gemma laughed. "I love it. What else? How was the work? Are you back permanently?"

"I think so," Brielle said. "At least for the time being. I have no other plans." She didn't want to elaborate on the "work" she'd been doing. It was one too many lies.

"Wonderful, darling." Gemma wrapped her arm around Brielle's shoulders and pulled her close. "We must do this more often, then." The waiter returned with another tray filled with shots. Gemma reached for two and pushed them to Brielle then grabbed two more. Holding both in her hands, she motioned for Brielle to do the same. She clinked her shot glasses against Brielle's and grinned. "It'll be just like old times." Gemma took the shots one after the other.

Brielle looked down at the shot glass. Tequila. She tipped back the first, followed by the second. As the burning liquid trailed down her throat, she knew it would be like old times, and tomorrow morning she'd likely wake up on her front doorstep, having lost her keys.

Chapter 17
Melanie Parker

Blaine reached over and placed his hand on Mel's knee. She was seated in the passenger side of his silver sedan and shifted in the seat nervously.

"You seem tense," Blaine said so only Mel could hear him over the thumping music and chatter of the girls in the back.

"I'm fine," Mel said. She wasn't.

"You're not staying until the end, right?" Blaine pulled his hand away. His jaw tightened at the question. He was asking if she planned on fucking anyone.

"No," Mel said. "I'm not staying any longer than I have to."

Blaine's shoulders visibly relaxed. "You look good."

"You sound surprised."

"Very funny." Blaine's eyes were fixed on the road and he said nothing else until they pulled up at the address Paul Dorian had given her. The girls in the back climbed out, leaving Blaine and Mel alone.

"You'll call?" Blaine asked.

"I'll probably head back when you return with the others," Mel said. He still had to pick up two more girls. The others would come on their own.

"Dorian wanted ten girls," Blaine said as if Mel hadn't been the one to make the plans.

"Yeah, I know."

"You make eleven." Blaine's grip on the steering wheel tightened.

Even reassuring him wasn't enough to get him to relax. Sometimes Mel felt like she was the only emotionally reasonable one in their operation. Did Blaine really think she'd give an extra girl to a job? If Mel intended to work, Dorian would have paid way more.

"Then I guess it's a good thing I'm not actually working." Mel turned and reached for the door handle, but before she touched it Blaine gripped her other arm and pulled her back toward him.

He planted a gentle kiss on her lips. "Be careful."

"If Dorian's party is what he said it is, then we have nothing to worry about," Mel said lightly. Then she slipped out of the passenger side before Blaine could answer.

He continued to gaze at her with concern.

"It will be fine." Mel gave him a small smile.

"I'll call when I'm back."

"Sounds good." Mel closed the passenger side door.

Blaine drove off and she turned to where Candy and Gabi stood. Jackie waved to her from the front step, having already arrived. Mel frowned, watching Jackie sway unsteadily in her stilettos. It was just like her to have one too many with her roomie before a job. She only hoped it was fun drunk Jackie, and not the sad one that came out from time to time.

"Ready?" Gabi asked, drawing Mel's scrutiny away from Jackie.

Mel waved toward the door. "Let's do this."

Candy went ahead to meet Jackie. Gabi held back. When Candy was out of earshot, Gabi fished into her purse and pulled out a grey and white pill. Taking Mel's hand, she thrust it into her palm.

"Take it," Gabi said. "It will calm you down."

"I'm fine." Mel eyed the long pill in her palm. It looked familiar. She closed her hand and offered it back to Gabi.

Gabi didn't move to take it back. "You're shaking like a terrified puppy. What's wrong with you?"

Mel shook her head. "Nothing."

"This isn't like you." Gabi planted her hand on her hips. "It's just a party. You're the queen of parties."

"I know."

Gabi nudged her hand. "Take the pill. Trust me. It helps with anxiety."

Mel glanced down at it again, certain she'd seen it before. "What is it?"

"It's an anxiety pill," Gabi said with a laugh. "It's not going to make your clothes fall off. It's just going to let you relax."

"Fine." Mel popped the pill into her mouth and swallowed it dry.

"We could have waited until you had a drink."

"I've swallowed enough pills in my lifetime." Mel got good at it when she'd been locked away in a psychiatric hospital. Pills every day. Pills kept people sane.

Before Gabi could answer, a large cab pulled into the long driveway. Glancing over her shoulder, Mel released a breath, glad more of the girls had arrived.

A petite blonde hopped out first and waved. "Hey, Mel." Four more girls piled out of the van behind her, then followed the blonde as she bounced to Mel's side. The girl stood a head shorter than Mel and was small around the middle. She wrapped an arm around Mel's waist and gave her a side hug.

"Long time, no see, hon," Christine said. She smiled at Gabi and bumped her hip against her. "Lookin' good, Gabs."

"Backatcha." Gabi winked.

The four remaining girls walked toward where Jackie and Candy waited. Now the others had arrived, Mel could leave when Blaine came back with the last two. As much as she wanted to make sure the party was only what Dorian promised, she hated the idea of being a part of the job.

One of the new girls whistled. "This place looks *way* worth it."

She wasn't wrong. The house before them was two stories tall and three times as wide. The brick was dark brown and the door bright white. The massive property was wrapped by an iron fence with a thick gate which creaked when it had opened for Blaine's car. The large hedges snaked through the yard and blocked the quiet country road from view. Whoever owned this place lived like a king.

When Gabi noticed Mel had stayed back, she excused herself from the giddy excitement and returned to Mel's side.

"Sure you don't want to work?" Gabi asked. "You seem like you need the tension release."

"You know I can't," Mel said. "And I won't."

"Of course, *Blaine.*" Gabi sighed.

Mel considered telling her off for insinuating Blaine had any control over her, then thought better of the confrontation, desperate instead to get her part of the night over with.

"I'm only joking," Gabi added in a softer tone. "I know you're here to play mother hen."

The nickname earned her an irritated look and Gabi quickly clamped her mouth shut.

"Let's just get this party going," Mel said. "Blaine won't be long and I'm leaving when he gets here."

Gabi smiled and waved her hand toward the house, indicating Mel should lead the way.

Mel approached the door and pressed the golden button next to it. A heavy ringing could be heard within the home and soon a man in a fancy suit opened the door—Paul Dorian.

"Ah, Ms. Parker," Dorian said. "Right on schedule." His eyes shifted from her and grazed over the girls behind her. "You are one short, and I didn't realize we were being graced with your presence."

"My associate will be here shortly with the remaining girls," Mel said, brushing past Dorian when he stepped aside and let the women enter. "I will be leaving when they arrive."

"No," Dorian said with a smile. "You must stay. It will be fun."

"You'll have plenty of fun without me." Mel motioned to the sitting room off the entrance hall of the home. "Shall we?"

Dorian nodded and cast a glance toward the girls. "Head down the hallway to the kitch—"

"Gabriela!" A deep voice called from behind Dorian, interrupting his instructions. A short, round man waddled toward the group of ladies with a huge smile on his face. Mel recognized him immediately as Liam Kyles.

Gabi stepped around the group. "Hello, Liam."

He caught her hand and pulled her down the hallway. "Come this way."

Mel nudged Jackie. "Go with them and take the girls."

Jackie motioned for the others to follow. As Candy passed by, Mel grabbed her arm and spun her toward Dorian.

"Mr. Dorian," Mel said. "This is Candy." Mel reached up and touched Candy's cheek. "She has promised me she will make sure you are very happy tonight."

Dorian gazed over Candy, his blue eyes trained on the end of her short dress.

Mel fought the smirk, turned to Candy, and leaned closer to her. "Anything he wants," she whispered before nudging her out of the room in the direction the others had gone.

Dorian watched her go. Candy didn't look back.

"Quite the group you've put together," Dorian said.

"Like I said, I have something for every taste."

"So I see."

"So we're clear, Mr. Dorian," Mel said. "Any problems and I'll have something to say about it. We are good at what we do, and discretion is our game. I won't hesitate to ruin you if you ruin anything I have going."

Dorian put his hands up. "Protective, I like it."

"Do we have an understanding?"

"Half before, half after. I understand completely. Your associate made himself very clear."

"Good." Mel turned from the room and headed to the kitchen. Footsteps behind her told her Dorian followed.

The kitchen was huge and overlooked the back of the property. From inside, Mel could see the large patio with several of Dorian's associates scattered about and her girls. A quick count told her there were eight men. Was he expecting more?

Gabi's bag was on the counter, already spilled open. From where Mel stood, she could see Gabi and Mr. Kyles doing lines off the patio table. Just like Gabi to jump right in.

Dorian appeared at her side with a martini in hand. "Dirty, if I remember correctly."

"You do." Mel took the drink from him.

"Make yourself comfortable," Dorian said. "Maybe you'll decide to stay."

Mel didn't answer as he proceeded through the kitchen and out the back door to the patio. She leaned against the counter, sipped the cool drink, and watched the party outside.

Jackie seemed to sense her gaze and looked up. Then she made her way into the kitchen.

"You okay?"

Mel nodded. "I should ask you the same thing. You took off today."

"I know." Jackie looked away. "I had something to do. It's okay now."

"You sure?" Mel asked. As much as she didn't want to pry, Jackie's glazed-over eyes gave way to her drinking. "Have you had too much to drink?"

"No." Jackie forced a smile, and her hand tightened on the drink she held. An amaretto sour, a favourite of hers. She'd forced the sickly sweet drink on Mel more than once. "Just had a couple of cocktails to calm the nerves. I'm good." She looked around before adding. "Will you stay?"

Mel shook her head. "I'm just waiting for Blaine."

"Things seem fine," Jackie said, glancing back at the patio party.

"Yeah," Mel agreed. "Dorian isn't a total prick. Plus, I have collateral now." Mel picked up her phone and snapped a quick picture of the party. Dorian was evident in the photo as he leaned over where Candy was sitting with a shot in her hand and a line on the table in front of her.

"Mel?" Jackie raised an eyebrow. They weren't in the habit of documenting their jobs.

Mel tucked her phone away. "I don't like being fucked with."

Jackie frowned. Mel's phone rang before she could say more.

Mel glanced down at the phone; Blaine's name flashed across.

"You here?" she asked when she answered it.

"Out front."

"Be right there." Mel ended the call and turned to Jackie. "Have fun. Blaine will drop me off at the hotel, usual room. Then he'll be back and waiting close by. He's your third number on speed dial. Hold it down if you need him fast."

"Melanie, I know," Jackie said.

"Join me whenever you're done," Mel turned to leave but hesitated and looked back at Jackie. "Dorian is for Candy. Keep the other girls off him."

Jackie cracked a grin. "I'll do my best."

Mel said nothing else before putting her empty glass down and heading back the way she came. Out front, she saw Blaine's car waiting. The last two girls were already up the walk, and Mel directed them into the house and toward the party. Then she went to the car.

"Everything look alright?" Blaine asked as he turned the car down the driveway.

"Yeah, fine," Mel said. "Dorian is a sleazy lawyer but not a total pig."

"And you're feeling okay about it?"

"Actually, yeah," Mel said. Whatever the pill was Gabi gave her had done wonders. She didn't feel anxious anymore. In fact, she felt entirely at ease.

"To the hotel?" Blaine asked.

"Yeah, then I need you back here."

"I know how it works," Blaine said, pulling out of the driveway.

"Keep an eye on Candy," Mel said. "Wherever she ends up."

"I will."

Chapter 18
Detective Ryan Boone

SINGH POKED HIS HEAD INTO RYAN'S OFFICE. "QUINN'S here now." Then he was gone.

Ryan glanced up from the page he was looking at and tucked it aside. He had asked the super to let him know when the rookie cop arrived. Ryan had barely seen Quinn since he sent him to track Lexi. Ryan knew they'd have to pull him soon with nothing coming up.

Leaving his office, he headed toward the pit where Quinn was socializing with some younger officers. They clamped their mouths shut when they saw Ryan approaching.

"Detective," a young female officer said in greeting. Ryan offered a stiff smile and continued to Quinn.

"Good Morning, Detective Boone." Quinn stood to meet Ryan.

"My office in five," Ryan said.

Quinn nodded. "Let me put my stuff away, and I'll be right in."

Ryan headed back to his office.

Quinn was only a minute behind; he closed the door after entering and took a seat across from Ryan.

"For a minute, I thought you'd maybe forgotten where the station was," Ryan said.

"I've been here," Quinn said with a small smile. "You've barely left your office so that you wouldn't know."

"I guess I've been busier than I thought," Ryan said. Quinn wasn't wrong. For days, Ryan had been arriving early and leaving late. He'd barely seen anyone other than Archer.

"I know the super is putting pressure on you," Quinn said.

"Really? And I thought Singh was so subtle with how he delivered his disappointment," Ryan joked.

"I wasn't going to say anything."

"Yet you did." Ryan laughed. "Don't worry about it. Tell me where we are with Ms. Chase."

Quinn dropped a file on the desk in front of Ryan. "That's what I have."

Ryan flipped it open and started going through the contents. It had a full report of Lexi Chase's movements. From the apartment to the office to a friend's house, along with her visitors.

"Did you get a good look at the boyfriend?"

Quinn shook his head, reached into the file, and pulled out a picture of Lexi at the door and the back of a man. He was Caucasian with dark hair. He was tall, thin. It looked like there could be a mark on his neck—a birthmark or a tattoo? The photo wasn't clear enough to confirm. "That's him, but he never turned toward me."

Ryan looked at the photo for a second, then continued through the file. He didn't stop again until he came across another picture of Lexi. The person she was with was a very familiar face.

"Is that..."

"Yeah," Quinn said. "Hotshot lawyer. Leslie Dunn's partner."

"With one of our top suspects." Ryan frowned. Dorian employed Lexi; it would only make sense they'd be together. He picked up the photo and examined it closer. The two were sitting at what looked like a patio table. Lexi appeared to be seated on the lawyer's lap.

"Yup." Then Quinn chuckled. "And from what I saw, let's just say the meeting wasn't business."

"So she starts a new job and then sleeps with her boss? Did you see her leave?"

Quinn shook his head. "I left after an hour of waiting around. Winters took my patrol."

"Are you back on the road today?" Ryan asked. He never liked Officer Winters and would prefer Quinn on the job.

"Yeah, I'm meeting Winters at noon. He's been trailing Ms. Chase since I left."

"Where are you meeting him?"

"Just a hotel on the edge of the city."

Ryan flipped the file shut but held onto the picture of Dorian and Lexi. Opening his top drawer, he slipped it inside.

"Boone?" Quinn asked, eyeing his placement of the picture.

"Just a little collateral. Don't worry about it." Ryan slid the file across the desk to Quinn.

"Okay," Quinn said as he picked up the file.

"Call me if anything strange happens with Ms. Chase,"

Ryan said. "We'll pull you from patrol in a few days if we don't find anything."

"Understood." Quinn exited Ryan's office without another word.

When he was gone, Ryan reached back into the top drawer of his desk and looked at the picture again. Something about it seemed unnatural. It wasn't the lighting or the angle. As he examined it, he realized it was the people. They looked uncomfortable with each other; they didn't reflect the normal faces of an office affair. It wasn't intimate in the way one would expect. They seemed like strangers. No, there was something much deeper in this picture, but Ryan wasn't sure what.

"Boone," Archer said as he stepped into Ryan's office. He ran a hand over his sweat-speckled forehead. "We just got a call about Kimball. He's been spotted at main station buying a ticket. Security is keeping an eye on him. We need to get over there, stat." Archer twisted his keys around his index finger.

"Got the arrest warrant?" Ryan grabbed his phone and wallet from his desk and pushed them into his jacket pocket before rounding his desk to Archer's side.

"Jade has it." Archer led Ryan from the office and toward their assistant.

Jade gave Archer the file as they passed. They headed to the parking lot and into the waiting cruiser. Lights and sirens on immediately, Archer raced down the street toward the main station, slowing down only for uncertain intersections.

In a matter of minutes, they were parked outside the train station and ascending the stairs in search of Allen Kimball.

Ryan spotted him on platform five, waiting as the train pulled into the station. He wore a dark hoodie pulled over his head.

He approached the man. "Allen Kimball."

Allen turned to regard Ryan. Kimball looked him up and down before his eyes widened, and he turned to run. Luckily, Archer was standing on the other side, and Kimball collided with the larger man's chest. There was nowhere else to go.

"Allen Kimball, you are under arrest for the burglary of Donovan Jewelers," Ryan said as Archer took Kimball's arms and cuffed them behind his back. "Know you have the right to remain silent and seek council through public or private means. Remember any words you speak from here on can be used against your case. Nod that you understand this."

Kimball gritted his teeth and nodded.

"Archer, take him out." Ryan waved for Archer to lead the way, following after. All bystanders' eyes were on them as they passed. Ryan didn't make contact with them, knowing Kimball's arrest would be all over the news in a matter of hours. High profile people never got away with secrecy for long.

Chapter 19
Melanie Parker

THE VIBRATIONS RATTLED THE SMALL GLASS TABLETOP and Mel reached for the phone to stop the awful racket. She sat forward in her lounger and pulled off her sunglasses to glance at the screen. The sun was shining off the pool in front of her, making it difficult to read.

"Mel here."

The deep voice on the phone was Blaine. "It's me."

"How did it go?" Mel glanced to her right. Jackie was lying face down on the blue woven lounger. A large black and white striped umbrella shielded them from the hot morning sun.

"Candy just left."

Mel glanced at Jackie's phone. Half-past ten. She stayed long. Most of the girls had already come and gone. "How did she look?"

"Fine. Happy, even."

"Good. Call me if there's anything else."

"Mr. Dorian hasn't left yet."

Strange. Mel frowned. "I'm sure he'll leave soon. Mr. Dorian does things on his own time."

"Should I wait?"

Mel hesitated. She always liked knowing what happened to their clients after one of her girls performed their services. It never hurt to keep tabs.

"Only until he leaves."

"Alright."

She hit end on her phone and looked back to Jackie.

"Who was that?" Jackie asked, propping herself on her elbows and pushing her bangs back with her sunglasses.

Mel leaned back in her chair and pulled her hair into a messy bun before putting her sunglasses back on and grabbing her magazine from the side table. The two girls were lounging by a large, curvy pool at Hotel Chapuys near the east end of the city. The pool was surrounded by tall, black spear-top gates. On the opposite side of the pool, a large, toned security guard dressed in a black uniform stood at the entrance gate, watching the guests.

"Blaine."

Jackie raised her right eyebrow. "Candy alright?" She was always so worried.

"She'll be back soon." Mel tried focusing on her reading with little success; Jackie was interested now.

"She do okay?" Jackie pushed herself to her knees.

"I guess we'll find out when she's back."

Jackie glanced around the pool, then lowered her voice. "Should I have left her there?"

Mel followed her gaze to the uniformed guard. She raised her magazine shielding him from her view, then looked to her friend.

"Jackie, it's fine."

"Are you sure?" Jackie asked, a frown plastered on her face. "You told me to watch her."

"I know," Mel said. "You had a job to do too. From what you said, Candy was having a great time. And Gabi was still there."

Jackie's light eyebrows knit together as her frown drooped further. "Gabi is hardly the person to be leaving Candy with."

"Gabi may be flippant from time to time, but she's experienced." Mel gave her friend a soft smile. "I trust her to do what's right. You too."

Jackie looked away, chewing on her lower lip.

For some time neither of the girls spoke; Jackie continued to look away. Finally, Mel sighed and put the magazine aside. She had never been able to stand Jackie being upset for long.

"Look, Candy knew what she was getting into. Besides, you said yourself when Dorian was all jacked up on coke he was very affectionate to her. I'm sure she had a wonderful night."

Jackie's fingers laced together in her lap. She still didn't look at Mel. "The party was intense."

"Nothing you aren't used to," Mel said, trying to mask the frustration in her voice. Couldn't Jackie just relax?

"Yeah, me. What about Candy?"

"Calm down. Wait until she's back, okay? For all you know, she loved it."

Jackie lay back on the blue lounger and pulled her sunglasses over her eyes. "Fine."

Mel reached out and took Jackie's arm, giving it a gentle squeeze of reassurance before retrieving her magazine to finish the gossip column. Feeling Jackie's steady gaze, Mel quickly gave up on trying to read. She put the magazine down for the tenth time in the past hour, flipped her legs over the side of the lounger, and sat on the edge.

"I'm getting in the pool." She stood, kicked off her flip-flops, and took off the black sundress covering her bathing suit. She stalked away from Jackie without waiting for an answer.

Mel glanced to the security guard again. The man watched her and Mel was almost certain he didn't recognize her. In her business, in this city, it was hard to know who recognized her.

She dipped her right foot into the cool water before starting down the white vinyl steps. The water felt nice against her warm skin, and she lowered herself to the stairs so she could sit with the water reaching just above her waist.

She tipped her head back and instantly felt several sets of eyes on her—the attention of all the middle-aged men resting along the poolside. Mel and her girls frequented this hotel often. She had a good relationship with the head manager, and security changed so often that no one seemed able to keep tabs on them. However, the manager asked her to use discretion in the past. The hotel was meant as a meeting place, not the house of their operation.

"I'm sorry to disturb you, Ms. Parker."

Mel glanced at the unknown voice. A man likely in his forties with greying hair and tired eyes smiled at her. He was short with a rounded middle and dressed in a fine suit.

She cocked her head to the side. "Can I help you?" She was never surprised when someone knew her name anymore.

Their business flourished on word of mouth. Her name had become renowned to a few.

The man reached into his jacket pocket, pulled out a small business card, and handed it to her. She flipped it over, examining both sides. It was for a marketing firm down the road from the hotel. "Derek Jeffries" gleamed as the sunlight reflected off the gold writing. *All you need is the market and a dream. We'll do the rest*—what a cheesy slogan.

Mel stared at the card for a while, chewing on her lower lip. She looked back at the man and decided he was innocent enough.

"Mr. Jeffries?" she asked, though she'd always imagined the oldest of Jeffries' cousins to be much more attractive. Didn't wealth make people more so?

The man shook his head. "My client, miss."

Mel looked back at the card. "Indeed."

The man shifted his weight back and forth as he glanced at the security guard. "Are you available tonight?"

"For what, sir?" Mel tucked the card into the top of her bikini.

The man glanced back at Mel and lowered his voice. "Your services."

A smirk spread across Mel's lips. She knew he wanted this; many of her clients were nervous when it started.

"Is that what you wanted?" she asked. The man glanced back at the guard. Mel continued to stare at him. She always enjoyed making people uncomfortable. "Rather last minute."

"Perhaps we should go somewhere more private," the man suggested, his eyes still darting between her and the guard. "Is now a bad time?"

"Anytime is a good time." Mel climbed out of the pool to

meet the man; she stood nearly four inches taller than him. She extended her hand in his direction, "Melanie Parker."

The man didn't take her hand; instead, he gawked at her toned body. Mel pulled her hand away and brushed a loose strand of hair from her cheek. A flash of red hair caught her attention, and Mel glanced toward the gate to see a woman dressed in a short black cocktail dress enter the pool area. Mel frowned. She shouldn't be here dressed like *that*. It was a dead giveaway that they weren't regular hotel guests.

The man cleared his throat. Mel held up her hand.

"Forgive me, sir, this will have to wait." She pulled the business card from her bikini top and waved it at him. "I will contact Mr. Jeffries shortly and arrange a meeting."

She brushed by the short man and waved at Jackie. The blonde collected their things as Mel proceeded to the pool entrance. When she reached Candy, she hooked her arm and steered her out of the pool area.

"Hey, what?" Candy said. Mel held a finger to her lips.

"Quiet, not here." Mel glanced over her shoulder and hesitated so Jackie could catch up with them.

"Hey, sweetie." Jackie smiled at Candy, who glanced up and returned it. "How did it go?"

Mel gave her a hard look. "Not now." She grabbed her dress and flip-flops from Jackie's arms and put them back on. "She can explain in the room." Mel waved them toward the hotel.

Jackie pushed open the green door marked one hundred and four. The room had two queen-sized beds and a light grey carpet, with white walls making the room bright and welcoming. A large watercolour painting of a sailboat on a clear sunny day was positioned above the beds in a wood frame. Their things were piled on the far bed. They rarely spent a night in these accommodations, though sometimes the girls wished they would. It was nicer than some of the other places they ended up. Not every paying customer had a beach house.

Candy fell to the first double bed and kicked the black pumps off her swollen feet. "Thank god," she mumbled.

Jackie lowered herself to the bed beside Candy and brushed her messy hair aside. "Are you okay? Was Mr. Dorian nice?"

Mel cleared her throat, and both girls looked to her. She leaned against the wall and crossed her arms. "Well, are you alright?"

"I am." Candy reached into her cleavage and pulled out the money, tossing it onto the bed beside her.

Mel stepped forward and picked it up. Then she looked at Candy with her right eyebrow raised. "He gave you more."

"Yes," Candy said.

Jackie beamed and caught Candy's hand before giving her a light squeeze. "He liked you."

Candy smiled. "He seemed to."

"How was the party last night?" Jackie asked, "Too much?"

Candy shook her head. "No, though I don't remember much." She looked at Mel. "I don't know what happened to Gabi. Sorry, I know you told me to lay off the coke, but Paul kept insisting."

"Paul?" Mel asked with an amused smile.

Candy blushed.

Jackie frowned. "Gabi probably left you at the party alone. That girl is always irresponsible."

Mel stacked the bills then shoved them into her purse. "Gabi can take care of herself." She looked at Candy. "Can you go again tonight?"

Candy glanced at her outfit and reached up, messing her cropped hair. "I'll need a shower first." She stood unsteady on her bare feet and stripped off her black dress, placing it on the dresser. Standing before them in her matching dark bra and panties, she motioned to the dress. "Sorry Mel, I think I ruined it."

Before Mel could touch it, Jackie grabbed the dress, sat back on the bed and examined it. The garment moistened the front of Jackie's clothes as she ran her fingers over the fabric.

"It's fine, just wet." Jackie placed the dress beside her.

Mel raised her eyebrow. "You got it wet?"

Candy looked away, a blush creeping up her neck. "Paul has some wild idea about swimming in our clothes. It seemed smart at the time."

Mel smirked as she walked to Candy's side. Mel placed a hand on her bare shoulder and Candy raised her eyes. Reaching up, Mel wiped away a drop of blood that trickled from Candy's nose.

"Actually, lay off the coke next time." Mel didn't release Candy. Instead, she ran her hands down Candy's arms and over her petite breasts and flat stomach. Then down each smooth leg.

"Is this necessary?" Jackie asked. She'd always found Mel's checkup routine tedious, but Mel had a good reason. A working girl could go every night if she was left undamaged.

Sometimes a nasty bruise went unnoticed for days. Besides, she needed to know how rough her clients could be and make sure the girls were okay after a wild night of work.

Mel didn't answer and Candy only gave Jackie a weak smile while waiting patiently.

"Ouch," Candy said when Mel pressed two fingers against the inside of her left thigh.

"What's this?" Mel asked, running her fingers across the ribbed wound.

Candy lifted her leg and examined the faint purple bruise on her thigh.

"He bit you." Mel pursed her lips.

"It got a little passionate," Candy said.

Mel frowned, said nothing more and continued her inspection. She circled and examined her backside. When she'd finished with her exam, she stepped back from the redhead and cocked her head to the side. "Anything else hurt?"

"No."

"Anything other than your nose bleeding?"

Candy shook her head.

"Good." Mel pulled a business card from her cleavage and handed it to Candy. "After you figure out how to cover that mark, here's your next customer."

"Who?" Jackie asked, snatching the card from Candy's hand before she could read it. She noticeably stiffened when she read the name. "Derek Jeffries?"

Mel gave Jackie a sharp look and didn't answer her, instead looking at Candy. "Okay?"

Candy nodded.

"Go and get cleaned up, then we'll get you something to

eat." Mel waved toward the bathroom door and Candy entered without another word.

Jackie pushed herself from the bed and stood next to Mel. She reached up and brushed a loose strand of brown hair from Mel's cheek and held a steady gaze.

"Don't look at me like that." Mel stepped away from Jackie.

"Have you thought this through?"

Mel squared her shoulders. "Now you're questioning me too?"

"No." Jackie looked at the floor between them. "It's just the Jeffries. They're ..."

Mel threw her hands up in exasperation. "They're what, Jackie?"

Mel was tired of her friend's secrets. What did Jackie have against an entire family?

"It's just ..." Jackie fidgeted, looking around as if for an escape. "They're dangerous, I guess. I don't know. I don't have great memories of Brielle and I just think it would be better to avoid their whole family."

"Seriously?" Mel frowned. "You think we should deny a well-paying client based on a friendship you had five years ago?" Or however long it was.

Jackie chewed on her lower lip. "I know it sounds stupid. It's just giving me a bad feeling."

"I'm not going to base my business off your feelings," Mel said. "I'm sorry if you feel like I'm putting your little pet in a situation you don't like. Candy is willing."

Jackie frowned. "My pet?"

"I know how you feel about her." Mel turned and walked away from Jackie. She reached into her purse and pulled out the money from Candy's job, followed by a pile of neatly stacked bills wrapped with a brown elastic band. She smoothed the crinkled bills Candy gave her and added them to the other stack. "She makes more than you did when you started. I'm not about to let her go."

"When I first found her, you weren't so keen."

"Things change."

"I don't want to frighten her." Jackie's fingers knitted together in front of her. "She's got nowhere else to go. If you scare her away, then she'll just go back to the alley we found her in, or worse, her abusive boyfriend."

Mel's hard gaze softened. "We have no reason to suspect this client will be any different than others. If you are worried she'll run away, then ask her. Do whatever you need to do to put your mind at ease." She picked up the money and waved the stack of bills at Jackie. "Because a few extra hundred bucks every session would be good for us."

Jackie bit her lip then draws a long breath. "You think it'll be fine?"

Mel placed her hands on Jackie's shoulders and leaned in so their foreheads were touching.

"When have I ever led you astray?"

"Never."

Mel pulled away. "You can trust me."

Before Jackie could answer there was a knock at the door.

"Let me in," Gabi called from the hallway.

Mel strode across the room and opened the door.

"Hey, girls," Gabi said, crushing her smoke on the concrete before entering the room.

The bathroom door creaked open and Candy rejoined the girls.

"Glad to see you're fine," Gabi said to Candy. "Which one got you in the end?"

Mel glanced from Gabi to Candy. What did she mean "which one"?

"What are you talking about?" Her lips formed a hard line as she glared at Gabi.

"Uh." Gabi's voice shook. "There were just two of them when I left with Liam. She seemed like she was having a good time."

"That's probably why the pig paid us more. He knew I'd be pissed. Who else was there? Dorian, and who else?"

"I—I didn't know his name. It was the tall one." Gabi's eyes darted between Jackie and Candy. "You remember, right?"

Mel grabbed the front of Gabi's shirt. "What are you doing, Gabi? You know better than this, after everything that's happened." She released her with a shove and Gabi stumbled backwards.

Then Mel turned her anger on Candy. "Did two of them have you last night?"

Candy's eyes widened and she stepped back, trembling.

Jackie grabbed Mel's hand, pulling her away from Candy.

"Mel, calm down." Jackie's voice was quiet. "This isn't Candy's fault."

Candy lowered herself to the bed and put her face in her hands.

Mel turned back to Gabi. "What the hell did you give her? Why the fuck can't she remember anything?"

"I don't know." Gabi stepped back, hands up in front of her face. "Maybe Geoff sold me some bad stuff. I don't know. She was pounding back the shots. Blame the booze!"

"There was only Paul with me this morning." Candy didn't look up at Mel as she spoke. She gently rubbed her temples. "I was drunk, but only remember him. Gabi left and I am pretty sure Paul sent the other guy away shortly after."

Mel took several deep breaths, trying to calm the anger. She hated when the girls didn't know left from right. Most of her veterans knew how to keep the party going without indulging too much. She should have known an amateur like Candy would have floundered at Dorian's party.

"It's okay," Jackie said, putting herself between Mel and Candy. "See? Nothing bad happened. Everything is okay."

Mel shook her head. "What happened after I left?"

Gabi looked at her hands and fidgeted with the edge of her shirt. "Nothing crazy. We were all fucked up. After you left, Mr. Dorian honed in on Candy. I don't think he stopped touching her once. At the end of the night, Liam propositioned me and I left Candy there. By then, only two guys were left—Dorian and one of his buddies. Wasn't Blaine watching Candy all night? Can't he tell you who had her?"

Blaine would have said something if the job seemed off. At least Gabi was smart about that.

Mel's hand shot out and grabbed Gabi's wrist. "Where's the money?"

"Calm down." Gabi pulled her arm from Mel's grasp and plunged her hand into her shoulder bag. Gabi handed Mel the cash; she grabbed it and started counting. One, two, three, four.

Mel narrowed her eyes and she looked up at Gabi. "Where's the rest?"

Gabi waved the last couple bills at Mel. "I figured you'd want me to pick up again."

"Fine," Mel added the cash to the pile she was handling before and returned it to her purse.

"How was Mr. Kyles' party?" Jackie asked.

Mel turned away from the group and walked toward the door, slipping out just as she heard Gabi begin explaining the lavish party Liam Kyles took her too. Mel had no doubt the man paraded Gabi around like his middle eastern princess. She was also gorgeous. It was no surprise Liam Kyles took a liking to her.

Mel glanced down at the screen of her phone as she stepped out of the front lobby and into the sunlight. She sought cover under an awning to shield her screen from the rays. She had a missed call and a voicemail from Blaine.

"Melanie, I'm heading back to the house. Call me if you need a ride."

Mel deleted this message then pulled out the business card and dialed the direct line.

"Derek Jeffries." His voice was crisp through the receiver.

Mel cleared her throat before speaking. "Mr. Jeffries, this is Melanie Parker. An associate of yours approached me about requiring some services for this evening."

There was a commotion on the other end of the phone and Mel waited patiently, certain the man was only finding somewhere more private to talk.

When he returned, his voice was lower. "What can you do for me?"

"Depends on what you want, Mr. Jeffries."

Silence.

"Do you have a preferred location?" Mel asked, trying to push the conversation further. "Perhaps a favourite hotel? If not, I can suggest one."

"I have a place. We can go there." He sounded rushed.

No real surprise. Most people tried to get off the phone quickly. It wasn't a conversation they seemed to like having.

"Will you give me an address? I can have my girls meet you there." Mel hit speaker on her phone, ready to type in the address when he gave it.

He didn't. "I will have a car meet you. Is the hotel where my associate met you okay?"

"The hotel is fine. Eight o'clock. I will have my associate contact you to confirm numbers and cost, as well as extract payment before then." She clicked end on her phone and dialled Blaine's number.

"Blaine?" Mel asked when she heard the phone click.

"Are you okay?" His voice was smooth.

"Fine," she said. "Dorian get off okay?"

"Shortly after Candy."

"Was there anyone else?" Mel asked. If there'd been two guys Blaine would have seen them.

"Only the lawyer."

"Good. Now I need you to do something for me."

Blaine didn't answer; he never did when Mel asked for a favour.

"I need you to do a background check on Derek Jeffries. Afterwards, meet with him and figure out how many girls he wants and price him out. We have an appointment with Mr. Jeffries this evening at eight. His car will pick us up at the hotel. I want you to follow us wherever we go. Jackie is freaking out about this one."

"I will let you know what I find. Tell Jackie not to worry. I'll make sure it's okay." Blaine paused. "Are you going again?"

"Not to work," Mel said.

"Yeah," Blaine said. "I get it. Text me Mr. Jeffries' number."

"I will now." She hit end on her phone, then quickly typed the phone number to Blaine. As the message sent she stared at the screen, wondering if she could have been nicer to him. Blaine was used to their brief conversations, and Mel knew how he cared for her. Sometimes she wondered why he even bothered. She was too cold to really love. She didn't know if she was worthy of it.

Mel turned and went back into the hotel. The three girls were still sitting on the beds while Gabi talked about her night.

Mel didn't listen as she grabbed her things and entered the bathroom. She changed from her bathing suit and sundress into a pair of tight jeans and a crop top, then ran a brush through her hair and tied the mess up in a bun. Glancing in the mirror, she knew she'd need to do something else to make it more presentable tonight.

When she finished, she exited the bathroom and turned to the girls. Candy looked up at her and almost instantly looked back down at her hands.

Gabi, clearly noticing the reaction, turned to face Mel. "What's up?"

Mel fished a few bills from her purse and tossed them at

Gabi. She'd need more than the few hundred she'd held on to. "Get the same as last time. We have another one tonight."

Gabi took the money and left without another word. Mel turned to Jackie and Candy.

"Mr. Jeffries' car will pick us up here at eight." She tossed a key toward Jackie, who caught it out of the air. "I have some errands to run before we get picked up."

Jackie chewed on her lower lip.

Mel stepped closer and lowered her voice. "Blaine will be looking into him first."

Candy gave her a questioning look but said nothing. The girl was likely too intimidated to voice any real concerns to Mel.

"What about us?" Jackie asked.

Mel plunged her hand into her purse and pulled out a few bills, handing them to Jackie. "Go get her something to eat. I can hear her stomach from a mile away. Then take her back to the house to get ready. See if you can cover up that awful mark and make sure she is in perfect condition."

Mel left the hotel room, leaving the two girls alone.

Chapter 20
Brielle Jeffries

BAGS IN HAND, BRIELLE EXITED THE EXPENSIVE boutique and beelined for a place to sit. In the center of the mall hallway there were four white benches. Two were occupied by resting shoppers. Brielle went to the farthest and placed her shopping bags down. Then she dug into her purse and took out her cell phone.

There was a message from Gemma. Since the previous night, the girl had been relentless. Now she was insisting Brielle attend a party with some of the other people from their high school.

"Brielle?" A voice came from behind her.

Brielle turned to be met by a blue gaze. It was her friend from high school, Patsy. Several shopping bags hung around her left wrist, and her right hand grasped a small black purse. She wore a long-sleeved, floor-length dress despite the stifling heat. Her dark hair was pulled back from her angular face in a tight, low bun. And the caked-on makeup Brielle had seen the last time was still in place. Brielle wondered what she was covering up this time.

"Oh, hi," Brielle said. "You threw a great function the other night; sorry I didn't get a chance to tell you."

She smiled. "Thank you, that's kind of you to say." Her eyes dropped to the bags at Brielle's feet. "It looks like you've been busy."

"Yeah, I guess." Brielle shrugged. "I've not much else to do."

"Me neither, to be honest," Patsy said.

"You've got the community stuff, at least."

Patsy looked away when Brielle said it. She forced a tight smile. "Yes, of course."

They stood awkwardly for a moment, neither speaking nor sure what to say until Patsy spoke once more.

"It was lovely to see you," she said. "I must be going. I can't be late getting home."

"Have a good night," Brielle said as Patsy turned and hurried off. Brielle watched her go, then shook her head. *Weird.* Glancing at her phone once more, she noted the time. It was after five. Her throat started to itch and she craved a strong drink. Gathering her bags, she headed to the parking lot and hopped into her car.

Back at home, Brielle went straight to her room with the intention of grabbing the small bottle of vodka cooling in her mini fridge. Her mother must have heard her arrive home and followed her into her bedroom.

"Did you go shopping?" Mary asked, sitting on the edge of Brielle's bed.

"Yeah." Brielle placed the bags next to her.

"Can I see?"

Brielle mumbled her approval and Mary opened the closest bag, pulling out the clothes Brielle had purchased.

"Did you have fun last night?" Mary asked.

"Yeah, it was good."

"Did you spend the night with Riley's girl? What's her name again? I assumed you slept there when you didn't come home."

"Gemma." Brielle remembered spending the start of the night with Gemma. She didn't remember where she slept. There were a few tequila shots, then, Brielle imagined, a few more; she couldn't really remember, though. The desire to drink still itched in the back of her throat.

"Right, of course." Mary smiled and took out a jean jacket Brielle had purchased. "This is nice."

"Thanks."

"So, did you have fun?"

"Uh, yeah I did. It was good to catch up," Brielle said. "Actually, she wants to hang out again."

"That's nice, dear. It's good for you to get back into seeing your friends and being social."

"Thanks, Mom."

Mary then reached into the next bag and pulled out a black tank top covered in tiny sequins. She passed it to Brielle.

"If you and Gemma go out somewhere nice, you should wear this," Mary said. "It will look lovely on you."

Brielle took the shirt from her mother. Maybe it was worth going out.

Mary dropped her gaze to her hands and her smile faded. There was something she wasn't saying.

"What is it?" Brielle asked, taking the chair in front of her mirror. The counter in front of her had her bag of makeup and hair products, as well as a square pill case, her required dosages pre-sorted. A half glass of day-old water was next to it.

"Nothing to worry about, honey," Mary said.

"You're going to tell me eventually." Brielle reached for the pill case and checked what day she was on. A quick count told her she was caught up. Her spotty memory didn't stop her from taking her meds, at least.

"Dr. Konch called," Mary said. "She wanted to see how you were."

Brielle looked over at her mother. "And how am I?"

"I told her what I thought."

"Which is?"

Mary stood and walked over to where Brielle sat, placing a hand on her shoulder. "You're doing well. You're young, beautiful, and healing. You seem happy."

Brielle couldn't remember a time when she was happy. She didn't think she was happy now. Still, she forced a smile at her mother.

"I think that was the right thing to say."

"I told her you would call." Mary moved toward Brielle's door. "I told her Monday, so you don't need to rush."

"Okay." Brielle tipped her required pills for the day into her palm and grabbed the old water.

"Brielle?"

Brielle looked at her, still holding the water and meds.

"This doesn't mean you have to go back to seeing her regularly," Mary said. "She just wants to check in."

Brielle hesitated. "I know."

"Good." Mary turned and left Brielle's room.

Brielle gulped back the water and swallowed the pills in one go. Then she looked up at the mirror and grabbed her brush. Before she finished with her hair, her cell phone chimed from within her purse. Brielle grabbed it and checked the message. It was another one from Gemma; a request to hit a local club. Glancing back at the mirror, Brielle sighed. She could really use a drink.

What was the harm in going out tonight? Maybe she needed a little fun, and maybe Gemma could clear up her previous night.

Brielle grabbed her phone and dialled Gemma's number. The girl picked up after the first ring.

"Aloha!" Gemma's voice came through the receiver.

"Hey, Gemma, it's Brielle."

"Hey, hon," Gemma said. "You're coming out tonight, right? You aren't allowed to bail on me like you did last night!"

Brielle frowned. "Bail? What are you talking about?"

"You don't remember?" Gemma laughed. "You must have been pretty wasted, darling."

"Must have," Brielle said. "Did I say where I was going?"

Gemma made a long humming sound as she considered the question. "No specifics. Said you had a job to do, and you left after your third sour."

"A job?"

"It's what you said," Gemma said. "So, are you coming out tonight?"

"Yeah, I think I'll try to make it," Brielle said.

"Good, and no bailing on me this time! It's been so long since we partied together. Let me enjoy your company."

"Sounds good," Brielle said. "I'll text you later."

"See you tonight," Gemma said, and the phone clicked, ending the call.

Brielle set the phone down and sat on her bed beside it. She was drinking amaretto again, a drink Brielle hadn't touched since before the clinic, or at least she thought. Maybe her drinking was getting out of hand if she couldn't remember picking up a bottle she hated. She resolved to drink less tonight and actually see where the night took her.

Chapter 21
Detective Ryan Boone

RYAN WAS HALFWAY TO THE OFFICE WHEN QUINN'S number flashed across the screen. The morning traffic had been killer, and Ryan was running late.

"You've got Boone."

"You sound chipper this morning," Quinn said.

"Cut it with the sarcasm, Quinn," Ryan said. "Your wit and brilliance can never compare to mine."

Quinn laughed.

"I'm surprised you're up." Ryan clicked a few buttons on the dashboard of his car, hooking up his hands-free call. "Did something happen?"

"I thought I had something interesting with Lexi Chase, so I tailed her for a bit."

"And?" Ryan turned off the highway.

"She got picked up in a shiny limo and attended a party in the Beaches with the same girls I'd seen before."

"Fancy place," Ryan said. He and Lilian used to visit a friend's summer house in the Beaches every year. Ryan hadn't had the courage to even drive through the area since her passing.

"Yeah, though not too sure what happened there since the property is gated. There was something else."

"What is it?" Ryan asked as he pulled into his parking spot and cut the engine.

"It looked like she was with one of the Jeffries clan," Quinn said.

Ryan frowned. "How would Lexi connect with that family?"

"I wouldn't know," Quinn said. "Struck me as weird, too."

"Which one?"

"Sorry, boss, I wouldn't know them by name."

"Anything else?" Ryan asked, glancing at the radio clock.

"That's it," Quinn said. "A rest for me, then I'll be in the office later."

"See you then, and good work, Quinn," Ryan said.

"Thanks."

Ryan hung up his cell phone. Two missed calls from the office. He climbed out of the car and headed inside. There, Archer waited by their assistant's desk.

"Morning," Archer said as Ryan passed by him. "I tried calling."

"You're early." Ryan headed for his office. "Did the baby wake you up or did your wife kick you out for snoring again?"

"Funny."

Jade wouldn't be in for another half hour, at least. Archer must have been hoping to catch Ryan alone.

"What's going on?" Ryan placed his briefcase aside and took his seat, booting up his laptop.

Archer sat across from him and folded his hands in his lap. "Kimball's lawyer called. He's coming in this morning to see you."

Ryan frowned. "Seriously?" He didn't appreciate how last minute it was.

"I said the same thing." Archer shook his head. "He wouldn't take no. He could be here any time."

"Who is it?"

Archer grimaced. "Dorian."

He meant Paul Dorian, the top defence lawyer in the city. Ryan had dealt with him on more than one occasion. He wasn't an unpleasant man, other than his chosen career path. He was cocky. Getting wealthy people out of their crimes for a living was bound to rub off on someone. It certainly had with Dorian.

"Isn't this a conflict of interest?" Ryan asked. "He's Lexi Chase's employer and she's the other suspect."

"Without evidence." Archer frowned. "So it doesn't count. I guess it pays to be a rich kid."

"It explains why Kimball has never seen the inside of a real jail cell. Maybe we can change that." Ryan heard the creak of the loose floorboard in the hall and footsteps outside of his office. He raised an eyebrow at the sound. "He's here already? I'm not prepared for this."

Archer headed for the door and Ryan followed him. Thankfully, it was only Jade. She settled into her desk with a large smile. She was dressed in a formal blue pantsuit, nicer than usual, and her hair was pulled back from her narrow face into a tight ponytail.

"Good morning, detectives."

"Jade, you're early," Ryan said.

She nodded. "Traffic was a breeze."

"Really? I can't say I found the same thing." Ryan retorted, thinking back to his own drive.

"Okay, fine," Jade said. "I crashed at a place closer to the office than usual. Do you want to hear all about my booty call?"

"I'll pass." Ryan grimaced.

Then Jade's smile faded. "Is something wrong? You have your panicked look on."

Ryan shook his head. "It's fine. We're expecting a visitor soon about the Kimball case."

"Name?" Jade grabbed a pen.

"Paul Dorian."

She hesitated and glanced at Ryan, eyebrow raised. However, she said nothing and scribbled it down. "I'll page when he's here."

"Good." Ryan turned to his partner. "Be in my office when Dorian arrives. We'll sort this out."

"Sounds good."

Back in his office, Ryan looked to his laptop and started going over the case notes and evidence the lawyer may ask about until his phone beeped and Jade's voice came through.

"Sorry for interrupting, detective," Jade said. She was speaking very formally today. Ryan assumed it just a show for the well-known lawyer. "Mr. Paul Dorian is here to discuss the case."

"Send him and Archer in," Ryan said.

The lawyer was tall and lean with shaggy dark hair that was usually slicked back, though not today. His eyes glinted at Jade as he passed her, though Ryan could see how tired he looked. His suit was clean, shirt untucked and tie loose. He didn't look like a lawyer ready to go to court, let alone meet with a client.

"Can I get you anything, Mr. Dorian?" Jade asked, batting her lashes at the lawyer. She was always overly kind to the attractive visitors at the office, and the rich. Jade loved the wealthy.

"I'm fine, thank you," he said. Jade seemed to hesitate by the door for a moment, gazing as the lawyer turned his back.

"That will be all, Jade," Ryan said. Her eyes widened and she left his office.

"Good morning, Mr. Boone." Dorian took the seat across from him.

Ryan offered a curt nod. "Mr. Dorian."

Archer slipped into the office and closed the door.

Dorian glanced back at him with a smile. "Excellent. Mr. Archer shall join us as well. I was wondering if our silent friend would grace us with his presence."

Archer only stared at him as he took the chair in the corner of Ryan's office.

Ryan leaned back in his chair and crossed his arms. "What do you want, Dorian? It's not like you to show your slimy face around here."

"A pleasure as always, Mr. Boone."

"I do try hard when it comes to you." Ryan tapped his chin. "I was just thinking about how much you reminded me of a gigolo we picked up last night, then I realized he only screws one person at a time, so I guess there's a big difference between what you two do."

Dorian raised an eyebrow but said nothing about the

insult. He straightened his tie. "I'm reaching out to the judge tonight. The bail hearing should be moved up to the end of the week."

"The judge will determine the best course of action, I'm sure," Ryan said.

"Of course," Dorian agreed. "Though my client will make bail. After all, the case isn't very solid."

"Why do you say that?"

Dorian grinned, then reached into his briefcase, pulling out a manila file folder and flipping through the pages. "You were at the scene after the crime happened?"

"Of course." Ryan narrowed his eyes, unsure of what Dorian was about to suggest.

"And you saw the surveillance video?"

"Yes."

Dorian produced two stills from the video. First, the man turning off the camera and two bright green eyes Ryan remembered seeing, and the second featured the woman and confirming the red hair Ryan thought he saw.

"You must realize neither of these are my client," Dorian said.

"Of course not," Ryan said. "He was spotted in the window."

Dorian shook his head. "A bystander. Innocent."

Ryan gritted his teeth. "It's not me you need to convince."

"You know me better than that, Boone." Dorian pointed to the two pictures again. "I always like to see you fail."

Ryan had dealt with Dorian on more than one occasion and the odds never turned out well. Ryan had to hand it to him. The man had a knack for arguing a twisted case.

"Your client helped with this crime," Ryan said. "There are a multitude of ways he could be involved. If he offered up the names of the two he was helping, this would be easier on him. Otherwise, I can only tell the prosecutor what I know."

"*Could* be, indeed," Dorian said. "The evidence you have is flimsy at best."

"We have a witness who saw him casing the store. He could have monitored the store's comings and goings for weeks."

Dorian frowned. "You can't win this case on this evidence alone."

Ryan didn't mention they were tracking Lexi Chase, nor did he bring up the photo in his desk. He simply crossed his arms. "I'm not trying to win a case. You have me confused with the prosecutor. I'm trying to solve a crime and put the guilty party behind bars."

"Of course," Dorian said, his hands up in defense. "Then you can understand where I am coming from, only trying to do my job as well."

Ryan looked away from the lawyer, wishing the conversation would end. Archer still hadn't spoken. He rarely did with company. "Are we done here?"

"Fine." Dorian stood. "As always, thank you for your time, detectives. I'm sure I'll have more questions for you after the hearing."

"I hope I've been of some help to you," Ryan said, though the sarcasm dripped off his words. "Please feel free to come by the next time you wish to question my cases, as I would love to hear it."

Dorian frowned and left Ryan's office. Jade scrambled to her feet as he saw his way through the lobby.

"Leaving so soon?" she said.

Dorian laughed uneasily and glanced back at Ryan. "I can't say I'm welcome here."

Ryan only watched him go, arms crossed over his chest.

"What happened?" Jade asked when Dorian was gone.

"Nothing," Ryan said, turning back for his office.

"Are you okay?" Jade asked.

Ryan grabbed the side of the door. "I'm fine." He shut it before Jade could press any further and fell to his chair. Archer was still seated in the corner, his thick eyebrows folded together in concentration.

Ryan glanced down at his desk, realizing Dorian left the two stills from the video facing him. He looked between the two figures. A redheaded woman, a green-eyed man. Who could these people be?

"He's an ass," Archer finally said.

"I know." Ryan chuckled. "You were quiet."

"You had it handled."

Ryan looked back at the picture. Archer moved across the room.

"What's this?"

"Back to work, of course." Ryan pushed them toward his partner. "We have two other suspects to find."

Chapter 22
Melanie Parker

"LOOK AT ME." HIS DARK EYES WERE UNREADABLE, TWO soulless pools of black staring through her. "Better."

He grazed her cheek with his thumb. She gritted her teeth against the pain, anything to avoid more. Leaning close, he captured her lips in a rough kiss.

"I want you now," he said as he pulled away.

She gazed up at him. "Where?"

"Upstairs." His voice was husky now, laced with lust.

She didn't lead. It wasn't her place.

His hand wrapped around her wrist, directing her up the stairs to the lush bed in the main bedroom. When he released her, she took the usual position, leaning over the side of the bed, exposing her rear end for his viewing pleasure.

The subtle zipper on his jeans was followed by the gentle sound of his pants dropping to the floor. He placed his hands on her hips and rubbed them over her backside before sliding one finger inside. It's his usual move, one to make sure she was ready for him.

To her surprise, he took his time, being slow and gentle.

A moan escaped her lips; it's the first time he's pleasured her in a long time. She instinctively pushed back against his hand, begging for more.

"You like that?" His voice was low.

She didn't answer.

He grabbed the back of her hair, pulling her up against him.

"I asked if you liked that," he growled.

"Yes." she whimpered.

He released her, and she fell back against the bed. He ran his free hand up her spine and pushed his fingers deeper.

"Good," he said, his voice softening once more. "I want you to enjoy this. Because after, I'm going to fuck you. I'm going to fuck you like the little whore you are."

MEL'S EYES FLEW OPEN. Something wasn't right. Her head pounded, and her memory was cloudy. *What day was it? Where was she?*

She sat up in the king-sized bed, surrounded by a large white duvet and wearing a torn nightgown. She didn't recognize the garment, yet the room was oddly familiar. In the far corner, beneath a large square window, was a white chaise lounge with a purse and her clothes piled on top. Getting out of bed, she hurried to her clothes. When she turned back, she noticed the streak of blood on the sheets.

Shit! Mel slipped her hand between her legs to assess the damage and pulled it out clean. At least it wasn't there. She pulled the nightgown over her head, wincing as it scraped against her elbow. Turning her arm, she saw where the blood was from. There was a clean gash on her arm. It had stopped bleeding now. Mel couldn't be certain how long ago the wound had happened or how long she bled.

At the other end of the room, a black door was ajar—a bathroom. The layout was familiar; she'd been here before.

Mel dressed and entered the large room. The glass frame shower was tempting; if she were anywhere else, it would be the first place she went. She settled for the sink and splashed cold water on her face. Her lip stung. She leaned close to the mirror to examine the damage. Her lips were swollen and bruised, cracked in several places. Seeing the damage, she realized she could taste the metallic tang of blood on her tongue.

Aside from the slit on her arm and swollen lips, Mel found love bites lining her neck and chest, cruel bruises. They looked painful. Mel ran her finger over one and winced. They *were* painful. She splashed some water on her face again, ignoring the pain in her mouth, and gently rubbed her eyes, black makeup coming off on her knuckles.

She ran her hands under the tap and wiped away the makeup on the plush towel hanging on the rack. Then she reached into her purse and pulled out her phone. It'd been on silent, and she had several missed calls and texts.

Why didn't she answer them? She squeezed her eyes shut. It was Saturday, the day after she scheduled Derek's job. According to Jackie's text, they went without Mel. What happened last night? Why didn't she make it to Jeffries' summer house? From the sound of the address, it was likely very nice. Hopefully, the girls were tipped well.

Mel scrolled through the rest of her unread texts before returning her phone to her purse. She'd call Jackie once she was in a cab. First, though, she needed to get out of this house.

Hurrying down the stairs, she noticed her black flip-flops sitting at the front door. To the right of the door was a small side table. On top were several envelopes addressed to Fraser or Patsy Morrison. This made her stop for a moment. No wonder the house was familiar. Fraser was her ex. One Blaine had nearly killed.

There was that name again, Patsy Morrison. Mel squeezed her eyes shut. Where had she heard the name? Did he have a wife? She couldn't recall Fraser being married, though she'd been avoiding the man for ages. She was certain he dominated whoever had been unlucky enough to tie herself to him. His forceful ways were what turned her off him in the first place.

Her eyes flew open. She remembered seeing the woman's full name before. On the pill bottles. Why did Blaine have this woman's pills?

She shook off the question and focused on the real issue. Mel hadn't been to Fraser's in nearly a year. Their relationship had ended violently. Blaine had tried to help, but he only made it worse.

Blaine would be pissed if he found out she was here. She grabbed her flip-flops and reached for the door.

"Hey! Where do you think you're going?" a man called out. His voice made her freeze.

She turned and locked eyes with Fraser. His dark stare was cold. Not one to be intimidated, Mel straightened her back and took two steps toward him.

"I'll be leaving now." She glared at him. "I don't know why I came back here in the first place."

Fraser's nostrils flared, and he took a menacing step toward her. Mel's hands flew up defensively, ready to attack. She'd trained in self-defence for moments like this. She'd used it on him before.

"I didn't say you could leave." His voice had lowered, trying to be threatening. It was exactly how he used to speak to her, and it made her angrier.

"I don't give a shit what you say," she said, moving back toward the front door.

Mel turned away to slip on her flip-flops, and as she did, his hand shot out and wrapped around her wrist, pulling her toward him. Mel struggled in his grasp but couldn't seem to pull free. He pulled her closer to him, his rancid breath warming her cheeks.

"There's your feisty attitude." His eyes gleamed with excitement. "I thought you'd lost all your fight. Maybe it means we can play some more." His grip on her wrist tightened.

She nearly winced from the pain. "We only play when I say it's playtime."

His eyes narrowed and his grip tightened further, cutting off her circulation. His hand flew to her throat. She saw it coming before he began to move and reached up, locking her right hand around his wrist and pulling it down. He lurched forward as she pushed her left wrist against where his fingers connected, breaking his hold on her. His eyes widened.

Mel grabbed his other wrist and jammed her knee into his groin. Releasing her hold, she grabbed his shoulders, pulling him down and slamming her knee into his face. She heard a sickening crack, and he fell to the floor groaning in pain.

"You'll regret this." He moaned.

Mel didn't look back before grabbing her shoes and leaving the house. She hurried down the street, pulled out her phone, and did a quick GPS check for the closest main street. It wasn't far.

Her heart raced as she waved down a cab and climbed in. Drawing several breaths to calm herself, she dialled Jackie.

"Where the *hell* have you been?"

"Cool it, Jackie; I got caught up in something else, okay?" Jackie didn't reply, so Mel continued. "How did last night go?"

Mel realized she was shaking. Fraser knew how to frighten her. She'd kicked enough asses in her time to know she could hold her own, but Fraser was worse than all the others. She'd loved him once, or she thought she had. It was strange how distant and different that past seemed to her now and how she'd been a completely different person. Or how he'd been.

Jackie's continued silence was unsettling.

"Did something happen?" Mel asked, visions of girls being attacked or harmed started swirling around in her mind.

"No, no, it's fine."

She didn't sound alright.

"Where are you?"

"I'm heading home for a few hours. I have something to deal with." The tone of her voice said she didn't want to share more. Mel didn't pry.

"Call me later," Mel said.

"Mel ..."

"What?"

"Candy disappeared last night."

Mel chewed on her lower lip. "With the money?"

"No, I have it. I don't know where she is."

Mel relaxed. "She'll turn up. Call me when you're leaving home."

It wasn't the first time a girl had disappeared after a night of work. Some needed a break, to wind down. Some spent their money and others ... well, Mel wasn't in the habit of asking too many questions.

There was silence on the other end for a moment. "Glad you're okay. We were worried."

"I'm sorry I scared you," Mel said.

"It's okay. I'll talk to you soon."

The line went dead. Mel slid her phone into her purse and leaned back in the seat. She glanced out the window and watched the buildings pass by, trying to shake the feeling that had followed her from Fraser's house. The blackouts were happening again. It wasn't something she could explain away with logic. Maybe drinking, though Mel knew how to handle her alcohol. No, something was very wrong. She'd have to keep it to herself. After all, unexplained blackouts meant she was crazy and crazy people were locked up.

BACK AT BLAINE'S HOUSE, the driveway was empty and the curtains pulled shut. Mel went to the front door and tried the handle. The door opened with a light push.

"Hello?" Mel called into the house. Blaine couldn't be home without the car.

"We were wondering where the hell you got to last night," Gabi said, coming out of the sitting room.

"Where is Blaine?" Mel asked.

"Looking for you," Gabi said, hands planted on her hips. "And I repeat, where the hell were you last night? You look like shit."

"Leave it. Something came up." Mel shrugged off the question and reached for her phone. She texted Blaine, letting him know she was home.

"Everything go okay?" Mel asked when she put down her phone.

"Yeah," Gabi said. "Candy serviced Derek, as requested. Haven't seen her since, though."

"Jackie told me. Don't worry. She'll turn up." They always did. A working girl came back when the money ran out.

Gabi waved toward the stairs. "I stopped by the hotel on the way back, and when I saw you weren't there, I grabbed our stuff. It's upstairs now."

"Thanks. How was the place?" Mel wished she'd been able to see the beach house in person.

Gabi smiled. "So nice. Those are the jobs that make me wish I was rich."

"I always wish I was rich."

"So, tell me what happened to you," Gabi said. "You were planning on coming, weren't you?"

"Like I said, something came up."

"Very cryptic."

"I said leave it, Gabi, okay?"

She opened her mouth to retort when the door swung open behind them. Blaine entered. His eyes were red like he hadn't slept, and his hair was mussed like he'd been ringing his hands through it.

"What the fuck?" he asked through gritted teeth.

"Nice to see you, too." Mel offered a small smile.

"Where the hell have you been? I've been searching for you all night. I almost called the cops."

"That would have been stupid."

Blaine stepped forward and grabbed her shoulders. "Disappearing and ignoring your phone is stupid."

Gabi slipped by Blaine and Mel and headed for the door. Mel almost forgot she was there.

"I'm gonna go," Gabi said. "And let you guys sort out your stuff." She was gone before either Mel or Blaine could answer.

"I'm fine," Mel said.

Blaine didn't release her, his voice still low. "You don't look fine."

"I'm okay," Mel said. "You can trust me."

Blane continued to scrutinize her. He didn't speak.

Mel carefully reached up and removed Blaine's hold from her shoulders. He let his hands fall to his side, never taking his eyes off her. As the moments ticked by, the anger in his expression dissipated and was replaced with relief.

"You're a tough girl, Melanie, but you are not unstoppable." The words came out quietly. There was fear in them. Fear that one day, she might not come home.

His words stung because it was true. She'd been in more than one precarious situation in the past and Fraser had proved he wasn't one to be trifled with.

Mel dropped his gaze—heat crept up her neck. "I know. I'm sorry."

Blaine released a long breath, then stepped to her side, wrapping his arms around her and pulling her into his chest. He rested his chin atop her head and held her for a moment.

"You scared the crap out of me."

"I didn't mean to." Mel pressed against his hold, and he released her.

"Tell me what happened."

Mel bit down on her lip and considered the previous day. She remembered leaving the girls at the hotel; she always liked to take a bit of time after a night of work. Blaine was often a strong silent presence but sometimes Mel just needed to be alone.

She had gone into town and spent the morning at a café where she knew the manager. After asking about potential clients, she sat and had her coffee. One man approached her, intending to chat. Mel flipped a business card his way, and he quickly retreated from the situation. Not all men loved a working girl.

She finished her coffee then went to the mall to get a few supplies for the house. What happened after?

"I was out with a friend." It could have been true; Mel just didn't know for sure.

"Who?" Blaine asked, taking her hands from her face.

"No one you know."

He stared into her eyes for several seconds before saying, "Are you having memory issues?" His voice had lowered, and his tone softened.

"No," Mel said quickly.

Blaine frowned. "You said you'd tell me if your memory went again."

"It's fine," Mel said. "Gabi gave me a pill, and then I drank a lot. Maybe it was just a delayed hangover thing."

Blaine didn't look convinced.

Mel moved toward the stairs, and Blaine followed her up to their shared bedroom.

"Should I be worried?" he asked, leaning against the door frame.

"No," Mel said again. She stripped off the clothes she wore to Fraser's house, wincing as her shirt brushed by the cut on her arm.

Blaine's eyes were on it, likely following all the marks on her body. "Melanie." Her name came out like a low growl. "What the hell?"

"It's nothing." Mel quickly covered up the marks with a new shirt.

Blaine's fists clenched at his side. "It looks like some asshole had his hands all over you."

"I can handle it." Mel turned away from him.

"It doesn't look like you're handling it."

"Blaine, stop it!" Mel said, turning back to him with a hard glare. "I've had a weird enough morning without dealing with you."

He crossed his thick arms over his chest and glared down at Mel. "I'm not an idiot. I know what those marks mean."

"No, you don't." Mel moved toward the bathroom.

"No memory, unknown bruises," Blaine said. "This has happened before."

Mel hesitated in the bathroom doorway. It had happened before. Too many times. It didn't matter. She wouldn't tell Blaine the truth. He worried too much. He'd want her to get help. Mel didn't need help. She just needed to be left alone.

"You've seen him again, haven't you?" Blaine said. His voice was low, this time filled with pain.

"You don't know what you're talking about," Mel whispered.

"Why?" His voice pleaded with her. "Why did you go back there?"

Mel didn't answer, instead closing the bathroom door behind her. For a moment, she leaned up against the door and drew an unsteady breath. She swallowed hard to fight the tears that wanted to fall free. *Why did I go back there?* If only she knew.

Chapter 23
Brielle Jeffries

SILVER FORKS CLATTERING AGAINST FINE CHINA WAS the chorus to the argument surrounding Brielle. She sat in a straight-backed chair as white as the framed table before her, mindlessly swirling the food on her plate. She'd lost her appetite long ago.

At the opposite end of the table, her father argued with his brothers while her mother and aunts ate quietly, staring at their plates. Her ever-patient grandfather sat with his elbows on the table and chin in his hands, listening to his sons disagree.

"That's ridiculous!" A hand slammed down, shaking the entire table. Silverware clattered from plates to tabletop, tabletop to the floor.

Brielle's uncle scowled at her father. When he glanced down the table and noticed Brielle and her three cousins watching, he leaned back in his seat, folded his hands in his lap, and muttered something inaudible. Their conversation quieted, and the cousins turned away again, uninterested.

Brielle stabbed her fork into her food and took a bite of

the overcooked chicken. A quick tap on the table in front of her drew her attention. Brielle glanced up, meeting two sets of bright blue eyes. Her twenty-two-year-old twin cousins wore matching smiles.

"Brie," Amanda called to her, tapping the table again.

"What?" Brielle asked, blowing her blonde bangs from her eyes with nonchalance.

Caroline's eyes flashed with excitement. "We're going to the bar tonight after dinner, right Derek?" She glanced around the table and received a mumbled yes from the only male cousin. Then her gaze rested on Brielle. "Come." It wasn't a request.

"Brie. You haven't seen us in years," Amanda said, probably trying to make Brielle feel guilty, something she was very good at doing to other people. Not Brielle, though.

Brielle glanced back down the table, watching her father and uncle argue. Her only other option was to stay and listen to pointless arguments. A night on the town sounded like a good idea; well, at least not a bad one.

When dinner finished, Amanda and Caroline went over to their grandfather. Brielle watched from a distance as they smiled and told him about their courses at school.

Spoiled rotten. Brielle rolled her eyes.

These conversations always ended with the twins being a few hundred dollars richer; tonight was no different. They came back with a handful of bills each.

"Papa says we can use his driver," Amanda said with a smug smile. "Isn't that *sooooo* sweet?"

It wasn't a question Brielle was expected to answer, and she followed Amanda and Caroline to their grandfather's stretch limo. Brielle climbed in and slid down the leather cushions, making room for the rest of her cousins. She'd never ridden in her grandfather's limo, though the pale blue lighting gave her a strange sensation of deja vu. The twins sat on either side of her, each grasping a hand.

"Oh my god, Brie," Amanda said, "Can you believe we're all doing this?"

"I know, right?" Caroline leaned forward, looking at Amanda over Brielle's lap. "Like, when was the last time we all were in the same city? Like, *sooooo* long ago." She tossed her hands up dramatically.

Brielle wanted to roll her eyes. Feeling a gaze on her, she glanced at her other cousin sitting in the back seat. He stared at Brielle intently and answered Caroline's statement.

"Nineteen years, Carol," Derek said.

The younger twin made a face, hating the short form of her name. Derek wasn't paying attention to her; he stared at Brielle. He'd been acting strange ever since she first saw him tonight.

"Nineteen years would make you what, Brielle, seven?" He cocked his head to the side, a knowing smirk on his lips.

She frowned. "Yes, Derek, seven. And how old would you have been?"

"Fourteen." He raised his right eyebrow, and she turned away, hoping he wouldn't act this way all night.

"It's certainly been a while," she muttered.

Derek leaned forward in his seat. "Has it?"

"What the hell is that supposed to mean?"

Derek's hands flew up defensively, and he leaned back in his seat. "Nothing, sheesh, calm down."

Brielle crossed her arms, glaring at him. "You've been weird all night."

"I haven't," he protested. "I feel like you've been lying to us. Like I've seen you recently."

Brielle looked at him dumbfounded. "You do remember the last time you saw me, right? Because I do. My isolation hasn't been an illusion all these years."

"Guys, you're ruining this." Amanda put on a whiny voice and a pathetic pout on her pink glossy lips. "Can't we all get along? I don't want to be like our parents."

Derek chuckled, placing his hands behind his head. "Always nice to have a family reunion."

Brielle glared at him, but before she could speak the car stopped and he pushed open the door, not bothering to wait for the driver.

"Where did you take us?" Brielle asked as she crawled out of the car between the twins. However, she didn't need them to tell her because she knew once she saw it.

A black carpet stretched across the sidewalk and to the white double doors of the club. Off to the left was a roped-off line packed with people trying to get in. A slim awning hovered over the door. The name—Trill—was written in cursive and lit up in white lights. Brielle followed her cousins as they hooked arms and hurried up to the bouncer, a large man dressed in uniform. They both kissed his cheeks, then he opened the door, and the twins motioned to their cousins to follow them in. There was a commotion in the lineup as they passed by. Saturday night at the city's hottest nightclub; it was no surprise people were complaining she and her cousins got in without waiting.

Music blared through the dimly lit club. Amanda wrapped her hand around Brielle's and guided her through the packed crowd. Sweaty, half-naked bodies pressed against one another, grinding to repetitive music. The bass shook the floor, pulsing through Brielle.

Someone bumped into her, pushing her sideways. Amanda lost her grip, and Brielle tumbled, lost among the crowd.

"Sorry," she heard. Hands wrapped around her arms, pulling her to her feet. She looked at her rescuer. Young, handsome. He smiled. His eyes were kind.

"It's okay."

He still had a firm hold on her arm. He shook his head. "Let me buy you a drink."

Brielle nodded, unwilling to turn down the handsome stranger.

He waved over at someone before steering her toward the bar. There he ordered her a drink, then turned back to her, hand out. In the dim bar lighting, she could make out his round face and dark eyes. His hair was raven black and he had a distinctive mole on his neck.

The bartender returned with their drinks and the young man handed one to her then smiled as he tapped his against hers. She kept his gaze, sipping the cool liquid, rum and coke; spicy and sweet. His eyes seemed to twinkle in the dull light.

"Do you want to dance?" he asked.

Brielle glanced down at her drink then around the bar. *Where did my cousins end up?* She had no idea. Glancing back into his kind eyes made her realize she didn't really care. She would find them later. It had been a while since she'd been given this kind of attention.

She tapped her glass against his again. "Let me finish this, then you can show me the dance floor."

"Deal."

AFTER A COUPLE OF SONGS, the handsome stranger disappeared into the crowd. Brielle hadn't gotten his name. Her head was cloudy and she was covered in sweat. It had been years since Brielle had been to a club scene like this one and she was beginning to realize why she'd left it.

The repetitive beat irritated the growing ache behind her eyes and she was exhausted, wanting only to find somewhere to sit down.

Unable to find her cousins, Brielle stumbled out of the club into the cool night air. The wind kissing her cheeks made the pain in her head ease, and she closed her eyes and breathed in deeply.

When she opened them, she looked around but couldn't find the limo anywhere. A taxi waited near the entrance and Brielle went for it, desperate to get home. And desperate to sit down.

She pulled open the door and slid into the backseat. The driver had his head turned away so she didn't see his face as she told him the address and tilted her head back against the seat.

The car jerked forward and Brielle glanced out the window, watching the streetlights pass by. Soon her eyelids grew heavy, and she couldn't keep them open any longer. Letting her worries go, Brielle allowed her eyes to close and for sleep to take her.

Chapter 24
Melanie Parker

MEL'S HEART THUDDED AGAINST HER CHEST. IT WAS THE second time in a few days she'd woken up in the familiar home with no explanation. This was more than just a memory issue. Had Fraser found her at the bar? Knocked her out and brought her home? Mel could think of no other reason she would end up here again. It had been a long time since Fraser was a kind person she wanted to spend time with.

Mel crept down the stairs, wary of running into him again considering the way she left their last interaction, and was relieved to discover he wasn't home. She was out the door and into a cab as quickly as possible. Her anxious heartbeat never settled for a moment.

In the cab home, she glanced over her missed calls, seeing four from Blaine. When she got home he would be mad—if he wasn't already. She almost didn't want to go, though knew she had to.

Mel tried to remember how she ended up at Fraser's again. The last thing she remembered was a dirty martini and a handsome face—a possible new client, another wealthy family.

After was a blur, did she drink too much? Did the man she met drug her? She shook her head on the second idea. It wasn't his house she woke up in. So, if she was drunk, why Fraser?

Shaking it from her head, she entered Blaine's house and hoped the explanation of a new client would be enough to deter any questions. It was late in the afternoon by the time she arrived home, and only two of her girls lounged around the room.

"Hey," Gabi said. "How did last night go?"

"Actually, not bad," Mel replied, knowing it was better to pretend the blackout never happened. "Possible new client, and another wealthy one."

"Oh," Gabi said, hoping to her feet. "Who's this one?"

"Brennan Drake."

Candy noticeably twitched when Mel said his name. She cocked her head toward the red-haired girl. "Someone you know?"

"No," Candy shook her head. "The name seems really familiar."

"The Drakes are a pretty well-known family," Gabi told her. "Aren't they, Mel?"

"Yeah, upper-middle class. Not the wealthiest, but they're up there."

"Sounds like a good party," Gabi said.

"We'll need Jackie for this one. You heard from her?" Mel asked.

"Not since Saturday. She's probably lying low. Give her a call. She'll answer for you."

"Okay." Mel turned and left the girls in the sitting room. She pulled out her phone to call Jackie, only to have the call directed to voicemail. She hadn't heard her friend's voice since the morning after the Derek Jeffries' job. Mel had left messages without any response.

After leaving another message, she climbed the stairs to her shared room with Blaine. She hesitated at the doorway when Blaine looked up at her and glared.

"You look like shit."

"Good to see you, too."

"I know," Blaine said with an accusing tone.

"Excuse me?"

He stood from the bed and moved closer to her. "I know where you've been," he said again. "First, you miss a job, and now you're back at *his* place two nights later? What the fuck is going on?"

"I don't know what you're talking about. I was out with a potential client."

Blaine snatched her phone out of her hand and swiped his thumb across the screen.

"What are you doing?" Mel snapped, grabbing the phone from him. The screen had gone to her text messages like he was checking who she was talking to.

"Getting tired of all the lies, Mel." Blaine reached up and ran a hand through his hair. The exasperated look on his face didn't fade.

"I'm not lying," Mel said. "I did meet with a client." And she had ... at least for the portion of the night she could remember.

"Until you went back to Fraser's."

Mel turned a hard glare on Blaine. "Are you following me?"

Had he been checking up on her this whole time? She'd found him with her phone more than once. What was he playing at?

Blaine looked away, angry and ashamed. "I wouldn't have to if you talked to me."

"That's fucked, Blaine. More than usual."

"I didn't want anything to happen to you."

"Nothing will." Mel stormed toward the bedroom door. "I can take care of myself."

"Can you?" Blaine asked, following her steps. "It doesn't seem like it when you come back a beat-up mess."

"I'm fine!" Mel said. She turned and left the room, heading for the stairs. She couldn't handle Blaine's tone or accusing stares. A part of her knew he wasn't wrong. Blaine was very rarely wrong. She could take care of herself. She didn't need him chasing after her, following her, protecting her. Worse, she didn't want him to get wrapped up in her mess. He'd been cleaning them up since they met over two years ago, and Mel was starting to wonder when he'd give up on her. Or worse, send her away, somewhere she couldn't escape.

"Where are you going?" Blaine called after her, standing in the doorway while she descended the stairs.

"To find Jackie," she said without looking back. Jackie could make sense of what was going on. Jackie could help her understand why she was making the foolish choice to return to a once-abusive ex. Jackie would talk some sense into her.

Mel reached the front door, grabbed the keys from the

hanger, and left without another word. In Blaine's car, she stuck the keys in the ignition and calmed her erratic breathing.

Mel snatched her phone and dialled Jackie. It rang twice before going to voicemail. Prepared to leave Jackie yet another message, the robotic voice on the other end informed her it wasn't possible and Jackie's mailbox was full.

Frowning, Mel shifted the car and backed out of the driveway. She didn't have anywhere to go, but she didn't want to stay at home with Blaine. So she headed to the first place she could think of—the café—and resolved to remain there until Blaine forgave her.

Chapter 25
Brielle Jeffries

BRIELLE WOKE UP TO A POUNDING HEADACHE, THINKING it was the worst hangover she'd had in a while, but as her vision cleared and her eyes focused, she realized she wasn't at home.

Her chest contracted. Where was she?

She lay on a hard cot in the corner of a square room. Four bare, slate walls stared back at her. There were no windows, and the room had a distinct chill to it.

Brielle's head spun. Black spots formed in her sight.

"No, no." The words came out soft. Breathless. She'd been here before.

Blood pumped in her ears, a deafening sound, as she drew a shaky breath and glanced at the bedside table. She expected to see a low-burning candle; instead, there was a small electric lamp.

That was different.

She tried to calm her now ragged breathing. Was this a dream? She pinched herself; nothing changed.

Sweat prickled on her brow. *No, no, not again.*

She threw herself out of bed. Her legs buckled when she hit the floor, and she felt behind her for support.

Glancing down, she noticed the strange clothing she wore. It wasn't the short dress from the bar but a flowy sundress she'd never seen before, not one she would buy. Her fingers ran over the foreign fabric. It was soft, though it didn't offer her any ease.

This was all too familiar. She trembled as she slowly took in the rest of the room.

At the opposite side was a dresser with a large round mirror hanging over the top. Another thing new to her prison.

Brielle walked over to the mirror and checked her reflection. She looked tired; her face was blotchy. She opened the drawers. They slid open easily and were stocked with clothing, toiletries, and even some of her favourite makeup. She pulled out a sweater. It was her size.

What is this place? It was a question she didn't need answering. Even the changes weren't enough to distract her. This was déjà vu.

Back at the bed, Brielle pulled out the mattress.

Her breath caught and tears welled in her eyes. There on the wall were the very marks she'd made as a young captive girl. Eleven single ticks, each marking a time *he* had come to her.

She stumbled back away from the marks. "No, no."

Brielle ran to the door, desperate to find an escape. He'd kept her locked behind closed doors the last time he took her. Why would this time be any different?

To her surprise, the knob turned easily. She carefully

pushed it open to find a narrow, windowless concrete hallway.

Placing her hand on the wall, a flash of memory returned to her. A hazy vision of her sprinting down this hallway away from his horrible screams. The way her bare feet pounded the cold bunker floor as she ran for an escape—anything to get away from him and what he did to her.

Brielle squeezed her eyes shut. He'd be an older man now. Around her parents' age. How did he find her again?

Brielle glanced down the hallway. At least she seemed to be alone.

She crept further and came across another door, one she couldn't remember. She tried this one as well, hoping for a way out.

It wasn't an exit.

Brielle slid her hands along the wall just inside the doorway and found a small switch, which lit up the room.

This time her stomach twisted with nausea.

It was similar to the one she'd woken up in, only weirder. If the pictures on the wall weren't enough to freak her out, then the eerily accurate timeline did it. Her heart raced as she gazed around the room. It was like a time capsule. Who had done this, and why?

Brielle walked further into the room to really gauge what she was looking at. They were pictures of her—hundreds of them, starting at the age of six until recent ones. There were pictures of her daily life, at the coffee shop with a fling, shopping with her mother. There were ones of her graduations— middle school, high school, college—and the picture from her prom with her first serious boyfriend. Next to it was a picture of them entering the hotel he'd booked. They broke up shortly after. There were even pictures of her at the clinic, which was supposed to be private. It seemed like someone had been keeping tabs on Brielle for her entire life.

Amongst the personal pictures, there were countless newspaper clippings about her family. Any picture featuring Brielle had been added to this wall.

Her eyes scanned the early pictures. Brielle couldn't have been much older than six. As if to confirm her thoughts, her eyes fell on a picture she never knew existed. A picture of *him*.

Her breath caught in her throat as she gazed over the young man. He looked exactly as she remembered him before she plunged the piece of metal into his arm in an attempt to escape. He grinned up at the camera, his dark hair parted and his arm wrapped around a little blonde girl who wouldn't look up. Brielle didn't need to see her face to know it was her.

She racked her memory. When would this picture have been taken? She reached out for the photo when she heard the shuffle of feet behind her.

"What are you doing in here?"

She turned, clutching the photo in her grasp.

A familiar man stood in the doorway, leaning against the frame with an amused expression on his rounded face. He had dark hair and a mole on his neck. His eyes were two emotionless pools of black. Brielle frowned. It was the man from the bar.

"Do I know you?" Brielle's stomach twisted. Who was this person and why had he brought her here?

The man smirked. "Let's just say I'm Sam."

Her throat constricted. "You're not Sam." She held the

picture of Sam in her hand. Sam would be an old man now. This guy couldn't be much older than Brielle.

She glanced down at the photo and realized this man could very well be the man in the photo. She looked back and forth between the two, wondering how it could be possible.

Exasperated, the man's amused expression faded.

"What's going on?" Brielle's voice shook. "Why did you bring me here?"

He stepped closer to her and Brielle looked around for a place to run. There was no way to escape without going by him and from the looks of his t-shirt straining against his muscles, Brielle wasn't sure she could fight him off.

"You ask a lot of questions," he said with a smug smile. "I don't think you need to worry." He moved closer to her and she stepped back.

"I'm going to need you to follow me." He grinned at her in a way that looked more like a dog baring its teeth than a human trying to smile.

"I'm not going anywhere with you," Brielle said, stepping back again and finding herself against a wall.

The man's expression drooped, and he let out a long, exhausted sigh, as if she were a child refusing to listen to her father. He seemed annoyed rather than angry.

"Either you come on your own, or I can take you by force," he said. "Or I can just toss you another vial of GHB. You were pretty easy to handle after."

"You drugged me?" Brielle said, eyes widening. "At the bar?"

"Yeah, at the bar and then again after," he said. "You should think twice before taking a drink from a stranger."

Brielle shook her head. "I left the bar. I took a cab."

"Did you?" he asked, tilting his head and amusement in his tone. He was having too much fun with her state of mind.

"Yes," Brielle said, though she wasn't sure. She hadn't seen the driver, and she'd fallen asleep on the drive. Oh god. She'd also given him her address.

The man chuckled. "You were pretty messed up. When I tried to stash you down here, you kept mumbling you weren't Brielle and that this was some mistake. Your name was Jackie and you shouldn't be back here."

Brielle dropped her gaze. The last thing she remembered was passing out in the cab. When did she pretend to be Jackie? Why would she say her name? Whatever he drugged her with at the bar must have been strong.

"Once you had these drugs in your system, you calmed right down. You were much easier to handle." He fished into his pocket and pulled out a vial of clear liquid with a covered needle. "Your decision."

Brielle didn't answer right away, and the man made a move toward her, popping the lid off the needle. She put her hands up and shook her head.

"I'll go," Brielle said. "Keep it away from me." She hated needles.

"Good choice." He slipped the needle and vial back into his pocket and Brielle thought he looked disappointed for a moment.

Brielle glanced around, looking for something to use as a weapon. Maybe she could hit him over the head and escape. Though as she thought it, she wasn't sure where she would escape to. Could she get lost in this place, wherever it is?

"Follow me." He turned and led her from the room.

Brielle fell into step behind him, weighing out her options. Her hands were free, but she couldn't overpower him. She would need a weapon, the element of surprise, anything to work in her favour.

The man turned when the hallway ended and in front of them was a set of stairs leading to a door in the ceiling.

Before he pushed it open, he turned back to Brielle and held a blindfold toward her. "Be a peach and put this on."

"No." Brielle stepped back, not willing to compromise her vision. She wanted to see where they were when they exited this bunker. Was it a basement in a house?

The man didn't seem annoyed with her; he only fished into his pocket again as if looking for the drugs he'd stashed away.

Before he had a chance to pull anything out, Brielle took the blindfold from his hands and covered her eyes.

"If you let me fall—" Brielle said, but he cut her off.

"Then you're a lot clumsier sober than you are drunk." He took hold of her arm and Brielle heard the creak of rusted hinges.

A puff of warm air caressed her cheeks and the sound of chirping reached her ears. She slowed her breathing, desperate to hear and feel as much as she could while he led her away from her prison. Anything to help her gauge where she was and where he had taken her.

The grass they crossed tickled her bare feet. It was damp with morning dew, or an evening of rainfall; Brielle couldn't be sure. Bright light leaked into the blindfold and the sun warmed her arms. It was likely mid-morning, possibly later.

Wherever he was keeping her, he didn't want her to get a glimpse of it. Though if everything was as Brielle remembered, and this was the same prison where she'd been kept, then there was a forest behind her and an unknown street ahead.

The sound of a screeching car seemed to answer her thoughts as if to tell her the road wasn't far off. Before she heard anything else, she was directed up a set of steps and through another door. There he removed the blindfold.

She stood inside a house; the windows were shuttered and she couldn't see anything outdoors.

"This way." He led Brielle through one of the open archways.

"Where are we?" she asked.

He didn't answer her, only continued through the house. When Brielle was young, she saw nothing beyond the bunker Sam kept her in. Seeing the house now, she didn't know if it was really the same place she'd been all those years ago. Either way, she didn't want to be here.

They reached the set of stairs, and he turned up them. Still free, Brielle turned toward the front door. The man was ahead of her and had his back turned away. There was no one around to stop her. She could make a run for it.

As if reading her mind, he said. "I wouldn't if I were you."

Brielle glanced at him. He wasn't even looking in her direction.

He turned his head to look at her. "Doesn't lead anywhere. By all means, try it if you don't believe me."

Brielle reached for the door and found it didn't open. It was either locked or, as he said, led to nowhere.

She glanced back the way they came, considering making a run for it out the back. She didn't know where she was but out there seemed better than in here. Or down in the bunker.

Brielle glanced back at the man who continued to watch her. He was only a few steps away from her. He could practically reach out and grab her. Would she be fast enough to get away from him? She definitely wasn't the high school track star.

The man seemed to grow tired of waiting and descended the few steps he had climbed. He grabbed Brielle's hand and pulled her toward him.

"Let's go."

Brielle twisted her arm in his grasp, trying to free herself, but his hand only tightened, causing her to cry out.

He didn't let up, only pulled her along.

Upstairs there were several rooms. The closest had a large man in a suit seated near the entrance. He looked buff from the way his broad shoulders strained in the suit jacket. He seemed uninterested in her and Sam.

"What's in there?" Brielle asked, curiosity getting the best of her.

The man loosened his grip on her arm and shoved her toward the open door. There she saw what the buff man guarded.

The curtains were half closed, allowing a beam of light to creep across the floor. It lay across a large bed where a man slept. Surrounding the bed was several machines. An oxygen mask covered the man's mouth.

She stepped further into the room, and neither man stopped her. Something about the sleeper seemed familiar. As she got a better look at his face, Brielle went cold. Her whole body froze; her hands shook as memories of his cruelty and her captivity came rushing back. She choked on bile as images of his rough hands touching her invaded her mind. Looking him in the face once more, she was reliving her worst night terror.

Except this wasn't the same man from all those years ago. Now he looked broken, dying. All those years ago, he'd been terrifying and dangerous and was now reduced to nothingness—

an older man attached to oxygen. Her eyes crawled through the room, looking for anything familiar.

Across the room from the bed was a desk. There, an ancient-looking desktop computer sat on top and on the chair was an aged briefcase with the inscription *H. Drake.*

Brielle looked back at the bedridden man, certain he was her abuser from so many years ago.

"Sam ..." she huffed out from memory, her voice breathy and frightened. She tried to steady it. To a six-year-old child, he was terrifying, but Brielle wasn't a child anymore.

"The original," the man behind her said.

She glanced back at the younger man, realizing who he likely was. His similarities to the dying man were uncanny. They were relatives. Maybe father and son.

"I guess it's hard to forget him."

"I don't think I would forget the man who stole and molested me," Brielle said with poison in her tone.

A moan escaped the dying man, and Brielle glanced to him, wondering just how much he had heard. Did he know she was here? Could he recognize her voice?

She wasn't given a chance to consider it further before the younger Sam took hold of her arm again and dragged her from the room. Brielle secured one final glance at the man.

He took her further down the hallway to another room and tossed her inside. Then he closed the door behind her. Brielle's heart started to race. Was he going to rape her?

Instead, he pulled out a cell phone from his pocket, her cell phone.

"What's that for?" Brielle asked.

"You really are a dumb blonde, aren't you?" He snapped. "I thought it was just an act." He thrust the phone into her hand. "Call your daddy and tell him we have you hostage. We want cash; five hundred grand." A cruel smile formed and he brushed her cheek. Then he pushed her to the bed. "Now, call him, before I decide the call can wait."

Brielle looked down at the phone in her hand. "What happens if I don't call him?"

He clicked the lock on the door and raised an eyebrow at her. "I think you're clever enough to know what happens to you if you don't. Sam may have liked to touch a child, but I've always found adult women to be more my speed."

Brielle's eyes widened. "My dad won't believe you. He'll think it's a setup."

The man smiled. "If he wants his daughter back, he'll ransom you."

"And then you'll let me go when you have the money?"

"If your daddy does as we tell him, then you'll be fine." He sat next to her on the bed and placed a hand on her bare knee, sliding it up her thigh. "Now call him."

Brielle shoved his hand away, then opened the contacts on her phone and selected her father's. It seemed like it rang forever, until the familiar male voice answered the phone.

"Hello?"

"Daddy," Brielle said. "It's me. I'm in trouble."

Once she was connected with her father, the man took the phone and began talking to the man.

"Mr. Jeffries, I'm sure it was pleasant to hear your daughter's pleas. I can assure you we are keeping her safe, for now, and for a price."

He walked away from her, still discussing his plans with her father. Brielle glanced around the room. The door had a simple lock on the handle, and the stairs weren't far. She wasn't dressed for running, but with him distracted, she thought she could be fast enough to make it outside before they caught her.

When he had his back turned, she hopped to her feet and ran for the door. She swung it open. It resounded off the wall as she bolted for the stairs.

"Stop her!" Brielle heard him yell. Footsteps thundered down the stairs after her.

Brielle ran for the back door, thinking freedom was right around the corner. She pushed her way into the yard, squinting in the bright sun. Running off the deck, she glanced around for the quickest way out. The backyard was large with the same dense forest behind it. There was a shed; otherwise, it was bare. She ran for the front, sure she'd find a road and people who could help.

The back door creaked open as someone chased after her. She didn't look back, only pushing forward to escape. Her heart raced. Her throat started to sting. She could see the road and pressed forward. Then she fell. Someone tackled her from behind, and she went crashing to the grass. Pain shot through every part of her body. A weight on top of her.

The bodyguard picked himself up off her and held her

arms as he led her back to the house. Brielle struggled in his grip. It was no use; he was too strong.

"Let me go," Brielle yelled. Her voice echoed despite the wind. He clamped a hand over her mouth before she could scream more.

Back inside the house, the man stood in the kitchen, still on the phone with her father. An older woman Brielle hadn't noticed before sat in the far corner looking at the floor. She glanced up at Brielle only once, and it was very quick.

"Quite the feisty daughter you have," Sam said, his lips still twisted in a cruel smile. "You have two days." He hit end on the phone and looked at Brielle.

"That was foolish, Brielle," he said. "We would have treated you nice." He turned and opened one of the drawers, pulling out a vial of clear liquid and a needle. He filled the needle then moved toward her. "You had to make this difficult."

The bodyguard pushed her to a chair and held her in place.

"I won't run anymore," Brielle said, keeping her eyes locked on the needle.

"I don't believe you."

He grabbed her arm while the bodyguard held her steady, then pushed the needle into her and emptied the contents into her bloodstream.

Her eyelids immediately felt heavy, and her speech slurred. The hold on her arms loosened, and she was helped to her feet and carried toward the stairs. Her head rolled to the side and her knees buckled. She felt arms wrap around her and lift her from the ground. It was the last thing she remembered before everything went black.

Chapter 26
Melanie Parker

MEL GLANCED AT HER PHONE. IT READ NINE O'CLOCK, Tuesday, June twenty-fourth in bold, black lettering. The old apartment building loomed in front of her, casting a cold shadow across the parking lot. Keys in hand, she headed to the front door and up to Jackie's apartment. First, she knocked. It was only a few seconds before Jackie's roommate opened the door.

"Melanie, right?" She said, cocking her head to the side. She was a short girl with bright blue hair and a layer of dark makeup. Mel had met her twice before but couldn't remember her name.

"I'm here for Jackie," Mel said. "Can I see her?"

The woman frowned. "I thought she was with you."

"What?"

She stepped aside and let Mel enter. "She hasn't been home in almost five nights. Last I heard, she was working with you." She waved toward her bedroom. "See for yourself."

Mel strode across the apartment to Jackie's room. It was

spotless. The bed was made, not a thing out of place. As her roommate said, it looked like she hadn't been there for days.

Mel began opening drawers and searching through her things for any clue or indication something had happened to her. At her vanity, she pulled open the top drawer and found an orange pill bottle. Her stomach flip-flopped. Though the bottle was generic to most pharmacies, she couldn't stop the sinking feeling that made her think of Blaine's secret stash.

She picked up the bottle. It seemed full, and the date indicated the prescription had been filled only seven days ago. The medication was the same—Solydexran—though Mel still didn't grasp its significance. All she knew was that it scared Blaine.

Stranger still, the prescription wasn't Jackie's. It belonged to the heiress, Brielle Jeffries. The one Jackie claimed she hadn't been in touch with. Mel frowned. Was that why Jackie had been so averse to the Derek Jeffries job? She'd been seeing a Jeffries behind their backs this whole time?

Mel exited the room to find Jackie's roommate sprawled on the couch watching some reality show.

"Have you spoken to Jackie?" Mel asked.

She shook her head. "Not since before the weekend."

"Did she have any friends over?" Mel asked. "Anyone named Brielle?"

Again, the girl shook her head. "Last I saw her, she stopped by quick to give me rent then she was gone again." The girl looked back to the TV. "Honestly, I'm starting to wonder why she bothers living here when she's barely around."

Mel couldn't stop her frown as the girl spoke. Jackie rarely spent the night at Blaine's house. She only stayed on occasion, usually leaving for a few days at a time then returning when there was work to be done. If Jackie wasn't going home, where was she going?

"If you hear from her," Mel said, digging into her purse and pulling out a business card, "call me. I'm getting worried."

"Sure thing," the girl said.

Mel placed the card on the coffee table and then left the apartment, heading back to Blaine's car. There, she dialed Jackie again. Straight to voicemail.

"Where are you, Jackie?" Mel said out loud when the automated message again informed her the mailbox was full. She shifted the car into drive and headed back to Blaine's.

At Blaine's house, Candy and Gabi were in the sitting room chatting. Knowing Candy was the last person to see Jackie in person, Mel went right for her.

"Where is Jackie?" she said the words very slowly.

Candy frowned and stood to meet her. "What are you talking about?"

"I've just been by her apartment and her roommate hasn't seen her in days."

"How should I know?"

Mel's hand shot out, grabbing Candy's wrist. "What happened on Friday night? You're the last person who saw her. I spoke to her Saturday morning. She said you disappeared. Where the fuck did you go?"

Candy's eyes widened. "I—I don't know ..." Candy dropped Mel's gaze and Mel tightened her grip. Candy cried out in pain, but Mel didn't release her.

Blaine entered the room, likely hearing the commotion

from upstairs. He moved toward the girls and pulled them apart. "What's going on?"

"Has Jackie called you?" Mel asked.

Blaine raised his eyebrow. "No."

Mel turned on Gabi. "Well?"

"She's probably fine." Gabi stood. "She's done this before. She's got a boyfriend or something, I'm telling you. What are you going to do about it?"

Mel turned her rage onto Gabi and lunged at her. Gabi stumbled backwards. Mel never made contact as Blaine's arm slid between them and scooped Mel off her feet. He carried her from the room like a screaming child. The girls watched them go.

"Put me down, Blaine," Mel said. "Right now!"

He didn't speak or release her until they were in their bedroom. Then he set her on the bed.

"You don't have to carry me away like I can't control myself," Mel snapped.

"You lunged at your friend." Blaine crossed his arms. "Don't try to tell me you were in control."

Mel's hands clenched at her side and she drew several deep breaths. "I was in control."

She knew she wasn't. She hadn't felt in control over the last few weeks. Everything was spiraling and now Jackie ... her once closest friend was lying to her about something.

"Mel, what is this really about?" Blaine asked.

"Jackie. What else would it be?" And all the other crazy things that had happened over the past few weeks. Memory loss, a mysterious drug of which no one knew the origins, seeing Fraser ...

Blaine frowned. "I have one idea."

"What are you talking about?"

"It's okay," Blaine said softly. "Maybe it's time you stop hiding."

Mel stepped back from him. Why was he speaking to her like this? She wasn't hiding. She was trying to find something.

"I'm not hiding."

"Patsy," he whispered the name so softly Mel wasn't sure she heard it.

"What did you say?"

Blaine looked away from her. "I want to talk to Patsy."

He didn't make any sense. First he claimed he didn't know a Patsy, then she found the drugs in his drawer. Now he wanted to talk to her? Who was Patsy, really, and why was Blaine so invested in Fraser's new wife?

Mel shook her head. "Fine, then go talk to her. I'm going to look for Jackie because right now I think she needs me and you aren't helping."

Blaine released a long breath, a look of sadness on his face. It wasn't the answer he was expecting, though Mel didn't know what he really wanted.

"Let me drive you."

Mel looked at him for a moment, then shook her head. "No."

"Melanie."

"No," Mel said. "I'm going alone." He'd been nothing but confusing these past several days. His anger would flare up, then fade in almost an instant. He followed her, searched her phone, hid drugs from her. Something was going on with him and suddenly she didn't feel as comfortable with him as she once did. Like the man she'd come to know over the past two years had changed.

"I think that's a bad idea," Blaine said. "What if something happens when you're gone?"

Mel frowned. What could happen? "I don't really care what you think right now."

She turned and left him standing in the middle of the bedroom. Downstairs, Mel found Candy standing near the stairs as if she'd been listening to Mel and Blaine argue. Considering Mel had nearly attacked Gabi, she wasn't surprised by the quiet girl's concern.

"Where are you going?" Candy asked.

"None of your business." Mel grabbed the keys from the small table beside the door.

"If it's about Jackie, I could help."

Mel turned a hard gaze on her. "Why do you care about Jackie?"

Candy flinched but quickly shook it off. "She's the only person I can call a friend. If you think she's in trouble, I want to help."

"And how could you help?"

"I could keep you company, at the very least."

Mel frowned. She didn't really care to have any company. If what Candy said about Jackie was true, then the girl was as important to Candy as she was to Mel.

"Fine," Mel agreed. "You have to do whatever I say."

"I always do."

Mel raised an eyebrow; then the two women headed out the door together in search of Jackie.

Chapter 27
Detective Ryan Boone

THERE WAS A KNOCK AT RYAN'S OFFICE DOOR. HE looked up and saw Archer standing in the doorway with two coffees in his hands. Ryan smiled at his partner of ten years.

"You brought me coffee?"

"You look like you could use it."

In the years they'd worked together, Archer had only brought him coffee a handful of times. Always on hard cases and always when Ryan wasn't sleeping. The man could read him like a book. Ryan was grateful for it. Archer was the person he was closest to in his life and had been ever since Lilian passed away.

"Please don't tell me you're coming to ask about the threesome your wife can't seem to quit pushing." Ryan laughed. "I promise, I'm *not* that lonely."

"Okay, maybe I'll keep this one for myself."

"I kid, friend." Ryan waved him in, and Archer took the chair across from Ryan's desk and handed him the coffee.

"Just what I needed." Ryan lifted the coffee in mock cheers before taking a sip.

"You've been here nonstop the last week," Archer said.

"Someone has to work around here."

Archer raised an eyebrow.

Ryan continued, "You know I never sleep when we're on a big case."

"You never sleep in general." Archer picked a file up off of Ryan's desk. "Singh has you covering the Jeffries' call on top of Kimball?"

A missing person's report was filed for the heiress Brielle Jeffries yesterday and already half the station was on the case. There'd been a ransom call and now they had to figure out their next steps. Her parents were understandably frantic. This was the second time Brielle Jeffries had been abducted.

"He wants me to put Quinn on it." Singh had dropped the file off in Ryan's office early in the morning. With the call coming in last night and the report just filed, it was all hands on deck in the Jeffries' case. Ryan wasn't done with the jewelry heist yet. Something just didn't make sense.

"Quinn is covering Lexi," Archer said.

"Yeah, Singh thinks it's a dead lead. So he's calling it off."

"I guess they do have Kimball for the crime. They don't really need anyone else."

"He made bail," Ryan said. "He may get off again."

"I heard he was pleading not guilty."

"Yeah." Ryan leaned back in his chair. "He wouldn't give up the other two involved either. And since he's pleading not guilty, he really has no reason to."

"You know that's not why."

"I know."

Dorian would have advised him against giving any

evidence on the others involved. It would only solidify his guilt and Dorian had a track record of acquittals to keep.

"I guess case closed on the jewelry heist then?" Archer asked.

Ryan shook his head. "Something isn't right about this case. There's more going on. I can feel it. This case is deeper than some shoddy burglary. And I can't just give up on a case when I feel this way. After what happened last time ..."

Archer grimaced but didn't speak. He didn't need to. Ryan and Archer both knew what happened the last time Ryan ignored a gut feeling on a case. It turned out they had the wrong perp, and someone ended up dead. It was a death Ryan could have prevented if he'd just pushed back against his superiors a bit. He'd never allow himself to forget it. And he'd never ignore a gut feeling again.

Another knock at his door stopped their conversation from going any further. Quinn poked his head into the office.

"Sorry, detectives. Singh said you wanted to see me."

"C'mon in, Quinn."

The rookie cop entered the office and took the seat next to Archer.

"How's your assignment going?" Archer asked.

Quinn cast a sideways glance at Archer before looking at Ryan. "It's bizarre. The whole thing has been off. Ms. Chase hasn't been home in over two days."

"Where is she?" Ryan asked.

"I've lost her. She's just disappeared."

"Did you check previous whereabouts?"

"All of them. She's gone."

"That's suspicious," Archer said. "What about her job?"

"Not going," Quinn said. "Her friend Marley hasn't seen her, either."

"You spoke to her?" Ryan asked.

"Yeah, as a former date. Saying she hadn't answered my calls."

"She probably thought you were a creep." Ryan laughed.

"No, she was genuinely concerned about her missing friend. She asked me to call if I heard anything," Quinn said. "I even dialed into Dorian to make sure it was true."

"I guess it doesn't matter anymore," Archer said. "Now you have a new assignment, anyway."

Quinn looked to Ryan. "What assignment?"

Archer slid the folder across Ryan's desk to Quinn. "The abduction of Brielle Jeffries."

"Yeah, I heard about that," Quinn said, flipping open the folder. "Singh is switching focus?"

"A ransom call came into the family last night. We don't have a recording, only their word to go on." Ryan glanced at Archer. "You know how Singh feels about the rich and the fabulous. She's been gone less than forty-eight hours and already cases are being pushed aside to find her." Ryan paused. "Why don't you get started on your work, Arch? I'll talk Quinn through the file."

Archer nodded and got up, leaving the room without another word. When he was gone, Ryan stood and closed the door behind him.

"So, do we have any idea where she might be?" Quinn asked when Ryan sat back down.

Ryan reached across the desk and took the file away from him. "I don't care what Singh thinks. I want you to find Lexi

Chase and keep following her. She has done nothing but suspicious things since we first spoke to her."

"What about the Jeffries' call?" Quinn asked.

"I'll cover for you and make sure nothing gets missed."

Quinn cracked a smile. "Is that smart? You're so busy already."

"I'll be fine. Just cover Ms. Chase, and I will cover the rest."

"Okay."

"Oh, and keep this between us," Ryan said. "If anyone asks, you're looking into this missing person."

"What about Detective Archer?" Quinn asked.

"He's included in anyone."

"Okay, between us." Quinn left Ryan's office.

Ryan picked up the file about Brielle Jeffries and started reviewing the notes. The ransom call came from her cell phone. They'd been unable to track it. Leonard Jeffries explained the voice he spoke to, a man with no accent detected. It wasn't very helpful information. Brielle was last seen at a club downtown on Saturday night. There might be video footage or something that would help them figure out if she met someone at the club. It was a place to start, at least.

Chapter 28
Brielle Jeffries

When Brielle woke next, she was back in her underground prison. She didn't know how long it had been since she tried to escape or how long she'd been in the drug-induced coma.

She threw herself out of bed and tried the door. This time she wasn't so lucky. It was locked, and she didn't have a way out. She stumbled back, dizzy. Her vision blurred as she lowered herself to the small bed and drew her legs to her chest.

Brielle was stuck.

She still wore the same sundress from her attempted escape and felt grateful at least the scumbag who abducted her hadn't had his hands all over her. She shivered in the dampness of the bunker and decided to find something warmer to wear. The drawers were full of clothing in her size, after all.

Brielle pulled out the sweater she'd found earlier and a pair of track pants. As she settled back on the bed, at a loss for what to do, she wondered why her prison seemed more accommodating this time. Did they intend to keep her after the ransom drop? Did they intend to leave her down here when they ran with the money, to be found or to die?

Brielle didn't know. All she wanted was to get out and go home.

When it happened all those years ago, something had awoken inside her. Her instinct took over and gave her the strength to harm the man who had been abusing her. She'd taken him by surprise, and she'd gotten away. This time, however, she didn't know what would happen. It wasn't the same man who had taken her. As much as she hated the man, Sam, who lay in the bedroom upstairs, he was dying. He didn't want her in the ways he had before. Perhaps he didn't even know she was here. So why did his son think she was such a prized jewel? Why, of all the people he could ransom, had he picked her?

The sound of a door closing made Brielle jump up from the bed. There were footsteps in the hallway outside her prison door, and she held her breath as they came closer. Had he come to do to her what Sam used to? Brielle squeezed her eyes shut and gently started patting her shoulders with her opposite hands, a calming tactic she'd learned in therapy.

When the door opened, Brielle risked a glance. She sucked in a sharp breath when she saw young Sam standing in the doorway.

She stepped back. "What do you want?" Her eyes darted to the bed and back, remembering those horrible nights by candlelight.

An amused smirk spread across his face, and he pushed the door open. "I want you to come with me."

He didn't wait for her response. He left the door wide open and turned down the hallway.

Brielle was unsure how to react. What did he want with her, and why was he allowing her the freedom to follow? She only needed to dart past him in the hallway or shove him into the second room to make a break for the bunker door. She would have to catch him by surprise.

She took a careful step into the hall, then looked up to where he waited. His face still held a steady smirk.

"The place isn't about to explode." He waved toward the second room, blocking the way to the bunker door. "It's in here."

Brielle walked toward the room and entered. It was the room of photos, the ones documenting her entire life. She immediately turned to leave. This room was the last place she wanted to be. He blocked the only escape.

"What do you want?" Brielle asked, cowering away from his broad form. The way he seemed to fill the doorway pushed pause on her escape plan. Brielle doubted he was stupid enough to let her roam freely without some sort of backup waiting for her outside the bunker.

For a moment, he didn't speak. His eyes traced the elaborate collection on the wall, seeming to scan each different photo of her. She followed his gaze to the intricate timeline of her life. She thought she'd lived in private, but this proved she'd been watched her whole life.

Brielle glanced back at him when he still remained silent. His eyes no longer rested on the photos; instead, he stared right at her. The look unnerved her and she looked down at the floor. She couldn't describe it. He wasn't desperate or hungry. He seemed confused, disappointed.

"He's been obsessed with you for years," he finally said. "I guess ever since he took you. He was always a very distant and unloving family man. He hit his wife and his children. Yet he was a man of the neighbourhood. He could woo a crowd. If only they knew what he kept hidden beneath his yard."

Brielle turned to the wall, looking at the range of photos. She reached up and touched one from her eighth birthday. Her hair was up in pigtails, and she wore a silver tiara. She didn't smile, only stared at the camera with round green eyes. She didn't look sad ... just lost.

"I didn't find this place until I was in college." He curled his lips in disgust. "I couldn't believe the warped fascination he had with you. He tried to tell me you were special and you belonged to him, but all I saw was a sick man with a twisted dream. All he wanted was you."

"Then why abduct me?" Brielle asked. "If you think he was so deranged, what am I doing here now? He's clearly dying."

He ran a hand through his hair, exasperation written on his face. "He spent his fortune tracking you, nearly bankrupting himself in the process. This seemed like poetic justice. A way to get him back for everything he did to me."

Brielle stepped back. "How so?"

"You will help give me back my fortune."

"You only want the money?"

"Yes," he said. "All I need is the money. After, I'll have no use for you."

Did he intend to release her, or kill her? Brielle wasn't sure.

"Why are you showing me this?" Brielle turned back to the wall.

He looked away from her. "I brought you here because I wanted to know why he loved you when he didn't seem to love anyone else in his life. What is so special about you?"

Brielle glanced over her shoulder at him. "And what is it?"

He looked her in the eye, his two dark pools of indifference. With a gentle shake of his head, he said, "Nothing at all."

He turned from the room. Outside the door, he stepped back, waving Brielle in the direction of her prison. Thrown by their strange interaction, Brielle took the path he indicated and returned to her room.

SHE DIDN'T KNOW how long she was sleeping when the door to her room opened again. This time it was the older woman she'd seen in the house right before they drugged her. She carried a steaming tray of food and didn't make eye contact. She closed the prison door and placed the food on the dresser.

"Wait," Brielle said before she could reach for the door. Brielle hopped to her feet and placed herself between the woman and the doorway. "Is there a way out?"

The woman still did not look her in the eye but slowly shook her head.

"You could leave the door unlocked." Brielle hoped the woman would pity her.

Again she shook her head.

"Please," Brielle begged. "You could."

"I'm sorry," her voice came softly. "He will lock it behind me."

"Who is he?" Brielle asked. "Why does he want me?"

This time the woman looked up at her, and Brielle could see the sadness in her eyes. "He is desperate for money."

"Who is he?" Brielle asked again, urgency in her tone. Then she remembered the briefcase she saw in Sam's room. "Who is H. Drake? Whose house is this?"

The woman clamped her lips shut and shook her head.

Brielle reached out and grabbed her arm, gently shaking her. "Please. I can't stay here."

The woman backed away, pulling her arm from her hold. "I am sorry," she whispered. "I wish I could help you."

Brielle sighed, realizing the woman wouldn't help her. Still, she had to get as much information as she could. "Who are you then? A housekeeper? Their maid? Why are you stuck here?"

"I am his nurse," the woman said, her gaze on the floor. "He's very sick and when he's gone, I will go too."

"Why would you help such a horrible man?" Brielle spat. "Do you know what he did to me when I was just a child?"

The woman shook her head, unwilling to look at her.

"He molested me," Brielle said. "Raped me. I was six years old."

The woman shook her head again. This time she looked up at Brielle and tears were forming in her eyes. "I am sorry," she said again.

Brielle had enough. She turned and reached for the door, prepared to leave despite what the woman said.

"No!" The woman roared. She reached for Brielle's

hand, pulling it away from the handle. "If you go, they will hurt you. I know Herold wasn't a perfect man, and I do not trust his son."

Brielle's eyebrows folded together. "Herold?"

The woman's eyes grew wide and she used Brielle's moment of shock to jump around her and hurry through the door. Brielle reached for it, trying to stop her, but she was too quick. The door was closed and locked by the time Brielle tried to pull it open.

She banged against it. "Please!" she called. "Please help me!" There was no response. Only the silence of her prison answered her wishful cries.

Brielle lowered herself to the ground, allowing tears to fall. She'd cried too many tears in this place, alone and frightened as a child, and now alone and stuck as an adult. How could she escape without someone helping her?

When she'd exhausted her tears, she picked herself up off the floor and looked to the waiting food. The steam had since disappeared. It wouldn't stay warm long down here. Brielle found she didn't care. Her hunger was gone, but she needed her strength, so she would force herself to eat.

Still, what the woman had said made her hesitate. Herold. It was a name she'd never heard before. Was Sam really Herold Drake? She closed her eyes, racking her brain. Why did the last name sound so familiar? She heard it somewhere before, yet she couldn't put her finger on it.

Grabbing the cooled food, she sat back on the bed and looked at the tick marks she had made all those years ago. They were the marks of her nightmares, and she wished more than anything she would never have to see them again.

Chapter 29
Melanie Parker

MEL DRUMMED HER FINGERS ON THE KITCHEN counter, waiting for Gabi to arrive. She had called, saying she wanted to talk. Mel had been waiting nearly an hour on her. She was irritated and stressed enough as it was with Jackie completely missing, and now Gabi was trying her patience.

"What do you want, Gabi?" Mel asked when the girl finally walked into the kitchen.

"Nice to see you, too," Gabi said with a smirk and her hands planted on her hips.

"Don't start with me. Just get to the point."

"I wanted to talk business," Gabi said. "I've been with you for a while now and I've brought in a couple of clients, some pretty nice ones. I think I deserve a bigger cut of our profit. I want to get a nice place."

"Are you serious?"

"Dead," Gabi said. "I've done a lot for you; you can't deny it. Even when you go crazy."

"What's that supposed to mean?"

"Look, I don't know what Blaine tells you, or how he

explains it, but I've seen my fair share of shit being here." Gabi shook her head. "I'm not trying to start shit or even get involved with stuff I don't fully understand. I've been loyal to you and I think it's fair I get a bit more."

"I don't think right now is the time to be discussing this," Mel said.

Gabi glared at her. "Then when is a good time, because nothing ever seems to be good with you."

The high-pitched ring of Mel's phone interrupted them, and she was quick to grab it, seeing Jackie's number light up. She showed the phone to Gabi, whose eyes widened.

"Pick it up!"

Mel answered the call with relief in her tone. "Holy shit, Jackie. Where have you been?"

"Thank God," Jackie's voice came through the receiver. The sound immediately made Mel relax, like all the stress of the past few days was completely washed away. Jackie was okay.

"I thought they might have taken you guys too."

Mel straightened. The hair on her arms stood on end as goosebumps formed. Taken. That word never sounded good. "What are you talking about?"

"Someone took me," Jackie said. "I don't know who. I woke up in this creepy place, unable to remember anything. I have marks on my arm. I think I was drugged."

"Where are you? I'll come get you."

"Don't worry," Jackie said. "I'm almost home. I'll try to head back to Blaine's tonight."

Mel paused, preferring to see Jackie right away, though she understood why Jackie would want to go home. Would she go to the police? They'd always avoided the law in their line of work, but this was serious, Mel admitted.

"Just keep texting me. You scared the shit out of me."

"Trust me, I had the shit scared out of me, too."

"And Jackie?"

"Yeah?"

"Send me your location. I'll feel better if I have eyes on you."

"Okay."

Mel clicked end on her cell and looked up at Gabi.

"She okay?" Gabi asked.

"She's alive." Mel turned and headed for the door.

"Where are you going? I wasn't finished."

Mel glanced back at Gabi. "I was."

"Mel!" Gabi called after her.

Mel didn't turn back. She headed upstairs, closing the door behind her.

Mel needed a minute to sit down. She needed a minute to compose herself. Hearing Jackie's voice again, the relief in knowing she was okay, overwhelmed Mel, and once she was alone, tears rolled down her cheeks. Tears of relief and joy. She wouldn't allow Gabi to see her this way. She wouldn't allow herself to show any weakness in front of her working girls.

She didn't have to; as soon as she heard the front door open and shut with a loud bang, she knew Gabi had left in a huff. Mel went to the window and watched her storm to her car and leave. She didn't care. Gabi would be back. Gabi always came back.

Chapter 30
Brielle Jeffries

BRIELLE BLINKED SEVERAL TIMES AS HER EYES ADJUSTED TO *the darkness. She sat up, glancing around. To her left was a small bedside table, a lamp on top. Hitting the switch, the light flickered on. The lighting was only a dull yellow. A tattered old wool blanket covered her legs, stretched out on the stiff bed she slept on.*

She pushed herself from the bed, only for a moment, as dizziness set in, and she needed to sit again. Her head spun and it took a moment before she could focus her eyes. She reached up, touching her face and quickly pulled her hand away. It was tender. Her whole body ached. Taking several breaths, she stood once more and walked over to the door, quickly testing the knob, only to discover it was locked.

She stepped back from the door, hesitating when she thought she heard one open in the hallway. Soon, there was a sound at her door like someone was trying the handle. Brielle stepped back, hoping it wasn't him.

There was a soft click, and the door opened a crack and

the nurse slipped inside. She was dressed in black and looked tired and beaten down even in the low light.

"Ms. Jeffries," the woman said, her voice hushed. "We haven't much time. He left the property and you in my care for only an hour. You must go now."

She pushed a bag into Brielle's hand and turned to leave.

Brielle caught the old woman's hand. "Come with me."

"Ms. Jeffries, you must go." She looked away. "Terrible things will happen to you if you stay. Terrible things have already happened."

"I'll come back and help you," Brielle promised.

"There is no helping me. You must go. Now." She reached for the door and slipped out before Brielle could say anything else.

Brielle glanced down at the bag, opening it slightly. It had the things she had with her the night they went to the club, her phone and party dress included. She exited the room into the long hallway and ran for the staircase at the end. She pushed open the door to the grounds and squinted in the bright sunlight. She was in the large backyard of the house. It was lined with a thin metal fence. The gate at the opposite end was open and Brielle headed for it. She hurried down the quiet street, glancing first at the house number and then the street sign. Seven fifty-two Queen Terrace.

She didn't look back.

BRIELLE JOLTED AWAKE.

"Honey," her mother's soft voice said. "Are you okay?"

Brielle glanced around, her chest heaving. She was in her

bedroom. Did she escape her prison? Her dream felt real, cloudy, almost as if it wasn't really her memory.

Her mother sat on her bedside with a hand on her forehead.

"What happened?" Brielle asked.

"You stumbled into the house yesterday slurring your words and completely out of it," Mary said. She ran her hand down Brielle's arm. "You said somebody drugged you and took you."

Brielle looked away. "It was him again."

"Sam?"

His name made her go cold.

"Yeah, and he had help. I know where they are this time. Who they are."

"You told us already. We've passed it on to the police."

"He's been following me. He had these pictures—a collection. My whole life mapped out. He could have taken me at any time. Or killed me," Brielle said.

Mary wrapped her arms around Brielle and held her daughter to her chest. "I'm so sorry, honey. I don't know who this man is, or what he wants. You're safe with us."

Brielle closed her eyes and didn't say anything. She knew exactly what he wanted. He wanted money. She wasn't safe. She would never be safe as long as he roamed free.

"The police will find him, and you won't have to be afraid anymore," Mary whispered. "I promise."

Brielle let her mother gently rock her. She was glad to be home and escape her underground prison. A part of her knew the police wouldn't find anything. They were too smart.

"Until then, your father and I will keep you safe." Mary

stroked her daughter's hair. "We have a nurse staying with us to monitor you and make sure those bastards didn't do anything awful."

Brielle didn't answer. Although she wanted to believe her mother, something inside her said different. Sam's son wouldn't give up his desperation. The nurse said they needed money, and whoever he was, he would get it, even if it meant coming after her again.

Chapter 31
Melanie Parker

SHE WAS OUT AT THE GROCERY STORE EARLY IN THE afternoon. When she pulled their car into the double garage, the house looked empty. Many of the rooms had curtains pulled over the window. She expected him. Perhaps he wasn't home. She scooped the grocery bags into her arms and carried them through the front door.

Craaaack.

A fist collided with her right cheekbone, knocking her and the groceries to the floor. She hit the ground with a thud and peered up at the menacing man towering over her. His eyes were filled with hatred. His nose was bent out of shape, and two purple bruises formed around his eyes. He looked as though he'd been in a bad fight.

"What happened?" She managed to say, though it was the wrong thing to ask because his fist knocked into her again, this time cutting open the inside of her cheek.

"Like you don't fucking know." His flat palm came flying toward her, slapping her wounded cheek, sending a sharp pain through it.

Her hand flew up to cover her cheek.

"Not so tough now, are you?" He smacked her again, now closer to her temple. A ringing pain resonated through her head.

She squeezed her eyes shut. Why? What did she do?

Curled into a ball on the welcome mat, she refused to look up at him, determined to hide from further pain. It didn't come. Instead, his footsteps retreated from her. She braved a look. He was leaving her alone.

"Clean this up!" he barked over his shoulder without looking back at her.

Her eyes scanned the groceries around her. Cans dented from being dropped. Apples rolling free from plastic bags and scattering in the front hall. She slowly got to her knees and gathered the groceries. She tiptoed to the kitchen, put them away, and hurried up the stairs to the bedroom. She cowered on the bed, hoping he wouldn't come looking for her soon.

MEL'S BODY ached when she woke in the familiar house again. Her lips were swollen. It felt like something should be broken—more than just a tooth.

Rage coursed through her body as she trashed the house. He was gone again today, and she'd had enough. Unable to stop herself, she grabbed the lamp from his bedside table and hurled it to the floor. The glass base shattered and the lampshade bent and rolled away. Mel went to his drawers and ripped out the clothing, tossing it everywhere. Anything she could grab and throw, she did.

The primary bedroom was a disaster by the time she finished. Admiring her work, she drew several quick breaths, unable to calm her rapid heartbeat or soothe her anger. She glanced at the clock radio and was thrown by the time. It was already past five. He could be home any minute. As angry as she was, she didn't want to see him.

Mel grabbed her bag and ran for the door. She glanced back at the house once as she dashed down the street. The cool wind whipped her face and pushed against her momentum; she ran faster, her heart still racing and eyes starting to water.

This was never going to stop.

In the cab, Mel tipped her head back and gently touched her swollen cheek. She didn't know what to do. No matter how hard she tried, she kept ending up there. She couldn't seem to stop herself from going, and why? Worse was she couldn't understand it. Nothing would stop Fraser. Mel's eyes shot open. Well, almost nothing.

When she arrived at Blaine's house, she fell through the door. She didn't look to see if anyone else was around and went right for her bedroom. Footsteps followed her up. Mel never looked back.

She flopped onto the bed and heard Blaine's familiar voice behind her. "You okay?"

Mel looked where he stood, resting against the doorframe with his arms crossed over his broad chest. "Can you stop asking me already?"

She wasn't okay. How could he think she was? He knew something he wasn't telling her. She was tired of all his secrets.

"What?" Blaine protested. "You don't look okay."

"I get it," Mel said, her anger still boiling inside her. "You've known me for two years. Stop acting like this is new, like I'm the one keeping secrets. You're the one keeping things from me."

"This is new," Blaine said. "You stopped working. Now you're back at it for that bastard? No, I'm not okay with this."

"It doesn't matter what you're okay with," Mel snapped. "Leave if you hate it."

Blaine looked away. "Do you like to be hit?"

"No," Mel said.

"Do you like to bleed?"

"No."

"Then you need to stay away from him."

"I tried!"

Blaine frowned. "You're a tough girl. I know, even tough girls need a chance to be vulnerable once in a while. Don't you realize what pain and fear can do to you if you choose to hold it in?" His gaze softened and he shook his head. "You don't want to be haunted by those demons. You need to stop."

"Leave me alone." She pushed herself from the bed and headed toward the bathroom door. She was already haunted by demons. Blaine didn't know what he was talking about.

"You can't just brush this off," Blaine said, stepping further into the room and closing the door behind him. "Tell me, Mel. Have you heard from Patsy lately?"

Mel shook her head. "I've told you I don't know any Patsy." Why would Fraser's wife call her?

Blaine frowned and walked closer to her. "Why did Fraser hurt you?"

"Because that's what Fraser does." She had hit him first.

"Then why did you go back?"

Mel closed her eyes, suddenly fearing the closeness

between her and Blaine. The moment passed quickly. "I don't know."

"I think you do."

"I loved him," Mel said, looking away. "He was everything to me." And he had been. That time had long passed.

"He's married. You left him." Blaine paused. "Why have you been going back? What are you planning?"

"I loved him, and he destroyed me," Mel said. "Now, I'm going to end this." It was the only way.

"Because he hit Patsy?" Blaine asked.

Mel's hands balled into fists. "He hit me! He used me. I hear his name and I feel sick. I look at my bruises and I hate him more." Anger and fear swirled around inside her, twisting together into a mess of rage and emotion. She couldn't think straight anymore. She could only think about next time. What would happen when she slipped up again? What would happen when she woke up in his bed next time? If she was lucky enough to wake up. No, there was only one way to end this.

Blaine cracked a half-smile. "He should know better than to hit you. You aren't his battered wife."

She reached up, gingerly touching her cheek. "He doesn't. And now he's going to pay for what he's done."

Mel didn't wait for Blaine to respond. This time she turned and threw open the door, letting it rebound off the doorstop.

Blaine thundered down the stairs after her. "What are you going to do?" He grabbed Mel's wrist, forcing her to look at him.

He'll never hurt me again. She looked away from Blaine. "I'm going to talk to him."

"Fraser doesn't talk," Blaine said. "We've tried before."

Memories of the previous months came crashing into her mind. Waking up at Fraser's disoriented, confused. Feeling beaten, broken. Facing his anger. Blaine had tried to protect Mel more than once. It only made Fraser angrier.

Mel pulled herself from Blaine's grasp. "Then I'll try harder."

"Let me come with you."

Mel shook her head. "I don't need you. You make him worse. You nearly killed him last time."

Fraser's bloodied lip and swollen eye had given her pleasure until she saw the rage behind Blaine's gaze. She had to scream at Blaine to get him to stop. She wouldn't let Blaine go down for something she'd caused. This was her problem. She had to fix it.

"He deserved it," Blaine said, looking away.

"That's not you. Let me handle this." Blaine had too much to lose. He was a good person before he'd met Mel. He would be better off without her.

"I don't like it."

"Too bad." Mel grabbed her bag from the front hall and headed into the sitting room.

Candy stood when Mel entered and immediately fidgeted with her bracelet.

Gabi, who was seated on the other side of the room, looked to Mel with a raised eyebrow. "What's up?" She exchanged a look with Candy.

Mel ignored the girls and walked over to the cabinet in the corner, slipped a small silver key in, and pulled open the doors. Inside was several thousand dollars in cash; their safe from their jobs. She took a stack and slid it into her purse.

Grabbing hold of both doors, Mel went to close the cabinet once more but hesitated.

She peered at the money for a moment before reaching in and grabbing another stack. She'd need money once it was all done. A quick escape. She would just disappear.

She'd call Blaine after. Make sure the rest of the money was properly divided amongst the remaining girls, then Blaine would get his wish. Her operation would be shut down and they could live free again.

Mel closed the doors and locked it, then turned back to the girls.

Mel gave Candy a once over. Candy had always been a pushover. She'd do what Mel said without the stupid questions.

"Candy, you're with me." Mel looked at Gabi. "You, get out. I don't want to see you around here for a few days." Better Gabi was gone when it happened.

Gabi stared back at her, confusion written on her face. "What did I do?"

Mel glared at her. "I said go!"

Gabi stood, her eyes wide, and exited the sitting room. Mel didn't speak again until she heard the front door close. She stared at Candy.

"You ready?" she asked.

Candy walked toward her. "You decide."

"You'll do." Mel waved her to follow as she went to grab her shoes and reached for the front door. Candy went through first and Mel hesitated, seeing Blaine staring at them from the staircase as she pulled the door closed behind her.

"So, where are we going?" Candy asked as they climbed into one of Blaine's cars.

Mel stuck the key into the ignition and the car revved to life. She looked at Candy with a wild smile. "Fraser Morrison's."

"New client?" Candy asked.

Mel stared at the road in front of them. "No."

"Old client?"

"We've had a complicated relationship."

"Are you going to tell me?"

Mel shook her head. "No." She cast a sideways glance at Candy and added. "How's your driving?"

Candy frowned. "Fine, why?"

"Okay, promise me no matter what happens you'll have the car ready to go and you'll drive me out of the city."

"Why? What are you planning?"

"Just promise," Mel said. "Or I won't get you to another job."

Mel glanced back at the road in front of them. The sun was setting, casting an orange and pink hue across the nearly empty freeway. The sky was peaceful, calming. Unsuited for the task ahead.

"Fine, I promise."

"Good."

The car radio read half past eight. Candy leaned forward and turned the dial, increasing the volume.

"... *looking at another week with high temperatures. Enjoy it while it lasts. Now in local news ...*"

"*Good Evening, this is Jennie Randall with your local updates. Breaking News. We've just received word Brielle Jeffries has been found. The search is called off. Details to come in one hour.*"

Mel's eyes darted to the radio before looking back at the

road. She grabbed the dial and turned down the news. She didn't need any distractions right now.

They pulled off the freeway at exit thirty-nine. Mel never decreased her speed. Not until they pulled into a nice, gated neighbourhood. They passed a long driveway where a blue car was parked. Mel pulled up to the curb beside it. Then she looked at Candy.

"You ready?"

Candy cocked her head to the side. "What's going on? You're so flushed."

"I asked if you were ready."

Candy shrugged. "Unless you can think of a reason I'm not."

"I can think of about a hundred. They don't matter now."

She climbed out of the car and Candy followed, taking her place in the driver's seat.

"Wait here for me. I won't be long." Mel's heart pounded as she looked up at the house. There were lights on in the rooms upstairs. The downstairs seemed empty. She reached the front door, leaned down, and lifted the welcome mat. She retrieved a key and slipped it into the lock. Mel looked back at Candy and then proceeded into the house.

The door squeaked when it opened. Mel didn't see him in the front hall. There was movement upstairs; the floorboards creaked slightly with each step.

"Patsy!" His angry voice echoed down from the floor above. "I know you're home. I heard the damn door. What the fuck did you do to the house?"

Mel froze like a deer in headlights. Her breath caught in her throat at the sound of his harsh voice.

"Patsy!" he called again.

Mel shook her head, regained her composure, and glanced to the stairs where Fraser appeared, red-faced, spit flying. His dark eyes narrowed at Mel. "Do you think it's funny to leave the house like this? You'll clean this up and you won't do it again."

"Like fuck I will," Mel said.

His hands clenched at his side, and he stormed down the stairs toward her.

Sensing his rage, Mel beelined for the kitchen in search of something to defend herself against his anger. She found the knife block and pulled out the largest chef's knife. She weighed it in her hand as Fraser entered the kitchen.

"What the fuck are you doing?" His voice was low and menacing, eyes dancing over the sharp knife in hand.

Before Mel could answer, Candy entered the kitchen. The younger girl's eyes widened when she assessed the situation.

Fraser looked at her. "Who is that?"

Mel didn't answer him. Fraser stared at Candy like he was a hunter and she was his prey. He turned his cool gaze on Mel when she still didn't answer him.

"Where the fuck have you been?" he asked in a low voice. He reached out to grab Mel, but she jerked back, knife poised to stab him.

"Don't touch me."

Fraser turned and stepped toward Candy. "And who's this little whore you've brought?" He raged. "I've told you I don't want these people in my home."

Candy backed away from him, knocking into the kitchen table and sending the lone vase toppling on its side. It crashed to the floor, shattering. With nowhere to run,

Candy gripped the table behind her and squeezed her eyes shut as he reached for her. His hand wrapped around her hair and yanked her toward him. She cried out and reached up to grab at his wrist, trying to free herself from his painful hold.

Knife in hand, Mel ran toward them and approached from behind. Candy opened her eyes and screamed as Mel plunged the knife into Fraser's neck.

His grip on Candy loosened and she stumbled away. She backed against the table and watched, her hand flying up to cover her mouth.

Mel stood over Fraser, who had fallen to his knees. She continued to stab the knife repeatedly into his neck. Blood poured from the wounds, soaking Mel, Fraser, and the floor in a dark crimson. He tried to reach out and stop her. It was no use. He fell to the ground, motionless. Mel's heart pounded against her chest as she stood over the body, her hands and arms covered in his blood. Breathing rapidly, she turned toward Candy.

"You okay?"

Candy managed a nod.

Mel stepped closer, and Candy drew a sharp breath, eyes still on the knife in her hand. Mel walked to the counter and placed the knife down before turning back to Candy. She held her blood-red hands up so Candy could see she was empty-handed.

"Do you have any blood on you?"

Candy glanced down at her body and shook her head.

Mel stepped closer. "Candy, we need to go." Candy didn't move. Mel grabbed the knife and hurried toward the door. "Let's go! Let's get out of here!"

Glass crunched beneath Candy's shoes and Mel heard her curse as she nearly slipped on the fresh blood.

Outside, Mel hopped into the front seat and shifted the car into gear. As they rushed down the road, Candy shook her head.

"Didn't you want me to drive?"

Mel stared at the road in front of her. "Change of plans. I'm dropping you at the bus and heading out of the city. Then I'll ditch the car."

"What just happened?" Candy asked.

Mel shook her head. "I can't explain it now. There's no time. Call Blaine. He'll make sure you're okay. Don't tell him what you saw."

She pulled up on the side of the street and waved Candy out of the door.

"What about you?" Candy asked before she closed the passenger side.

"Don't worry about me. I'll be fine."

Candy closed the door, and Mel rushed off. She glanced in the rear view in time to watch the redhead fiddle with a bracelet that was no longer there. Mel swallowed hard and reached for her phone. One call to Blaine, and then she was ditching it. It was only a matter of time before the cops found Fraser and came after her.

Chapter 32
Detective Ryan Boone

RYAN STOOD IN THE CENTER OF THE VICTIM'S KITCHEN. The coroner had already removed Fraser Morrison's body to do an autopsy. Procedure, but unnecessary; Ryan could tell what killed him from the scene alone. There was one knife missing from the expensive block and several stab wounds in the man's neck. Still, procedure was everything.

Before him was a large pool of blood. The scene reeked of death. The sickly, sweet stench of too much blood. Archer waited outside, having never liked being on the scene of a murder, especially one so graphic. Ryan, however, was an expert. It had been a long time since blood made him squeamish.

He scanned the kitchen. There was a bloody handprint on the counter and a smudge of blood next to it, as if the murder weapon had been placed down after the crime. There was a smear of blood coming from the pool like someone had carelessly walked through it.

There was no forced entry; the door was unlocked on their way in. If not for a call from a nosy neighbour, the police probably wouldn't have found the body for a few days. At least this community was always watching.

It didn't take much detective work to figure this one out. Patsy Morrison had murdered her husband. Ryan could guess why, but he didn't vocalize it, knowing he had to study the facts.

Ryan glanced back at his partner, who had appeared in the kitchen doorway, arms crossed. A few other officers stood behind him, speaking quietly.

"Did you hear the one about the husband who died under mysterious circumstances?" Ryan quipped.

Archer kept a straight face. "Jokes about homicide aren't funny, Boone."

"Hey! That's not true." Ryan grinned. "They just have to be properly executed."

Archer groaned. "Are we done here?"

Ryan glanced back at him and then shook his head. He carefully moved around the pool of blood toward the kitchen table. The out-of-place chairs told him the table had been knocked, likely because there was shattered glass piled beneath it. Something had been knocked off, possibly during a struggle.

"It doesn't make sense," Ryan said.

Archer ran a hand through his hair before moving further into the room. He scrunched his nose as he passed by the pool and stood beside Ryan. "What doesn't?"

Ryan straightened and looked back at the blood. "Morrison was attacked from behind." He turned away from the pool to show Archer what he meant and pointed to the side of his neck. "The knife got him here, and he crumbled forward." They had found him face down in the pool of his blood.

"So?" Archer asked. He shifted from side to side; the amount of blood made him uncomfortable. If he weren't a sucker for a good mystery, Archer would have never gotten into the business.

"So," Ryan continued. "It seems like he was taken by surprise. Then how did the table get jostled and the glass shattered? Why does it look like there was a struggle, and if they were struggling, why would Morrison turn away from his attacker? Why would he willingly expose a weakness?"

Archer's eyebrows furrowed together, and he glanced around. "You think there was someone else here?"

"It's possible," Ryan said. He walked away from the blood and back toward the moved table. "Someone else being here would explain why he would turn away from his attacker. Maybe he was pursuing someone else when he got killed."

"Could he have been rushing his wife, and someone else got him from behind?"

Ryan held up his hand to silence Archer when something caught his eye. "Hold that thought."

He moved around the table and crouched in the corner of the kitchen nearby a door leading to a backyard patio. There, resting in a heap on the floor, was a sparkling bracelet. Ryan reached down with a gloved hand and picked up the bracelet, examining it from all edges. Archer walked up behind him.

"Looks like Donovan's bracelet."

It looked *exactly* like the bracelet Mr. Donovan had worried about. One of the missing pieces.

"One of the robbers came here."

Or they sold it to someone. Maybe even to Patsy herself.

"Think now Kimball will be willing to talk?" Ryan gripped the bracelet and looked around. He ducked low and glanced below the table. It was faint, but there against the tile floor were a few short strands of red hair. Ryan glanced at the other officers and waved over one of the assistants.

He pointed at the hair. "Collect that. We'll get it back to the lab for testing." Now he was certain. Whoever robbed the store had been here and wasn't as careful.

When the assistant stood with a sample bag of hair, Ryan motioned to the bracelet and they placed it in another bag, which the assistant retreated with.

"Alright," Ryan said. "Let's get out of here. Maybe we can get a few answers out of the neighbours."

Archer shook his head. "Quinn already went around the street. He's out front."

Ryan waved toward the door and followed Archer from the kitchen, leaving the crime scene to the rest of the officers and the cleanup crew.

The front yard was roped off by police tape, and several of the neighbours peered out their windows at the various police vehicles and the active crime scene.

Quinn was standing next to the superintendent, flipping through a page of notes and speaking quietly. They glanced up at Ryan and Archer as they emerged from the house and waved them over.

"Someone else was here," Quinn said.

"Boone seems to think so," Archer said.

"Really?" Quinn looked to Ryan with his eyebrow raised.

"Yeah," Ryan said. "We have reason to believe this

murder might be connected to the burglary." Ryan pointed at the notebook in Quinn's hand. "What did you find?"

Quinn flipped the page. "Most people didn't see much, weren't around. There was one woman who said she saw two people leaving the house together in a black car. One matched Patsy's description and the other a slender redhead. The timing fits with the murder."

"That would explain the red hair." Ryan looked to Archer.

"Why do you think the burglary is connected?" Singh asked.

"We found Donovan's bracelet," Archer said. "Or a look-a-like."

"We're going to head back to the station. Call us if you find anything else." Ryan turned for the car when someone called out, stopping him.

A young forensic officer who had also worked on the burglary hurried down the walkway with a plastic bag in hand. "You should see this," she said when she got to his side.

Ryan reached out and took the bag. Inside was an orange pill bottle prescribed to Patsy Morrison. He turned the bag in hand and saw what was so interesting. On the side, it said Solydexran—the pill they found at the jewelry shop. The prescribing doctor's name, Dr. Miranda Konch, was in the top corner.

"What are the odds?" Ryan asked, passing the bag to Archer. "Where did you find it?"

"In her bathroom drawer." The woman pointed to the side of the bottle. "Seems like this is the fifth time she has filled the prescription."

"We'll have to contact the good doctor." Archer handed the bag back to the forensic officer.

"Maybe we can get a better idea of just how sick she is." Ryan glanced at the female officer. "Thank you. Confirm it's the same medication we found at Donovan's."

The woman nodded and returned to the house. Ryan turned, and Archer followed him down the cobblestone walk and under the police tape blocking the street. He climbed into the passenger side and Archer went around to the driver's seat.

"Think they'll match DNA from the hair?" Archer asked as he started the car.

Ryan shrugged. "We'll be lucky if they do."

"You think the killer is the wife?"

"Almost definitely."

"Why?"

Ryan pulled out a photo of Patsy and Fraser Morrison, one given to him when they arrived on the scene. "I've seen her before. Him, too."

"Really?" Archer asked. "Where?"

"They were at the police function, and she didn't look good," Ryan said. "I think he was hurting her. The way he stared at me after I spoke to her ..." Ryan shivered. "Even creeped me out."

"You think she snapped?"

"Who knows? Would you be surprised? How long has she been living like this? It wouldn't be the first time a woman killed her abusive partner."

"And the bracelet?" Archer asked.

"I guess we'll see if it's a match. Sure looked like it."

"What about the pills?"

"All seems very convenient, doesn't it?" Ryan said.

Archer sighed. "Why did a simple burglary have to turn into murder?"

"Simple?" Ryan chuckled.

Archer didn't answer.

Ryan glanced out the window as they left the gated community. "I think you and I have a very different definition of simple."

Chapter 33
Brielle Jeffries

HER FATHER PACED BACK AND FORTH IN FRONT OF HER. He was dressed in a fine, tailored suit, only having arrived home from work an hour before. Brielle sat in one of their straight-backed dining room chairs. It was specifically brought into the living room for this lecture, as it often had been when Brielle was a child. Across the square room, her mother sat in the far-right corner. Her back was straight, and she was looking at her hands, at the ceiling, at her pacing husband— anywhere but at her daughter.

The two windows on the left wall were open just a crack, letting the cool evening wind blow in. The blinds were drawn. The stars were still waking up in the inky night sky. Brielle wasn't certain how late it was or how long she'd sat here with her father pacing. She shivered as she stared at him, but not because she was cold.

"I thought we were beyond all this lying," her father mumbled.

Brielle's eyes widened. "How can you say that?"

His face went red, and his fists tightened as he spoke.

"They found nothing. I called the police, had the entire city searching for you. Your family in chaos—"

"Because someone abducted me!" Brielle interrupted. "You saw me when I came home. I was a mess. I was drugged."

"Brielle, the police investigated the address you gave us. There was only an older woman—a nurse—and a very sick old man. She said the rest of the Drakes have been out of town for weeks."

Mary finally looked at her. Her eyes were sad. "I'm worried about you, honey. I thought you were better. Miranda said you were healthy now."

Mary stood and walked over to Brielle's side. She took her arm and ran a thumb over the needle marks from when he drugged her.

"Why are you shooting up again?" Mary asked.

Brielle's jaw dropped and she yanked her arm from her mother's grip. "What about my face?" Brielle motioned to her swollen lip and bruised cheek. "Can you explain where this came from?"

"I'm sure getting into drugs brings out a rough crowd," her father snapped. "Which one of your friends did you pay to make a fake ransom call?"

"What? No one!" Brielle's stomach flip-flopped. She put her face in her hands. "I don't know what else to tell you," she said, begging them to listen. "They're smarter than we think; they set it all up." Tears threatened to spill. "I swear. There was an underground bunker on the property, the one I told you about. Did they look for it?"

Her father frowned. "That neighbourhood is expensive, and the Drake family well known, of status, and you choose to place the blame on their house. Foolish. Childish. The police aren't about to search a property based on the accusations of a silly girl who's been doing drugs and having a psychotic break!"

"It's a rouse! I swear." Brielle tried again. "The nurse rescued me. She seemed like she was in trouble. Was it her? She was coerced. He probably hurt her, too." She looked to her father, pleading with him. "Did you speak with Amanda or Caroline? I was with them; they know I disappeared."

Mary frowned. "Yes, your drunk, twenty-two-year-old cousins were a wonderful help. They told us the last time they saw you: dancing with a stranger. It sounds exactly like it did before the clinic. Why would you do this to yourself? You were doing so well."

"I'm not lying." She stood, challenging her parents. "He knew about Jackie. He said I was pretending to be her."

Her father stopped and glanced over his shoulder, exchanging looks with Brielle's mother.

Mary draped her arm over Brielle's shoulders. Her tone had softened, her face riddled with pity. "Do you pretend to be Jackie often, honey?"

Brielle pushed away from her mom and the concerned looks on her parents' faces. "No. I don't know why I would."

Again, they exchanged worried looks.

"Have you seen her, Brie?" Leonard asked, taking a step closer to her. His anger had subsided; his voice was quiet.

What was wrong with them? Brielle instinctively backed away. "No." She knew they didn't like Jackie, but did it warrant this reaction? Brielle wasn't crazy.

"Should we call Miranda?" Mary asked, though the question was directed at Leonard, not Brielle.

"No," Brielle protested. "She said I was fine."

Her parents didn't even look at her. It was like she never spoke.

"Maybe we should," Leonard whispered.

Mary frowned. "If it's serious, we can send her back for a few weeks."

Brielle backed away from her parents toward the archway leading into the kitchen. Her parents continued to discuss sending her to the clinic again, and she hurried up the back stairs leading from the kitchen and entered her large bedroom. Without another thought, she quickly threw some of her things into a backpack. She didn't know where she would go, only that she couldn't stay here. Whatever her parents were planning wouldn't help the poor nurse who rescued her.

Backpack on, Brielle descended the back stairs. Stopping by the kitchen arch, she listened to her parents.

"We can send her next week," Mary said.

"Do you really think this is necessary?" Leonard asked, running a hand through his grey hair.

"You heard her," Mary insisted. "If Jackie is back, then Brielle isn't safe. You remember what happened last time."

Leonard looked away from his wife. "We aren't speaking about that."

Mary shook her head. "I won't have it happen again. We had to leave the city, for god's sake!"

Leonard took hold of her shoulders. "Mary, calm down. Wait until we talk to the doctor."

Mary lowered herself to the chair. "I thought we were past this."

"So did I, but it will be okay," Leonard said. "We'll help her through this."

"I don't know if I can do it again," Mary whispered. "The medication was supposed to help."

Leonard closed his eyes. "We may not have a choice." He let out a long breath. "Go get Brielle. I'll call Miranda; hopefully, she'll be able to meet with us soon."

Brielle hurried to the back door and slipped into the cool night air. If her parents didn't worry before, they could now. She wouldn't let them send her away again.

Brielle opened the back gate and crossed her front yard to her quiet street. She lived in a gated community with large houses lining the paved road. Hurrying through the dark complex, she noticed an unfamiliar car parked on the street two houses down from hers on the opposite side of the road.

She stopped and glanced at the mysterious car. The moon and few streetlights provided enough light for Brielle to see, though it was impossible to see inside from this distance. Was someone sitting in there? Glancing around at the empty driveways, she wondered why the car didn't park in one. It wasn't often cars were parked on her street, and for some reason, this one gave her chills. She shook it off and continued down the street, reaching for her phone.

Chapter 34
Melanie Parker

MEL OPENED THE MOTEL DOOR A CRACK TO SEE WHO knocked. Blaine stood waiting, holding a plastic bag.

"Did you get it?" Mel asked, closing the door behind him after he entered. He said nothing but handed her the plastic bag. She took it, pulling out the requested supplies: hair dye, tanner, makeup, coloured costume contacts. The works.

Mel smiled and placed the bag aside. "Thanks."

She moved closer. She slid her hands up his biceps and hooked them behind his neck. She leaned in to kiss him. His response was rigid, uninterested, untrusting. He removed himself from her hold and perched on the edge of the stiff double bed with a frown plastered on his lips.

"Are you going to tell me what it's for?" Blaine asked when Mel turned away from him. "Or what you did? You scared the hell out of Candy. She wouldn't even speak when I saw her."

"No." Mel grabbed the bag and kicked open the small bathroom door. Blaine moved, watching her in the bathroom as she pulled her brown hair from the bun on top of her head.

He stepped forward and ran a strand of her soft, long hair between his fingers. She watched him as he did. He looked remorseful. He always loved her hair.

Mel reached out and took the strand from his hand. "It will grow back," she said as she mixed the dye solution he purchased. Soon her chocolate locks would be maroon.

"You've never dyed your hair," Blaine said. "What about a wig?"

Mel glanced at her reflection in the mirror and started to cover her hair with dye. A wig wouldn't be enough.

Blaine frowned and leaned against the door frame. "If you don't tell me what happened, I can make assumptions." His black t-shirt hugged his chiselled body and strained under the stress of his rapid breathing.

Mel stared at him as she ran her gloved hands through her dye-soaked hair, making certain it was coated properly. "Then make the assumption, Blaine." She twisted her hair back into a bun and put a shower cap overtop. Then she removed the gloves and tossed them into the garbage. "It's what you do anyway."

While her hair colour set, she grabbed the self-tanner from the packaging. Blaine continued to watch her as she placed the bottle aside to be ready for use after she washed the dye from her hair.

"You're going to look so fake." His jaw clenched as he looked away. He meant it as an insult.

"At least I'll look different."

"Why?"

"It doesn't matter," Mel said, then she put on a playful

grin and stepped closer to him. "Aren't you excited to see me look a little different? It will be like roleplay. And you can pretend you're fucking someone entirely new."

It was the wrong thing to say because Blaine's nostrils flared, and he took a step closer to her. "That's enough." His voice hardened. His shoulders squared. He took hold of Mel's wrists and stared into her eyes. She struggled against his hold, but he tightened and wouldn't let go.

"Blaine, you're hurting me," Mel whispered.

"After what I've seen, you can handle a little pain," he said and held steady. "Now tell me. What the fuck are you running away from?"

The sound from the TV drew both of their attention. The commercials had finished, and the upbeat music told them it had returned to the evening news. A pretty young reporter was centered in the screen and announced the arrival of Detective Ryan Boone live.

"Good evening, Detective," she said. "Thank you for joining us." The TV screen was now split with a handsome police detective opposite the reporter interviewing him.

"It's my pleasure."

"Please, go ahead," she said. "Tell us about Patsy Morrison."

Blaine stiffened. His hands dropped to his side, and he turned toward the TV.

"Yes, of course. First, we can't be certain if she is dangerous," he said, speaking in a low voice. He pronounced each word clearly when he spoke and carried himself as an experienced officer would. "Patsy Morrison may just be a scared woman, hit one time too many. Still, don't approach her if you see her as she is still a suspect. I urge you to contact your local police. We will make sure she gets the help she needs."

"And what about a second suspect?" The reporter asked.

Mel stopped listening.

Blaine turned and stared at her. His eyes wide and mouth agape. "Tell me it isn't true."

Mel grabbed the remote and turned off the TV. "I can't."

"You murdered him?" Blaine said, taking a step toward her.

Mel immediately backed away, feeling intimidated by his closeness. "I did what I had to."

Blaine said nothing, only stared down at her with a hard expression.

"It was me or him," Mel said.

Blaine stared hard at her for what seemed like forever. Then his expression melted away and he pulled her into his arms. He didn't care she was covered in hair dye, he only held her against his chest.

"I'm so sorry," Blaine said. "I should have stopped you. It shouldn't have come to this."

Mel rested her head against his chest and said nothing for several seconds, shocked by his apology. Eventually, she managed to say, "It's not your fault."

Blaine only continued to hold her until Mel pushed away.

"We need to get out of here," Blaine said. "Right away."

Mel shook her head. "I can't leave Jackie." She hadn't seen Jackie since last week, and since she ditched her phone, she hadn't been able to call.

"Jackie will be fine," Blaine said. "You're the one who will be in trouble. We have to go."

"They're not blaming me." Mel motioned to the TV. "They're blaming his mousy wife."

"They'll figure it out," Blaine said. "Especially if they find Candy."

Mel gritted her teeth. Of course, Candy. Why hadn't she just stayed in the car?

"I won't leave without seeing Jackie."

"Mel," Blaine said, his tone hardening.

Mel planted her hands on her hips. "I need you to go get her and bring her here."

"What?"

"I said, go get her. It's what you want to do." Mel waved him off. "I need to see her, and I can't go looking for her. You can." She turned to the bedside table and glanced at the time. "Go find Jackie."

Blaine lowered himself to the bed and fidgeted with his hands in his lap. "Mel ..."

"Go get her," she said, stepping closer to him. "I need you to."

Blaine shook his head. "She has a car. She can meet us. Let me stay with you. Let me protect you."

Mel almost smiled at his desire to save her but she knew better. She reached out and touched his cheek. "I need you to trust me."

He took her hand and kissed her palm. "I want to stay."

"It will be too many cars here. Go pick her up. Then we'll know she's safe." She pulled him from the bed, leaned in, and kissed him. He didn't respond, but he didn't resist either. "Don't be long."

"What about Candy?" Blaine asked.

Mel hesitated and drew a long breath. She was in this because of Mel. "If you find her, bring her with you."

Blaine grabbed his keys and left the motel room. Mel locked it behind him. She removed the shower cap, entered the bathroom, and tossed it into the waste bin. Mel stripped and turned on the shower, stepping in and letting the warm water rinse away the extra dye. The white tub turned maroon as the coloured water poured down her nude body. She admired her complexion as the water dribbled down. Soon, her skin would be a few shades darker, and she would miss it. She'd always loved her look, but now some things were more important.

After washing her hair and rinsing the dye from her body, she stepped out of the shower and grabbed a large towel. She dried herself, then wrapped the towel around her newly coloured hair. Grabbing the self-tanner, Mel rubbed it over her legs and arms.

Blaine would look at her differently now. Would he still love her after all this? She was still the same person, wasn't she?

Mel applied the tanner to her arms and face, making sure it was even, and when finished, she removed the towel from her hair. Still damp, her long, now red-tinted hair fell to her now tanned shoulders. She looked different at first glance, but the same blue eyes stared at her from behind her new skin and hair. She glanced down at the green contacts and decided she could do without them for now.

Mel tilted her head to the side and stared at her reflection for some time before retrieving her clothes from the floor. Perhaps in looking so different, escape wouldn't be so hard.

Chapter 35
Detective Ryan Boone

Ryan grabbed his phone and hit Quinn's name, tapping his desk as he waited for the call to go through.

"Boone, good to hear from you," Quinn said.

"Quinn, we need to find Lexi Chase," Ryan said. "Immediately."

"What happened?"

"I got a call about the hair. She was at the murder scene. And Kimball named her and Brennan Drake as the suspects in the video at the burglary." Word about the murder had made the rich kid panic. He admitted to his crimes and had traded their names for a lesser sentence, following his lawyer's advice. No trial. An easy win for Ryan.

Ryan could only imagine how Dorian had taken the loss. Or maybe he considered no trial a win. What was the joke about lawyers being money hungry and lazy? Ryan would have to remember it for when he next had to testify in a case where Dorian represented the accused.

"Okay," Quinn said. "Where should I meet you?"

Ryan glanced at the time. It was late in the day and Lexi

had likely left work already, if she had gone at all. "I'll meet you outside her condo building."

He hung up and headed to Singh's office.

"I'm going to Lexi Chase's house now," Ryan said.

Singh looked up from his paperwork. "The arrest warrant hasn't gone through yet."

"We have probable cause, and the warrant will be issued soon. I don't want to lose her before then. Quinn has reported some strange activity to me."

Singh raised an eyebrow. "I thought Quinn stopped his surveillance."

"Oh," Ryan said, forgetting he'd kept it secret. "I asked him to continue. No other job has suffered."

Singh regarded him coolly. "I'll send a squad car after you with the processed warrant."

"What about Brennan Drake?" Ryan asked.

"Archer is already en route." Singh stood and rounded his desk. "He'll call when he's found anything."

"Good. I'll do the same." Ryan left the building for his car.

QUINN WAS WAITING outside the condo building door when Ryan arrived. He was dressed in casual clothes and leaning up against the wall.

"Did you see her come home?" Ryan asked.

Quinn shook his head. "No."

"Let's head up." Ryan reached for the door.

"We're alone," Quinn said.

"More are coming."

"Are you arresting her?" Quinn asked.

Ryan flashed his badge at the concierge—a short, round man with a large beard—who quickly opened the door and allowed them to enter.

"Do you have a master key for the units?" Ryan asked.

The concierge nodded.

"You'll need to come with us."

The man placed a sign on the counter saying he'd return soon, then followed Ryan and Quinn to the elevator.

"Lexi Chase?" Ryan said as he knocked on her door. "This is the police. Allow us entry, or we will have to enter by force."

No answer on the other side.

Ryan tried again. Still, there was no sound on the other side. He stepped aside and let the concierge use his key.

Gun drawn, Ryan entered the apartment to find it empty. The bedroom was spotless. It looked like she had cleaned up or hadn't been home in weeks. He ran a finger along the bedside table, collecting dust in the process. There wasn't a thing out of place except the black day planner resting alone on her dresser. He took it to review.

"Clear!" Quinn called from one of the rooms on the opposite side of the unit.

"All clear over here, too," Ryan stepped out of her bedroom and lowered the gun.

"Where did you see her last?" Ryan asked.

Quinn frowned. "With the brunette I told you about on the other side of town."

"Right." Before Ryan could ask more, his phone started ringing. "You've got Boone."

"Ryan." Archer's thick voice came through. "We need you."

"What happened?" Ryan could hear sirens in the background of his call. "We're at Lexi Chase's. It looks like she hasn't been here in days."

"No time for that," Archer said quickly. "We got to the Drake residence, and it wasn't a pretty sight. Possible triple homicide."

"You've got to be kidding me."

"Negative. I'll text you the address. Bring Quinn and get here, quick."

The phone clicked before Ryan could agree. Tucking his phone back into his pocket, he thanked the concierge and directed Quinn out of the building and to his waiting car.

"Chase will have to wait," Ryan said. "There's been a possible triple homicide."

"A triple, really?" Quinn asked.

"Why only kill one person when you can kill three?"

"Shit."

"It's been some month." Ryan slipped into the car and quickly checked the address—the very house they'd been to only days before that Brielle Jeffries had claimed she'd been held captive in—then headed down the street. He could hear the sirens in the distance. At least they were close.

A GUNSHOT WOUND to the head had killed Brennan Drake. The second victim was unidentified, though he wore a suit and an earpiece—possibly security. Perhaps hired help who got caught in the crossfire? Ryan couldn't say for sure.

The third murder was less gruesome, however, as it was clear from the state of the bedroom that Herold Drake was not a healthy man. An oxygen mask had been carelessly discarded and a blood-stained feather pillow tossed aside. He had likely been suffocated.

"I think we've got our guy," Archer said, sifting through the bags of jewelry they'd found on the property.

Ryan glanced around the room. There were pictures of the family on the mantel. One in particular caught Ryan's attention: Brennan Drake with a slender red-haired woman Ryan almost immediately recognized as Lexi Chase. Now they had reason to connect her with all three unsolved crimes. The hair found at the Morrison's house was confirmed as her DNA which they had on file from a previous assault charge. Quinn further confirmed Brennan was the man he saw go by Lexi's apartment. This must be the Bren Marley had referred to as Lexi's ex.

"Does the property have surveillance?" Ryan asked.

"We caught Ms. Chase," Archer pointed to the photo of Lexi, "on video, following who we suspect to be Brielle Jeffries."

"Brielle Jeffries." Ryan frowned. "Maybe this is not such a surprise—she claimed this was the address of her abductor."

"And she killed them?" Quinn asked. "An heiress out for revenge."

"They say revenge is best served cold," Ryan said. "And I've heard it's sweet. Hey guys, I think I just figured out revenge is ice cream."

Archer shook his head and looked to where Singh stood

on the opposite side of the room. "Hard to say who committed what crime. We can't find the gun."

"Angry ex-girlfriend murders her boyfriend?" Quinn said. "Sounds plausible."

It all seemed a bit cliché to Ryan. "Then why bring Ms. Jeffries?" Better, how did Lexi even know her?

"Sounds like she had reason to hate these guys too," Archer said. "Her parents said Brielle was pretty convinced she was abducted, despite their assertions she had been on a bender. Maybe they both wanted revenge?"

"We need you two back at the station," Singh said when he tucked his phone into his pocket. "You too, Quinn."

Ryan nodded and followed Archer out to the cars.

"How would someone like Lexi Chase connect with an heiress like Brielle?" Archer asked.

Ryan shrugged. "Honestly, I haven't stopped thinking about ice cream."

Chapter 36
Brielle Jeffries

"JACKIE, WHAT ARE YOU DOING?" THE REDHEAD BEHIND *her hissed as she carefully crept up the stairs. "We have to go."*

She wasn't wrong. The neighbours would have heard the gunshots. Brielle wasn't finished yet.

"Then go," she said. Brielle had her own business to attend to. She didn't look back as she topped the stairs and made for Herold's room.

The door was wide open and she carefully stepped in, listening to the machine breathe for him. She couldn't believe the man she'd feared for years had been reduced to this. He had no life; he was only dying.

She walked to his bedside and his eyes opened. For a moment, he seemed confused. His expression changed when he recognized her, his eyebrows lifted and eyes widened.

Bile swirled around inside Brielle as she grabbed a pillow from the floor. She thought for a long time about what she would do if she ever came face to face with Sam again. Never had she expected it would be like this, where she now held all the power. She wanted nothing more than to take it from him.

In one fluid motion, she ripped the breathing mask from his face. Sam gasped for breath. Brielle didn't give him a chance, pressing the pillow into his face and using all her might to push down.

He tried to struggle, but his movements were weak. Brielle held steady, as tears began to roll down her cheeks. She let go of all her anger and fear. Everything he had caused all those years ago was ending here.

Soon his movements stopped and there was no life left in his aged body.

"Jackie?"

Brielle jumped back at the voice. The redheaded woman stood in the doorway, concern written on her face.

Brielle dropped the pillow. "We have to go."

BRIELLE'S HEART thudded against her chest as she tried to clean the red stains from her hands and clothes. Where the blood had come from, Brielle wasn't sure, but a sinking feeling in her stomach told her whatever happened was her fault.

"C'mon," she muttered, scrubbing at her palms so hard they started to ache. She gave up on her clothes. They were ruined. Worse, her phone was nowhere to be found. Had she lost it at the scene of whatever crime she committed? Had Sam died?

Drying her hands on a hanging towel, she exited the bathroom and returned to the room she'd come from. Jackie's room. Brielle wasn't sure how she got back here, or where her friend was; she was only glad to wake up in a somewhat known place looking how she did.

She stripped herself of the soiled clothing and got something from Jackie's closet. It wasn't Brielle's taste; still she'd always fit into Jackie's clothes fine when they were younger. Jackie's closet was nearly empty, like she'd cleaned out and left only what she didn't care about. In fact, her entire room was barren. Brielle grabbed a tattered pair of jeans and a sweater.

As she dressed, Brielle noticed something on Jackie's desk. There was a single piece of paper spotted with blood. On closer investigation, Brielle recognized the writing as her own. It was an address for a place on the other side of the city. Written beneath the words were "Pack and leave" again, in her handwriting.

She grabbed the piece of paper and shoved it into her jeans pocket. She didn't remember writing it, but she trusted her own writing and with no other options, it was where she was going to go.

She gathered the soiled clothing and packed it into a plastic bag, then quickly assessed the room to make sure nothing more belonged to her before leaving. She had only a small bag with a leather jacket and a mickey of vodka. No wallet, no ID, no phone. Only enough to get drunk and a pile of cash to get her out of the city.

In the main room, Brielle stopped to use a desktop computer in the corner. Luckily, the machine wasn't password protected, and she pulled up the internet. Quickly typing the address in, she mapped the location from the note to a motel outside of the city, almost half an hour away from where she was. Would she know what to do once she was there?

She pulled the paper from her pocket and noticed the

number 106 written in the corner, likely to indicate a room number. Whatever was at this motel and in this room would hopefully help. Brielle wiped the search history, then ran her sleeve over the keyboard, wiping away the evidence she'd used it. Then she grabbed the dirty clothing bag and left the apartment, throwing the clothing down the garbage shoot. It would hopefully be taken away with the rest of the trash before the cops had a chance to find it.

She headed to the elevator and out to the street. The kindly concierge waved to her as she left. Brielle didn't make eye contact with him as she hurried out the door and waved down a cab.

She gave the driver the address and he tutted.

"Gonna take a while," he said. "Bad accident on the Gardiner."

"That's fine," Brielle said. "I can afford a few minutes. Take a detour if you need to."

"I'll do my best," he said as he pulled the car into the street.

Brielle leaned back against the seat and watched the outside world pass by. Everyone moved about their everyday lives as if nothing had changed. And for a moment, Brielle couldn't help but envy them. Her life had never been normal or easy, and now it looked like it was about to change more than it ever had before.

⁓

THE CAB PULLED up to the dingy motel, and Brielle found the room she'd recorded. She tried the door. It was locked, and when she knocked no one answered. Unsure what else to do, she went to the front desk. An older woman with rounded glasses sat on a low chair with her nose in a romance novel. Brielle stood there for nearly two minutes before the woman looked her way.

"Booked up," the woman said, then turned back at her book.

"I have a room," Brielle said. "One-oh-six, but I can't find my key."

The woman regarded her for a moment. "You're the girl they said would come." She reached under the desk and pulled out a key. "There you go, love." She looked back at her book.

Brielle took the key but couldn't keep silent. "Who are they?"

"Your friends, of course," she said, then shook her head. "That handsome fellow with the feisty woman. They said you'd be coming."

"Thanks," Brielle said, moving from the front desk and back toward the row of motel rooms. Outside room 106, she slid the key into the lock and it opened with a simple click. She slowly pushed the door open, unsure what she would find inside. It was empty.

Brielle entered the motel room and closed the door behind her. On the bed she found a note, and beside it a bag.

Glad you made it. We were worried about you. Use what's in the bag. We'll try to be back soon.

It wasn't signed or addressed. It was just four short sentences and beside it was a plastic bag. Brielle opened it to find a bottle of hair dye and a box of coloured contacts. Someone wanted her to disguise herself. Someone wanted her to escape. Whatever crime she committed had to have been awful for someone to react this way. However, she suspected as much from the blood and strange memories.

Looking at the brown hair dye, Brielle considered her options. Dye her hair and take off, risking those people coming back in the process, or just run. Brielle didn't know where she would run.

The dread built up inside her as her eyes darted around the hotel room. She should leave, trust what she knew instead of waiting for the unknown. Brielle took the bag of supplies and turned for the door. As she reached for the handle, she heard voices outside and the lock turned. Whoever was staying here had come back.

Chapter 37
Detective Ryan Boone

BACK AT THE STATION, RYAN SAT AT THE ROUND TABLE with four other men, three officers in blue uniform and his partner, Archer. Across from him, Higgins tapped the table nervously, his usual habit; a bead of sweat escaped his wet, dark hair and ran down his chubby, red cheek. Ryan looked away. Winters stared at him with dark, beady eyes. The giant of a man had never liked Ryan, and Ryan had never cared for him, finding the hulking man to be moronic and power-hungry. He ran a huge hand over his buzzed hair, wiping away his own sweat.

The room was so damn hot. They'd been waiting on Singh for nearly an hour.

"How long do we have to wait?" Quinn groaned. He was the youngest of the group and tugged aimlessly at his wavy blonde hair.

Archer sat closest to Ryan but seemed the furthest away. The Black man leaned back in his chair, arms crossed over chest, staring at the board in front of them. His dark eyes gazed at the pictures, unblinking.

Ryan had looked at them too, seeing nothing more than suspects. Archer seemed to see more, as if he saw through the photos. Ryan tore his gaze away from his partner and glanced back at the board.

Three women stared back at him, all young and attractive. Ryan saw the motive but didn't get the connection. He wasn't the only one. Since the burglary, things hadn't added up.

Before he could consider it further, the door to the conference room swung open and Singh entered, closing it behind him. The superintendent walked to the board and looked at the pictures for a moment before turning to his men.

"An heiress, a middle-class working woman, and an abused housewife. Three different women from three different worlds. How do they connect?" He stared at the photos with his piercing blue eyes. His uniform was clean and pressed. Even in this heat he wore his hat, his graying hair visible beneath.

No one answered him. None of them could.

"Angry women's club?" Ryan suggested. "Or maybe the classifieds. Abducted heiress seeks angry woman to help murder terrible men."

Singh ignored him and tabbed the board behind him, picture by picture. "Brielle Jeffries, the pretty blonde, Lexi Chase, the spunky redhead, and Patsy Morrison, the tired brunette."

"No connection we can find, yet all guilty." Singh pulled out a chair and collapsed in it with an exhausted sigh. "Winters, Higgins? Anything?"

Higgins nervously wiped his brow with a handkerchief

he pulled from his pocket. Winters only shrugged. The super stared directly at Ryan.

"Boone?"

"Perhaps we have it wrong," Ryan said.

Singh leaned forward in his chair, glaring at Ryan. "Four murders, Boone, and a burglary. These three women are somehow involved in these crimes. How can you suggest otherwise?"

"Once again, you misunderstand me, sir. I'm not suggesting they didn't do it. It's the connection doesn't make any sense; I think we're missing something."

"Archer?" Singh barked.

The larger man leaned forward in his chair. "Perhaps Detective Boone isn't wrong." He spoke softly; his voice was smooth and had a tone of authority. The other officers instinctively leaned forward in their seats.

Singh cocked his head to the side. "You think so?"

"You say they aren't connected, but perhaps we are looking for the wrong connections," Archers said. "Maybe it isn't them we need to connect."

Singh's brows scrunched together in deep thought. "You think there's someone else."

Archer leaned back in his seat. "I'm saying we could be looking at the wrong thing."

Singh turned in his chair gazing back at the board of pictures. The other officers looked as well. Ryan continued to stare at Archer. The man's dark eyes stared back, unreadable.

Ryan turned away when Singh pulled the three photos from it and laid them on the table in front of them.

"There is something going on with these three women,"

he said. "I need you three to assist Boone and Archer with whatever they need to figure out what, and fast. Before another body turns up."

Singh turned and left the conference room.

Winters stood, pushing back his chair and stretching his arms. "Guess that's it for me," he said, grabbing his jacket off the back of the chair.

"Why am I not surprised?" Ryan quipped. "No, by all means, please head out. I'm sure your assistance isn't necessary."

Winters gave him a hard stare before turning and leaving the room.

"Oooph." Ryan nudged Archer. "Think I struck a nerve? I mean, he was useless on our last case."

"Detectives?" Higgins asked.

Ryan waved Higgins and Quinn off. "We'll speak in the morning. Go get some rest."

"You know where to find me." Quinn stood and Higgins followed, leaving Ryan and Archer alone.

Then Ryan looked at Archer. "You don't think they did it?"

Archer shook his head. "No, they did it. The evidence is clear. I just don't think it's as simple as plain murder."

Ryan stared at the pictures. Blue, grey and green eyes stared back at him. Could these three women really be capable of what they were accused?

THE ROOM WAS plain and void of distraction. Even her desk was spotless, with nothing but a small lamp and pen on top of it. The white walls were disrupted by a small square window with dark grey curtains and a single painting. A room for an imperfect mind—as Dr. Konch described it. Ryan had arranged a meeting with the doctor as soon as she returned, desperate to learn more about Patsy. He'd arrived alone with a warrant for Patsy's files.

The woman's greying hair was pulled so tight it stretched her aging skin. Her plain fingernails tapped against the arm of her grey bergère chair, yet she wore the hint of a smile.

"How can I help you, detective?" she asked after inviting him to sit. Her hand lifted to her chin.

"I'm sure you've heard the one about the therapist and the skier?" Ryan joked as he sat down opposite her.

Miranda frowned and looked to the painting on the wall. It featured a vast mountain range. "Uh, no, Detective, I can't say I have."

"Oh, just that their life had been going downhill." Ryan grinned.

Miranda only continued to stare at him with a perplexed expression.

"Sorry." Ryan cleared his throat, produced the bag with the pill bottle and passed it to the doctor. "We'd like to know more about your patient, Patsy Morrison."

"Mrs. Morrison?"

The surprise in her tone made Ryan hesitate for a moment.

"We found this medication at the scene of a homicide."

"Oh god," Miranda said, clutching the bag tighter. "Is Patsy okay?"

"We believe so," Ryan said. "She is a suspect in a murder investigation."

Miranda's jaw dropped. "It's not possible. She was so quiet, frightened."

Ryan took out a pen. "What were you treating Patsy for?"

"I am her doctor." It was a plea for confidentiality.

"She may be a murderer. I have a warrant," Ryan said. "Was she very sick? Is that what the medication was for?"

Miranda looked away for a moment and pursed her lips. When she looked back, the slight smile she wore upon his arrival had vanished.

"Patsy was horribly abused for a very long time," Miranda said. "First by her father, then by her husband. She needed support. I did what I could to provide it for her."

"And the drugs?"

"They are calming." She glanced down at the bag in her hands. "They allow my patients to see the truth in their fear, to release the burden of stress and to invite a more positive way of thinking. This medication helps people."

"Did it help Patsy?" Ryan asked.

"I believe it did."

"Why didn't you encourage her to seek help for her situation?"

"I did!" Miranda protested. "Nearly every session; it's why she stopped coming to me."

"Doctor, this prescription was filled only two weeks ago; when was the last time you saw Patsy?"

"She stopped coming to sessions nearly six months ago," Miranda explained. "She only came back for a refill on her meds."

"Did you request a meeting?"

"Of course," Miranda said. "Though she constantly refused. I thought the medication was the least I could do."

Ryan paused his notes and looked at her. "I'd like to see her files."

"Very well." Miranda stood and went to her desk. She pulled open the top drawer which revealed a comm system and paged the front desk, requesting Patsy's files.

Then she returned to her seat and waved to the door. "My assistant will have those files for you at the front."

"Thank you," Ryan said as he stood to leave. "Though, I must ask ... you seemed surprised when I inquired about Patsy, as if you expected me to ask something else."

Miranda frowned. "Honestly, Detective, I thought you came here to talk to me about Brielle Jeffries."

"What do you know about Ms. Jeffries?"

Miranda stood to meet him. "I assumed you'd discovered she was one of my patients. She stayed at my facility for some time."

Ryan hesitated. "Did Patsy spend time at your facility as well?"

"For two months, no more," Miranda said. "It is all recorded in her files."

"Did she know Brielle Jeffries?" Ryan asked. Perhaps Patsy was the reason Lexi was involved.

"From high school," Miranda said. "Though I didn't realize it was the same woman I had treated. I never learned her last name from Brielle."

Ryan glanced at the floor before asking the last thing on his mind. "Did you ever treat a woman named Lexi Chase?"

"The name isn't familiar to me, detective," Miranda said. "Sorry."

Ryan stood. "Thank you. I'll be back for Brielle Jeffries' files."

"Of course, detective." Miranda waved him out and returned to her seat.

In the lobby, Ryan fetched the files about Patsy and her treatment off the front desk and retreated to his car. At least they'd found one connection.

Chapter 38
Melanie Parker

MEL STARED OUT THE WINDOW AS THEY RACED DOWN the empty freeway. The trees whipped by, blurring together in a mix of greens and browns. In front of them, the open road stretched for miles. As they drove toward the red and orange sky, the sun dipped below the horizon.

Mel sat in the front seat of Blaine's black sedan. Candy and Jackie were in the back while Blaine drove. The four of them hadn't spoken since they left the motel.

Jackie's once blonde hair was now dark brown, not unlike how Mel's was before today, and Candy's red locks were now black. Mel glanced back at the girls but neither met her gaze, only staring out the windows and watching the world go by.

"You okay?" Mel asked Jackie.

Jackie looked to Mel with a tired gaze. "I've never shot anyone before."

"Yeah," Mel said. "I get it."

"Do you?" Jackie cocked her head to the side.

"I shoved a knife into a guy's neck," Mel said. "I get it."

Jackie dropped her gaze and Mel looked away from her

and back to the passing world. The sun had nearly disappeared and the bluish night was taking over. She stiffened when she heard sirens in the distance, and Blaine rested a hand on her thigh, giving it a light squeeze.

"It's okay," he said.

She looked at him with narrowed eyes, brushing her maroon hair from her sight line. "You don't know that."

"Trust me, okay?" His voice hardened.

"Where are you taking us?" Mel asked. Blaine had forced her into the car once he arrived with Candy. He didn't say where they were going, didn't give any clues.

Blaine's hands tightened on the steering wheel. He had been getting irritated quickly with Mel since they left the motel. "I trusted you; can't you trust me?"

Mel glared at him with her arms crossed over her chest. She didn't think she could trust anyone at this point.

He sighed. "The farm."

The conversation ended there, and Mel turned back to looking out the window. Blaine had inherited a farm on the outside of the city when his father had died the previous year. Mel had only ever been out to the overgrown property once. Blaine didn't like to spend time at the farm he grew up on; he said it brought back bad memories. He never expanded on what those memories were.

Now it seemed they didn't have a choice. It was their best option to get out of town—as of this moment, Blaine wasn't connected to them. The cops wouldn't know to look there. They'd be safe for a week, at least.

Jackie leaned closer to Mel's chair and tapped her shoulder. "Are you going to tell us the plan?"

"It doesn't matter." Mel kept her gaze on the road. She'd

been short with Jackie since they found her, and Mel knew it wasn't fair. It wasn't Jackie's fault they were here. Mel had made rash decisions too. She was tired of being questioned. She'd gotten them this far. Couldn't the girls just trust her?

"Why not?" Candy asked. Her tone was stiff.

Mel turned her cold gaze on Candy. "Because it's none of your fucking business."

"Are you kidding me?" Candy's hands clenched into tight fists. Her grey eyes darted between Jackie and Mel. "I watched both of you commit murder and you tell me it's none of my business? It became my business the second you took me with you. Both of you."

"You weren't supposed to come inside," Mel barked. "You did this to yourself."

"Fuck you," Candy hissed. "I'm supposed to sit in the car while some guy chases you around the house? If I hadn't come in, you'd be dead. You brought me into this, and you know it."

Mel's jaw dropped at this outburst from the normally timid young woman. She turned away from Candy and said nothing. It would have been fine if Candy had done as she was supposed to. Fraser wouldn't have killed Mel, right?

Blaine cast Mel a sideways glance. He looked unimpressed, keeping his lips clamped and saying nothing. Behind her, Candy and Jackie engaged in quiet conversation.

"What now?" Candy asked.

"Nothing's different," Jackie said. "We're in this together, and we'll escape together."

"And if we don't?"

Mel had grown tired of her whining. "Then you know nothing about this, and we'll cover for you." She didn't look at them when she said it. Neither responded to her, and feeling uncomfortable, she glanced over her shoulder at Candy and added, "Blaine will make sure you don't go down with us." Her gaze shifted to Jackie. "We can handle it."

Jackie nodded her agreement, though her unsure expression said otherwise.

Mel turned back to the front. "How much farther?"

"We're close," Blaine said.

"Good."

"You do realize he's an accomplice too," Candy said, not done with their conversation.

"We'll be gone before *they* realize it," Mel told her. "I have a plan. Trust me." She didn't, really. She was relying on Blaine and her disguise. If the police figured out the truth and caught up with them before they were able to get far enough away, she wasn't sure what she'd do.

Chapter 39
Detective Ryan Boone

"I REALLY DON'T KNOW HOW I CAN BE OF HELP, Detective," Jamila Cham said, glancing between Archer and Ryan. "I haven't seen or heard from Patsy in weeks. She no longer works with the committee."

Ryan and Archer stood outside the large home, several blocks from where Patsy and her late husband lived. Jamila Cham was the head of the neighbourhood committee Patsy used to work closely with.

"She stopped working, yet still attended your events?" Ryan asked, remembering the event where he ran into Patsy. "Didn't you see her then?"

"Yes," Jamila said. "Her husband liked to get out in public as often as he could. I suppose I did see her at the events; we barely spoke, though."

"When did she stop showing up to committee meetings?"

Jamila frowned for a moment, her dark eyebrows knitting together, and she ran a hand over her black ponytail, twirling the end around a finger.

"Maybe about half a year ago?" Jamila said. "She started showing up looking rough—bruised, scratched, cut up. She tried to cover it, but the makeup never did what she wanted. To be honest, it was distracting to the other members. We were glad when she stopped coming. Though now I feel guilty myself. Maybe I should have said something."

"Maybe you should have," Archer retorted.

Jamila didn't miss a beat and ignored Archer's comment. "I'm sorry I can't tell you more. She was one of the youngest on the team and didn't connect much with the other women."

Ryan glanced behind him as a red SUV pulled up to the house.

Jamila groaned. "Sorry, Detectives, my daughter is here. I can't say it's expected."

The girl who hopped out of the front seat looked almost identical to her mother. She had long, sleek raven hair, smooth tawny skin and a curvy build. Dressed in a short miniskirt and white crop top, she wandered up the front walk and regarded the detectives with a cool look.

"What's going on, Mom?" she asked, brushing by Ryan and entering the house. She peeked around them at the waiting squad car and Ryan wished they had taken Archer's car instead of the assigned vehicle Singh gave them. "Why are the cops here?"

"We're just here to find out about a woman your mother used to work with, Patsy Morrison," Ryan said, gazing at the girl. "Would you know anything about it?"

"The beaten housewife who murdered her husband?" she said. "Yeah, the whole city has heard."

"Did you know her?" Archer asked.

"Didn't she have a severe mental disorder?" The girl looked at her mother.

Jamila gasped. "Gabi, that is not polite."

"What? I've heard you say it like a hundred times," Gabi said.

"Did you know her well?" Ryan asked Gabi.

She shook her head. "Never met her. I only know what I have heard from bored, gossiping housewives."

Jamila took her wrist and pulled her further into the house. "My daughter chooses not to be a part of the community activities, despite my attempts to make her," Jamila explained, then she turned back to her daughter. "I specifically told you not to come by today. I'm having company this afternoon. You can't be here when the ladies arrive."

Gabi pursed her lips and shot another cool glance at the men. "I'm just grabbing a few things."

Jamila didn't release her daughter's wrist. "Did you find a job? A place to live? You haven't called in days and the one time I ask you not to interrupt is when you decide to come. What have I done to deserve a daughter like you?"

Gabi's eyes narrowed at her mother, and she pulled her arm out of her grasp. "I'm fine. I've been fine since you kicked me out months ago. Now I have somewhere to go, but it doesn't mean you deserve to know." She said nothing else to her mother or the detectives before turning and storming up the staircase leading from the front hall.

Jamila sighed. "I'm sorry, Detectives. I haven't spoken to my daughter in several days. I should probably make sure she's okay. Is there anything else?"

"What about this mental disorder?" Ryan asked. It was

not an idea they'd ruled out since the discovery of the pills. Dr. Miranda Konch had implied as much in her notes.

Jamila shook her head. "I'm sorry for my daughter, Detective. Petty gossip, I'm afraid. An excuse to explain Patsy's departure. Sorry, I can't be of any more help."

Ryan flipped his notepad shut and held his hand out to her. "I'll call if I need anything else.

Jamila grasped his hand. "Good luck. I can't say this is something I expected to happen in our quiet neighbourhood."

Archer followed Ryan back to the car silently. Ryan climbed into the front seat as Archer took the passenger side. His dark eyebrows were knit together, and his eyes stared straight ahead.

"What's wrong?" Ryan asked as he pulled the car out of the gated neighbourhood. "You look pissed."

"I am," Archer said, folding his arms over his chest and staring at the road.

"Why?"

"You heard her," Archer rolled down the window and spit. "It's sick. They see a woman obviously in need of help, obviously being abused, and rather than do anything about it, they complain it's a simple distraction to the other women? What the hell."

Ryan frowned. "I know, but look where we just came from. It's clear their image is everything." Besides, Ryan had offered her help too, and Patsy refused. Who knew how many others had done the same?

"And Patsy wrecked that image," Archer said. He rolled up the window. "It makes me sick this is how they treat someone in need. They'd rather she suffer in silence and hide away then seek help." Then his expression softened, and he sighed. "I feel for this woman. She was stuck and had no one to turn to. Who knows how long he hurt her, who knows how much she suffered."

"I know," Ryan said. "We're going to help."

"No, we're going to find her guilty of murder and lock her away," Archer said, his tone stiffening again.

"You know that's not what I want." Ryan had been exploring the option of a psychiatric hospital. For the criminally insane.

"It's the truth."

Ryan didn't say anything, just stared at the road in front of him. He didn't disagree with Archer. He understood his partner's frustration. Patsy had been living under duress for what seemed like years. He wished there had been a way to help her.

"It was probably self-defence," Ryan said as they pulled into the station. "We'll find a way to prove it."

"I hate cases like this." Archer shook his head. "I feel we're going after the innocent party, even though they committed murder."

Ryan turned off the car and followed his partner up to the station. He didn't answer because he wasn't sure what to say. It did feel that way.

"These arrived for you," Jade said when Ryan passed by her desk. She held out a large envelope.

Ryan took it from her. "Thanks." He retreated into his office.

Sitting at his desk, he set his things aside and dropped the envelope in front of him. He tore it open to reveal several file folders, each with a white label at the top read *Brielle Jeffries*, accompanied by a date. The oldest folder was weathered like it had been stored for ages.

After some coaxing, Miranda had revealed some of Brielle's background and after hearing more about her childhood abduction, he knew he had to see the facts for himself.

He flipped it open and read over the report. At the age of six, Brielle disappeared from a family function. No one noticed until the close of the evening. There was a city-wide search for her almost immediately, commissioned by her grandfather. When they didn't find her right away, they alerted the entire country to be on the lookout for the young heiress.

There was never a ransom demand, never any real reason why she was taken. Nearly two weeks after her disappearance, a pair of hikers came across her in the woods sleeping at the base of a large tree. She was disoriented and frightened. She wouldn't speak.

He flipped to the next page. There were faded pictures of a child's hands and other parts of her body, showing defensive wounds. The doctors examined and confirmed she'd been sexually assaulted. Brielle couldn't say who it was. It was nearly a year later before Brielle finally spoke again.

The door to Ryan's office creaked open while he was reviewing her cut-up and bloody knuckles. "What are you looking at?"

Ryan glanced up to see Quinn standing in the doorway. "Brielle's file from her childhood."

Quinn leaned against the doorframe. "I'd heard something about that. You think it's connected?"

"I have no idea," Ryan said. He glanced over another page. Brielle finally gave a statement over a year later. She called her attacker by name, the same name she used only a week ago. Sam. "It seems like she believed they were connected."

"Well, it doesn't sound like her mind was all there," Quinn said.

Ryan had stopped listening. He flipped another page and found something they could actually use. He looked up at Quinn. "Do we still have access to Herold Drake's DNA?"

Quinn frowned. "Yeah, why?"

"Come take a look at this," Ryan said, waving Quinn over.

Quinn entered the office and glanced at the page. "It's just the report from forensics. What are you thinking?"

"They still have this information on file," Ryan said, handing the report to Quinn. "Get this and a sample of Herold Drake's DNA for testing. I want to see if we have a match."

"You don't think Brielle was lying?"

"I think she was a scared girl who constantly relived a terrifying past," Ryan said. "At least this will confirm if she was right, or simply projecting the situation onto the Drake family."

"What about the son?" Quinn said. "Where does he come in?"

"Maybe it was just part of the plan. It was clear Herold was not a healthy man capable of kidnapping a grown woman." Ryan frowned.

"What's wrong?"

"The only thing that doesn't add up is the ransom call," Ryan said. "There was no demand for money when she was abducted the first time. I don't know what to think of it."

Quinn held up the report. "This is the first step. I'll get it down to the lab as soon as possible."

"Thanks," Ryan said and Quinn turned, leaving him in his office. Ryan looked back down at this file.

"Quinn was out of here fast."

Ryan glanced up again, and this time, Archer stood in his doorway. His partner entered and shut the door behind him.

"What's going on?" Archer took the chair across from him. "What are you looking at?"

"Brielle's abduction."

"I thought it was a hoax."

Ryan shook his head. "I'm not looking at the recent one."

Archer raised a thick eyebrow. "Have you spoken to her parents?"

Ryan shrugged. "Briefly. They didn't want to say much, though you would think they would, since their only daughter is being accused of a triple homicide. I got the files from Dr. Konch today."

Archer leaned back in his chair. "Ah, yes, the doctor. I still can't believe Patsy and Brielle shared the same doctor. Good catch on the connection."

"Thanks." Ryan reached into his briefcase and handed over the notes he had made on the last call with Dr. Miranda Konch.

"She deemed Brielle healthy?" Archer asked as he read over Ryan's notes.

"Yeah, I guess her parents arranged another meeting

right before Brielle disappeared." Ryan hesitated. "Right before she committed the crime, after the supposed abduction."

"Who's Jackie?" Archer asked.

Ryan's lips twitched. "Keep reading."

Archer's eyes continued to scan the page. He stopped when he reached the bottom. "So she was taking Solydexran."

"Yeah, one of ten drugs she was prescribed over the years," Ryan said.

"And with the doctor and their past with high school ..."

"Maybe it's all finally coming together."

"What about Chase? How does she fit into their world?"

"Other than her apparent mutual hate for the Drake family?" Ryan flipped the folder shut. "I can't be sure. It's still a mystery."

Archer rubbed his tired eyes. "Now what?"

"Quinn is looking into the connection Herold Drake has with Brielle's previous abduction," Ryan said. "I'm hoping that will answer some questions."

"Until then?"

Ryan reached up and scratched his chin. "I think we need to do a very thorough search of Herold Drake's property."

"He owns half the woods behind his backyard," Archer said. "It might take a while."

"Then we should get on it."

Ryan and Archer stood, leaving Ryan's office and his files on his desk.

Chapter 40
Melanie Parker

THE SUN WAS DOWN BY THE TIME BLAINE PULLED INTO the long farm driveway. The tall farmhouse loomed before them, cast in shadow by the bright, full moon behind it. The windows were dark and covered, the front walkway overgrown. The first and only time Mel had been to this property with Blaine was nearly seven months ago, shortly after he inherited it. She hated the country because it was bad for work. Besides, the bit of Blaine's history with his father she did know was enough to make her understand his disinterest in this place. She didn't like making him relive it. Still, the farmhouse didn't seem like such a bad place to be when everything was considered.

Blaine shifted the sedan into park and turned to face Mel. His dark eyes were laced with concern in an expression she was getting tired of seeing. She turned away from him, looking at the girls.

"Grab your bags, and I'll show you your rooms," Mel said, reaching for the door handle. "We don't want to stay here too long. We probably have a week to sort things out."

Pushing the door open sent the cool night air whipping into her face and blowing her hair like wild. The back doors opened, and Candy and Jackie got out on their respective sides. Neither had looked at Mel or spoken to her since she snapped at them.

Mel regretted it and grabbed Jackie's hand when she passed by. Jackie pulled it from her grasp almost immediately.

"Don't." Jackie's eyes blazed and Mel was taken aback.

Mel shifted her gaze to Candy. Her friends seemed to only have glares for her, while Blaine only had pity and concern. There wouldn't be any comfort from them tonight.

"I'll show you the guest rooms." Mel turned and followed Blaine up the front steps.

He slid the small silver key into the aged lock. It turned easily, and Mel heard a soft click. She didn't wait for Blaine to move and pushed past him into the darkened front hall. Reaching for the light, her hand met Blaine's, who made the same move. Mel quickly pulled away and headed for the staircase.

"Girls." Mel started up the stairs expecting Jackie and Candy to follow. When neither did, she shot them both a cold gaze. "Fine. Blaine can show you where to stay. I'm not sitting around so you can glare at me. This isn't my fault."

"You could be less of a bitch about it," Candy said, dropping her bags at her feet.

Mel stared at her, mouth agape. "Excuse me?"

"The way you're treating us is bullshit," Candy snapped.

"Then fucking leave!" Mel yelled at her, descending the stairs she climbed and now standing directly in front of Candy. Blaine stepped closer to them.

"You're serious, aren't you?" Candy said.

Mel didn't back down. "The last thing I need is to listen to your whining."

"You really think me leaving would be a good idea?" Candy looked between the women with wide eyes. "And when they catch me, who the fuck do you think I'm going to rat on?"

Mel grabbed her arm, but Candy pulled it from her grasp almost immediately.

"No," Candy said, putting distance between her and Mel. "You don't get to threaten me. I've put up with your shit and attitude since day one. Enough! I want answers. What is going on with you two?"

Blaine took Candy's arm and steered her toward the stairs.

"It's been a long day, an even longer week," he said. "Now isn't the time to be fighting about this. We'll figure it out in the morning."

Candy fought against him for a moment, then looked at him with tired eyes and let him lead her up the stairs. "I am pretty tired."

"Jackie," Mel said, staring at her friend.

Jackie shook her head. "Blaine's right. It's been a long day. Let's talk in the morning; right now, I just can't." She turned and followed Blaine and Candy up the stairs.

Mel watched her disappear before following her steps and turning for the primary bedroom.

She dropped her bags on the floor and headed into the bathroom to get ready for bed. When she emerged, Blaine was sitting on the large bed in a pair of pyjama bottoms. His chiselled chest faced her, and she smiled at the nice view.

"Are you still mad at me?" Mel asked, leaning against the door frame and crossing her arms.

Blaine's eyes danced down Mel's body. She wore only an oversized T-shirt. Her toned legs were bare and Blaine's eyes lingered there.

Mel smirked. "I guess you don't hate the new look too much."

Blaine looked away. "I didn't say I wasn't angry."

"Your cock isn't, no matter how you try to deny it." She stepped toward him but stopped when he glared at her.

"You don't need to be so crude."

She crawled across the bed toward him. "You like it."

Her hands snaked around his neck and she planted a kiss on his lips. He reached around, unhooked her hands and moved away from her.

"And you like to tell me how I feel." Blaine stood.

"What the fuck?" Mel said. He had been sulking since they left the motel.

"Yes. I'm still mad," Blaine said. "You act like you've done nothing wrong. You act like a total monster to the people who love you most. Honestly, it's like you're the innocent one and your friends caused all this."

Mel's eyes widened. "Jackie did it too!"

Blaine turned to her, eyes wide and wild. "Where do you think Jackie learned everything? Where were you when Jackie needed you? Right, you were hiding because you killed a guy."

"He would have killed me!"

"He's been abusing you for years," Blaine said. "What changed now?"

Mel frowned. "What are you talking about?" Mel

crawled off the bed and stormed toward Blaine. "He fucked with the wrong person."

"Maybe I did, too," Blaine said it so softly Mel wasn't certain she heard him right.

"What?"

"You heard me. I made a mistake."

Mel swallowed the lump in her throat and stepped back. "With me?"

Blaine looked away.

"You don't love me anymore?" She felt for the bed behind her and lowered herself to it. Blaine had been her support since the beginning of all this. Did she ruin their relationship? She'd held him at arm's length for as long as she'd known him. She never thought he'd actually regret it. Didn't he love her?

His expression softened, and he stepped closer to her, taking her face in his hands and brushing his lips against hers.

"Of course I love you. I only help you because I love you. I'm angry because I love you."

"Then what was the mistake?"

Blaine shook his head. "I'm going to check on the girls. I'll tell you in the morning."

He turned and left the room before she could say anything else and Mel was left wondering what his big regret was.

Chapter 41
Detective Ryan Boone

RYAN AND ARCHER STOOD ABOVE THE STAIRS THAT WENT deep into the ground. The door in the ground had been discovered only moments before by one of the officers and a police dog. The stairs descended into darkness and the smell of death wafted toward them when they opened it.

"I guess it's true what they say: people sure like to keep their secrets buried." Ryan flicked on a flashlight and descended the stairs. He wore plastic gloves and held his sleeve to his nose. It reeked down here. Archer followed behind him with another light.

The underground area featured a long hallway with a low ceiling. Ryan located a switch and hit it. The lights on the ceiling flickered on one by one, casting the hallway in a white light. Ryan squinted until his eyes were used to the sudden change. He flicked off his flashlight and proceeded down the hallway slowly. There were two rooms Ryan could see off the hall. He waved Archer forward toward the furthest room.

Ryan approached the first room with his gun drawn. He

kicked open the door and entered. His flashlight scanned the room, and he found no one inside. There was something on the far wall. He located a switch and when the light flickered on, he was taken aback. The entire wall was a mural of Brielle Jeffries and the Jeffries family. A perfect collage following her every step through life. It was surreal. Brielle had told the truth.

"Boone, get in here!" Archer called from the other room. Ryan turned and left the pictures behind, knowing they'd have to go through each one to see if they could find any evidence.

Ryan headed to the second room and located the source of the awful stench. There in the center of a small bedroom lay a dead body, recently deceased.

"Wonderful," Ryan said sarcastically.

Archer only nodded, sleeve covering his nose and mouth.

"Get out of here." Ryan waved to the exit. "We'll need the coroner."

Archer darted from the room without answering.

Ryan surveyed the scene quickly. It was a small bedroom, with a dresser table and large mirror. The drawers were all filled with clothing to fit a young woman. There was makeup and other toiletries, and even a tiny bathroom through a door that looked to be part of the wall.

From the look of the body in the center of the room, it had been there for over three days. A woman, possibly in her sixties. There were grotesque blisters coating her bloated skin, and a yellow fluid leaked to the stone floor below. Ryan couldn't be sure how this body was related to his mystery. He hoped the coroner would provide him with some answers.

He turned and left the room, heading for the entrance

and desperate for a breath of fresh air. Outside, Archer stood near the entrance with Singh and Quinn.

Archer wore a steady grimace and looked as though he might be ill. Ryan thought after so many years on the force his partner would have gotten used to dead bodies.

"Deep breaths, buddy." Ryan patted his partner's shoulder.

"This doesn't look good." Singh took off his hat and wiped at his damp brow.

"There is a room down there filled with photos of Brielle Jeffries," Ryan said. "I want those photographed, then collected and brought back to the station. We need to take a look at them."

Singh waved an officer forward. "We'll get them sent to you as soon as possible."

"Did you contact the coroner?" Ryan looked to Archer.

"They're on their way," Quinn confirmed.

Ryan directed his partner away from the bunker in the ground and toward the deck where he pushed him to a sitting position.

"Stay here," Ryan said. "Clear your head. You look like you could vomit."

"I'm fine."

"Wait until the body is gone," Ryan said, walking back toward the others. "Then you really will be fine."

It was later that day, and they were back at the station. Archer frowned, staring at the report. "The nurse?"

"So it seems," Ryan said, taking the report from his partner. The coroner had been quick to process. According to dental records, it was a woman named Margaret Grindle. The story checked out when they confirmed she was working in the Drake household. A gunshot to the head had killed her. The bullet was lodged in her skull. It was the same model of gun used to kill both Brennan Drake and the bodyguard.

Archer stood and paced across the small boardroom. "Are we supposed to believe Brielle shot this woman?"

"It's just a theory," Ryan said. "If she already killed three people, it's possible."

"In her statement, she said a woman rescued her from the bunker." Archer shook his head. "It doesn't make sense she would go back and kill her. There isn't a motive for this one."

"No good deed goes unpunished. Or what's the staying?" Ryan leaned back in his chair. "Maybe it's a cover? Something to throw us off the case?"

Archer dropped another file in front of him. "I doubt it. This sounds more like a scared girl than anything else. We've got a motive for the Drake deaths, not for Ms. Grindle, and the bullets match."

Ryan crossed his arms. "And the gun?"

"Still missing. Probably with Brielle. Any clue who it's registered to?"

Ryan shook his head. "Herold Drake had .357 Smith & Wesson Classic registered to him. We can't find it anywhere."

"Could someone have shot Ms. Grindle before Brielle's arrival?"

Ryan hesitated. "Good point."

"What about these pictures?" Archer asked. He took one of the photos from the file and tossed it on the table in front of them. "Or this one." Another one followed the first.

The pictures both featured Brielle Jeffries with the other two suspects. The first was her poolside with Patsy Morrison, but Patsy didn't look like the beaten, tired woman she was. She looked strong, confident, and angry.

The other picture was Brielle with Lexi Chase seated on a patio with what looked like several lines of cocaine on the table in front of them. There were two men in the picture. The angle of the photo cut off their faces, and Ryan could only see their chests.

"At least we know there is a connection." Ryan straightened the photos side by side. "Though I'm not completely sure what it is, yet."

"What else did they find about the room?" Archer asked.

"The blonde hair was definitely Brielle's," Ryan said. It matched the DNA they got off one of the heiress' hair brushes, provided by her parents.

"So, they *were* keeping her there," Archer said.

"It seems like it." Ryan scratched at the stubble on his chin. He needed to shave. He needed a shower.

As if reading his thoughts, Archer shifted, sending his metal chair scraping across the tiled floor. "I need a break."

"Head home." Ryan waved him off. "We'll pick up again tomorrow afternoon. I have a meeting with Derek Jeffries in the morning. He offered to speak to us about Brielle, and I'm hoping he can shed some light on her whereabouts. Should I count you in, or do you want to meet after?"

Archer grabbed his coat and threw it over his broad

shoulders. "Give me a ring before you head over. I should probably tag along."

"See you in the morning." Ryan followed Archer out into the crisp night air.

～

"You look like shit," Archer said the following morning when Ryan arrived at the station. He took one last drag from his cigarette before tossing it on the road.

Ryan chuckled. "You look no better." He looked to where the cigarette had been discarded. "I thought you quit."

Archer shrugged. "Stress."

"How does the wife feel about that?" Ryan asked.

"She'll never know because big-mouth detectives will keep it locked down."

"Noted." Ryan chuckled. It was just past ten, and neither had slept much, if at all. Ryan rarely slept well when working on a heavy case.

"Shall we?" Archer waved toward his car.

At Derek Jeffries' mansion, a young woman answered the front door after two knocks and directed the detectives into the large sitting room.

"Mr. Jeffries will be with you soon." The woman smiled and disappeared out the same door.

Ryan glanced around the large room as Archer settled into one of the armchairs. Ryan's gaze stopped on the fire-place mantle and he walked toward it. He picked up the closest frame, a family photo. Ryan recognized Robert Jeffries and his sons, each famous in their business and well-known in the area. Poised beside Robert was his young wife, and each son had an attractive woman on their arm. The children were seated on various levels in front of the adults. Ryan imagined it was a difficult picture to take with so many family members having to cooperate.

"I was almost fourteen in that photo," a voice said from behind him. Ryan turned and regarded the tall man in the fine pinstripe suit. "The infamous Brielle would be near seven. It was one of the last times I saw her, until recently." He walked to Ryan's side and pointed at the petite blonde girl in the centre.

"She looks unhappy." Ryan placed the photo back on the mantle. "Detective Ryan Boone." He offered his hand.

"Derek Jeffries." The man returned a firm shake. "Brielle wasn't a happy child, at least not most of the time."

"What do you mean?" Archer asked.

"Detective Brad Archer," Ryan said when Derek looked at him.

"Brielle has a complicated history," Derek said as the woman returned to the room.

"Sorry, sir," she said. Her blonde hair fell into her sight line. "Can I get you and your guests anything?"

Derek paused and stared at her for a moment. The look was more than friendly and Ryan was certain this woman did more than serve his guests drinks.

"A coffee, please, Amelia," Derek said, then he looked to the detectives. "Anything for you, gentlemen?"

They both refused and Amelia smiled at Derek before hurrying from the room.

Derek sat across from Archer and met the larger man's gaze. "I'm sure you know about the scare Brielle had when she was very young. She disappeared for two weeks, then was found in the woods, frightened and alone. After that, she was difficult to be around. Her parents kept her at arm's length from us. She went on several different medications. I babysat her a few times when I was younger but that quickly stopped."

Ryan pulled out his notepad, nodding along with him. "We spoke with Dr. Konch. We know all about Jackie Biggs."

Derek half smiled. "I'm sure you don't know all."

"Brielle thinks she saw her again."

"She did see her."

Archer raised an eyebrow. "You sound sure."

"I am sure." Derek leaned back in his chair. "Because I saw her."

"Brielle's parents suggest very few people had contact with Jackie. They said most of your family doesn't know her." Ryan glanced at Archer.

Derek chuckled. "And had you asked me two weeks ago, I would have agreed."

"What about Brielle's time at the clinic?" Ryan asked.

Derek frowned and leaned forward. "What clinic?"

Ryan exchanged a look with Archer before answering Derek. "The one where she spent most of her early twenties."

"I don't know anything about that, Detective."

"Sorry," Ryan said. "I assumed since you knew about Jackie ... forget it. Tell me, how do you know about Jackie?"

Derek's frown broke, and his grin returned. "The reason you can't find Brielle is because she's hiding behind Jackie. And you can't find Jackie because of Mel."

"Who?"

Derek reached into his jacket pocket and pulled out a small business card, handing it to Ryan.

"Melanie Parker." Derek nodded at the card. "Call this number for a good time."

"Prostitutes?" Archer asked when he snatched the card from Ryan's hand.

"It's much more advanced. These girls are party pros. Drugs, sex, and alcohol. You call a number, and you have the service." For a moment, Ryan recalled the pill bottle from Patsy's home. It had a clear warning to avoid alcohol consumption. Was this how Brielle disappeared?

"They can't be alone." Archer flipped the card in his hand, examining each side.

Amelia stumbled back into the room with a cup of hot coffee shaking on the saucer. She batted her eyes at Derek before turning and leaving the room again.

Derek sipped his coffee and looked back at the detectives, shaking his head. "No, Mel runs the show but has a bodyguard."

Archer grabbed his phone and dialled the number on the card. When he pulled the phone away from his ear, he looked at Ryan.

"Disconnected."

"If they have Brielle Jeffries, I'm not really surprised." Ryan's gaze switched to Derek. "Anything else?"

Derek shook his head. "I wanted to get you that information."

Ryan's phone chimed. He pulled it from his pocket and checked his email.

Meeting confirmed.

"If that is all, Mr. Jeffries, then we should go. Thank you for all your help."

"If you don't mind me asking," Derek said. "What will happen to Brielle when you find her?"

Ryan and Archer exchanged another glance. "It all depends on what we find when we find her," Archer said, turning away from him.

Derek looked to Ryan as Archer retreated from the room. Ryan stayed back and held his hand out to Derek. "I'm going to try to get her the help she needs."

Derek grasped his hand again. "Best of luck finding her."

"What did you say to him?" Archer asked when they were back in his car.

Ryan offered a half smile. "I just reassured him."

"You can't play the sympathy card in this case," Archer said. "We have five bodies to account for."

Ryan looked away. His partner had been the sympathetic one only the day before.

"You're one to talk. Besides, I don't think it's as simple as five murders. There is something deeper going on here."

"You mean the escorts?" Archer asked.

"Yeah, I guess. Something just feels off here. Like Brielle isn't the only one. And the pictures from the Drake bunker ... it's all very strange."

"You think we need to find this Mel?" Archer flipped the business card onto Ryan's lap.

"If we can."

Archer turned the keys in the ignition. "Back to the office?"

Ryan shook his head, pulling out his phone. "We have a meeting at Dunn & Dorian."

"The law firm?" Archer raised an eyebrow. "Not that asshole again."

"So, you do remember Lexi Chase's employer."

"What a great idea, because the first time wasn't bad enough." Archer drove the car down the long street. He referred to the visit Ryan had from Dorian when he'd been representing Allen Kimball.

"Yeah, well, this time I'm the one with the questions."

Archer nodded and it was several minutes in silence before either man spoke again.

"How will we find her?" Archer asked.

Ryan cast a sideways glance at him. "What?"

"The girl, the leader or whatever, Melanie."

Ryan glanced at the card again. "I still have to figure that one out."

Archer chuckled. "I agree; that one's on you."

"It's not like the man with the baby is putting in the hours."

"I'm so glad you understand how complicated my life is."

Archer pulled the car up outside of the tall law office. Ryan squinted as he looked up at the glass sides. They were going all the way to the top.

They were greeted by a slender blonde whose nameplate read Marley—the same girl who vouched for Lexi a few weeks back. She had since assured the detectives she had no contact with Lexi or any idea about the crimes she was involved in.

"Mr. Dorian is waiting for you in his office. I can take you there."

They followed the admin assistant down the narrow hallway and past the open offices. She stopped at the largest one near the end of the hallway. Here Ryan saw an empty reception desk and an open door at the opposite side.

Marley waved toward it. "He's in there." She turned and left the detectives alone.

Archer waved to Ryan and stepped back, so Ryan could lead him into the large office.

Paul Dorian was seated at his desk. He stood when they entered and motioned to the long black couch in the center of the room.

"Fancy seeing you two again. I didn't think I would after my client confessed." Dorian moved around his desk. "What on earth could this be about?"

Ryan pulled out his notepad. Lexi Chase was working as his assistant before she disappeared, and since the desk outside his office was empty, Ryan assumed Dorian had yet to replace her.

"And here I thought you'd jump at the opportunity to see me again," Ryan said. "Who knows! Maybe I'm in the process of finding you a new client. You must be desperate; I mean, how else will you get your billable hours without a trial?"

Archer intervened. "We are here to discuss your former employee, Lexi Chase."

Dorian settled into a nearby armchair. "Former? I wasn't aware I had fired her."

Ryan frowned. "She's under investigation for a murder case."

"It's of no matter whether she works here now or if she

did before," Archer chimed in. "We need to know more about her."

Dorian tipped his head toward Archer. "Not so silent today." A cocky smile spread on his lips. "Between you and me, Detectives, Lexi Chase has worked for me for less than two weeks. I don't know a thing."

"A mystery to you as well?" Ryan leaned forward.

"Completely. The weirdest thing about the whole situation was I could have sworn I had seen her before."

"Outside of work?"

"Very outside of work."

Ryan pulled out the photo Quinn had given him during his surveillance and dropped it on the coffee table in front of Dorian. "Like at a party?"

Dorian picked up the photo, his mouth hung open. "How do you have this?"

"We were running surveillance on Ms. Chase," Ryan said, he pointed to the photo. "This came up in the process."

"You're wrong, Detective, this isn't Lexi Chase," Dorian said. "It's someone different. Trust me, I thought the same thing at first. This girl is part of a whole different group of ladies."

Archer and Ryan exchanged a glance. "Any chance the group of ladies is headlined by Melanie Parker?"

"How did you know?"

"The operation was mentioned to us earlier," Archer said. "So, you think Lexi is a part of this?"

Dorian stood and walked toward the large window at the back of his office. "Her, or a sister, possibly a twin. I confused her when we first met, mistaking her for someone else. I'm afraid I helped to drive her away."

"What happened?" Ryan asked.

"I approached Lexi, asking her what her relationship with Candy was. She recoiled from me and stormed out of the office." Dorian turned back to them. "I haven't seen her since."

Ryan made the note on his page. "Do you think she was afraid you found out the truth? Maybe she thought you recognized her from the theft?"

Dorian scratched his chin. He was unshaven, and his clothes were wrinkled. Despite the attempt to clean up the room, there were dishes piled in the sink and the garbage near overflowing. It looked like Dorian had spent several days at the office.

"Maybe. While I was certain I'd seen her, she looked at me like I was a complete stranger." Dorian laughed. "And how we spent the night, well, we wouldn't be strangers. Even an amazing actor couldn't have been both of those girls. She didn't know me."

"It seems a part of her knew you," Ryan said.

Dorian raised an eyebrow. "Why do you say that, Detective?"

Ryan pulled a black day planner from his pocket and tossed it on the coffee table in front of him. Dorian took it.

"We found that at Ms. Chase's apartment. She has you pencilled in four days before she started with you," Ryan said. "Any ideas?"

Dorian flipped open the book. "The nineteenth was my night with Candy." He looked up at Ryan. "What are you saying, detective?"

"They are the same person, and Ms. Chase is a better actress than you think."

Dorian shook his head. "She didn't know me. You didn't see her reaction."

Ryan stood. "Maybe, but all the evidence says otherwise." He held his hand out to the lawyer, who reached out and grasped it. "Call us if you hear from Ms. Chase." Ryan paused, then added, "Or Candy."

"What now, if you don't mind me asking?" Dorian said as he saw the detectives out of his office.

"We try to find them before anyone else ends up dead." Archer shrugged. "Mind if we search her desk for anything she may have left behind?"

"Be my guest, but don't be going through any case files."

Ryan and Archer left Dorian's office and turned to the L-shaped desk. Archer slipped on a glove and started sliding open drawers in search of anything left behind. He was on the third drawer before he found anything.

"Now we have our connection," Archer said, pulling out an orange pill bottle prescribed to Lexi Chase.

"Solydexran?" Ryan asked.

"Yup." Archer tossed the pills to Ryan. "Looks like the good doctor lied to us as well."

In the top corner, Dr. Miranda Konch was printed in small text. The third and final connection. Konch treated them all and prescribed the drug. What did it all mean?

Ryan slipped it into his pocket. "Maybe she didn't find my joke so funny."

"None of your jokes are funny," Archer said. "I've tried telling you this." He turned back to the desk and searched the remaining drawers. When he found nothing more of value, he pulled the glove off and tossed it into the trash bin.

Back at the elevator, Ryan frowned. "So the medication connects them, but it doesn't explain everything."

"Sounds like we might need to pay the doctor another quick visit," Archer said.

"And this time, we're getting the whole truth."

Chapter 42
Brielle Jeffries

BRIELLE JOLTED AWAKE, HER BREATHING RAPID. SHE'D had it again, the nightmare. This time it was different. It wasn't Sam who had her; instead, it was an unfamiliar man with large muscles and wide, dark eyes. He was keeping her on a farm. Despite the unfamiliarity of the situation, Brielle didn't feel about this man the way she did about Sam. She trusted this unknown person for some reason.

Her eyes slowly adjusted to the room around her. She wasn't in her bedroom but tucked into a twin bed. The moonlight leaked through the open window, and a cool breeze touched her cheek, messing her already tangled hair.

There was a creak to her right and she glanced at the other twin bed, only just noticing her company. Another girl rolled over onto her side making the bed move. Brielle froze. Who was that?

When the girl didn't stir, Brielle threw off the covers and slipped from the bed. She noticed a bag in the corner with clothing. It seemed familiar, even if it wasn't really her style, and she threw on a pair of jeans and a T-shirt over her under-clothes. Then she tiptoed across the floor and left the room.

The house was quiet and dark. The upstairs had only three rooms Brielle could see; she didn't wait to find more, instead hurrying for the stairs and toward the front door. Something about this place felt different than the last time she was taken. She wasn't in a bunker, she wasn't confined, and, although she couldn't remember how she got here, there wasn't the same feeling of dread she had when she woke up at Sam's house.

At the front door, she hesitated, thinking it might be worthwhile to grab some supplies before she left. She didn't know where she was after all; the house looked old enough to be anywhere.

Glancing around, she squinted in the dark and headed for the archway leading to the kitchen. She opened the fridge and grabbed a few bottles of water and any food she could carry—it wasn't much. She tried the cupboards. They were nearly empty. Whoever brought her here hadn't come prepared. Then the freezer. There, she found what she really wanted; the vodka she'd had before she reached the motel.

Brielle stopped when she heard the creak of the staircase, and with the supplies in hand, she slipped out the back door into the cool night air.

The moon was bright, leading a clear path across the dark, overgrown fields. She was on farmland, just like in her dream. She couldn't remember where there was farming close to the city. In the distance, Brielle could see headlights passing on the street.

"Jackie, wait!" Brielle heard someone behind her. She

glanced back and saw a slender girl with short dark hair following her from the house. "Where are you going?"

This was the second person to mistake her as Jackie. Brielle looked back at the road, wondering if she could outrun the girl and make it to the road. She turned and started running through the fields.

"Jackie, wait!" The girl called again, picking up her pace and chasing after Brielle.

"I'm not Jackie," Brielle said as the girl neared her.

"What?" The girl's face contorted with confusion. "What are you talking about?"

"You've got the wrong person," Brielle said. "I'm not Jackie."

"No." The girl shook her head. "Stop it."

Brielle backed away. "I'm leaving."

She reached out and grabbed Brielle's arm. "You can't leave!"

"Yes, I can," Brielle said. "I'm going home."

"If you go home, they'll arrest you," the girl said.

This made Brielle stop and she immediately thought of the blood and the memory of Sam from what felt like only a day earlier. "What do you mean?"

"For killing Sam," she said. "You smothered him. I watched you. If you leave, you'll ruin everything, and Mel will lose it."

Brielle's head started to spin. So, the memory she had of killing Sam was real. Brielle scrutinized the girl. She looked familiar.

"I'm sorry," Brielle said. "I can't stay here."

The girl reached to grab her again, and as she made contact, a loud, high-pitched scream came from the farmhouse. The girl dropped her hand to the side and, with wide eyes, beelined it back to the house. Brielle watched her go, then looked back at the road. Her conscience wouldn't let her leave the woman who screamed, whoever she was, so Brielle followed the other girl back into the house.

They darted up the stairs and toward the bedroom at the end of the hallway. The door was closed. Brielle could hear the commotion behind it.

"Mel?" It was the voice of a man. "Mel, what's wrong?"

"I'm not Mel! Who are you? Why have you brought me here?" It was the screech of a woman. "Leave me alone!"

The unknown girl threw open the door. "Blaine! What is going on?"

Brielle glanced between the three people in the room; an unknown girl, the large man from her dreams called Blaine, and the woman with maroon hair cowering on the floor with her arms wrapped around her head. Blaine never looked away from the woman on the floor.

"It's okay," Blaine said. His voice was soft, caring, and oddly familiar. "Patsy, it's okay. You know me. We've met before. I'm Blaine."

"What did you do to me?" Patsy cried, scratching at the tanned skin on her arm and pulling at her maroon hair.

Brielle took a step into the room. "Patsy?"

The woman looked up at Brielle. There was a hint of familiarity behind her eyes. "Brielle, where are we?"

"What's going on?" the other girl said, glancing between them.

"Candy, it's okay," Blaine said.

"What are you talking about?" Candy asked.

Blaine looked from Brielle to where Patsy sat on the floor. "It's okay," he said. "I can explain this."

Candy shook her head and glanced around Blaine at Patsy. "Mel, what's wrong?"

Patsy stared at her, cocking her head to the side. "I'm not Mel."

Blaine straightened and held a hand up to Candy. "Let me handle this." He turned back to Patsy and crouched before her. She looked terrified and shook with every ragged breath she took.

"I promise I won't hurt you," he said. "I only want to help you. That's all I've ever wanted. Do you think you know who I am?"

Patsy looked to Brielle before answering. "I think so."

"It's been a while," Blaine said.

Patsy dropped her gaze to the floor. "Why did you bring me here? They're coming for me. It can't be safe, even if I didn't do it. You'll all be considered accomplices."

Blaine cocked his head to the side. "You didn't do what?"

"Kill him," she whispered though it was barely audible.

Brielle swallowed hard. *How many people were dead?*

The floor creaked as Blaine shuffled toward her on his knees. Patsy's breathing grew louder and more rapid, but she didn't stop him.

"Patsy."

She looked up at him.

Blaine held his hand out to her. "I know you didn't do it."

She offered him a weak smile before taking his hand. "The police are looking for me. I can't let them find me."

He lifted her to her feet. "I know. Don't worry because I know who did do it."

Her tired eyes lit up. "You do?"

Blaine glanced back at Brielle and Candy before continuing. He brushed a strand of messy maroon hair from her face. His hand rested on her cheek, turning her to face him as his thumb slid over her skin in a circular motion.

"Did he hurt you, Patsy?" Blaine asked. "Did he hit you a lot?"

Brielle knew he was referring to Patsy's intimidating husband Brielle had seen at the charity function. Brielle had guessed at the time he'd been abusing Patsy.

Patsy's eyes welled with tears. "It was my fault," she whispered. "I couldn't help him. I only made him angry."

Blaine's jaw tightened, but as quickly as he tensed, he relaxed and moved his hand from her cheek. He treated her very carefully, as if he knew about her difficult past. Brielle started to feel uncomfortable watching the intimate conversation between them.

"Don't say that," Blaine said, his words soft. "It is not your fault he took his anger out on you. It is not your fault he chose to be abusive. You have done nothing wrong."

Patsy looked away, glancing toward Brielle for a moment.

"He was killed for hurting you," Blaine said after Patsy didn't respond.

"What is going on?" Candy demanded, stepping into the room now. Brielle glanced at her, unsure why she seemed familiar. She had a short, black pixie cut and chewed on her lower lip.

Patsy shot Candy a frightened glance, and Blaine stepped between them.

"Go downstairs."

"You have to tell me," Candy said.

Blaine shook his head. "Go." He waved them out the door. "Let me calm her down, and then I'll try and explain."

Candy glanced back at Brielle, then, after letting out a long breath, she stormed out of the bedroom.

"You too, Jackie," Blaine said.

Brielle shook her head and blinked at him several times. "I'm not Jackie."

Blaine nodded. "Go with Candy, Brielle."

Unsure what to say or how to react, Brielle did as he asked and followed the steps Candy took down the stairs and into the sitting room.

Chapter 43
Detective Ryan Boone

ARCHER DRUMMED HIS FINGERS AGAINST THE DESK between them. His annoyance was clear despite his passive expression. "How can she disappear?"

Ryan didn't mention that seemed to be the case with all their suspects lately. At least Konch's assistant had been able to obtain the patient files for Lexi Chase, even if the information was minimal.

Lexi had been a brief patient of Konch's shortly after her first arrest. The notes claimed she was a cooperative patient who had trouble getting past the incident. Solydexran had been prescribed with a refill every other month over half a year ago. There was even a recent meeting, one week after the robbery, where Lexi had requested an early refill, claiming to have lost her bottle.

"We'll find her," Ryan said, though his tone was more confident than he felt. They weren't having much luck with finding people these days.

"Before or after another person is murdered?" Archer muttered.

Ryan didn't get a chance to answer as the door to his office swung open.

"Uh, sorry, Detectives," Jade said, looking down.

"What is it?" Ryan asked

"There's a woman here to see you. She says you spoke a few days back."

Ryan frowned. "Who is it?"

"She says her name is Gabriela Cham," Jade flipped her hair over her shoulder.

"Send her in," Ryan said, recognizing the last name. "I'd like to hear what she has to say."

Jade turned for the door.

"Interesting." Archer leaned back in his chair.

"Very," Ryan said and cleared his desk, packing the file of the three women up and placing it aside.

"In here, Ms. Cham," Jade said as she directed the young woman into the room.

"Thank you," Gabi said.

Jade closed the door behind them, and the detectives stood to meet her.

"Good afternoon, Ms. Cham," Ryan said, holding his hand out to Gabi. She was dressed in an expensive pants suit that made her look older than she was, despite her young features.

"Gabi is fine, Detectives," she said, taking the offered hand. Her shake was firm, authoritative. One Ryan would expect from the daughter of Jamila Cham.

Ryan motioned to the chair on the opposite side of the desk and returned to his own. A small pad of paper was the only thing on the desk except for the computer and compiled file folder.

"How can we help you?" Ryan leaned back in his chair, unsure why she had come to his office. She glanced down at her hands and fidgeted with the edge of her blazer.

"My mother can't know I've come to speak with you," Gabi said. "I can't tell her what I've done to get by."

Ryan scratched at his chin before reaching for his pen. "We haven't had any contact with your mother except to discuss Mrs. Morrison."

"She'd kill me," Gabi said.

"We understand," Archer interjected. "We won't speak with your mother about what you discuss here. She isn't a part of our investigation anymore."

Ryan slid the notepad closer to him.

Gabi bit down on her lower lip and seemed to consider what to say. Ryan waited; he was used to it with interviews when people had things of value to share.

"I haven't been completely honest with you, Detective," Gabi said. "You asked me if I knew Patsy Morrison, and I told you I didn't. That wasn't true. I do know Patsy, only not by that name, and I didn't know it was her at the time."

Ryan still didn't speak, only making notes as Gabi did.

"About six months ago, I met a woman named Mel," Gabi explained. "I wasn't in a good place. My mother had kicked me out days before, and I struggled to find anywhere to stay. I met Mel at a party I slipped into. She'd been in a rough state and promised me a life of freedom and money as long as I could help her."

Ryan hesitated, lifting his pen off the page and exchanging a look with Archer. "Melanie Parker?"

Gabi cocked her head to the side. "You've heard of her."

"She ran an intricate operation of party girls," Ryan said. "We've had two people confirm this."

Gabi's hands twisted together in her lap. "When I saw Patsy on the news, I knew it was Mel. I thought it was strange an abused woman would masquerade as the leader of this group."

"Did she ever speak to you about her life outside of work?" Archer asked.

"No, she was a very private woman," Gabi said. "There was only one time I got a taste of her old life. She told me about an ex who turned abusive. When it was late, and she swore he was gone, she took me back to their old house and went inside to take a few things."

Gabi shook her head. "It was in my neighbourhood, but I was never going to tell her that. I didn't know the house or the ex she referred to. It wasn't until the murder I figured out it had been the Morrison's house all along."

Ryan frowned. Why was this woman running an escort operation?

"I asked her about her past once," Gabi continued. "She brushed it off. I even tried asking Jackie, a girl Mel was close with, but she didn't have anything to tell me."

"You met Jackie?" Ryan asked, making the note on his page. Another part of the story was connecting.

"Yes," Gabi said. "She was the kindest of them all."

Ryan flipped back in his notepad. "What about a woman named Candy? Did you meet her too?"

Gabi nodded.

"Was there anyone else?" Archer pressed.

"A few other girls who would come and go, and a man. Mel's guy," Gabi said. "He went by the name Blaine."

Ryan jotted the name down. "Do you know where they are?"

Gabi shook her head. "A few days ago, I stopped hearing from any of them." She slipped her hand into her purse and pulled out a list of phone numbers. "These were given to me. I've tried calling, but there's been no answer. Some are disconnected. Maybe you can find something of value in them."

Ryan glanced over the numbers. Maybe they'd be useful.

"And I can give you an address," she said. "Where Blaine lived." She reached for the pad in front of Ryan.

He hesitated before sliding it toward her with a pen.

Gabi jotted down the address and slid it back to him. She stood. "That's all I know." She paused. "They aren't bad people. I don't know what happened, but from my time with them, I would have never expected it."

Ryan stood and reached out to shake her hand again. "Thank you. This can only help." He followed her to the door and saw her out of the office.

"That reaffirmed the stories from Mr. Jeffries and Mr. Dorian," Archer said when Ryan returned to his seat. "She worked with those women."

"We need to find this Melanie Parker, wherever she is," Ryan said.

Archer sighed. "I guess we have to go check out the house."

Ryan opened his mouth to agree when the phone chimed, and Jade's voice came through. "Sorry for disturbing you," she said through the speaker. "I have Singh on the line for you. He said it's urgent."

Ryan hit the com button. "Send him through." He hit speaker.

"You've got Boone and Archer."

"You were right with your lead on the drug," Singh said.

Ryan exchanged a look with Archer. He'd requested they look more into Solydexran after finding it connected to all three of their suspects.

"What about it?"

"It's complicated, but long story short, we need you on scene," Singh said. "Now."

"Where?"

"Turns out Dr. Calvin Wright was one of the drug's creators."

Ryan scratched at his chin. Calvin Wright—the name Quinn told him when this case first started. The owner of the house Lexi kept visiting. He glanced down at the address. He thought it had been familiar.

"So what?" Ryan asked. A doctor owned some land he rented out to a group of misfits. It wasn't criminal. It didn't even seem suspicious.

"Boone, Dr. Wright has been dead for almost five years," Singh said.

Ryan's brow furrowed, and he looked to his partner as Archer spoke.

"Wait, how does he own property if he's deceased?"

"As I said, I need you both on the scene."

"You there now?" Ryan said.

"On our way," Singh said.

"Is it 9189 Grove Street?" Ryan asked, looking over the note Gabi had left.

"Yeah, how did you know?"

Ryan stood. "I'll explain when we get there. We'll head over now." He ended the call and looked at his partner

Archer was already standing and reaching for his keys. "I'll drive."

Chapter 44
Melanie Parker

BLAINE WAS SITTING UP IN BED WHEN MEL EXITED THE bathroom. He wore a steady grimace.

"What's wrong?" Mel asked. He'd been withdrawn since the previous day and wouldn't say why. Candy kept her mouth shut and hadn't spoken a word since their arrival at the house. She only looked between Jackie and Mel with a confused but empathetic look.

Mel had long grown tired of her gazes and retired to the bedroom. Here, Blaine was sullen.

"It's nothing," Blaine said.

Mel sighed. "Look, I know I put us in a bad situation. I know I could have been better and I could have been there for Jackie and maybe things would be different. We can't change that now. We have to look forward. We have to escape."

Mel lowered herself to the bed. The distance between her and Blaine seemed like a cold and vast lake, and she wasn't sure she should try to touch him.

"When should we leave?" Mel asked.

Blaine frowned. "And go where?"

"Anywhere," Mel said. "We have a car. We have cash, and we have our whole lives ahead of us." Mel didn't expect him to be happy about her committing murder, but she'd removed Fraser from their lives. Her actions uprooted their lifestyle, which didn't matter since Blaine had grown tired of the whole operation. He wanted her to retire. He wanted a quiet life. Now they could have it. Why couldn't he see it?

"We can't go," Blaine said. "We'll be spending our whole lives running."

Mel's body stiffened. "So, what, you're just going to let them arrest us? Let them charge us for what we've done?" She stood and stepped away from him. "I thought you supported me. I thought you would keep me safe."

Pain crossed Blaine's face. "I don't think I can."

"Why?" Mel demanded.

Blaine stood and approached her. His movements were slow and deliberate. When he reached her side, he gently took her into his arms.

"I can't stop the pain each of you carries," Blaine said softly, burying his face in her hair. "I can't fix what's been done." His body crumbled in her hold, his shoulders sagged forward, and she swore she heard him sniffle. She'd never seen Blaine cry.

"You can," Mel said. "You have."

Blaine pulled away. His face was dry. His eyes were sad. "I can't do it anymore. It's not working. I was wrong."

Mel reached out and rested her hands on his biceps. "You're not making any sense."

"I know," he said. "Because I've been hiding something from you. I've been hiding it from you for a long time."

Mel dropped her hold and stepped back. "What are you talking about?"

Blaine released a long sigh. "I know more about the medication than I let on. A girl I knew was on it and she took her own life. She believed she was going crazy."

Mel frowned. Why was he telling her this? So, he'd found a bunch of medication someone used to take. It wasn't like any of them were regularly using.

"Those meds I found," Blaine said. "I was trying to hide the truth from you." He lowered himself back to the bed. His shoulders slumped forward. "I thought if I could remove it from your system, then maybe you'd be okay. Maybe you could separate the two and be who you are supposed to be. I thought, maybe, this was you."

Mel shook her head. He didn't make any sense. She hadn't been using any medication in months. "I don't get it."

"I know, and it's my fault." He reached for her hand and she stepped closer, allowing him to take her and pull her to his level. Then he wrapped an arm around her shoulder. "I need to tell you about Patsy, about Lexi, and about Brielle."

He breathed in deep, as if trying to bring her closer to him. "And I need to tell you about Calvin and what happened."

Mel sucked in a sharp breath and let him share his story.

Chapter 45
Detective Ryan Boone

THE HOUSE LOOKED LIKE ANY OF THE OTHER PROPERTIES on the street. The only difference was the brick, a shade darker than the other houses. A cobblestone path led from the sidewalk to the front door of a large two-story home. The three front windows on the lower level were shuttered, and the house was dark. The red front door was open; the roped-off house turned into a crime scene. Ryan and Archer headed inside to find other officers already searching the property.

"Glad you're here," Singh said, emerging from the kitchen.

"What's going on?" Ryan surveyed the scene. From where he stood, it looked like the place had been cleared out. The front hall closet doors were wide open, and nothing was inside. There were hangers on the rack; some had fallen to the ground as if clothing had been yanked from them. There was furniture but nothing else indicated someone lived here. There wasn't a single picture or decoration. "Do we know anything about this guy other than what he did? What about a picture? A family?"

Singh shrugged. "We can't find any pictures. There is very little background information on Dr. Wright. It's like he was erased."

"Why?" Ryan asked.

"Maybe it has something to do with his dismissal," Archer suggested.

"Anything in the house tell you about him?" Ryan asked. Glancing around, he thought it was impossible.

"The place has been cleaned out," Singh said, waving for Ryan and Archer to follow him as he headed up the staircase. "All except useless possessions. Though we did manage to find one file."

"Really?" Ryan said. "That seems strange."

"It wasn't easy to find," Singh said. He turned at the top of the stairs toward a door at the end of the landing. It was open, and a uniformed officer with plastic gloves was going through the shelving. "It was in the left desk drawer. It had a dummy bottom."

"So, Dr. Wright was hiding it," Ryan said.

Singh crossed the office to the large desk in the corner. He picked up the file and passed it to Ryan. "This will be of interest to you."

"Oh?" Ryan raised an eyebrow and flipped through the information. It was a report on the development of Soly-dexran and its known side effects. When he finished, he glanced up at Singh. "Why wasn't this information ever reported?"

Singh shook his head. "I don't know."

"What is it?" Archer asked.

Ryan handed him the file to review. Before Archer could

comment, Quinn rushed into the room with a serious look on his normally relaxed face.

"We have to go," Quinn said, looking between the detectives and Singh.

"Why?" Singh asked. "We're not done here."

"I just got a call from the office," Quinn said, speaking directly to Ryan now. "We have a potential location for the suspects. They're all reported to be together."

"Are you sure?" Singh asked.

Ryan was already making his way to the door.

"Bring that information to the station," Ryan said. "We'll need it later."

Ryan followed Quinn from the office with Archer on his tail. "Are they far?"

"About thirty kilometers outside of the city."

"Call the office and get back up to follow us," Ryan said.

"Quinn, you can ride with me," Singh called from behind them. "The other officers will finish up here, and we'll head to the scene."

"No siren," Ryan said. "We need to keep our profiles low."

Archer and Singh nodded their agreement.

"Good. Let's go break this case." They turned for their cars and headed to the suspects' location.

ARCHER DROVE their assigned cruiser as they raced down Highway 34 toward the farmhouse. A neighbour had been walking by when they called in the tip. She claimed the farmhouse hadn't been used in ages, and three women and a man had recently moved in. She managed to get a photo. They found recent ownership in the last year had been transferred from Jonathan Roche to a Blaine Roche upon the former's death.

Glancing in the side view mirrors, Ryan eyed the other cars following behind them. No sirens or lights were on.

"Do you think we'll find them?" Archer asked, eyes locked on the highway.

"Mrs. Roylends seemed pretty insistent. A car arrived a few days ago at the Roche's farmhouse." Ryan grabbed his phone, looking over the blurry photo sent to the station. "It's hard to tell; they seem to match the profile." He looked back to Archer. "At the very least, the timing is right."

"Who's the guy?" Archer asked.

Ryan looked back at the picture. A large man was with the three girls outside the farmhouse. "My guess? Blaine Roche. Mr. Jefferies did say they had a bodyguard of sorts, and Gabi confirmed the story."

"Think he'll be a problem?"

"I guess we'll find out," Ryan said as the cruiser pulled off the highway and turned down a country road.

In the distance, the farmhouse came into view. The sun was setting behind it and the windows looked dark. If not for the black car in the driveway, he would have suspected no one was home.

They pulled into the long driveway, and the other cruisers followed. Near the house, each car cut its engine, and the officers climbed out. Ryan looked to the back car and motioned for the officers to go around the side of the house, surrounding the property and preventing any escape.

Guns drawn, Ryan and Archer approached the front

door. Ryan stepped forward and called, "Mr. Roche, this is the police. Open the door; we have the place surrounded."

No answer but a thump from the upper floor. Ryan looked to Archer and stepped aside. The larger man placed a hand against the door.

"Mr. Roche," Archer said. "We have a warrant in hand to enter the premises. I insist you open the door, or we will enter by force."

Still no answer.

"Your go," Ryan said.

Archer stepped back and lifted his leg, kicking down on the handle of the door and breaking it from the frame. It swung wide open. There was a scream upstairs, and Ryan ran into the house and up the stairs with his gun drawn. A frightened woman with short black hair cowered in the corner of the room. Ryan immediately recognized Lexi despite the hair colour change.

A commotion broke out on the floor below him. There was shouting and a gunshot went off, causing Lexi to cover her head and start crying again.

"Lexi Chase," Ryan said. "You are under arrest. I won't hurt you unless you resist."

Lexi looked at him; her eyes were wide and frightened, brimming with tears. "Don't hurt me."

"Just slowly stand up and place your hands behind your back," Ryan said.

Lexi stared at him for several seconds before she stood on shaking legs and turned her back to him.

Ryan lowered his gun and cuffed her. Lexi continued to cry.

He led her down the stairs repeating the word required

by law. "You are under arrest by the rules of federal legislation. Know you have the right to remain silent and seek counsel through public or private means. Remember, any words you speak from here on can be used against your case. Nod that you understand this."

"I understand," Lexi squeaked.

At the base of the stairs, Ryan saw Archer leading a handcuffed Brielle Jeffries from the house.

"Jackie!" Lexi yelled when she saw her.

Brielle gave her a weak smile. "Don't worry. It will be okay. Just keep your mouth shut."

Lexi clamped her lips closed.

Ryan passed her off to a waiting officer and returned to where two officers were handling a struggling Patsy Morrison.

"Get your pig hands off of me!" she yelled, squirming in their grasp.

"Patsy, you have to calm down," Ryan said. "We will be required to tase you if you don't stop resisting."

It seemed to work because Patsy immediately stopped moving and turned a vicious glare on Ryan. She spat in his direction, but it fell short of hitting him.

"Where is Blaine Roche?" Ryan asked. "The man who owns this place."

"Fuck off, pig," Patsy hissed. "I'm not telling you anything. You'll never find Blaine."

Ryan waved to the cars waiting in the driveway. "Get her in one of the cruisers."

Two officers escorted her away, each holding onto one of her shoulders.

"What about Mr. Roche?" Ryan asked.

Quinn shook his head. "It was only the girls in the house. None of them would tell us where he was."

Ryan scanned the surrounding land. It was long and overgrown. He could be out there.

"Have the dogs go through the field," Ryan said. "Have an officer at the door waiting to see if he comes back. I want to get this guy." He walked back to the driveway with the waiting cars. The ones carrying the girls had already begun the ride back to the station. Archer waited out front, leaning against the hood.

"Find the pimp?" Archer asked.

Ryan shook his head. "Looks like he's gone. We're searching the area. If he's close, we'll get him."

"I hope so," Archer said. "I'm getting tired of this case."

"Tell me about it." Ryan climbed into Archer's cruiser.

Archer followed and shifted the car into drive, following the route the other police vehicles had taken.

"At least it's almost over," Archer said.

Ryan grimaced. "I'm afraid it's only beginning."

"Why do you say that?"

"Because you saw those girls. We've studied them for the past weeks, and none of them matched their suspected personalities. It took two officers to even handle Patsy. She wasn't the terrified woman we've been profiling."

"Maybe we were wrong," Archer said.

"No," Ryan shook his head. "I know what it was. I can't believe it."

"Yeah. What a strange case."

Chapter 46
Brielle Jeffries

THE DETECTIVE ENTERED THE QUESTIONING ROOM. His head was cocked slightly to the side, and he regarded her cautiously. There were two folders in his hand and a notebook in the other. Brielle had to admit he was handsome, with crew-cut brown hair and dark eyes. He clearly worked out by the way his suit fit nicely to his buff form, though the stubble lining his chin and bags under his eyes implied he had been working around the clock. How much trouble had she and the other women put the police through?

"Ms. Biggs?"

Brielle shook her head. "I only told them I was Jackie so you would see me, Detective." The truth still caused her confusion. How could she not have known for all these years?

"You know you don't have to speak to me until your lawyer is present," Detective Boone said, taking the seat across from her and placing the files on the table. "Your parents requested we don't speak with you until then."

"I don't care," Brielle said. "Make it off the record if you're so worried. I have to know."

"What did you want to speak to me about?" Boone asked. He retrieved a pen, poised to make a note in his book.

"I heard the officers talking," Brielle said. "Saying my abduction wasn't fabricated. Does that mean you believe me?"

"We found the bunker, Ms. Jeffries," Boone said. "I have no doubt you suffered a very traumatic experience."

"And they are really dead?" Brielle asked. Her mind immediately went to Sam and how she pressed a pillow into his face in her dream. How *Jackie* had killed him. How Jackie was her.

Boone grimaced but didn't ask who "they" were. Instead, he slid the two files across the table. "Are these them?"

Brielle flipped open the first folder, and a picture of Sam stared back at her. It was his victim profile, detailing his death. Her breathing hitched for a moment. She checked the second one and saw his son. Then she pushed them back toward the detective, uninterested in learning more.

"That's them," Brielle said. "How did they die?"

The look on his face told her she should know. He sighed, scratched his chin, and played along.

"One was shot in the head," Boone said. "The other, suffocated."

"Wow ..." Brielle stared at the table in front of her. Whatever vision she'd had was true. She'd pressed the pillow into his face and ended it all. Or Jackie did. The whole idea was still so baffling. "I don't know what happened. I wish I did."

Boone collected the files but didn't speak.

The silence unnerved her, and she continued, "I don't know what I would have done if I hadn't escaped. For years, I've lived with this. I used to dream about being taken. I used to remember him coming into my room at night. I don't know where the will to escape came from. I guess it was from Jackie ..." Brielle blinked back tears.

"Can you tell me where the gun is?" Boone asked. "Or how you got it?"

Brielle shook her head. "Maybe it was my dad's? We used to shoot on my great-granddad's property up north when I was just a kid. Shooting a gun is something I've always known how to do. I guess Jackie used that part of me. She probably knew where the gun was hidden too."

"We'll look into it." Boone jotted a note down on the folder.

"What about Jackie?" Brielle asked. "Is it true what they say about my condition?"

Boone looked away for a moment. "It's complicated, but yes, it's true."

"How could I have never known?" Brielle looked down at her hands, trying to think back over the years, over the time she'd spent with Jackie, or what she believed. Her parents had hidden the truth from her, convincing her Jackie was nothing more than a bad friend. That she was the reason Brielle did drugs. Little did Brielle know Jackie had been inside of her all along, something her parents had hoped to keep buried.

Brielle couldn't properly describe what she felt when the truth had first come out. Disbelief, certainly, but perhaps almost relief. Like she wasn't losing her mind. She wasn't some hopeless drug addict and Jackie wasn't someone who seemed to vanish without a trace, but, in reality, a part of her. Something that maybe Brielle suspected all along.

"Like I said, it's complicated." Boone folded his hands on the table in front of them.

"My parents hid it from me," Brielle said. "Why did they want me to think it was drugs?"

Boone frowned. "I'm afraid I don't know. Your parents will have to explain that."

Brielle shook her head. "They won't tell me what I really need to know." She paused for a moment before continuing. "What about Patsy and the other girl? Are they like me?" Blaine had implied as much before he left them behind.

Boone's expression remained solemn. "They are. Though it seems different." He paused. "Each one of you was a patient of Dr. Miranda Konch. Did she ever allude to anything about the drug you were taking or the other girls?"

"No," Brielle said. "She has been my doctor for several years. I didn't know Patsy had seen her, and I'd never met the other girl."

Boone grimaced. "Konch has vanished. If you have any information on her, it would be greatly appreciated."

"I'm sorry, Detective, I wish I did." Brielle sighed. "I'm still having a hard time believing this is true." A part of her held some reassurance, however, as if this was the answer to so many questions that had been unanswered for years. The explanation for all of Brielle's memory loss or strange happenings, something that had held such a mystery for years.

"If I hadn't seen it, Ms. Jeffries, I would be the same."

"What do you think caused this, Detective?" Brielle asked.

"I'm still working that one out," Boone said. He leaned back in his seat and eyed her for a second. "Do you know about the other death?"

Brielle shook her head.

"She was a woman working for your abductors. In her sixties, working as a nurse."

Brielle frowned. "She released me."

"Yes. Do you know what happened to her?"

"I don't," Brielle said. "I'm sorry. I had hoped to save her from them. She looked pretty beat down when she came to my rescue."

"Anything else, Ms. Jeffries?"

Brielle tilted her head to the side. "Is Patsy okay?"

"Under the circumstances," Boone said. "She'll be just fine."

"I think she's been through a lot."

"We only want to help."

Brielle looked away. "It sounds like we've needed help long before today. I think you're too late." Then she glanced back at Boone and forced a smile through the tears formed in her eyes. "Thank you, Detective. That's all I need."

"I'll have more questions for you once your parents and the lawyer arrive," Boone said.

"Yes, of course." Brielle dropped his gaze and folded her hands on her lap. "I'll do my best to remember all I can."

The detective regarded her silently for a few seconds before he stood and left the room.

Brielle glanced toward the mirrored window where other officers likely watched her. Perhaps that was why her parents kept her condition a secret. Even in the psychiatric hospital, she never felt as watched and studied as she did in this tiny room.

Chapter 47
Melanie Parker

"Look who it is." Mel smirked, leaning back in her chair and arms crossed over her chest. "Detective Hotshot here to learn all my dirty little secrets."

"Ms. Parker," the lawyer seated beside her said. "Please."

Mel shot him a cold look. "No, I want this bastard here to know exactly how I feel about him."

Detective Boone lowered himself into the chair across the table from Mel and her public defender. Her lawyer was an older man with greying hair and nearly twenty pounds overweight. His cheap suit strained around his large middle. He'd mentioned his name twice already, but Mel didn't care enough to remember it. Still, she knew better than to reject the free legal aid.

"Mrs. Morrison," Boone said. "I assure you I'm only here to learn the truth. I want to help you as much as I can."

Mel stiffened at the mention of Fraser's last name. She still felt so separate from the woman Blaine claimed she really was. From the wife who'd married the bastard Fraser. How was it possible she was merely a creation in someone's mind, that she wasn't a real person. That she inhabited the body of the woman Patsy.

Mel spat on the table in front of Boone. "That's exactly how I feel about you helping me." She uncrossed her arms and leaned forward, placing her hands on the cold metal table. In a low voice she said, "Where were you, Detective Hotshot, when we needed help before? Where were you to stop all this from happening?" She leaned back again. "I don't think you can help. I don't think you understand what helping us means."

Boone pulled out his notepad. "I'm not sure I know what you mean."

"I guess *not* such a hotshot." Mel chuckled.

"Ms. Parker," the lawyer said. "Please try to be a bit more respectful."

"It's okay, Mr. Phillips," Boone said.

Mel could admit the detective was a good-looking guy, in his late thirties, likely, and determined. Were she meeting him in another situation, she may have felt differently. Now he was here to change things, to separate her from Jackie and reprimand her for her crime.

"Mrs. Morrison," Boone said again.

Mel looked at the lawyer and laughed. "This fool can't even get my name right." Looking back at Boone, she said, "How did you get here if you have such trouble with names, Detective Hotshot?"

She wished he'd stop reminding her of it. That she could pretend she never learned the truth and go on like Melanie Parker was real. Instead, she was stuck trying to sort out two conflicting personalities and learned that some of the things she believed she'd run from were still very much a part of her life when her body was taken over by another.

At least the strange phenomenon seemed to explain things. The mornings she woke up at Fraser's or the missing bits of memory, how she'd dream about Patsy, and it would all feel too real. It wasn't a dream. She'd lived it, somehow.

Boone frowned and glanced at the notebook on the table. "Very well, Ms. Parker."

"See, not so hard."

"Are you willing to let me speak to Patsy?" Boone asked. "I'd like to hear her side of things."

Mel's amused expression contorted into an angry grimace. "If she wanted to speak to you, she'd be here." However it worked, Mel still wasn't sure.

"Very well," Boone said, making a note on the page. "Then why don't we talk?"

Mel crossed her arms again. "I'm sure a smart guy like you doesn't need my help figuring this out."

"Perhaps you're right," Boone said. "I could certainly work faster with your assistance."

"I hate to ruin your day, Detective, but—" Mel stopped and smiled. "Actually, I'd love to ruin your day." She motioned with her hands, zipping her lips closed and then winking.

Boone sighed. "It's not just my day you're ruining."

Mel said nothing and turned her head away from him.

The page crinkled as Boone flipped it. "Okay, let's start with a few questions. Why did you kill Fraser Morrison?"

"You don't have to answer," Mr. Phillips said.

Mel glared. "I'm not stupid, thanks." Then she turned her cold gaze on Boone. "Got anything better?"

Boone made a mark. "What is your relationship with Patsy Morrison?"

Mel looked to the lawyer, who nodded.

"I don't know, Patsy," Mel said. "Not in a way I can help."

"Are you sure?" Boone asked.

"C'mon," Mel said. "You must have better questions than this, Hotshot."

Boone flipped the page. "Very well, what is your relationship with Brielle Jeffries?"

Mel raised an eyebrow. "She's a rich bitch that lives in town. A co-worker fucked her cousin."

"And Jacqueline Biggs?"

Mel glowered at the detective. "Leave Jackie alone."

"Actually, Ms. Biggs has been a big help," Boone said, flipping back in his book several pages. "She told me a man abducted her around the same time Ms. Jeffries was reported missing. Do you have any memory of Ms. Biggs' disappearance?"

Jackie had disappeared only to come back freaking out about an abduction. At the time, Mel thought she'd had one too many drinks, but maybe her story held more weight than Mel had given it.

"I might remember something along those lines."

Boone made another mark. "Might is better than no."

The lawyer cleared his throat. "Not binding."

Boone looked at him. "No, Mr. Phillips, not binding." His eyes shifted between the two of them. "I know you don't believe me, but I really am trying to help. I don't want to trap you. I just want to know what happened and why."

Mel looked away.

"Can I ask you about Lexi Chase?" Boone asked.

"You can," Mel said. "Not like I could tell you anything. I've heard her name twice in my life, and one of those was in the last two hours."

"Okay, then what about Candy?" Boone reached up and scratched at the stubble on his chin.

Mel looked back at him. "Is Candy okay?"

Boone smiled. "She's fine, though confused."

"Candy is always confused." Mel scoffed.

"She hasn't said a word on the case," Boone said. "Your friend Jackie advised her against it."

Mel leaned back in her chair and narrowed her eyes. "She always listened to Jackie. Good luck getting anything out of her."

"Do you think that's the best idea?"

"I don't really care."

Boone shook his head. "I'd like to ask you about Blaine Roche."

"Ask away," Mel said. "It's not like I'll answer."

"Was he your pimp, as he's been so referred to?"

Mel laughed. "Pimp, really? That's funny."

"I'll take that as a no," Boone said. The chubby lawyer next to Mel cleared his throat. "I know, Mr. Phillips, it's not binding."

Mel glanced at her lawyer. "I wouldn't worry." Mel looked back at Boone. "This asshole won't get anything out of me." Mel folded her hands on the table in front of her and glared at Boone. "You have no idea who Blaine is or what you're dealing with."

"That's why I'd like you to enlighten me," Boone said.

"We've been given reports you and Blaine were very close. I wonder why he left you at the farmhouse alone."

"I told him to go," Mel said. When Blaine had told her the truth, everything he knew, she made sure he left. He'd been hesitant, unwilling to leave her behind. Mel knew better. If what he said was true, then he couldn't help her. She was beyond his help. He could still help others. She wouldn't let him give up.

"Why?"

"He isn't finished yet."

Boone frowned. "What does that mean?"

"You're the smart guy," Mel smirked. "You figure it out."

"Why were you staying at Calvin Wright's home?" Boone asked.

Mel cocked her head to the side as her eyebrows furrowed together. "I don't know what you're talking about."

Boone slid a picture of Blaine's house across the table. "Do you know this residence?"

"Yes." It was home for her.

"This house belongs to Calvin Wright," Boone said.

Mel shook her head. "No, it's Blaine's home. He told me he'd been living there for over five years." Blaine had told her about Calvin but never implied the house belonged to anyone other than Blaine.

"It doesn't matter what he told you," Boone said. "The house is owned by a dead man."

"Dead man? That's not possible," Mel said.

"It may not seem possible, but I assure you it is. There has been a lot of this case that has made the impossible seem very plausible."

Mel pursed her lips. What was this guy talking about?

"Tell me about the doctor," Boone asked. "Miranda Konch."

Mel frowned. "I don't know her."

"Patsy was quite familiar with her. She stayed in her facility several towns away," Boone said.

"So?" Mel had memories of time spent in a psychiatric hospital. Could those have been Patsy's memories and not hers? Everything was blurring together.

There was a knock at the door and a uniformed officer poked her head into the room.

"Detective," the officer said. Boone glanced over his shoulder to regard her. "Brielle Jeffries' family and lawyer have arrived."

"Thank you, Collins," Boone said before the woman left the room.

Mel waved toward the door when Boone looked back at her. "I suggest you go and talk to the sweet little heiress you have in custody because I have absolutely nothing more to say to you."

Boone glanced toward the large one-way mirror on the wall where someone was likely watching the interrogation. He then placed a pill bottle on the table in front of Mel.

"Ever seen these before?" Boone asked.

Mel reached for the bottle and the detective didn't stop her. Taking it in her hand, she flipped it around, reading the label. The Solydexran was prescribed to Patsy Morrison by Dr. Miranda Konch. It was the same bottle as the one she'd found on Candy and the one Blaine had freaked out about. The same bottles she'd found in his office.

Mel popped off the top and poured one of the pills into her palm. It was a cylinder capsule, white and dark grey.

Come to think of it, this pill looked exactly like the one Gabi had given her at Dorian's party. She tilted her palm and dropped the pill back in the bottle then sealed it and rolled it back to the detective.

Shaking her head, she lied. "I can't say I have."

"No?"

"You heard me."

With a frustrated sigh, Boone said, "Are you sure you have nothing more to share with me, Ms. Parker?"

Mel crossed her arms again. "I've never been so sure in my life, Hotshot."

"I'm very sorry for that." Boone stood, and the lawyer did the same. "Good day, Mr. Phillips." They shook hands and then Boone looked at Mel. "If you have anything to tell me, or perhaps if you hear from Patsy, please do." He left without another word.

Mr. Phillips looked at Mel. "You could be more pleasant with the detective. Your attitude doesn't help you."

Dolt. Mel looked away, pleased the hotshot left her alone, and hoping Patsy didn't try to talk to him.

Chapter 48
Detective Ryan Boone

ARCHER STOOD OUTSIDE THE ONE-WAY WINDOW WHEN Ryan emerged from the room where Patsy Morrison was sitting with her lawyer.

Archer gave him a sympathetic smile. "That went well."

"Really?" Ryan reached up and scratched at the stubble on his chin. "I don't think that would have been my first thought." Ryan turned and retreated to his office.

Archer followed. Once they were there, Archer closed the door behind them and took the seat across from his partner.

"I guess Wright knew what he was talking about," Archer said.

Ryan reached for the file from Calvin Wright's house and flipped it open. The page he'd found was still on top and the results stared him in the face. The report was seven years old and dated two years before Wright's death. For some reason it had been missed or hidden, but Ryan knew it was true. He'd seen it with the women. It seemed impossible this would be allowed to reach the market with such substantial findings.

While Solydexran is highly respected for its ability to suppress negative or anxious thoughts in a subject, heavy use of the drug or consumption of alcohol or another medication slowly changes the compound of the narcotic. Testing studies show an overwhelming rate of subjects who suffered from minor side effects, such as dizziness or nausea, to extreme disorders.

Studies show Solydexran enhanced the symptoms of dissociative identity disorder (DID) in subjects already suffering from a previous traumatic life experience or living in an unstable environment by helping the brain create new personalities to stave off trauma. Studies also indicated an alarming number of test subjects, as high as five percent, suffered some type of psychological disorder ranging from minor schizophrenia to enhanced anxiety disorders.

"I still don't understand how this drug hit the market," Ryan said. "Especially if it causes a disorder this extreme."

Archer only shrugged his response.

Ryan's phone pinged with a new email, and he instinctively reached for it. The subject line was blank. There was only a link to a video in the content. The virus scan came back clean and indicated the file was safe. The email address was a jumble of letters, numbers, and symbols. Whoever sent this email was trying their hardest not to be tracked.

"What is it?" Archer asked, likely seeing the perplexed expression on Ryan's face.

"A video." He clicked the button. It popped up on his phone screen and slowly loaded. Archer moved around his desk and watched the video over Ryan's shoulder.

When it loaded, Ryan saw who had sent it. Pictured in the center of his screen was Blaine Roche. He was seated in a small room with darkened walls; only his face and torso were lit up.

"It's the pimp," Archer said.

Ryan didn't answer, only listening as Blaine's low voice came through the video.

"Good evening, Detective," Blaine said. He stared into the camera with dark, focused eyes. His expression was sombre, and his hands were folded in front of him. He was the picture of perfect calm. "I have no doubt you have several of your men searching for me. I have no intention of sounding cocky, but I also have no intention of being caught. Your people won't find me. I'm further than your jurisdiction allows."

Ryan frowned. "Can we track this video or the email?"

Archer didn't answer his question, only continued to watch the video.

"You're probably wondering why I'd bother to reach out to you," Blaine said. "You see, Detective, I love Melanie Parker with all my heart, whoever she is. And because of that, I have to tell you my side of the story."

Blaine drew a long breath and reached up, rubbing his eyes. When his gaze returned, it was just as focused as it was before.

"I bet you've formed your own opinions about the women in your custody," Blaine said. "I'm sure you can forgive me when I tell you you're wrong. Every thought you've formed, every clue you've solved, won't tell you about them. It will tell you what they should be like, not who they are. Only I know."

Blaine cracked a small smile. "I'm going to try and explain it to you. I met Melanie Parker over two years ago at a bar downtown. She looked like she'd had a rough night. Her lip was split and hair a tangled mess. Her dress was ripped. There was a cut on her arm. I must have stared at her for a full ten minutes before she noticed me."

His gaze shifted away from the camera and seemed to shine in the light as if tears were forming. The memory seemed happy for him.

"I don't know what made me walk over to her, but something did. I ordered a drink and told her my name. She looked at me like I was crazy. I guess she scared away a lot of people with her attitude, but all I could think about was how beat-up she looked. I thought she needed help or at least a friendly ear. She put up a front, but eventually, I knocked down her walls."

"Why is he telling us this?" Archer asked.

"Maybe he needed to confess and couldn't find a priest who would listen."

"We were together after," Blaine said. "I became her confidant and I quickly fell in love. It seemed she loved me, too. Until one morning, I woke up and she was gone, and I had no idea where she went, or why.

"Three weeks later, she returned with more wounds." Blaine's expression hardened. "I asked her what happened, and she shrugged it off, claiming she'd been working and clients were rough. I didn't fight her on it; I hated fighting with her. Besides, she eventually got more girls and she quit working herself. Things got better. Or at least, I thought they did." He forced a sad smile. "I guess things had never really gotten better. A lot about Mel was an act."

Blaine drew another long breath. "So, while I thought things were improving, I relaxed and kept what happened to myself, until Melanie woke in my bed one morning and she wasn't Melanie. That was when I met Patsy. I tried to keep her calm. I got her downstairs and started speaking. It wasn't until I found the drugs in her purse that I knew the truth."

"He knows about the drugs?" Archer said.

Ryan frowned. "It seems like he does."

"Patsy was quick to trust me," Blaine said. "Perhaps because Mel told her to subconsciously. Patsy told me about her husband, and I quickly understood the bruises Mel constantly returned with. I tried to keep Patsy at the house, but her fear of him was too much, and she felt forced to return, sure he would find her.

"I tried to stop her so many times, but she'd never stay with me. I confronted him once, but when I saw Mel, I knew I couldn't help. He nearly broke her arm after I went by. I always tried to save her, yet Patsy always managed to slip through the cracks."

Blaine looked away for a moment again. "A few times, I tried to explain to Mel what she was suffering from, and each time Patsy returned and went home to him whenever I did. I thought it was better to separate the two personalities in the hopes Mel would dominate and save Patsy from him. I would cover for Patsy during Mel's extended visits. I could always find an excuse to keep her husband off her back. Visiting her sister, out of town, at a wellness retreat. I never knew how much Fraser knew about Patsy's condition. I did whatever I could to keep her away from him and keep him off her trail. I only made it worse."

"Did this guy think he was a psychiatrist or something?" Archer scoffed.

Ryan shook his head. "I think there is something else going on here."

"What do you mean?" Archer asked.

"I'm not totally sure," Ryan said. "It just feels off."

"You're probably judging me, Detective, and I have to ask that you don't," Blaine said. "You see, I was in love, and I saw Melanie as the dominant personality or the safest personality. I never thought she would go this far. This was never supposed to happen."

Blaine's stiff shoulders collapsed forward. "You're dealing with a group of women who need serious help, through no fault of their own, and for a reason they won't be able to fully understand. I'm still working on understanding it all.

"I'm sure you have a lot of questions, Detective. I'm afraid there aren't answers for everything," Blaine said. "I had hoped by removing the drugs their minds would settle. Then they could try and figure out the two conflicting personalities living inside them. From what I understand, Jackie had been around for a long time as a result of the trauma Brielle faced as a young girl. Candy, well, she showed up at my home not long ago. She carried around the prescription for Lexi Chase. It didn't take me long to figure out who she was."

There was a sound in the background of the video, and it seemed to distract Blaine for a minute. He glanced over his shoulder before focusing back on the screen.

"Your work has probably shown you the connection between the girls by now." Blaine's expression tightened. "Miranda Konch played a role in ruining all their lives, and she will pay for the damage she's caused." He reached out and angled the camera lower, cutting off the top half of his forehead and changing the view to cover just himself. "Though she may have been the cause behind it, she was also the person who brought the girls together. Mel met Jackie at the clinic weeks before she joined the group. It seemed like their alters found comfort in one another.

"Girls came in and out of Mel's life due to her work, but Jackie was different." Blaine shook his head. "I knew who she was right away. Who wouldn't? Brielle Jeffries is an heiress to a powerful family. I confronted her about it once. Jackie freaked out, and Mel vouched for her. So, I just let it go. Mel tended to lie, and it wasn't worth confronting. I didn't want to risk waking up Patsy. When I found Brielle's medication, I knew the truth and did everything I could to keep the medication from them."

"He definitely knows more about this drug than he's letting on," Archer said.

As if answering Archer's thought, Blaine continued on. "I'm sure the medication is perplexing, perhaps almost fantastical. I neither know what you've discovered about it nor will I pretend to be an expert on the subject. The make of the drug seems to affect each person differently. Some take it and never see a side effect, and they live a better life for it. For others, the reality of the side effects is too much. Devastating, as it was in this case. It was never supposed to hit the market, and those that put it there will pay for what they've done."

Blaine paused a moment. "They aren't bad girls, Detective. They are troubled, with complicated pasts. They would never harm anyone undeserved. You can't argue these deaths were unprovoked."

Ryan didn't disagree. Still, murder was murder, whether it was deserved or not.

There was another commotion behind him, distracting Blaine from the camera once more. When he looked back this time, his voice seemed rushed.

"You have the girl I love in there," Blaine said. "Maybe she's no one. Maybe she's a part of Patsy she doesn't know. All I can say is this was never supposed to happen, and I will do everything I can to make it right. Starting with Konch."

The screen went black as the video cut out. Archer and Ryan stared at the screen in silence for several seconds before Ryan spoke.

"So he knows everything and plans to act against this woman."

"It seems like it." Archer agreed. "We need to find her first."

Exiting the video, Ryan forwarded the email to their IT department hoping they would find some way to track it.

"Do you think they'll find him?" Archer asked, moving back to the seat across from Ryan.

"If that video told us anything, Blaine Roche is not a man to be taken lightly," Ryan said. "He knows more than we do, and without our resources."

"You said it felt off," Archer said. "What were you talking about?"

Ryan scratched his chin. "His reasons. Why did he take these women in when he knew about the drug? We're missing a piece of the final picture."

"Hopefully, they can track him down and we can get an answer."

"Until then, we have three very confused suspects to process. Sending them to prison won't help. They need psychological help. Each of those girls is fighting her own demon."

"What are you going to do?" Archer asked.

Ryan glanced down at his notes. "I'll give my recommendation. If they don't get help, it's possible the condition will worsen. Then we may be dealing with more than one alternate personality."

"It depends on how the drugs tie into it all." Archer stood. "It's strange, isn't it?"

"Real strange." Ryan went down the list of the girls. "The leader, Melanie, was the alter of Patsy. Mel was a strong woman Patsy created to escape the abuse she endured. Fairly simple explanation there."

"And the others?"

"From what I gather, Jackie saved Brielle," Ryan said. "Jackie was the strength and endurance to escape her captors, twice. She came from a completely different life and gave Brielle the freedom she never had. As for Lexi ..." Ryan trailed off.

"If abuse can bring out anger, I'm sure it could pacify it too," Archer said.

"Like Candy was the result of Brennan Drake?" Ryan asked, thinking back to how Lexi described her ex as violent.

"Wasn't she found in an alleyway, left for dead? Maybe he beat her and left her there. Candy was the personality she chose to survive."

Ryan reached up and scratched at his chin. "It's hard to say what sort of trauma would bring out the timid change."

"Whatever you decide, I'll back you up."

Ryan held out his hand to his partner. "I'm glad to have your approval. You were a huge help on this case. It's been a crazy one, even if it's not completely over."

Archer grasped his hand. "You took the lead. I only came along for the ride. This will set a precedent."

"I hope it does," Ryan said. "We've never come across anything quite like this. I want to make sure they get the help they need to avoid any crime they could commit in the future."

"I hope it ends well for them," Archer paused then added, "And you."

"Thanks. I'm glad this part of the hunt is over."

"Me, too. You sticking around long?"

"I have a few things to finish up here, plus I still have to talk with Brielle while her lawyer is here."

"Grab me when you do," Archer said. "I'd like to listen in."

"Sure thing." Ryan looked back down at the notes in front of him. A prescription medication tied them all together with a complicated condition. He didn't know if removing the drug would help. He didn't know how much treatment it would take. A part of Ryan suspected he'd never really know the whole truth. The doctor on the project was dead; the girls on the drug were split and had two different stories; and the man who tied it all together was only a video message and a jumbled email.

Ryan reached for the report by Calvin Wright again

when his office phone chimed, and Jade's voice came through the pager.

"Detectives, there is someone here to speak with you."

Archer and Ryan exchanged a glance.

"Send them in."

The doctor looked frazzled as she entered his office. Her grey hair was pulled back in a messy bun, and her makeup was smudged like she'd been crying and tried to wipe it away. Above all, she looked terrified. Her eyes were wide, and her lips trembled. She clutched a folder between her shaking hands as she sat across from Ryan and next to Archer.

"Dr. Konch," Ryan said. "You've been a difficult woman to find."

"I'd be lying if I didn't say that was my intention." Miranda placed the folder on his desk. "I thought hiding was the best choice." She glanced at Archer with nervous eyes before continuing. "Until Dr. Wright tracked me down. I had no choice but to come here and ask for your protection."

Ryan raised an eyebrow. "What are you talking about?"

"Calvin Wright," Miranda said. "The research doctor. He's been following me, and yesterday he got too close."

"Calvin Wright is dead." Archer crossed his arms, his eyes fixed on the doctor.

"He's not," Miranda protested. "I saw him." She flipped open the folder to reveal an old newspaper clipping. The edges were weathered, and the page had yellowed, the picture in the center was still clear. A familiar man in a lab coat with the caption, *Dr. Calvin Wright discovering the innovative effects of Solydexran.* The smooth curve of his face and focused gaze in his dark eyes was unmistakable.

Ryan picked up the photo and studied it. "This can't be Wright."

"It's the pimp," Archer said, reaching for the photo.

"That's Wright," Miranda said. "I got a call a few days back from a man claiming I'd pay for what I'd done. I didn't know the drug trials had been faked and I'd contributed to ruining the lives of my patients. Then someone tried to break into my house, so I ran." She shook her head. "I started looking further into the drug and its trials. I didn't know the extent of what I had gotten involved in. Then *he* started showing up everywhere I went."

"How did you come by the drug?" Ryan asked.

"A couple of years back, a sales rep came by the office with a new formula," Miranda explained. "The results spoke for themselves. At the time, I had other methods and I wasn't ready to just move to a newly, untested product. So, he offered me money, payment to use the drug and an assurance it would help my clients and grow my practice. I didn't know about the intense, possible side effects. No one did."

"Are there other clients you've prescribed the medication to?"

"Of course." Miranda flipped another page and provided Ryan with a list of names. The records stretched back for over two years. Ryan couldn't be positive how many suffered similar fates as the women in his custody.

"It's widespread," the doctor continued. "I'm not the only one who worked with it. I know of at least three other practices in the direct vicinity distributing it."

"So why is Roche targeting you?" Archer asked.

"It's Wright." Miranda insisted, pointing to the photo. "The voice on the phone told me what I'd done. I swore I didn't know anything about the false results. He didn't believe me."

Ryan glanced at Archer. "How much do we know about Wright's death?"

"Not much; the records were sketchy."

"Could they be false?" Ryan glanced back at the photo; the image of Blaine's video was still clear in his mind. The test results had been fabricated; could the death be fake too?

"What are you suggesting?"

Ryan focused his attention back on the doctor. "Did this man say anything to you? What was your interaction like?"

"Other than the phone call, he never got a chance. When I recognized him as Wright, I ran."

Ryan's brows furrowed together; Ms. Parker had said Blaine claimed Wright's house as his own.

"What are you thinking?" Archer pressed.

"Maybe Wright isn't actually dead."

"He's not," Miranda interjected. "I've seen him."

Ryan disregarded her comment and stayed focused on his partner. "What if we're dealing with another alter, one out for revenge?"

"Then we're missing something," Archer said. "Something about this drug and the bigger picture."

"Yeah, more people might be in danger."

Archer stood, and Ryan followed.

"What about me?" Miranda asked.

"We have more questions for you." Ryan buzzed his assistant. "Jade will take you to a room for further questioning, assuming you're willing to cooperate."

"I will help however I can," she said, though her wide-eyed expression hadn't vanished.

"That would be best," Archer said as Jade entered and invited Miranda to follow her.

When they were alone, Archer turned back to Ryan. "Do you really think we're dealing with another alter here?"

"I think it's a safe bet." Ryan reached for the photo of Calvin again. It was Blaine. There was no mistaking it. Ryan would have the lab do facial recognition from the video to be sure.

"So, what now?" Archer crossed his arms.

Ryan retrieved the file containing the women's information and the one for Blaine. With a small smile, he said, "One case closes, and another opens wide. Sounds like a typical month." He headed to the office door and nudged his partner as he passed. "After all, you wanted a heavy caseload. So consider your wish answered."

Archer chuckled as he followed Ryan. "Not exactly what I had in mind."

"Who doesn't love a good mystery?" Ryan said.

THE STORY of *Twisted* will continue with *Wicked*, releasing October 2024.

Acknowledgments

This book has been in my heart for far too long. I started writing *Twisted* back in 2013 after a day out with two of my best friends. Jillian (My real-life Jackie) insisted I write a story about our "alter-egos". Mine, hers and our third Celeste's (real-life Candy) with names she picked herself that remain in the book. Immediately on my return home I wrote Candy's scene when she woke up from a night with Paul Dorian.

Twisted started as a seven-point-of-view story about three very confused women and one dedicated detective. After several rounds of revisions and ideas, it turned into the story it is now.

When my amazing publisher first asked me what I hoped my sophomore novel would be I was quick to pitch *Twisted*. It was a story I had stuck in a drawer years ago but knew there was potential. Thankfully, Rising Action Publishing Collective saw that potential too.

Thank you to my publishers, Alexandria Brown and Tina Beier, for recognizing the story in *Twisted* and helping me take Ryan Boone from bland to the awkward-dad-joke-making detective he is now, for seeing the depth in Melanie and helping me bring some light to all her abrasiveness and for building out Brielle and the confusing situations she faces. Without you and your thorough input, *Twisted* wouldn't be the book it is today.

Thank you to Kathleen Foxx for proofreading my messy words and bringing some clarity to the endless typos you likely had to fix.

Can we take a minute to appreciate this beautiful cover? Nat Mac, you are a freaking rockstar when it comes to designing covers and I am so proud to call this one mine. I can't wait to see what you come up with next.

To Marissa Fuller and Jessica Schmeidler for helping me knock my POV count down from seven to three and narrow the focus for each character many, many years ago.

An author would be lost without beta readers, which I was lucky to have a few. Thank you to Dustin Fife, Laura Reynolds, Derek Cummings, Jefferson Hunt, Dave Cushing, Simone Downie, Shellah Inman, Gravis Kartweeler, and Dee-Ann Brown. All courtesy of the Uber Group. Without your support, I'd still be floundering.

To Denise, Jessica, and Kristen aka the Sexy Train. These last two years with you ladies have been unforgettable. I am so grateful that Bianca Marais connected us back in 2021 and that we've all grown as writers together. I would be lost without our therapy sessions, writing hours and text chain. I hope we continue writing together for years to come.

I'm so thankful for all the connections I've made along this journey. To ladies of the Hot Author Summer group, the Toronto Area Women Authors, Same Story Different Year, and everyone else I have connected with across various platforms or events, thank you so much for commiserating, supporting, and reading.

To Sam Bailey, thank you for being a massive cheerleader and constantly encouraging me to strive for more all while wearing the biggest smile. Your positive light is an absolute joy to be around.

To my family, I am forever thankful for the support you've given me and for being my biggest fans.

To my Collingwood friends, my high school girls, and my amazing partner, thank you for your willingness to hear about my trials, read a new book and listen to me yammer on about something that won't come out for years. Your patience and understanding will never be forgotten.

And finally, to all my readers. Thank you so much for picking up my sophomore novel. It's been an amazing journey to get this book to you and I hope you love these characters as much as I do.

Stay tuned for part two, coming 2024!

Book Club Questions

1. Detective Ryan Boone has just had the case of his life. It's taken him on a wild ride, laying out evidence that didn't add up. He's obviously gotten invested in the crime. Did you question any of his choices when pursuing the case?

2. Did the twist about Solydexran surprise you?

3. Mental illness is a theme throughout the book. Do you feel that the women were innocent of the crimes their alters committed?

4. Blaine and Mel have a complex relationship. Did you ever question why Blaine was so dedicated to Mel and her operation?

5. What do you think happened to the women after their arrest?

6. Brielle is a very well-off heiress, yet seems to have a tragic home life, and has spent many years in and out of psychiatric care. Did you ever question her relationship with Jackie and why they may have cut ties?

7. Patsy and Brielle's connection is revealed early on, then you learn the truth about Mel and Jackie. Do you think this past played a role in their alters finding each other?

8. Were you surprised by the connection between Brennan, Lexi and Brielle?

9. Which character did you relate to the most?

10. Mel is clearly invested in her less-than-legal operation. Do you believe she cared about the girls in her employ or that she was only in it for the money?

11. What did you think of the ending, knowing that a sequel is forthcoming? Did you feel the first mystery was wrapped up? Where do you think the next part of the story will go?

*Now a Preview
of Wicked...*

One

Blaine Roche

The article on the local news page of the *Ottawa Citizen* beckoned him, trying to draw his attention away from surveillance. Blaine drummed his fingers against the glass table in the quaint corner café, eyes darting from the headline to the front door of the office building across the road.

He'd kept an eye on the door for nearly twenty minutes now, having finished his coffee after only ten. She was taking her time today. He had been about to leave, thinking perhaps he'd missed her when the server sauntered by with a refill and the local news page.

Blaine had declined both, but the young woman didn't acknowledge him. He wasn't surprised, having spotted the two white earbuds nearly hidden beneath her messy, purple hair. The paper wouldn't have been of interest to him if not for that one little word sticking out.

Giving in to the temptation, he reached and grabbed the

newspaper, flipping it flat and laying the article in front of him.

HERON MAN ARRESTED IN CONNECTION WITH SANDY HILL MURDER

A suspect has been charged with first-degree murder after top ACE Pharmaceutical investor was found dead in Sandy Hill condo.

Police said Julie Kanner, 28, was found dead the morning of September 5 by her roommate. Rickie Hastings, 34, was arrested yesterday morning (September 9) at 11:50 a.m. Police won't say at this time how, or if, these two people are related.

The investigation is ongoing.

Anyone with information is asked to contact Ottawa Police or Crime Stoppers.

Blaine placed the paper down and reached for his phone, Googling Julie Kanner. Her LinkedIn page confirmed his suspicions. Julie wasn't just an investor; she was an employee of ACE pharmaceuticals. She had a connection to Solydexran.

He put his phone away and looked back at the article, wondering if the infamous drug would make an appearance in this case or if it was all just a terrible coincidence.

Before he could consider it further, the office door swung open and Doctor Miranda Konch emerged from within. Abandoning his coffee and leaving a crisp bill on the table, Blaine exited the café, quickly crossed the road, and fell into step behind her. He slipped his hood over his head.

Miranda had disappeared after Blaine's girls were arrested. In fear, perhaps, though Blaine couldn't be sure. She abandoned her downtown Toronto office and vanished into the depths of Ottawa, starting a new, quiet practice in the suburb of Orléans.

Blaine had expected the doctor to come out with the truth, to reveal that she'd been paid off to distribute a new and seemingly flawless medication. In fact, Blaine had counted on it. But the good doctor surprised him. She didn't try to save herself, as she had so many times before—instead, she slipped away silently. Blaine couldn't understand why.

He'd been watching her for two weeks now, noting where she went, who she met, and who was also keeping an eye on her. It was the only way he could conceal himself under the radar.

Blaine had been desperate to confront her since the day he found out about her involvement with Solydexran, but after she went to the police, Blaine had to be careful.

Now, several months later, Blaine was sure it was safe. It didn't appear she was under police surveillance or protection, and she lived alone.

When Miranda turned off the main street for the alleyway shortcut she often took, Blaine considered nabbing her then, pulling her aside, and drilling her for all the answers he needed. But that wouldn't be discreet. He needed her to trust that he wasn't there to hurt her, despite what she'd told the police.

When they neared her apartment complex, Blaine stayed at a comfortable distance, slipping into the building behind her just as the door was closing. He followed her to the elevator. The once-paranoid doctor seemed unaware of his presence behind her as she waited for the lift, or her guard had lowered after months of nothing.

When the elevator doors slid open, Blaine followed

behind her and pressed a button on the floor above hers. Blaine was careful to keep his face hidden beneath the oversized hood.

The doors opened on her floor, and she stepped out without so much as a nod in his direction. Blaine waited only a few moments and slipped out before the doors closed. She was at her apartment door now, sliding the key into the lock, then she disappeared behind the door.

Blaine strode towards it and knocked three times. She couldn't have gone far into the unit. When the door swung open, Miranda looked around with wide eyes. When they fell on Blaine's face and registered who stood at her door, she quickly tried to close it.

"Miranda, wait," Blaine said, placing his palm on the door and holding it open. He was too strong for her to fight him off. "I just want to talk to you."

Miranda seemed to struggle for a moment longer before admitting defeat. The fear in her eyes said she didn't trust him but also conceded she couldn't stop him from entering her apartment. As Blaine slipped through the door, he saw her eye the discarded cell phone on her counter.

"I'd rather you didn't," Blaine said, putting himself between her and the phone.

"What do you want, Dr. Wright?" Miranda backed herself away from him, though the wall behind her stopped her from going too far. The way her eyes darted around the apartment told him she was considering any escape possible. Still, she didn't scream, which meant that despite being frightened, she was curious. That would work to his advantage.

"I just have some questions for you." Blaine glanced to

the couches beyond the open kitchen, ignoring the formality. "I promise, I'm not here to hurt you. I just need you to tell me some things."

"I don't believe you," Miranda said. "You called me and threatened me."

Blaine frowned. He'd done no such thing. The most he'd done was keep an eye on the doctor; he'd never made contact before today.

"Then you tried to break into my house," Miranda snapped. "Why do you think I left Toronto?"

Slowly, he raised his hands. "I didn't call you and I didn't try to break in, but I think I know who did. If you could talk to me for a minute, maybe I can help you out too." He waved to the couches.

Her raised shoulders didn't lower as she cautiously stepped around him and moved to the couches. Her eyes found the phone again as she passed him by. He followed her steps, keeping the distance between them. She was an older woman, with grey hair and a frail frame. He could overpower her any day, and Blaine knew his stature didn't instill much confidence in his assertion of meaning her no harm.

"What do you want to know?" Miranda moved to fold her hands in her lap but instead she fidgeted and threaded her fingers together.

"Were you paid off to distribute Solydexran?" Blaine asked.

For a moment, the doctor seemed taken aback by the questioning. "You want to know about the drug?"

"Yes," Blaine said. "Were you offered something to start prescribing it?"

"Yes, of course," Miranda said. "It came with a selling

bonus. I was deterred at first, as it's important my clients only receive the best care, but after I refused a few weeks later, the gentleman returned with substantial results and an increased incentive."

"So, you took it," Blaine said, trying to keep the judgment from his tone. It was difficult to see past the falsified testing and understand how professionals could have classified such a new medication as effective and safe.

"I saw no reason not to," Miranda said. "I started prescribing it to my clients who showed increased anxiety and began to see substantial results."

"You treated Brielle Jeffries for many years, correct?" Blaine asked, referring to one of the women he'd taken into his care.

Miranda nodded. "Since she was a child."

"And you knew about her second personality." Blaine paused, remembering the person that had lived inside Brielle. Though he'd known the truth about her from the beginning, Blaine struggled not to find the alter, Jackie, endearing. Like Mel, he'd let her in when he should have kept them at arm's length.

Again, Miranda nodded. "Yes, she sought treatment at my facility for several years as an attempt to recover from drug use and to help quell the voice inside her."

"And did you help her?" Blaine asked though he knew that whatever aid Miranda had given failed years later when Solydexran came into the mix.

"For a time. Until Jackie surfaced again only a year after her departure."

"You realize now why that was?" Blaine asked. He'd seen

the results; he knew the consequences. It was only a matter of time before everyone else did too. He hoped.

Miranda looked away. "Look, before Brielle began on Solydexran, things were looking up and the results with the drug had been as flawless as the original testing implied. I saw no reason to not start her on it. If anything, I hoped it would alleviate some of the pressures of her home life."

Blaine didn't answer, as they both knew how poorly that turned out. Solydexran had only worked to amplify Brielle's childhood traumas and bring life to the other being that lived hidden within in her subconscious. The one Blaine had come to know.

"You said you knew who was threatening me," Miranda said.

Blaine nodded. "The same people who have been after me for years. A lot of shady shit went down when the drug came into creation, and someone is trying hard to keep it hidden."

Miranda shook her head. "What does that have to do with me?"

"You know the truth," Blaine said. "You've seen the original reports, you've seen the damage it has done, and it's already destroyed you. You have nothing left to do but come clean about Solydexran and the conspiracy around it. But you haven't. Which means you're scared and someone is keeping you scared."

"I'm scared of you," Miranda said, straightening her back as if to show her strength in the words.

"That's probably what they want," Blaine said. Fear had been their tactic in the past. If they knew he was still working against them, then it was only a matter of time before they got to the doctor or perhaps the detective. Anyone and everyone to clean up their tracks. "Tell me about the guy who brought you the drug. Do you have his contact or a card?"

Miranda shook her head. "It was years ago. I had a sales rep come into my office, he was new to the area and new to the drug trade. He was looking to break into the market with a breakthrough drug."

Blaine couldn't stop his grimace at her response. He'd hoped she would give him more to go on.

"What about names?" Blaine asked. "Do you have information on who you have provided the drug to? Others who could have suffered?"

"That's confidential," Miranda said stiffly. "I could lose my license."

Blaine raised an eyebrow at her. "Are you really worried about that now? The best thing that can happen for you is that the truth comes out and you're far away when it does."

Miranda seemed to consider his words but didn't respond.

"I am trying to fix all of this. Solydexran should have never been created for mass distribution." Blaine shifted, remembering when he'd first discovered the forged reports and the mayhem that followed: the payoffs, the denial, the deaths. "If you give me the names of those who have used then I can trace how far and deep the damage goes. I can get closer to revealing the truth, and you may survive."

Miranda still didn't answer him, but she stood and retreated from the room. For a moment Blaine worried she'd call the police, but when she returned with a folder in hand, he forgot his concerns.

"This is what I gave the cops months ago," Miranda said. "I'm sure they looked into it, so I'm not sure what you'll be able to find."

Blaine nodded his thanks and took the folder.

"Should I be worried?" Miranda asked. "About my safety?"

Blaine hesitated. "You should be cautious. Continue to keep your profile low and I think you'll be fine. You aren't the biggest player in this, and you don't have the evidence to be a major threat to them."

For a moment, he pondered the report he'd so willingly given Detective Ryan Boone back in Toronto. It was the first officer of the law that he'd felt confident in trusting. Now, he realized his mistake as the reports stayed buried and Boone's work on the case had all but vanished.

Blaine turned and headed for the door.

"You surprised me," Miranda called after him.

Blaine stopped but didn't turn back to her. "Why, you really thought I'd hurt you?"

"I suppose I always thought that was inevitable, considering what I'd done to someone you loved. But no, I am surprised you didn't ask about *her* or where she is."

Blaine looked over his shoulder at the doctor. He'd tried not to think about Mel in the months that had passed since their separation, but it had been futile.

"She isn't who I thought she was," Blaine said.

Miranda nodded. "You're right about that. But you're not who she thought you were either, are you?"

Blaine stiffened at the question and looked away from her. "You don't know what you're talking about."

"I know more than you think," Miranda said.

"Then I'd be careful to keep your mouth shut." Blaine didn't give her a chance to respond before he dashed out the door. He gripped the folder tightly as he returned to where he'd parked his car and didn't risk a look inside at the contents until he was parked at a motel outside of the city.

When he flipped it open, stuck to the list of names was a yellow post-it note. Patsy's name. The hospital where he could find her and a phone number to reach her.

Mel had been Patsy's alternate personality brought on by abuse and the use of Solydexran. Blaine met her when he'd hoped to help her through her struggles, only to fall head over heels for the woman that was Mel. After her arrest, Blaine couldn't be sure that the woman he loved still existed.

As he stared over the nine digits, his heart fluttered with hope for the first time in months. He really could hear her voice again; the only question was if he really wanted to.

About the Author

Maggie Giles is the author of the award-winning novel *The Things We Lost*. She has been a member of the Women's Fiction Writers Association since 2014, where she works as their Social Media Director. A Canadian author who is usually daydreaming about fictional characters, she lives in Collingwood, Ontario. Her third novel, *Wicked*, will be releasing with Rising Action on Oct 22, 2024.